Contents

George I m. Sophia Dorothea of Celle

George II m. Caroline of Ansbach — Sophia Dorothea

Frederick Louis m. Augusta of Saxe-Gotha — Anne — Amelia — Caroline — George — William, Duke of Cumberland — Mary — Louisa

Augusta — George III m. Charlotte of Mecklenburg-Strelitz — Edward — William — Henry — Frederick — Caroline Matilda, Queen of Denmark

George IV m. Caroline of Brunswick — Frederick — William IV m. Adelaide of Saxe-Coburg Meiningen — Charlotte — Edward m. Victoria Mary Louisa of Saxe-Saalfeld-Coburg — Augusta — Elizabeth — Ernest — Augustus — Adolphus — Mary — Sophia — Octavius — Alfred — Amelia

Charlotte

Victoria

The Royal Sisters

THE Duchess of Kent, seated at her bureau, her gown a mass of lace and ribbons, her hair piled high under her enormous feathered hat, was smiling with some complacency at her extremely handsome Comptroller of the Household, Sir John Conroy.

Such a treasure of a man! thought the Duchess. *Dear Sir John.* And if people liked to speak of them scandalously, let them. Heaven knew there were scandals enough in the family, and *if* she were a little more friendly with Sir John than his position made necessary, who could blame her? She was eight years widowed, still young and vital and even her enemies must admit decidedly attractive so surely it was to be expected. She might have married again on the death of her Duke, but that would have been most unwise. Her position was unique; she was no ordinary widow. She was the mother of the most important little girl in the Kingdom, a fact which she would never forget—nor allow anyone else to.

"So the arrangements are completed," she said.

"As we could wish, dear Duchess."

"My *dear* Sir John, everything you do is for *our* good, I know well."

"It is not only my duty, dear Madam, but my utmost pleasure to serve the interests of the family."

"Within a day or so the Prince will arrive. The Clarences are taking him as their guest." The Duchess grimaced. "Poor dear fellow. William is such a buffoon and Adelaide so dowdy. Still, she has a good heart, and of course she adores my darling Victoria."

"She wishes our Princess was hers. I see it in her eyes."

"But there is no malice in her . . . unlike some. As for

9

William, he is a fool. God help England if ever . . . I really don't think there is much to choose between them. His Majesty is either living in that odd way with Lady Conyngham at that ridiculous cottage of his in Windsor or like some Eastern potentate at the Pavilion or Carlton House. It is really shocking. It's a state of affairs that can't last."

They exchanged glances. They shared an ambition to see the Duchess's daughter Victoria on the throne and a Regency established; and of whom should that Regency consist but of the little Queen's mother? And who would be her adviser, at her right hand to guide and care for her? Who but her handsome Comptroller of the Household, Sir John Conroy.

Sir John's expression had become slightly apprehensive. His dear Duchess was a little indiscreet; she was apt to talk too loudly and too much; and although they conducted their conversation in German—the Duchess's English was not always intelligible—there might be spies in the household.

"I suppose when we speak of His Majesty and his brothers we should whisper," he suggested.

The Duchess nodded so vigorously that the enormous pale blue feather momentarily covered her right eye.

"How right you are! And how clever to have made a friend of that woman, who is extremely vulgar. I really cannot understand His Majesty. He has always been said to have such exquisite taste."

Sir John bent closer to the Duchess so that his mouth almost touched her ear.

"His Majesty is failing fast. They say his eyesight has almost gone and he is so full of water that he is too heavy to walk and has on some days to be carried up and down stairs."

"He can't last."

"And Clarence could be as unstable as his father."

"Poor George III. I never knew him. But what a tragedy! A mad King of England!"

"The people won't want another."

"Do you really think William . . . ?"

"They say that but for Adelaide he would have been in a strait-jacket by now."

"Adelaide is a far more significant person than people are led to believe."

"Your Grace speaks with your accustomed wisdom. If she were not so devoted to Victoria . . ."

"She is devoted to all the children, but I believe she has a special feeling for Victoria."

"How could she help loving our plump little pet."

"Dear me! Such storms! She will have to be guided."

"Indeed yes . . . and with such a mother . . ."

She returned his fond glance. "Who is so fortunate to have such a faithful . . ." She hesitated. She could not call him a servant. He was an extremely proud man. ". . . helper," she concluded. "And I was saying it was clever of you to have won the favour of that odious Lady Conyngham. It's so helpful for knowing what is going on at Windsor . . . even though she is so vulgar."

There was a glint in the Duchess's eyes. Sir John did seem to be able to charm rather easily; and there was no doubt that he had made an impression on the King's mistress. He must not alienate the Duchess because she was essential to his success. It was comforting, of course, to be on good terms with the King's mistress but once the King was dead—and that could happen at any moment—Lady Conyngham's power would be non-existent. She was only useful as long as the King lived.

He said quickly: "Indeed, I have often wondered what His Majesty saw in her. The Princess Lieven said that she is at a loss to understand that too. All the lady has, so says that Princess, is a hand for taking jewels and a magnificent balcony on which to display them."

"He always liked those large-bosomed females . . . or almost always. Maria Fitzherbert was his ideal and she was almost as lavishly endowed—as far as balconies are concerned—as Conyngham."

"It is fortunate that she is friendly towards . . . us. It is so useful to be informed of the King's intentions. And with Cumberland so close to him . . ."

The Duchess shivered. "That man. My God, he is evil. I tremble sometimes to think of him and what may be going on in his mind."

"Never forget that you have good friends who are ever watchful of your interests and would stop at *nothing* to further them."

The Duchess was sober. He was forgiven his friendship with Lady Conyngham. Of course *everything* was permissible if it kept them informed of what was going on in the King's household.

"She was exceedingly helpful when we were at Windsor," went on Conroy, stressing the point. "Your Grace will remember how His Majesty laid speculative eyes on the Princess Feodora."

"I remember full well. Everyone noticed. He kept her at his side and it was clear what was in his mind. Even Victoria said that she thought he liked Feodora better than he liked herself and that he wanted to marry her." The Duchess smiled fondly. "That child is too precocious."

"She is certainly bright but in need of control as we have agreed."

"She shall be controlled. But in spite of her storms and waywardness I am proud of her."

"Justly so, Duchess."

"And proud of my dearest Feodora, too."

"Your Grace should be justly proud of all your children."

The girls, at least, thought Conroy. He was not sure of Charles, the young Prince of Leiningen, the Duchess's son by her first marriage, who, he had heard, was expressing his desire—and more serious still, his intention—to marry a woman who was most unsuitable.

This was not the time to refer to the affairs of the young Prince of Leiningen; it was the Duchess's two daughters with whom they must concern themselves. The constant concern being Victoria, the Duchess's daughter by the Duke of Kent, fourth son of King George III.

Feodora, the Duchess's daughter by her first marriage, was a delightful creature—twenty-one years old and a real beauty—as he believed their "plump little partridge" Alexandrina Victoria would never be; and as a sister to the future Queen of England, Feodora was a very desirable *parti*.

She might have been the Queen of England, for his ageing Majesty had been very partial. So much so that the Duchess had been apprehensive. It was a great compliment to darling Feodora, of course, but such a match would spoil Victoria's chances if it were fruitful. The Duchess would be the mother of the Queen Consort which was very different from being the mother of the reigning Queen. She was certain that Victoria would be Queen of England and that was what she wanted more than anything in the world.

So she had whisked Feodora from the King's circle, with the willing assistance of Lady Conyngham who had no desire to see her ageing lover divert his attention from her to a young and beautiful wife, and poor George, weighed down with his physical afflictions, so that he was often more dead than alive, had ceased to think of her; and her mother—

aided by Sir John—had arranged that the dear girl should pay a visit to her Grandmamma, Augusta, Duchess of Saxe-Coburg, who had with Teutonic efficiency set about finding a suitable husband for her.

Grandmamma's choice had fallen on Prince Ernest of Hohenlohe-Langenburg who had just succeeded his father to the sovereignty of his little Principality. He was a sober-living man, a phenomenon in these days, and turned thirty which was not a bad thing; and in fact the Duchess of Kent agreed with her mother that this was an ideal match; and the sooner it was completed the better.

It was for this reason that Prince Ernest was on his way to England to stay first as the guest of the Clarences until the marriage could be arranged, and then enjoy a brief honeymoon at the Duchess's brother Leopold's house, Claremont, before he took Feodora to her new home.

The Duchess leaned forward and lightly laid a hand on Sir John's arm.

This little matter had been so satisfactorily concluded.

In another part of the palace the Princess Sophia sat over her fire making a net purse. She could not see very well for her eyesight was failing. How terrible if she were to be unable to work at her embroidery and net her purses and do her knotting! What else was there to do nowadays?

What else, she asked herself, had there ever been to do?

She was not bitter; she had accepted her fate years ago when they had known that Papa would not allow them to marry if he could help it and Mamma was a tyrant and jailer at the same time. Once one of them had said: "I'd rather be a watercress seller down by the river or go round the streets crying sweet lavender than be a Princess of England." But Sophia had reminded them that if they had depended on watercress and lavender for their bread and butter they might soon have been wishing they were back in their completely boring utterly monotonous captivity.

And now they had all escaped. Death had brought about their release. The death of Mamma, Queen Charlotte, that was, for Papa living his crazy life behind the grim walls of Windsor had ceased to be of any significance to them when he had been put away because of his madness.

George had become King . . . dearest of brothers, adored

by all his sisters without exception; and he had given them freedom—but it had come too late.

Click-click went the steel needles—a comforting and familiar sound.

"I wonder if dear Sir John will call on me today," murmured Sophia. She touched her wispy hair and sighed. Too late, she thought . . . everything is too late.

She closed her eyes to rest them a while. Here she lived in these rather secluded apartments in Kensington Palace and her near neighbours were Edward's wife, the Duchess of Kent, with her dear little daughter Victoria and that pretty girl Feodora for whom they were now arranging a match. And close by in the Palace too was brother Augustus, the Duke of Sussex, with the hundreds of clocks which he tended as though they were children, his rare books and bibles and his pretty flower garden which was a source of great delight. And with him—alas for decorum—was that very merry plump little widow Cecilia Buggin. What a dreadful name—although she had not been born with it and had acquired it through marriage with a certain Sir George of Norfolk and was in fact a daughter of the Earl of Arran. Augustus was devoted to the lady and she to him, but of course he could not marry her since he considered himself married already, although the State did not recognize the marriage.

"Oh dear," sighed Sophia. "What a mess our lives are in and all on account of our not being able to live naturally like other people. Papa's Marriage Act has been responsible for so much discord in the family."

But for that she supposed dearest George might be married to Maria Fitzherbert and how much happier he would have been if that union could have been recognized! It was sad now to see that dearest of brothers reduced to his present state and with that harpy Lady Conyngham perpetually at his side.

Sad indeed! A long way they had come from that time when George had been Prince of Wales, then Regent and so concerned with Mr. Brummel about the cut of his coats. And how exquisite he had looked and how proud they had been of him! No woman could have loved him more than his sisters did. If George had been in power earlier how different their lives would have been! He would not have made prisoners of them; he would have helped them to marry, not prevented them from doing so.

But the girls were settled now and only she and Augusta

had remained unmarried. Charlotte the eldest had married long ago and become Queen of Württemberg; Elizabeth had married the Prince of Hesse-Homburg (and how the people had jeered at her and her husband—the ageing bride and the husband who had to be bribed to take a bath); Mary had married her cousin, the Duke of Gloucester ("Silly Billy" in the family, although he had become a tyrant since his marriage. Mary, though, preferred a domineering husband to a demanding parent); dear Amelia—so beloved of their father —had died at the age of twenty-seven, which sorrow, some said, had sent poor Papa completely mad; that left Augusta and herself, the old maids.

"I could not exactly call myself that," she said aloud. "And I don't care. At least I have something to look back on."

She looked back frequently on the great adventure of her life, on that occasion when her affairs had been talked of in hushed whispers among her sisters and how they had planned and plotted to keep her secret from Mamma.

Colonel Garth, Papa's equerry, was not exactly a handsome man. Far from it. But it had been wonderful to be loved; and she had been really happy for the first time. She should have been more careful. But how could she be? Adventure had come to Kew and while she sat with her sisters working on her embroidery, filling her mother's snuff-box, making sure that the dogs were walked at the appropriate times, she had dreamed of Colonel Garth and romance; and she had slipped away whenever possible, to his apartments— or he came to hers. Life had become filled with intrigue.

And the inevitable consequence!

Augusta had anxiously enquired: "Sophia, are you ill?"

And Mary: "What is wrong?"

And Augusta: "You had better tell."

And there in the prim drawing-room at Kew she had whispered her secret: "I'm going to have a child."

"It's impossible," Augusta had said. How could an unmarried daughter of the King be pregnant? How could it possibly happen?

"In the usual way," she had said defiantly, not caring very much.

"It will send Papa mad," Mary had said.

Anything that was alarming was always reputed to be likely to send Papa mad.

"Mamma will be furious."

Knowing this was true she had merely looked helplessly at

them while in her heart she did not greatly care for anything but the fact that she was going to have a child.

They might have told George; he would have helped; but they did not do this. Instead the sisters had made a protective circle about her; the dear Colonel was very helpful; and so he should be since he was the child's father. But he had been loving and tender and she was grateful. Kindly fashion had made skirts so voluminous that they might have been designed to disguise pregnancy. Dear Sophia was peaky, said Mary. She needed a little holiday by the sea.

So to the sea they went and there she gave birth to her boy who was adopted by a worthy couple; and the Colonel who had become a General doted on him and arranged his future for him and he was indeed a fine fellow now, almost thirty— a son to be proud of.

He came to Kensington to see her now and then. He knew of the relationship and was proud of it; but although brother William might openly acknowledge his ten FitzClarences borne to him by the actress Dorothy Jordan, it seemed a very different matter for a royal Princess to admit she was the mother of an illegitimate son.

"So many scandals in the family," she murmured and picked up her netting. Was there another family with so many? The dear King's life was one long scandal; her second brother Frederick, now dead, had created the biggest scandal of all when he had been accused of allowing his mistress Mary Anne Clarke to sell commissions in the Army of which he was Commander-in-Chief; then William, who had set up his house with Dorothy Jordan who had given him ten children; and Edward, Victoria's father, who had lived with Madame de St. Laurent for years (respectably it was true but without marriage lines); and Ernest, Duke of Cumberland . . . the less said of him the better. Many people shuddered every time they heard his name. Augustus, now living in this Palace tending his collection of clocks and bibles, accompanied everywhere by his dear friend Lady Buggin, though mild enough was scarcely without reproach; and only Adolphus in far away Hanover lived the exemplary life of a married man.

There never was a family so deep in scandal, thought Sophia.

And how strange that she should have had her share of it!

Perhaps her son would come today, by way of the back stairs. "Madam, a gentleman to see you." And they talked of course, for they knew. It was impossible to keep royal scandals secret.

My boy . . . my very own boy, she thought. At least I did something.

And if the boy perhaps did not come someone else would —perhaps that tall commanding gentleman whom she admired so much and was so charming and so courteous to her that he reminded her of the days when Colonel Garth had loved her so devotedly.

There was no doubt that Sir John Conroy was a very charming man. The Duchess of Kent realized this. Or course she was younger than Sophia; and beautiful too in a flamboyant way. Dear George did not think her attractive, but then he had his own views of beauty. She secretly believed he compared all women with Maria Fitzherbert. No, the Duchess was too showy and she was not of course of the same rank as a daughter of the King of England.

So it was rather pleasant sitting by the fire, dreaming of the past. I wouldn't have had it different, she thought.

Perhaps he'll come to see me today. And if he doesn't, perhaps Sir John will look in.

It was comforting to have something to look forward to.

In the nursery the Princess Victoria was whispering to her dolls.

"Darling Feodora will soon be leaving us. She is going away . . . to Germany to be exact and although she says we shall see each other often. I believe she says it only to comfort me." She shook the doll with the ruff impatiently. "You are not listening. *You* would not. You are more interested in your own affairs, I daresay."

The wooden face stared back, as Victoria clicked her tongue and smoothed down the farthingale. This was the most glittering of the dolls and the one singled out for abuse. It was amusing to slap Queen Elizabeth now and then. "You may have been a good Queen," said Victoria now, "but I do not think you were a very good *person*." And dear Amy Robsart with her satin gown and ribbons was picked up and hugged to Victoria's plump person.

"Feodora is going to be married," she went on, "and my only hope is that Ernest Hohenlohe-Langenburg will make her a *good* husband." Then Victoria began to realize what it would be like in the nursery without Feodora and tears filled her eyes.

Baroness Lehzen rose from her chair in the window and came over.

I am never allowed to be alone for a minute! thought Victoria resentfully. They watch me all the time.

The Baroness could never quite control her features when she looked at her charge. The words might be stern, the rule rigid, but the devotion was always obvious—and to none more than Victoria herself. Dear Louise Lehzen—so recently Fräulein and now awarded with a Hanoverian title in accordance with the dignity of her role in life. Lehzen—and of course Mamma, the Duchess of Kent—ruled Victoria's days as they had Feodora's, but now the bonds which bound Victoria's half-sister were slackening. Feodora was going to be married.

"Talking to the dolls again?" enquired Lehzen.

"I was telling them about poor Feodora."

"Poor Feodora! When she is going to marry the man your dear Mamma has chosen for her!"

"I think she would rather stay with me."

"Nonsense!" said the Baroness. "And what have you been doing to Queen Elizabeth's ruff?"

Lehzen loved the dolls as much as Victoria did; in fact she had made some of them. And because many of them represented figures of history it was decided that they were a frivolity with some educational advantages.

Lehzen adjusted the ruff. She sighed to herself. Marriages were disturbing. She was fond of Feodora but the little Victoria was her life; and when she had been selected to become her governess she had entered into the task with the dedication of a nun taking her vows. Victoria was no ordinary child. If all went as the Duchess of Kent and Lehzen nightly prayed it would, this plump lively child could be the Queen of England. But what a torment it was to contemplate that all might not go as they wished. There were obstacles. At the moment only William, Duke of Clarence, stood between her and the throne; but William had a youngish wife, Adelaide, and although she had had several miscarriages she had at least proved that she could conceive—and there was no doubt that this was her main object in life—and if a child of hers should live . . . away would go Victoria's chance of mounting the throne.

It was unbearable! It was unthinkable. Neither the Duchess

nor the faithful Lehzen would allow themselves to believe for a moment that it would really happen; but there was always the lurking fear that it might.

In the meantime dear little Victoria must be guarded at every moment of the day, because not only did William stand before her but there was her wicked uncle, the Duke of Cumberland, who the two watchdogs—as Cumberland had called the Duchess and the Baroness—knew was capable of any unscrupulous action to remove Victoria from his path. The old King was still living between melancholy solitude in his Gothic cottage in Windsor Park and oriental splendour at Carlton House and the Pavilion. He was on the point of death—but then, for the last ten years he had been in that situation—so depressing for him but so exciting for others as the Duchess had remarked to Lehzen. And the fact remained that it was for those two women—so united in their dedicated cause—to keep Victoria safe for the throne.

The Duke of Cumberland was a constant bogy; he and his Duchess had unsavoury reputations; both may well have been guilty of murder; the Duke was once in a very awkward position over the death of his valet who had been discovered dead in his master's blood-spattered apartments; and the Duke had been wounded too. As the Duke's reputation with women was well known and the valet had an exceptionally pretty wife, certain conclusions were drawn—although not proved. For how could a royal Duke be expected, or allowed, to stand in the dock of a court of law? With the Duchess it was a question of husbands. Two who had become a trial to her had died mysteriously.

The Duchess of Kent often whispered of these matters to the faithful Baronesses Lehzen and Späth (both German members of her household and therefore to be trusted) and asked: "If they were capable of murdering a jealous valet and unwanted husbands might not they be capable of acting similarly towards one who stood in the way of their path to the throne?"

Lehzen, shivering, agreed; and in consequence the Princess Victoria was never allowed to be alone. Some trustworthy person must always be in attendance—her mother, one of the Baronesses, her sister Feodora or one of her tutors.

In the past it had been easier but now that Victoria was growing up—and showing a certain imperiousness it must be admitted, for how difficult it was to keep the knowledge of her importance from her—it was becoming something of a problem to keep her under constant supervision.

But the Duchess was certainly mistress in her own household. A woman who was capable of conducting a feud with the reigning King was undoubtedly equipped to rule her own circle. Victoria was made well aware that in all circumstances she must obey Mamma. But Victoria was wayward. Only the other day her music master had reported evidence of this to the Duchess—for all the tutors knew that the Duchess wished every little incident concerning her daughter to be reported to her. The Princess Victoria was very fond of music and had on occasion been known to attempt to cajole her tutors, that there might be music instead of some less interesting lesson. But even in music she did not always work as she should and on this occasion her tutor had seen fit to reprove her.

"There is no royal road to music, Princess," he had said. "You must practise like everyone else."

Whereupon Victoria had assumed her most imperious expression and had promptly shut the piano, locked it and put the key in her pocket. Rising haughtily and with the air of the Queen her mother and Lehzen longed for her to be, she said: "There now. You see there is no must about it."

Arrogance which must be punished, had been the Duchess's verdict. "And yet," the doting Lehzen reminded her, "a certain queenliness, does not Your Grace agree? A royal determination not to be dictated to?"

The Duchess nodded; but they agreed that such waywardness must not go unchecked.

The child was truthful; one of the finest traits in her character was her frankness and her inability to tell a lie even to extricate herself from an awkward situation. She was subject to sudden outbreaks of temper. These "storms" were regrettable and must be controlled. Only recently when the Duchess had come into the nursery where Victoria was with Lehzen she had asked of Lehzen how Victoria had behaved that morning.

Victoria had in fact been rather more "wayward" than usual and on two occasions had shown temper. The Baroness, not wishing to complain overmuch about her darling but realizing that Victoria must always be shown examples of truthfulness, admitted that Victoria had once been a little naughty.

"No, Lehzen," said Victoria. "You have forgotten. It was twice."

And when her mother told her that when she was naughty she made not only her dear mother unhappy but herself also, Victoria considered this and said: "No, Mamma, I only make *you* unhappy."

They could not be displeased with such a child. In any case she was the centre of their lives. Once Feodora had told her mother that she loved Victoria far more than she loved her, to which the Duchess had sternly replied that a good mother always loved her children equally and was Feodora suggesting that she was not a good mother?

Feodora had merely been wistful, for she loved Victoria dearly; and now knowing that her little half-sister was in the nursery and that at this hour of the day she would not be at her lessons but in the charge of Baroness Lehzen she came to see her so that she might explain to Victoria about her coming wedding.

Victoria cried out in pleasure when she saw her sister; she immediately left her dolls and ran to her.

"Darling dearest Feodora!" Victoria put her arms about Feodora's neck and swung her feet off the floor. Lehzen looked on critically. Scarcely the manner in which a young lady—old enough for marriage—should greet her young sister who was destined to be a Queen; but perhaps as they would soon be parted such a boisterous greeting would be permitted this once.

"I've been telling the dolls that you are going to leave us, darling Feddy, and they do not like it at all."

Too much fantasy, thought Lehzen. It is time she grew out of the dolls. But the stern Lehzen had to admit that she herself could not grow out of them, so what was to be expected of an eight-year-old girl?

"Feodora, let us walk in the gardens. May I, Lehzen?"

The Baroness conceded that they might. "But put on your fur-trimmed coat and bonnet. The wind is cold."

Feodora knew the rule: Victoria was never to be left alone; and if the two girls did not stray too far from the Palace a little saunter in the gardens would be permitted. Victoria must not forget that the Reverend Davy would be waiting to give her a lesson in exactly half an hour's time.

"We shan't forget, Lehzen," said Feodora, holding out her hand. "Come, Vicky."

Such a beautiful girl, Feodora! thought Lehzen. It was

well that she was marrying. A reasonably good match but was it good enough for the sister of the future Queen of England? Would Victoria ever be as lovely as Feodora? Perhaps not. She took after her father's family so much, which was as well, as it would be from that side that the Crown would come to her. But Victoria was Victoria—beauty would not be of such importance to her. There could not be a Prince in Europe who would not be excited at the prospect of marrying Victoria—and perhaps even now in all the Courts of Europe ambitious parents with sons of eight, nine, ten . . . or older had their eyes on the little jewel of Kensington Palace.

Hand in hand the sisters came into the gardens.

"Oh, Sissy," Victoria said, "it is going to be *dreadful* when we're parted."

"Dreadful," agreed Feodora.

"You will write to me?"

"Such long letters that you will tire of reading them."

"How can you say that when you know it is not true."

"Vicky darling, I know. But I'm so frightened. I'm going to lose you all and have a new husband and I don't really know him very well. But the worst thing of all is saying good-bye to you."

Victoria wept openly. She displayed her emotions too readily, said Lehzen; but the Duchess was of the opinion that it showed a tender heart and the people would like it.

"What is your Ernest like, Feddy?" asked Victoria. "Is he handsome?"

"Y . . . yes, I think he is."

"As handsome as Augustus d'Este?"

Feodora sighed. Victoria had reminded her of that passionate attachment which had not been allowed to continue.

"It used to be such *fun*," said Victoria. "And Augustus was after all our cousin."

"But . . . he was not accepted as such by the family," Feodora reminded her.

"It is all so *complicated*," complained Victoria. "I do wish people would *tell* me things. Why should Augustus be my cousin and yet not be regarded as such? You know how he always called us 'cousins' when we went over into Uncle Augustus's garden."

Feodora nodded, recalling those days when she was quite a child, being just past eighteen—she was now a mature twenty-one—and she had been put in charge of Victoria and told not to let her out of her sight. There had been no harm in it. Uncle Augustus, the Duke of Sussex, had a garden among those of the Palace and Victoria had loved to water his plants. And how she used to get her feet wet in the operation and had to be smuggled in before Mamma or Lehzen or Späth saw and feared she would die of the effects. In the garden Augustus would often stroll. He was the son of Uncle Augustus and in truth their cousin, but not accepted as such because the "family" did not regard his father's marriage to his mother as a true marriage, although Uncle Augustus had been married to her both abroad and in London. It was something to do with that tiresome Marriage Act which said that the sons of the King could not marry without his consent. Well, Uncle Augustus had married without his father's consent and as his father was King George III who had brought in the Act, the case of Uncle Augustus's marriage was taken to court and the court gave the verdict that it was not legal. But Augustus the younger believed that it was and that he had every right to court his cousin.

They were happy days, with little Vicky wielding the watering-can and pretty seventeen-year-old Feodora sitting under the tree fanning herself and Augustus coming out as if by accident to talk to her and tell her she was beautiful. How exciting this was after the stern rules laid down in the Duchess of Kent's apartments in Kensington Palace.

Sometimes the Baroness Späth was with them. Dear old Späth was not nearly such a dragon as Lehzen, and very romantic, thinking how charming it was with Victoria tending the flowers and Augustus and Feodora falling in love.

Victoria had been aware of the intrigue although she was not quite six at the time. In any case it was pleasant to get away from the strict observance of Mamma and Lehzen, for she was allowed deliberately to pour the water over her feet and no one said anything, Feodora being so wrapped up in Augustus's conversation and Späth being so intent on watching Feodora and her cousin Augustus.

Cousin Augustus was old but very handsome, particularly in his Dragoons' uniform. As for Feodora she had grown prettier than ever; she had been constantly receiving letters and the Baroness Späth was always tripping from their apartments in Kensington Palace to those of the Duke of Sussex carrying notes from Feodora to Augustus and from Augustus to Feodora.

Once when Victoria had walked in the gardens with Feodora, her sister had whispered that she was going to marry Cousin Augustus and showed Victoria the gold ring he had given her.

"Then, Feodora, they will be *your* flowers I shall water."

"Yes, dear Vicky."

"I shall water them even more carefully because they are yours. And I shall come often to visit you, shall I not?"

Feodora said solemnly that if Mamma permitted it Vicky should be her very first visitor.

Victoria went back to the nursery and told the dolls the exciting news; but shortly afterwards there was trouble in Kensington Palace. This was when Feodora had told Mamma that Cousin Augustus wished to marry her, at which Mamma was "Painfully Surprised" "Disagreeably Shocked" and "Very Angry." It was nonsense it seemed to *imagine* Cousin Augustus could marry Feodora because Cousin Augustus was not considered to be legitimate and Feodora was the daughter of the Duchess of Kent and although the Duke of Kent had not been her father—for her father had been the Prince of Leiningen, Mamma's first husband—she was after all connected by her mother's second marriage with the royal family and was half-sister to Victoria.

Poor darling Feddy! That had been a bad time. Victoria had done her best to comfort her sister. Poor Späth had been talked to very severely by Mamma and had gone with averted eyes for days afterwards; Lehzen had clicked her tongue every time she saw her, and Victoria was not allowed to water the flowers in Uncle Sussex's garden because he was in disgrace too.

It was all very sad and poor Feodora had wept and confided to Victoria that her heart was broken.

Victoria presumed it had mended again because Feodora soon began to look almost as she had before those afternoons —though never quite so gay as when she had sat under the trees in Uncle Sussex's garden; and when not so long ago Uncle King—the most important of all the uncles—had expressed a desire to see his important little niece, Feodora had accompanied Victoria and Mamma to Windsor. Uncle King had been the most impressive man Victoria had ever seen. He was very very old and even fatter than he was old; and when she was lifted on to his lap to kiss him she had seen the rouge on his cheeks. Very strange, but she had liked him— better than Uncle William or Uncle Sussex—and most certainly better than Uncle Cumberland. Uncle Cambridge she did not remember seeing. He was abroad looking after Hanover. But the point was that while Uncle King liked his little niece Victoria very much and took her driving and smiled benignly on her, he could not take his eyes from Feodora and made her sit beside him and kept patting her knee and showing in several ways that he thought her very pretty.

"I do believe," said Victoria, after having witnessed the effect Feodora had on Augustus, "that Uncle King would like to marry Feodora."

Victoria was not the only one who thought that, and shortly afterwards Feodora was sent to Germany to stay with her grandmother, the Dowager Duchess of Saxe-Coburg, and there she had met Ernest, Prince of Hohenlohe-Langenburg, who, Grandmamma had made perfectly clear, would be a good husband for her; and what Grandmamma thought proper so would Mamma; and there was no fear of anyone's being horribly shocked about such a union.

"He's a soldier," said Feodora, "and he's past thirty . . . like Augustus."

Victoria brightened. The more like Augustus the better.

"He is a very good man," said Feodora. "There is no scandal about him. Not like Aunt Louise."

"What about Aunt Louise?"

"I don't know exactly except that Uncle Ernest has parted from her. I think she has done something very *wrong*. I didn't see her, but I saw the two little boys, Ernest—named after his father—and Albert, who is a little younger. Grandmamma told me he is three months younger than you."

"The little boys are our cousins, are they not?"

"Yes, they are. I wish you could have seen them. Albert is much prettier than Ernest."

"I am not sure," said Victoria, "that boys should be pretty."

"Oh they may be at that age; he's only eight years old, remember."

"Yes. Three months younger than I am."

"Dear little Alberinchen has the most lovely blue eyes and dimples. He will be very good-looking when he grows up."

"And who is Alberinchen?"

"Albert. It is Grandmamma's name for him. *He* is her favourite.'

"I think I should prefer Ernest."

"Why, when you have never seen him?"

"Because it seems to me that this Albert may be a little spoiled."

"Indeed he is not. It is only Grandmamma who shows how much she loves him; and she was the same with us."

"And we are not spoiled," admitted Victoria. "So why should Albert be? I should like to see our cousins."

"I am sure you will. Grandmamma was always saying how she would like you to be friends . . . with your boy cousins."

Feodora looked at Victoria to see if she had grasped the significance of this but Victoria had ceased to think of her cousins and had remembered how sad it was going to be when Feodora went away.

"How much happier it would have been if you had married Augustus and lived close by. I shouldn't have minded your marrying then."

"Alas," sighed Feodora, "marriages are made for us. It will be so for you one day, darling."

Victoria stared into the distance. That day was very far away.

"And there is our brother Charles . . ." began Feodora. "I believe he is going to find some opposition."

"Do tell be about Charles," said Victoria eagerly.

Feodora hesitated. She was reckless today; it was because she was soon going to leave her little sister. Victoria ought to know something of the world, she decided. How difficult it would be for her if she were suddenly thrust into marriage without any fore-knowledge. She was busy with her tutors for a greater part of the day; she was taught music and dancing; but what, Feodora asked herself, did the child know of human relationships and life? She had almost blurted out the scandal just now concerning Uncle Ernest and his wife Louise; what if she had let slip that Louise was an unfaithful wife and that Uncle Ernest had divorced her? Mamma and Lehzen would have been furious. They wanted to protect Victoria; but could ignorance be considered a protection?

And now she had betrayed the fact that Charles was heading for trouble. Well, what harm could there be if she told it discreetly?

Victoria loved her half-brother Charles; it was wonderful to have a grown-up brother—he was three years older than Feodora. It was true she saw very little of him, but when she did, she thought him charming. He was often in Germany, which was after all his home, but he loved to have news of him.

Feodora looked over her shoulder and whispered: "He is in love with Marie Klebelsberg and swears he'll marry her. It will never be allowed."

"Who is Marie Klebelsberg?" whispered Victoria.

"She is the daughter of Count Klebelsberg. Aunt Louise . . . before . . . before she left the Court met her when she was travelling with Uncle Ernest and was so taken with her that she made her her lady-in-waiting. That was how Charles met her. He says nothing on earth will stop his marrying her."

"Not Grandmamma? Not Mamma?"

"We shall have to see."

"Poor darling Charles! I believe people should marry for love."

She looked fondly at her dear Feodora and saw an idyllic picture—herself watering the flowers and Augustus and Feodora laughing under the trees and darling old Späth looking so pleased and happy.

Feodora, fearful that she had said too much, went on quickly: "It's a secret. You must not mention it. Mamma would be cross."

Victoria nodded conspiratorially; and Feodora, to take her mind from dangerous subjects, started to play the favourite game of "Do you remember?"

Victoria enjoyed hearing stories that concerned herself; and because she was sad about the impending departure, Feodora decided to cheer her up. The story of Victoria and the Bishop never failed to delight the little girl.

"He picked you up in his arms and you were not very pleased."

"No I was not," agreed Victoria. "And what did I do then, eh, Feodora?"

"You pulled off his wig and started to pull his hair out of it."

"How . . . wicked of me," cried Victoria delightedly. "And what did he do?"

"He could do nothing. Poor man, he was smothered in powder, and he only grew very red in the face and waited for Mamma to come to the rescue."

"Of course I was talked to *very* severely afterwards."

"Oh yes, there was quite a storm."

"Indeed I can be very wayward."

"Darling Vicky, you are often very good."

"Oh, am I?"

"Do you remember when your Uncle York was dying how

you used to send him a bunch of flowers every day?"

"I picked them myself. I thought he would like to know I was thinking of him."

"There. It shows you can be kind and thoughtful."

"He gave me my beautiful donkey. Poor Uncle York! He was a very kind man. He was the heir to the throne then and now it is Uncle Clarence."

Feodora sighed. Did Victoria know who was next to Clarence in the succession? One did not mention it. Mamma and Lehzen had decided that since Victoria was so frank and apt to speak her mind, it was better if her future prospects were not made too clear to her. She must, said Mamma, be made to feel that life would offer her great responsibilities, but what these should be must, for the time being, be a little vague to her.

"Darling Aunt Adelaide," said Victoria. "I love her very much. She gave me the Big Doll, you know. She is kind, although Mamma thinks her a little dowdy."

"Don't mention that. Mamma would not be pleased."

"No, but I heard her mention it to Sir John."

Feodora looked quickly at her sister. Victoria's mouth had tightened a little. She did not greatly care for Sir John Conroy, the Comptroller of her mother's household, and she did not quite know why.

"Look!" said Feodora. "Dear old Späth is coming. I expect it is for you."

The Baroness's yellowish face lit up with pleasure when she saw her two darlings. It was both a joy and a sadness to contemplate them. Victoria was a dear child, so vivacious, so passionate, so determined to have her way and yet so eager to be good, and always so ready to sympathize with the troubles of others. Often one saw the rather prominent blue eyes fill with tears at the sight of some poor person in distress.

The Baroness had never really recovered from the shame of having displeased the Duchess over the Augustus d'Este affair. Poor darling Feodora had been so much in love with the young man and if she dared go against the Duchess's wishes—which of course she would not—the Baroness would have said that a marriage with the son of the Duke of Sussex was not such an ill match. If the young couple were in love that, in Späth's opinion, should have been reason enough.

But the dear Duchess had been so displeased. Poor Späth trembled now to remember how angry she had been.

And now Feodora was betrothed and was soon to be married and that meant a sad separation.

"Have you come for me, dear Späth?" asked Victoria.

"It is time for your lesson, Princess."

Victoria walked between them a little soberly. This was how they used to walk when they went to Uncle Sussex's garden. Alas, that Mamma had not approved. If she had dearest Feodora would not have been on the point of going away.

A Wedding at Kensington

IN the house at Bushy—the favourite residence of Adelaide, Duchess of Clarence—she was preparing for the arrival of the Prince of Hohenlohe-Langenburg. This was in the nature of a State visit and State visits never made her very happy. She much preferred the rural life at Bushy where she and William could live quietly surrounded by the Fitz-Clarence grandchildren who were growing numerous and whose parents looked upon the mansion as the family home.

Adelaide was delighted that this should be so. She, who had longed for children of her own and been denied them, could find some solace in the children of others. People had ceased to remark on the extraordinary manner in which she had taken her husband's family by Dorothy Jordan to her heart. It certainly had won William's. She might be a little dowdy; she was certainly no beauty—she was pale and her skin was often spotty at certain times of the year; people were inclined to ignore her; but those who knew her well loved her. William her husband was delighted with her; he treated her with respect; he even listened to her; and one of his greatest delights was to see her with his grandchildren—behaving as though they were hers too. She, a Princess—albeit of a little German state—could be a fairy godmother to the actress Dorothy Jordan's grandchildren.

Soon she hoped to have with her her nephew by marriage —young George Cambridge whose father Adolphus, Duke of Cambridge, was at present Viceroy of Hanover. George's mother, Augusta, had written to her saying that it was time her young George came to England to be educated and she would be happy if Adelaide would take him under her wing.

Of course she would. She loved children; she had a way with them too; there was not one of them who did not respond at once to her affection and her gentle discipline. She herself was only happy when the house was full of them; and she gathered together all her young relations and gave parties for them; she was frequently devising new presents for them, something which would delight and enchant them. It was small wonder that they all loved Aunt Adelaide.

Even the Cumberlands' boy, George, was a frequent visitor. What a dear boy—so different from his parents who rather terrified Adelaide. She could never quite be sure what they were plotting.

There was one absentee from the parties: Little Victoria from Kensington. It was a shame. Adelaide often thought of the child—a lively, pretty little creature, bubbling over with affection. But her mother would not allow her to come to Bushy while the FitzClarence grandchildren were there. She implied that Adelaide should banish the youngsters—as if she could! They were William's grandchildren, and therefore hers. But the Duchess of Kent did not wish her Victoria to be contaminated by what she called the "bastidry." Really, she was a difficult woman! She incensed William who could grow incoherent with rage when he discussed her. The King himself was irritated by her. Adelaide had tried to make harmony in the family, but with a woman such as the Duchess of Kent who had such grand ideas of her position in the country—through her daughter, of course—it was certainly difficult. So dear little Victoria was not allowed to join the gay parties at Bushy and share in the fun. It was wrong. Children were not meant to be so serious—even if there was a possibility of their mounting the throne. Childhood was a carefree time. Poor little Victoria!

Had Adelaide's own darling Elizabeth lived, this glittering possibility might have been banished from Victoria's ambitious Mamma's mind; but all that was left to Adelaide was a stone statue of her reclining baby—so lifelike, so beautiful that often when she was alone she would kneel by it and shed tears of sorrow.

She did not believe that she would ever have a child now. There had been so many disappointments. It was not so much that she desired an heir to the throne; it was a baby of her own that she wanted. Alas, that blessing was denied her and she must console herself with other people's children.

William never reproached her. He was kind in his rough nautical way. He was devoted to his FitzClarences. They were bastards and could never mount the throne, but William did not really mind that he had no legitimate heir. As long as he himself was King—that was all that concerned him.

And there was another worry. He was becoming obsessed by the fact that the Crown could be his.

Adelaide sighed and went to his room.

"Ah, my dear Adelaide." He always seemed genuinely pleased to see her. He was a faithful and affectionate husband; he had not wanted to marry her particularly and had done so for expediency, but he had soon discovered the fine qualities of his dear Adelaide. He often said now in his brash way that if the most beautiful Princess in the world was offered him he would think twice before changing his Adelaide for her. It was meant to be a compliment of course. But unlike his elder brother George, the King, William had no grace of manners.

He came towards her and embraced her. He was shorter than his brothers—red-faced, weatherbeaten and showing his sixty-three years.

"The Prince will soon be arriving," Adelaide reminded him.

"Oh yes, yes. Why we should be expected to look after the fellow, I don't know. He's come to marry that damned Duchess's daughter, not one of mine."

Adelaide did not mention that if the young man had been coming to marry one of his daughters there would be no need for him to be received by a member of the royal family.

"Her girl," he grumbled. "A pretty creature. I don't doubt she's glad to escape from the interfering old woman."

"Let us hope she will find happiness in marriage."

"Couldn't be worse than living in Kensington Palace with that woman. And I suppose we've got to have a dinner party to entertain the fellow, eh?"

"We must remember he is a visitor."

William was further irritated. He was enjoying the domesticity of Bushy to which he had retired in great dudgeon after having been obliged to resign his post of Lord High

Admiral. That had been an intensely worrying time, when he had put on a uniform and attempted to command the Navy instead of treating the post as the sinecure Wellington, the Prime Minister, and his brother, the King, had intended it to be.

She had been afraid, for there had been rumours at the time that William was going the way of his father—towards madness. Such rumours had doubtless been circulated by Cumberland, and William's behaviour did suggest that there might be some truth in them. However, he had come through that difficult period, had given up parading in his uniform, attempting to reform the Navy and making grandiloquent speeches to the sailors. He had come to Bushy, to Adelaide and the children; now he lived quietly there, rising early, breakfasting with Adelaide and some of the children at nine-thirty, playing with the children until midday and after the meal taking a nap and later discussing the gardens with the gardeners or riding or walking and in the evening settling down to a game of Pope Joan with the family, never staking more than a shilling at a time.

In such surroundings he became calmer although he always talked a great deal and excitedly, making speeches at the least provocation even though Adelaide was his only audience.

But there could be no doubt that in the domestic atmosphere of his home his physical and mental health improved and he was his old affectionate and jaunty self. It was the thought of greatness that unnerved him, but its fascination for him was immense.

Since the death of his brother, the Duke of York—which made him next in the succession if the King did not have a child, and it was scarcely likely that that mass of corrupting flesh could beget a child even if he were suitably married—William had thought constantly of the Crown. He dreamed of wearing it as persistently as in her apartments at Kensington Palace the Duchess of Kent dreamed of her daughter's doing so. The thought of what his brother's death would mean would suddenly occur to him and Adelaide would fearfully watch the enraptured expression dawn in his eyes. Then the excitement would grow; the wildness would develop, and she would be terrified that what he said might be construed as treason.

Even now his eyes gleamed as he came closer to her. "He's failing," he said. "He's failing fast . . ."

No need to ask to whom he referred; the rising note in his

voice was enough. She drew away from him, wondering how
he could show this near elation at the thought of a beloved
brother's failing grip on life.

"Seventeen leeches they applied to his leg yesterday. He
was rambling badly."

"Poor George! He has always been such a good friend to
us."

"He's "He's a good fellow, George. But he's had his day."

"He is not so very old . . . only three years older than you,
William."

She hoped the comparison would have a sobering effect.

"Ah," said William craftily, "but think of the life he has
led. He has eaten and drunk too well. He's not a healthy man.
Any moment now, Adelaide. He can't last another year."

"We must pray for him," she said.

Yes, she thought, pray for him. Pray for him to live because what will happen when William comes to the throne
who can say? She shivered to remember his brief period as
Lord High Admiral. But how much more he would strut as
a King than he had as an Admiral, George *must* live; she
was terrified of what might happen when William became
King.

"It is very pleasant here at Bushy, William. The cozy inti-
mate life we lead here—and the dear, dear children."

He nodded; like his brothers—with the exception of Cumberland—he was excessively sentimental.

"Poor sweet Louise," she went on, luring him farther away
from dreams of kingship, "she is so interested in this wedding.
Dear child, I fear there will never be a wedding for her."

He nodded. "But she is fortunate," he said brightly, "to
have her Aunt Adelaide looking after her."

"I know she is happy here."

Poor little Louise, indeed she was. She was the daughter
of Adelaide's sister Ida, Duchess of Saxe-Weimar, and had
been crippled from birth. Adelaide had more or less adopted
her and her brother Edward, the little boy who had been
born in England when Ida was visiting her sister. This niece
and little nephew formed part of Adelaide's family of children; they adored her and she did everything she could to
make their childhood happy.

"So she should be. Why, my dear Adelaide, you look after
us all . . . every one of us."

His calm was restored; he was momentarily the country
squire of Bushy, but one word could bring back his dreams

of greatness. Adelaide lived in terror of what he would do. He was not only tactless but extremely insensitive. She was never sure when he was going off to the House of Lords to deliver a speech which at best would set the peers yawning and at worst set fire to some inflammatory matter which would set the people raging, the lampoonists and cartoonists jeering and given credence to the rumours that the Duke of Clarence was on the way to becoming as mad as his father.

"I think," said Adelaide, "that the bridegroom has arrived."

"Then," replied William ungraciously, "I suppose we should go down to greet him."

The Duchess's brother, Leopold of Saxe-Coburg, called at the apartments at Kensington Palace to see his sister. He came regularly every Wednesday afternoon, very dignified, very benign, expecting affection and homage, for the Duchess lived on his bounty and he was one of the few people in England whom she was sure she could trust.

On Wednesday afternoons Victoria was on her best behaviour because that was how dearest Uncle Leopold would wish her to be. She believed that she loved Uncle Leopold more than anyone else in the world. Dearest Feodora she loved tenderly; Lehzen she respected and loved; secretly in her heart she was not altogether sure of her feelings for Mamma except that one *must* love one's Mamma because it would be extremely wicked not to do so, but if loving meant being excited and happy to be in the presence of the loved one, that was not always the case with Mamma. But with Uncle Leopold she had no doubt whatsoever. Her other loves were female and Victoria believed that while she could love her sister and her governess deeply she could not feel quite so protected in their company as she did in that of a man; and therefore there was something beyond love in the emotions Uncle Leopold aroused and this set him apart from all others.

"He is the most *beautiful* man in the world," she told the dolls. "He has almost *commanded* me to love him best. Oh, he has not said so, but there is an understanding between us which does not need words."

So Wednesday afternoon was the great day of the week.

She would watch from her window for his carriage—usually with Lehzen beside her—and he would look up, knowing she was there. Once she had not been and although he was not reproachful he was very sad.

"Lehzen," she would say, "may we not go down to greet him?"

And Lehzen would say, maddeningly: "I think we should wait until we are sent for."

The summons would come quickly; and she would go to Mamma's drawing-room and she would throw her arms about him and say: "Dearest, most beautiful Uncle Leopold." And Mamma would say: "My child, your uncle will think you have never been taught how to enter a drawing-room." "Oh, but Mamma, this is *dearest* Uncle Leopold and I am *too* happy to have good manners."

And if Mamma was not pleased, Uncle Leopold was. He would have his dearest Victoria just as she was. He loved her tenderly and he was delighted when she showed him that she loved her uncle with a devotion almost as great as that he felt for her. "Oh, more so, dearest Uncle." "No, my love, that could not be." And they would play the delicious game of "I love you more than you love me," each trying to prove that the other was mistaken.

Then Uncle Leopold would wish her to sit on his knee while he twirled her hair in his fingers and he told Mamma how he suffered with his rheumatic pains and his chest cold, for poor darling Uncle Leopold, in spite of his beauty, was often very sick.

Mamma listened and mentioned a few symptoms of her own, and then Uncle Leopold would want to hear about Victoria's lessons because he was always so interested in what she did. But today was different as everything was with the wedding so close. Victoria was not summoned immediately to the drawing-room because Uncle Leopold wished to talk to Mamma alone.

He now sat in one of the blue-and-white-striped chairs regarding his boots with the high soles to make him look taller. His wig, which he wore not so much for the sake of appearances as to keep his head warm, and prevent his catching cold, gave him an added air of elegance.

"Soon," he was saying, "Feodora will be settled. It's a fair enough match. And Charles will have to be prevented from doing anything foolish."

"Charles will never be such a fool," said the Duchess.

"My dear sister, your son has sworn to marry this woman.

He's a ruler in his own right. I doubt he can be prevented . . . only persuaded."

"He shall be persuaded," declared the Duchess.

Leopold regarded her with faint irritation. She was a most domineering woman. She needed a man to guide her; all women did. His own wife Charlotte had been a hoyden but she had improved considerably under his guidance. Ah, if only Charlotte had lived, how different everything would have been. Charlotte would have been on the point of becoming Queen—for King George was surely on the point of death—and he would have been her consort, the power behind the throne, the real ruler of England. But his dear hoyden had died in childbed and this most unsatisfactory situation had arisen. The King's brothers had hastily married and Leopold's own sister had fallen to the Duke of Kent (he, Leopold, had helped to arrange *that* marriage) and now they had a child, dear little Victoria who, once George and Clarence were out of the way, would be Queen of England.

Some compensation, but how much better it would have been to have guided his Queen-wife than his Queen-niece.

And his sister, the Duchess Victoria, could be a nuisance. She talked too much; she wished always to be in the centre of the stage and if she was willing to accept Leopold as one of the little Queen's counsellors, she was determined that her mother should be another.

Leopold shrugged aside the affair of his nephew Charles and Marie Klebelsberg. The important issue was, as always, Victoria.

"The King has taken a turn for the worse," said Leopold giving a little cough and laying his hand delicately over his chest.

"He will die very soon, I'm sure," said the Duchess with blithe optimism.

"The life he has led!" Leopold raised his eyes to the ceiling. He had never liked his father-in-law and the feeling was mutual. A sanctimonious fellow who didn't drink could hardly be to the King's taste; besides, he had wanted his daughter to marry the Prince of Orange, not link the family with the little house of Saxe-Coburg.

The Duchess shuddered. "I can't understand how he keeps living. It seems as though he does it to spite us."

Leopold said: "You should speak with greater discretion, sister."

She shook her head, elaborately dressed as usual. The bows and ribbons fussed all over her gown and she glittered as she moved. She was overdressed, thought Leopold painfully. They would say it was bad taste.

"Everyone knows it," she said. "Everyone is saying it. And then it will be that fool William's turn. He can't last long."

Leopold put his fingers to his lips. He guessed that Sir John Conroy was not far away. That gentleman would make it his business always to be at hand when Leopold was with his sister, although he doubted not that the Duchess Victoria kept him informed of all that went on. Still, nothing was ever so accurate as that gleaned first-hand.

Should he warn her of Conroy? It was hardly the time. He himself was engaged in an adventure of the heart with Caroline Bauer, a charming actress, who was a niece of his favourite physician and friend, Dr. Stockmar. He was not given to such conduct and this was a rare lapse; but he consoled himself that Charlotte would have understood; and being so certain of this he could even entertain Caroline at Claremont where he had lived with Charlotte during those months before she had died.

His sister had learned of this attachment and expressed her stern displeasure. That Leopold should have behaved like the immoral people of the Court was distressing. This was perhaps because he had hinted at her relationship with Conroy.

It was clearly better for them to turn a blind eye on each other in that respect. There were ample excuses for both of them, and neither was promiscuous.

So not a word about Conroy. That could come later.

"Does Victoria understand the position?"

"Not exactly. She is aware that some great destiny awaits her but she is not quite sure what."

"I daresay she has a shrewd notion," Leopold smiled affectionately. "She is a clever little minx."

"I would not have her *talk* of the possibility. She is so . . . frank."

Leopold nodded. But not so indiscreet as her mother.

"Everyone should take the utmost care," he said pointedly. "This is a delicate matter. And I believe Cumberland has his spies everywhere."

She shivered. "I believe he would stop at nothing."

"She is guarded night and day?"

"She sleeps in the same room as myself. Lehzen sits with her until I come to bed. She is never allowed to be alone. I have even ordered that she is not to walk downstairs unaccompanied."

"I suppose it's necessary."

"Necessary. Indeed it's necessary. You know those stairs. The most dangerous in England, with their corkscrew twists and at the sides they taper away to almost nothing. It would be the most likely place that some harm would come to her."

"I have Cumberland watched. He wants the throne for himself first and for that boy of his."

"But he can do nothing. He comes after Victoria."

"And there is no Salic law in this country as in Hanover. But Cumberland would like to introduce it."

"He could not do such a thing."

"I do not think the people would wish it, but often laws go against the people's wishes. You know he is Grand Master of the Orange Lodges. I heard that one of their plans is to bring in a law by which females are excluded from the throne."

The Duchess put her hand to her be-ribboned bosom.

"It could never be!"

"I trust not. But I tell you that we should be watchful. William is an old fool; he's almost as old as George. His health is no good. He suffers from asthma, and that can be dangerous. Moreover, it is just possible that he'll follow his father into a strait-jacket. They are taking bets at the Clubs that William will be in a strait-jacket before George dies."

The Duchess clasped her hands. "If that should happen . . ."

"A Regency," said Leopold, his eyes glittering.

"A mother should guide her daughter."

"Her mother . . . and her uncle."

The prospect was breathtakingly exciting.

Leopold said: "I have been offered the Greek throne. But I have decided to refuse it."

His sister smiled at him. Of course he had refused it. What was the governing of Greece compared with that of England? When oh when. . . ? Just those two old men standing in the way. One on his deathbed—although it must be admitted that he was always rising from it, rouging his cheeks and giving musical parties at the Pavilion—and the other a bumptious old fool tottering on the edge of sanity and who was not free from physical ailments either.

It was small wonder that the marriage of Feodora and the pending indiscretions of her brother Charles were of small moment compared with the glittering possibilities which could come through Victoria.

Sir John Conroy, hovering close to the drawing-room, was disturbed. He was always uneasy when Leopold was in the Palace. Leopold was his great rival, for the Duchess's brother had marked for his own role that which Conroy had chosen for himself. Adviser to the Duchess. In the Saxe-Coburg family Leopold was regarded as a sort of god; he it was who had married the heiress of England, although a younger son and no very brilliant prospects to attract; he had won not only the hand but also the heart of the Princess of England and would have been to all intents and purposes ruler of that country. The Duchess was completely under the spell of her brother.

Hypochondriac! growled Sir John. But he had to admit that for all his brooding on imaginary illnesses Leopold was a shrewd man. Sir John, who made it his business to be informed on everything that might affect his career, had learned that there was a possibility of Leopold's accepting the Greek throne. That had been joyous news; and when Leopold had refused no one could have been more sorry than Sir John Conroy. He had to accept the fact that Leopold intended to rule England through Victoria, and that was precisely what Sir John wished to do. But how could he hope to influence the Duchess while her brother was beside her?

A lover should have more influence than a brother; and Sir John had always been able to charm the ladies. Lady Conyngham was prepared to be very agreeable; and the poor old Princess Sophia was always excited when he visited her; as for the Duchess, she was devoted to him. One would have thought, in the circumstances, that all would have been easy; but Leopold was no ordinary brother. And Leopold had shown quite clearly that he did not very much like the friendship between his sister and the Comptroller of her household.

What was Leopold saying now? He, Conroy, had made sure that the Duchess was aware of her brother's affair with Caroline Bauer. That would make him seem slightly less admirable, more human. Leopold was a sanctimonious humbug and it was not surprising that the King could not bear him.

Still, the Duchess did depend on his bounty. It was shameful the way she was treated. Even the King, who was noted for his chivalrous behaviour towards all women, expressed his dislike of her. As for Clarence, he spoke disparagingly of her publicly. But then no one expected good manners from Clarence.

While he hovered close to the drawing-room the Princess Victoria appeared with Lehzen.

Victoria was saying: "I do hope dearest Uncle Leopold will not be too upset because I was not at the window. He has come early. Oh dear, how I wish I had been there."

"I daresay His Highness will understand," said Lehzen.

This adoration of Leopold was really quite absurd, thought Conroy.

A sneer played about his lips. Victoria noticed it and did not like it. She had come to the conclusion that she did not really like Sir John. There was something about him that disturbed her. It was when he was with Mamma. Sometimes when he was with Aunt Sophie too; and there were times when his eyes would rest on Victoria herself speculatively.

She had never spoken the thought aloud but it was in her mind. She did not like Sir John.

"Have you something on your mind?" The sneer was very evident. He never treated her with the same *respect* as she was accustomed to receive from the Baroness Späth—and Lehzen who, for all her sternness, always conveyed that she was aware of her importance.

"I did not care to keep my uncle waiting," she said coldly.

"He hasn't waited long. You were here almost before the summons came."

"If I wish to be here, I shall be," she said in her most imperious manner.

But Sir John Conroy was not to be intimidated as a music master some years before. Doubtless, she thought, he will report this to Mamma and say that I was arrogant and haughty. But if I wish to be arrogant and haughty, I shall be.

"Ha," laughed Sir John, "now you look exactly like the Duke of Gloucester."

What a dreadful thought! The Duke of Gloucester. Aunt Mary's old husband and cousin. Silly Billy, they called him in the family; he was looked on as rather stupid and now that he had married the Princess Mary, had become a difficult husband.

"I have always been told," she said coldly, "that I resembled my Uncle, the King."

"Oh no, no. You're not a bit like him. You grow more like

the Duke of Gloucester every day."

She swept past, with Lehzen in her wake. Sir John laughed but with some misgiving. It was silly to have upset the child just because he was angry about Leopold. Old Lehzen too! She was no friend of his.

He would get rid of her if possible. But he could see he would have to be careful with Victoria.

Smarting from her encounter with her mother's Comptroller of the Household Victoria went into the drawing-room where the sight of dearest Uncle Leopold seated in his chair, his dear pale face *beautiful* beneath his curly wig, made her forget everything else.

"Dearest Uncle . . ."

She ran to him, throwing ceremony aside. After that horrible encounter with Conroy she needed the protective comfort of Leopold's arms more than ever.

Feodora, being dressed for her wedding, was a little fearful, a little tearful. She was not afraid of her bridegroom; in fact she liked him. Since her match with Augustus d'Este had been frowned on she had faced the fact that she must marry a Prince who was chosen for her; and her Ernest was by no means unattractive. She had compared Ernest with Augustus and now that Augustus was out of reach it seemed to her that Ernest did not suffer too much from the comparison.

All the same she was leaving Kensington which had been home to her for so long; but she had to admit, though, that apart from leaving Victoria and dear old Lehzen and Späth, she would not mind so much. Her recent trip to Germany had made her feel that she could be very happy there. It was leaving her dear little sister that was so upsetting.

She realized that she had not included Mamma in those she would miss. Well, to tell the truth, she would not be sorry to *escape* from Mamma. There, she had admitted it. But she would not allow herself to say it. Dear little Victoria was condemned to imprisonment . . . because that was what it was . . . in a way.

She should therefore be gay and happy; and so she would be if it were not for leaving Victoria.

Victoria had come in to see the bride. Lehzen hovered. Oh, why could we never be alone even for a little while!

"Dearest Sissy! You look *so* beautiful."

"All brides look beautiful. It's the dress."

"No bride looked as beautiful as you."

"Vicky, you always see those you love in a flattering light."

"Do I?"

"Of course you do, you dear Angel. And you look lovely yourself."

Victoria turned round to show off her white lace dress.

"I am going to miss you so," said Feodora tremulously.

"It is going to be *terrible* without you."

"But you will have Uncle Leopold, dear Lehzen and Späth . . . and Mamma."

"And you will have Ernest. He is very handsome, Feodora, and Uncle Leopold says he is a good match."

"Oh yes, I *like* Ernest."

"But you must *love* your husband. And just think there will be the darling little children."

"Oh, not for a while," said Feodora.

"What a lovely necklace."

"It's diamonds. A present from the King."

"He loves you. I think he would have liked to marry you."

"Oh, he is an old, old man."

"But a very nice one. I think that next to Uncle Leopold he is the nicest man I know. And he is a King."

"He is coming to the wedding. He has promised to give me away."

"I don't think he will like that . . . giving you away to Ernest when he wants you himself."

"Oh, Vicky, what extraordinary things you say!"

"Do I? Perhaps I say too rashly what comes into my mind. Lehzen says I do."

"Oh dear, when I think of you here without me, I shall weep, I know I shall."

"But you will come to Kensington and perhaps I shall pay a visit to Germany."

"I shall have to come to Kensington for they will never let *you* out of their sight."

Victoria sighed. "I wish they would let me be alone with myself . . . just for a little while."

"I know how you feel, darling. I think I am going to be freer now."

"You will have Ernest."

"But he will not be a jailer like . . ."

Silence. She was going to say like Mamma, thought Vic-

toria. And it's true. Mamma is like a jailer. How I should
like to be free too.

Feodora put her arms about her.

"But I must not spoil your pretty dress. When I go away,
Vicky, I want to take your dress with me. I want to take
it out and look at it and remember just how you looked
today."

"Oh, you shall," cried Victoria. It was a notion which
greatly appealed to her sentimental heart. Then the realization of her loss came back to her and tears filled her eyes.

The bells were ringing all over Kensington to tell people
that this was Feodora's wedding day. There were crowds
gathering outside the Palace because people had heard that
the King was coming to give the bride away, making this
a royal occasion.

The Duchess, overpowering in lace ribbons and feathers,
presided noisily in the Grand Hall. Everyone must be in
exact order of precedence. There was Victoria, looking very
pretty—and what was more important, healthy—in her
white dress, her fair hair specially curled for the occasion.
Lehzen had spent a long time on it. Everyone, thought the
Duchess, must be aware of the child's blooming looks. There
was Clarence—what a ridiculous old fellow!—and Adelaide,
her eyes on Victoria with that amused affection she had for
all the children. And Victoria was speaking to her, telling
her about the dolls, which was most unsuitable. Victoria must
be told of this later. But it was really Adelaide's fault for
encouraging her. One would have thought this was a cosy
family meeting in some quite inferior country gentleman's
home, instead of a wedding in the royal family with the
King due to arrive at any moment.

The wedding was to take place in the Cupola Room—so
suitable for such ceremonies. Victoria had been christened
here. What an occasion when the King had been so *unkind*
to the baby's parents and refused to give permission for the
child to have the names they had chosen for her. They had
wanted Georgiana, Elizabeth. Queen's names both of them.
And the King—Regent he had been then—had insisted on
Alexandrina Victoria. But it was amazing how one quickly
grew accustomed to names. Victoria now seemed as much
like a Queen's name as any of them.

Oh dear, the King was late. Was he going to *humiliate* the Duchess of Kent again?

"It looks to me as though the King is not coming," said bluff Clarence. Trust him to put it as crudely as that.

Adelaide as usual tried to disguise her husband's crudity. "I heard that His Majesty had begun to feel unwell again."

"He's always up and down," said Clarence. "One of these days there'll be no up."

A shocked silence, during which Clarence noticeably became more royal. He was waiting for George's death, thought the Duchess, almost as eagerly as she was waiting for his quickly to follow that of the King.

"His Majesty's resilience is wonderful," said Adelaide. "As we have often seen."

Clarence, seeing himself as King, decided to take charge of the situation. They weren't going to hang about any longer. It was clear to him that George wasn't coming.

He took Feodora's hand. "Come, my dear, your Uncle Clarence will do the King's job. He'll give you away to your husband, but you look so pretty that I'd never want to give you away unless it was necessary."

The Duchess's chagrin was obvious. An insult! How dared that rouged roué treat her so? No excuses. No apologies. This was the second time the Cupola Room had seen her humiliated.

But everyone was glad for the ceremony to proceed and Clarence—who would soon be King in any case (but not for long, prayed the Duchess) led the bride to the altar which had been set up and Victoria the bridesmaid followed her sister looking so sweet that many found it difficult to take their eyes from her.

So was Feodora married to Ernest, Prince of Hohenlohe-Langenburg; and afterwards Victoria went among the company carrying a ribbon-trimmed basket from which she gave the guests mementoes of the occasion.

And, as the Duchess later remarked to Sir John, in spite of the discourteous behaviour of that old man who called himself a King, the wedding had been a great success.

The day after the wedding the Duchess of Kent decided to travel to Claremont to see how the newly married couple were getting on.

"Poor Feodora," whispered Charles when they were in

the carriage. "I'm sure she would like to be alone for a while with her husband, but Mamma must be in charge of everything and everyone."

Victoria regarded her brother with awe. There was some secret in his life and she wished she knew more of it. Something to do with a lady named Marie Klebelsberg whom he wished to marry but who, like most people members of her family wished to marry, was Most Unsuitable.

How sad, thought Victoria, that both Feodora and Charles had chosen unsuitable people. Not that that affected Feodora now because she was suitably married.

Charles sat staring ahead of him while the Duchess watched him uneasily; Victoria, who loved to go on journeys, forgot Charles's unsuitable behaviour and enjoyed the countryside; she was delighted at the prospect of seeing Feodora again even though very shortly her sister would be leaving Claremont for Germany.

And there was Claremont—the house she loved to visit because it was the home of dearest Uncle Leopold and there he had been so happy when he was married to Princess Charlotte who was Victoria's cousin by birth and aunt by marriage with dear Uncle Leopold.

At Claremont she had known the happiest days of her life; and Feodora had agreed that she had enjoyed the same at Claremont. Not only was Uncle Leopold there but also Louisa Lewis who had served Princess Charlotte and stayed on as a sort of chatelaine of Claremont. Louisa declared that the happiest days for her, now that she had lost her beloved Charlotte, were those when Victoria came to Claremont because she saw in Victoria so much of Charlotte.

It was so comforting to give such pleasure to people merely by being oneself and listening to entrancing stories of the mad behaviour of Princess Charlotte.

And there was Louisa waiting to greet them and ready with such a sweeping curtsy for Mamma that even she was satisfied.

"And how are our young couple today?" she asked.

"Your Grace, they have gone for a walk round the gardens. I will have them informed of your arrival."

Uncle Leopold had appeared, and Victoria noticed with gratification that his first smiles were for her.

"Welcome, my darling, to Claremont."

"Dearest, dearest Uncle." How beautiful he was—even more so at Claremont than in Kensington because it was his home and he seemed more comfortable here. Victoria's heart overflowed with love. She really believed that she *did* love Uncle Leopold more than anyone else in the world.

They went to the drawing-room which was not large by Kensington or Windsor standards, but homely. She supposed that Bushy was rather like this, although she was never allowed to go there. Mamma would not permit it, which hurt dear Aunt Adelaide; there was some reason why it was not suitable for her to go. Thank Heaven, it was suitable to come to Claremont.

Would dear little Victoria like to take a walk over the lawns with Uncle Leopold? The view of Windsor Castle was better in the winter than in the summer.

Victoria would love to be anywhere alone with Uncle Leopold. So he took her hand, and while Mamma talked to Louisa Lewis about the arrangements she had made for the honeymoon, and Charles went off on his own, Victoria and Uncle Leopold walked in the gardens and assured each other of their undying love, admitting that they could feel no such love for any other. So that was very comforting since she was soon to lose Feodora.

"You are sad because your dear sister is going away," said Leopold, "but I am here, my darling. Do you know that I have just refused the offer of a crown . . . for your sake."

"Oh, Uncle Leopold!"

"Yes, the Greeks wanted me to become their King. That would have meant leaving England. I could not endure that. Not when my dear little love of a niece is here."

She clung to his hand, tears in her eyes; they stood and embraced; Uncle Leopold wept too; like the King, he wept in a pleasant way without any reddening or swelling of the eyes. It was elegant weeping. I must learn to weep as they do, thought Victoria; because hers was the kindly sentimental nature which demanded much shedding of tears.

But how pleasant it was to walk with Uncle Leopold through the gardens which he had helped to create and which he loved, and to hear him talk of Charlotte and the great tragedy of his life.

"Of course," he said, "I had to guide Charlotte. She was a hoyden, a tomboy, which is not really very becoming for a prospective Queen. I was constantly warning her. Dear Charlotte. Sometimes she would get a little angry with me and accuse me of being over-critical."

"Angry with *you*, Uncle Leopold!"

"Not really angry. She was devoted to me. The short time we were married was the only time she was ever happy. She said so often. Every criticism was for her own good."

"Did she know that?"

"I think she realized it. She was not always wise. I think my dear little Victoria may well be wiser than Charlotte."

He pressed her hand. She would be wise. She would listen. She would not complain at criticism—especially the loving tender criticism such as Uncle Leopold would give her.

"Dearest Uncle, you will always be near me?"

"While you need me."

"I know I am going to need you all my life."

It was the answer he wanted.

When they returned to the house Feodora and her bridegroom were there. Feodora looked rather flushed and excited and she whispered to Victoria that she was full of hope that she would be happy.

And while the grown-ups talked, Victoria was allowed to visit Louisa Lewis in her own room which was a part of the ritual at Claremont and when the door shut on them Louisa said, as she always did: "There now, we can be comfortable."

And comfortable they were, for it did not matter what one said to Louisa. She thought everything clever and so like Charlotte, which was the highest praise she could bestow. Victoria was growing fast; Louisa was astonished every time she saw her. She was getting more like Charlotte every day.

"Charlotte was not pretty, was she?"

"Charlotte had no need of prettiness. She was the most lively, attractive girl I ever saw."

"Was she a little like the Duke of Gloucester?"

"Good gracious me, what a question. The Duke of Gloucester! The Princess Mary's husband . . . now what put it into your head that Charlotte could be one little bit like him?"

"Someone told me that I was like him."

"You . . . a dainty pretty little girl like you! That was nonsense."

"I thought it was," said Victoria. "I think the person who said it was angry with me and wanted to alarm me."

"Nobody could be angry with you for long. In any case, my love, don't you believe it. Oh dear, you've torn your dress. Let me mend it. How Charlotte used to tear her things! She kept me and Mrs. Gagarin busy. I can tell you. Poor

Gagarin, she adored Charlotte; every stitch was put in with loving care."

Louisa threaded her needle. "I'll mend this so that no one knows you ever tore it. And where did you do it? On the stairs? It wasn't like that when you set out this morning, I know. The Baroness Lehzen would have seen to that."

"I think I caught it on a bramble in the garden."

"What a neat clean little girl you are. Now, Charlotte . . . there was nothing neat about Charlotte. She used to come in sometimes, bounding in so that she would well nigh knock you over; and would be so excited she wouldn't be able to get the words out. She'd stutter and grow quite angry with herself. You speak beautifully."

"I have to learn how to pronounce my words; I have to read a great deal."

"I'm sure you do. And very nice too."

"But I think you liked Charlotte's stutter."

"Oh, Charlotte!" Louisa laughed. "She could be a very naughty little girl sometimes . . . but in a lovable way, if you understand."

It was rather difficult to understand, thought Victoria, because Louisa somehow managed to convey that Charlotte's naughtiness was more attractive than other people's goodness and her stutter far more to be desired than the clearest form of speech.

"Such a time she had with them all on at her. Her father . . . her mother. Oh, it wasn't natural. And then your Uncle Leopold came like Prince Charming in the fairy tale and they were all set to live happy ever after. I never saw Charlotte so happy as on her wedding day. He was the sun, moon and stars to her; he was the whole world. He was the only one she would listen to. She used to comb his hair herself when he came back from riding. She wouldn't let anyone else touch it. Then she'd take off his boots. Never a cross word between them; and when she knew she was going to have a child she said to me: "There can't be more happiness in Heaven than this.""

Louisa released one hand from the mending to search for a handkerchief in her pocket. She wiped her eyes.

"Poor dear soul. Little did she know that she and her sweet babe would soon be in Heaven."

Victoria wept. There were always tears at these sessions because Louisa's accounts were so touching.

Then she finished off the lace and said brightly: "What

about a nice cup of tea?" And she made it in her room and Victoria always felt it was an adventure to drink tea with Louisa—just like a grown-up visitor.

But the visit came to an end and the Baroness Lehzen came up to tell her that her presence was required in the drawing-room.

And there was Feodora with her husband and Mamma and Uncle Leopold, and Mamma was saying that she would give a *déjeuner* at Kensington when the bride and groom would have an opportunity of saying their last farewells to the family before they set out for Dover.

So Victoria took leave of Feodora feeling that she had lost her already, although Feodora whispered that they would write to each other often.

Then she drove back to Kensington seated in between Mamma and Charles.

There was one more trip to Claremont; this was to say good-bye to Feodora.

The sisters clung together.

"We will write to each other," whispered Feodora.

"I shall wait impatiently for your letters and treasure them always," Victoria assured her sister.

Then Feodora's husband helped her into the carriage which would take her to Dover and across the sea.

Victoria wept and went back to Kensington to tell the dolls that nothing would ever be the same again.

The Cumberland Scandals

IN the Gothic house at Windsor, known somewhat inac-curately as The Cottage, the King was sleeping, scarcely aware of the passing of the days. Servants walked about on tiptoe, certain that this day or perhaps the next week would see the end of the reign.

The master of the King's household could be said to be the Duke of Cumberland; he had the ear of the King and indeed George seemed afraid of him. For what reason no one could be sure, but in view of Cumberland's reputation nothing, however sinister or shocking, need be ruled out.

The Duke of Cumberland was the most feared man in the kingdom. Even the Duchess—herself a formidable character —was somewhat in awe of him, although she was of no one else. Ernest was unlike his brothers; he was tall and thin almost to gauntness, very odd when the family's tendency to fat was considered. He had lost an eye and the patch he sometimes wore over it made him appear almost as forbidding as he did when the gaunt socket was exposed. His face had been scarred in battle; he was quick-witted, clever, shrewd and ambitious. It was clear that he deplored the fact that he was not the King's eldest brother; he wanted the throne, and when the Duke of Cumberland wanted something he went out to get it with no lack of enthusiasm.

His marriage to Frederica of Mecklenburg-Strelitz was, oddly enough, a happy one. He and Frederica were contented with each other; they understood each other. They were two of a kind, both adventurers and both ruthless towards those who stood in their way. The Duchess was reputed to have rid herself of two husbands who had become tiresome; the Duke had been suspected of murdering his valet. Their reputations were considerably tarnished but they did not care. It meant that people thought twice before offending them, a very desirable state of affairs.

The Duke was amused because the King had not attended the marriage of the Duchess of Kent's daughter and as he talked of this to his wife, a rare smile appeared on his grotesque face; she was lying back on a couch sharing his amusement.

"How I should have liked to have seen her face," said the Duchess. "She must have been furious."

"She's the most arrogant woman in England."

"Imagining herself Queen-Mother already."

Anger showed itself in the twitch of the Duke's lip. "By God, what ill luck. That fat infant . . . between me and the throne."

"We are unlucky," agreed his Duchess.

Indeed they were. Dark thoughts of removing the child had

been in his mind. He had set rumours in progress concerning her health. But the artful Duchess of Kent only had to parade her child for all to see to make nonsense of that. He had tried to get the young Victoria to Windsor "to live under the same roof as the King," he had said; but that meant living under the same roof as Cumberland, and the Duchess of Kent had sworn that should not be. That old fool Wellington had been on her side and the little scheme had fallen through.

Frederica was regarding him a trifle cynically. His schemes did seem to fail.

"Perhaps," she said, "you have not given enough thought to this important matter."

"Nonsense. I think of nothing else night and day."

"Except Lady Graves."

"That." He snapped his fingers. "I don't need to take my mind off Victoria for Graves's wife."

"Graves is piqued, I hear."

"Let him be."

He looked at her sharply. Was she jealous? They had an understanding. Their ambition was the same—the throne for him and then for their son George. The fact that he amused himself now and then was unimportant. He had made that perfectly clear. He might amuse himself with other women but there was only one he really cared for—his wife Frederica. She knew that. And he allowed her perfect freedom too.

"We don't want more scandal," said the Duchess. "There has been enough. If your reputation was not so . . . vivid . . . your schemes might not be perceived until after it is too late to foil them."

She was right. His schemes with regard to Victoria had failed and it was partly because people were prepared to suspect his motives.

It was true that Clarence, the heir to the throne, was generally believed to be unbalanced, verging on insanity; but was that due as much to Clarence's own odd behaviour as to the rumours his brother Cumberland had set in motion?

"Well," she said, "what do you propose?"

"There is only one safe way. I don't see why we shouldn't do it. Introduce the Salic law which excludes the right of females to inherit the throne."

The Duchess caught her breath. "Is that possible?"

"All things are possible."

"With Ernest, Duke of Cumberland," she added lightly.

"The Orange Lodges are against the female succession."

"I see," said the Duchess. "And you are their Grand Master."

Cumberland's one eye was shining with purpose.

"This could mean civil war . . ." she began.

He leaned closer to her. "Who's afraid of war . . . for the right cause?"

"Do you think it would come to that?"

"I'd have the support of the Lodges. It's to their advantage to see me on the throne . . . rather than that girl. Why, her mother and Leopold would rule the country. I'd never have that. Nor would the Lodges."

Frederica wondered how powerful the Lodges were. They had been formed by the Peep o' Day boys, those Ulster Presbyterians who had formed a union to fight the Catholics. Cumberland who, professing to be an ardent Presbyterian, had been elected their Grand Master, had never neglected them and was certain of their allegiance. Obviously they would prefer to see him on the throne than this little girl, with her ridiculous mother as Regent, aided by that hypocrite of a Leopold.

"You think they would make an effective force?"

"There are 145,000 members in England alone; and the Irish would be ready to come in."

"It's an ambitious scheme."

"We need an ambitious scheme."

"I would rather see Victoria go into a decline."

"She's as plump as a partridge, they say, and full of blooming health."

"It's a different story with Clarence."

"Oh, he won't last. He's half mad, I tell you."

"I wish I could be sure it was true."

"Well, you see Adelaide. What do you learn from her?"

"You know Adelaide. She would keep her mouth shut if she thought anything she said might be detrimental to him. Your Orange Lodge is the best idea—but wars don't always go as one hopes."

Cumberland nodded. He would only wish to resort to war if all other methods failed.

What ill fortune that he had not been born earlier. If only he had been the third son instead of Clarence, or even the fourth.

His elder brother Frederick, Duke of York, was safely dead; William was destined for the strait-jacket; Edward of

Kent was dead and if it were not for that wretched little girl at Kensington Palace . . . It was the old wearying theme.

The door opened and a young boy looked in.

The Duchess's face softened. She held out a hand: "George, my dear."

Cumberland watched his son and was proud of him. It would not have been possible to find a more handsome boy; nor a more honest and upright one. He was a continual source of surprise to his parents who marvelled that they should have such a son. He was a few months older than Victoria and whenever he looked at his son the Duke ground his teeth in fury that that girl at Kensington came before this beautiful boy whom he wanted to see on the throne when he himself was forced through death to vacate it.

"You look pleased," the Duchess was saying, her voice gentle as it rarely was. "Has something pleasant happened?"

"I have an invitation from Aunt Adelaide."

How the children loved that woman! She was harmless enough, more suited to be the mother of a large family than a Queen of England—which she would be if William didn't go mad before George IV died.

"And you wish to accept it?"

"May I?"

"I believe you would be a little sad if I said no," smiled the Duchess.

"Well, Mamma, I should. Aunt Adelaide's parties are so amusing. She thinks of the most exciting things for us to do."

"And your cousin Cambridge—how do you like him?"

"Very much, Mamma."

"I expect he misses his family."

"He did at first, and now Aunt Adelaide is like his mother. I think he is beginning to feel that Bushy is his home."

The Duke said: "I trust she remembers that you take precedence over your Cambridge cousin."

"There is no precedent at Bushy, Papa. We never think of it. It's great fun there."

"Well, don't forget, son, that you come before him; and if there should be any attempt to set him ahead of you . . . at the table shall we say . . ."

"There couldn't be. We just sit anywhere."

The Duke shrugged his shoulders.

"It's all right when they're young," said the Duchess. She turned to her son. "So your Aunt Adelaide has written to you, not to us?"

"She always writes to me, Mamma."

"It is a little odd. But that's your Aunt Adelaide."

He smiled and he was so beautiful when he did so that the Duchess, hard as she was, was almost moved to tears.

"Oh yes," he said, "that is Aunt Adelaide."

"So you want our permission to accept."

"Yes, Mamma."

"Then go along and write your letter and when you have written it bring it back and show it to me."

He went off and left them together.

"So," said the Duke, "he goes off to mingle with the bastidry."

"It's true. But he'll come to no harm through them. Remember William and Adelaide may well be King and Queen."

"That's true enough and it does no harm for George to be on good terms with them."

"What will happen if William gets the Crown? What of the family of bastards?"

"They'll plague the life out of him, I'll swear."

"William is a fool over his bastards."

"That's because he can't get a legitimate child."

"But we are wise to let our George go to Bushy. You can imagine what would happen if we didn't. Adelaide would become too fond of George Cambridge and you don't know what schemes might come into her head."

"Schemes? How could Adelaide scheme?"

"It may well be that Adelaide thinks George Cambridge might make a suitable husband for Victoria. Oh, I know you don't think she will ever grow up to need a husband, but we have to take everything into consideration. What if Adelaide makes a match between young Cambridge and Victoria. What I mean, Ernest, is this: Suppose Victoria *does* come to the throne . . . suppose there is no way of stopping her, then her husband should be *our* George, not George Cambridge."

The Duke was silent. He could not with equanimity let himself believe that Victoria would come to the throne; but he saw the wisdom of his wife's reasoning. Consort would be the second prize if it should prove to be impossible to achieve the first.

The Duchess went on: "George must accept Adelaide's invitation. I know we are determined that—if it is humanly possible—Adelaide shall never be Queen of England, but just suppose she is. Then she will be powerful; she leads William now. What she says will be the order of the day. So . . . as my second string . . . if George can't be King of England he shall at least be the Queen's Consort."

The Duke regarded his wife shrewdly. She was right of course. He was going to fight with all his might to keep Victoria off the throne, but if by some evil chance she should reach it, his George should be there to share it with her.

"Oh yes, it is well to be on good terms with Adelaide," he said.

The Duchess nodded. They saw eye to eye. Let him have his little philander with Graves's wife. What did it matter? What was fidelity compared with the ability to share an ambition?

It was very lonely in Kensington Palace without Feodora, but true to her word the older sister wrote regularly to the younger one and it was the delight of those days to have a letter from Feodora. Victoria read them all again and again and could picture the fairy-tale castle which was Feodora's home. It was Gothic and seemed haunted; there were so many dark, twisted little staircases, so many tall rooms with slits of windows from which Feodora could look on Hohenlohe territory. Her husband was very kind and she was growing more and more fond of him.

"I don't believe she ever gives a thought to Augustus now," Victoria told the dolls.

She sighed. How much happier it would have been for her if that marriage had taken place. She liked calling on Uncle Sussex and gazing with awe on his collection of rare books and bibles. The clocks were amusing too, particularly when they all chimed together. Victoria especially liked the ones which played the national anthem. She always stood to attention when she heard that and thought of dearest Uncle King and the time when she had asked his band to play it for her. Dear Uncle Sussex; he really was *one* of the favourite uncles; and how she loved his flowers and still liked to water them, although it made her feel rather sad because darling Feodora was not sitting under the tree. But Lady Buggin was amusing and very kind and nice. It was such a pity that Mamma did not like her and that she was told to keep away when Victoria paid a visit. Victoria liked people who were affectionate and laughed a great deal; and Uncle Sussex seemed much happier when Lady Buggin was there. Uncle Sussex was very tall and he looked grand in his gold-trimmed dressing-gown which he wore a great deal in the house. His little black page was always in attendance—also grandly dressed in royal livery. Uncle Sussex treated him with respect and always called him Mr. Blackman. Yes, it would have been much more comforting if Feodora had married Augustus and Uncle Sussex had become her father-in-law.

But it seemed Feodora was happy enough in her castle. She hoped, she wrote to Victoria, that before long she would be able to tell her some very exciting news. Victoria should rest assured that she should be one of the very first to hear.

"Now I wonder what that can be," said Victoria to the dolls.

Lehzen was seated in the room, ever watchful; this was a little respite after her drawing lesson. Of all lessons she much preferred music and drawing. Mr. Westall who was an important artist was very pleased with her; and she loved best of all sketching people. It was fun to send her drawings to Feodora—particularly those of herself which was, Feodora replied, almost like having darling Victoria with her. Mr. Westall said that had she not been a young lady of such rank she might have become a distinguished artist. What praise! But when she repeated it to Lehzen that lady had smiled wryly and said: "But as it happens you are a young lady of rank."

It was the same with singing. Mr. Sale of the Chapel Royal was delighted with her voice. It was true and sweet, he told her; lessons with him were always a joy, as were dancing lessons with Madame Bourdin. She would have cheerfully given herself to study if this meant learning subjects like music, dancing, drawing and riding! French, German, Italian and Latin, to say nothing of English and arithmetic, were less inviting; but because she was so much aware of her vague importance—which was never exactly mentioned but constantly implied—she did her best; and the Rev. George Davys who was in charge of her general instruction was pleased with her.

Victoria had been called a little vixen by some; she admitted to waywardness and storms; but at heart she was determined to do her duty however unpleasant this might be and always she was aware of the watching eye of Lehzen, and the effect her failure would have on dear Uncle Leopold. Mamma too, but it did not hurt in the same way to disappoint Mamma. Indeed there were times when some perverse little spirit rose in her and she felt a desire to plague Mamma. But the thought of losing Lehzen's approval or saddening Uncle Leopold always sobered her.

Lehzen came over and said that it was time for their walk.

"Do you know what I wish to do today, Lehzen?" said Victoria. "I am going to buy the doll."

"You have the money?"

"Yes. I have now saved enough." She thought of the doll. It was as beautiful as the Big Doll which Aunt Adelaide had given her; in fact it bore some resemblance to it and would be a pleasant companion for the Big Doll. As soon as she had seen it she had wanted it. She had pointed it out to Lehzen in the shop window and Lehzen had reported her desire to the Duchess. Together they had decided that it was not good for Victoria to have all she wanted; she must therefore save up her pocket money until she had enough to buy the doll. It was six shillings—a high price for a doll, but then it was a very special one.

"Is she not growing a little old for dolls?" wondered the Duchess.

Lehzen could not bear that she should, so she remarked that she thought there was no harm in her fondness for them . . . for a year or so. Many of the dolls represented historical characters and it was amazing how quickly she learned the history of those who were in the doll family.

So it was decided that she should save for the doll and add this one to her collection. The owner of the shop, although he had left it in his window, had put a little notice on it to say Sold. Every time she passed Victoria gazed longingly at the doll and exulted over the little ticket; and gradually she was accumulating the money.

"We will go now," said Lehzen, "and then we shall be back in time for Monsieur Grandineau's French lesson."

They were talking of the doll as they came out of the apartment and there was Sir John Conroy smiling the smile which Victoria could not like.

"Going to buy the doll?" he asked. What a pity, thought Victoria, that he knew. It was a lesson not to talk too much in future. She sighed. There seemed to be lessons in everything. What tiresome things lessons could be! But perhaps Mamma had told him.

Lehzen replied shortly that they were.

"And the Princess saved her money for it," went on Sir John. "That is quite admirable. I know how careful she is with her money. She is getting more and more like her

Grandmamma Queen Charlotte. She was very careful with money."

Victoria coloured hotly and pulled at Lehzen's hand. I hate him, she thought. I wish he would go.

Like Queen Charlotte! Queen Charlotte was ugly; she was unattractive. Nobody had liked her. Although poor Aunt Sophia and Augusta never actually *said* so, one could tell when they talked of their Mamma that they had not really loved her.

"Am I like Queen Charlotte?" she demanded as they walked through the gardens.

"Not in the least," comforted Lehzen.

"He once said I was like the Duke of Gloucester."

"I do not think," said Lehzen in a chilly tone, "that we should take any notice of what that man says."

Lehzen could not have told her more clearly that she disliked Sir John, and Victoria was comforted. If Lehzen disliked him, then she could do so and know that she was right to. Only Mamma did not dislike him. That was the odd thing. Mamma liked him in a strange sort of way.

But they were getting near to the shop and the thought of clasping the doll in her arms at last, of seeing it in the nursery with Queen Elizabeth and the rest drove from her mind such unpleasant thoughts as those conjured up by brooding on Mamma's relationship with Sir John.

"I have the money," she told the man in the shop and he was so pleased, not she was sure because he wanted to sell the doll but because he knew how pleased she was to have her.

She laid the money carefully on the counter and the doll was taken out of the window.

Would the Princess like it wrapped, or would she carry it?

Wrapped! She could not bear it to be wrapped. The doll was for her a living person. One did not wrap up people.

"I will carry her," she said.

And the doll was laid in her arms and Lehzen touched its face lovingly and said it was a very fine doll indeed, and compared favourably with the Big Doll.

The man at the door opened it with a bow and Vicotria, holding the precious doll, smiling, happily, walked out. She was glad, she told Lehzen, that it had taken so long to save up the money because this made the doll more precious.

It was a good lesson learned, said Lehzen; and then Victoria was staring in horror at the beggar in the road. His clothes were so ragged that she could see the flesh of his poor

thin legs and arms, which were blue with the cold. He looked
hungry. Such sights affected her deeply. Louisa Lewis had
told her how Princess Charlotte felt the same and used to give
all the money she had to the poor people she met, going without what she wanted herself to do so.

And there was this poor man—cold and hungry and his
eyes were on the plump little girl in her warm cloak and her
pretty bonnet, holding in her arms the smiling beautifully
dressed doll.

She said to the man: "You are hungry, I believe."

He nodded.

"Wait here a moment."

"Princess," said Lehzen, "what are you thinking of?"

But Victoria had gone into the shop. "Please," she said to
the shopman, "may I have my six shillings? You may take
the doll and put her back in the window, but please put the
ticket Sold on her. I will start to save again for her but I
must have my six shillings."

Lehzen looked on smiling softly; and Victoria, taking the
six shillings, went out of the shop and gave them to the
beggar man.

"It was a most affecting incident," said the Baroness Lehzen to the Baroness Späth.

"I am sure it was. The dear sweet soul!"

"And she needed no prompting."

"The people will love her. She has so much heart."

"That man sneered when he heard of it."

"He would. What a pity he has so much influence with the
Duchess."

The two Baronesses sighed.

"He will have no influence with the Princess, of that I'm
sure," said Lehzen. "She already begins to dislike him."

"Do you think she is aware . . ."

"She is so innocent, but I believe she senses something."

"Prince Leopold dislikes him."

"Oh yes, there is discord there."

They nodded and the Baroness Späth looked hopefully at
the Baroness Lehzen hoping for confidences. But Lehzen,
while recognizing the trustworthiness of Späth and her great
desire to serve Victoria, thought her something of a fool. She
remembered how stupidly she had behaved over the affair of
Feodora and Augustus d'Este. Foolishly romantic, that was
Späth and Lehzen was far from that; and if they shared an

antipathy towards that man who was trying to rule the household, that did not mean that Lehzen was prepared to take Späth into her confidence over other matters.

They talked for a while of Feodora who, Späth believed, was already pregnant.

"How I should like to be with her," sighed Späth. "But alas that would mean leaving our darling Victoria."

"It had to be," said Lehzen. "The time had come for Feodora to marry." She looked at Späth severely . . . "How *any*one could have imagined a marriage with that Augustus d'Este would have been desirable I cannot imagine."

The Baroness Späth looked suitably discomfited and hinted at some duty she had to perform. She could not endure another lecture over her folly on that occasion. The Baroness Lehzen, knowing that Victoria was safely taking an arithmetic lesson with Mr. Steward of Westminster School, went off to make sure that the new supply of caraway seeds, which she used liberally on all her food, had arrived.

Something strange was going on. Victoria was aware of it. There were whispers which ceased when she appeared. It was something very shocking and she believed it concerned that bogy Uncle Cumberland. When someone had mentioned his name Mamma had visibly shuddered; and on another occasion when someone had said his name Lehzen had pursed her lips in the way which told Victoria she thought it unwise even to talk of him.

Wicked Uncle Cumberland was like the witch in a fairy story; the evil ogre, the bad fairy. She had seen him once or twice and he certainly looked frightening, with that dreadful face, and he was so tall and thin that he looked like a shadow. When she thought of Uncle King with his bulky body—like a feather bed she had thought it when she had sat on his knee—and his kind face with all the pouches and hanging chins, she had to admit that although he was King and therefore very important he did not frighten her in the least. But Uncle Cumberland . . . he was the wicked magician whom the good fairies had to be fighting all the time.

She had met George Cumberland and she had liked him very much. She was delighted to have cousins; and she was growing very fond of George Cambridge who was living with Aunt Adelaide now that he had come to England to be educated. He liked to tell her about his Mamma and Papa in

Hanover and how he missed them and how they missed him.
He was certain of this because his Mamma, the Duchess of
Cambridge, was constantly writing and telling him so. He
would be very unhappy, he assured Victoria, but for the fact
that he had his Aunt Adelaide whom he loved so much that it
really made up for being without his mother.

Victoria listened eagerly; she too loved Aunt Adelaide and,
although she would not admit this to anyone, secretly thought
what a pleasant Mamma she would make and how strange it
was that she should not have children of her own.

So George Cumberland was quite different from his father;
and she wished that she could ask her cousins what it was
that people were whispering about. But Aunt Adelaide was at
Bushy and she was not allowed to go to Bushy. There was
some reason why she must not and she knew too that Uncle
William was not very pleased about this.

What a lot she discovered; and yet she could not quite
understand what it was that made so much shocking.

Suddenly she discovered this matter not only concerned
Uncle Cumberland but also Aunt Sophia.

The Princess Sophia kept to her apartments in the Palace.
She wished to see no one. It was all so distressing.

Her sister Augusta called on her. Augusta was nine years
older than Sophia and she was beginning to look her age,
which was sixty.

She embraced Sophia compassionately. She did not blame
her for this new scandal which was now being whispered in
all the Clubs and in fact throughout the Court and the City
of London. Augusta knew it was not true.

"My dear Sophia!"

Augusta had become more reconciled to her position than
her sisters. It had always been so. She had her music and this
had absorbed her; her compositions were delightful and gave
a great deal of pleasure to herself as well as others. Being a
musician Augusta had not minded so much being kept in
captivity as the others had. Nor did she seem to care that they
were the only two who had not—however late in life—found
husbands.

"This is terrible for you, my dear," she said.

"I am afraid to look at the papers," Sophia admitted. "And
yet if I do not I imagine the worst."

"It is dreadful . . . dreadful."

"How could such a rumour have been spread?"

"I believe it was whispered long ago. George's wife started it, I've heard."

"What could Caroline have known about it?"

"It wasn't what she knew. It was what she made up."

"But she's been dead nearly ten years."

"Rumours sometimes don't die entirely and this is directed more against Cumberland than against you. He did himself a great deal of harm when he set loose stories of Victoria's infirmity. Her mother soon proved them false and people began to ask why he should have done such a thing. To plot against an innocent child was a wicked thing to do. That's why people think he is capable of anything."

"Even . . . incest," said Sophia.

"Even incest."

"It's so . . . stupid. General Garth is the boy's father. You know it, Augusta."

"I know it. But many want to believe that Cumberland is his father."

"My own brother . . . the father of my child."

"That's the story."

"It must be denied."

"How? Are you going to come forward and say that you, a royal Princess, thirty years ago gave birth to a child while you were living under the roof of your father, the King, and were unmarried? Are you going to tell the world how you became the mistress of General Garth and how we smuggled you out of the Palace to give birth to a child . . . a son . . ."

Sophia covered her face with her hands. "It's all so long ago. Why need it be remembered now?"

"Such things are never forgotten. To have a child . . ." Augusta spoke almost wistfully . . . "I mean, there is the living evidence of one's act."

"He is such a dear boy, Augusta. I *live* to see him."

"I know. I understand. And it is wanton wickedness to accuse you of incest. Even Cumberland is not guilty of that."

"What can I do?"

"Nothing. They will get tired . . . in time."

"Oh, Augusta, sometimes I wish I'd died like Amelia. Darling Amelia, what a happy life she had."

"Happy. She was constantly in pain!"

"But she had no worries. Papa adored her. It was her death which finally sent him mad, I believe. Oh, Augusta, think of us . . . living so quietly as we did at Kew . . . sitting there with Mamma, one of us reading while the others sewed, or looked after the dogs or saw that Mamma's snuff-box was always full and at her elbow! It was all so incredibly dull . . . nothing happened, we used to say. And this happened . . . and now here we are two old women and people are telling these lies about me."

"But our lives were not as they seemed, were they, Sophia? No one's life ever is. There we were, as you say, sitting with Mamma, and all the time we were planning how to smuggle you away so that you might have your baby and no one know . . ."

"I shall never forget that time," said Sophia, shivering with recollection. "It was so frightening . . . and so exciting. And now . . . even now . . . I wouldn't have it different. Augusta, play to me. Sing to me one of your songs."

"Is that what you want?"

"It would comfort me. It takes me back. Do you remember how Papa used to listen to your songs?"

"Yes, as though I were a child who had done a good piece of work."

"He never believed anyone could write music but Handel. Oh, Augusta, how different everything might have been if Papa and Mamma had been different. The Princesses of the Royal Court. It sounds so wonderful, does it not? And how dull it was . . . how unbelievably dull. And yet . . ."

Augusta went to the harpsichord and began to play. Sophia picked up the purse she was netting.

Augusta was right. It would pass. It was just one of the scandals which were hurled now and then at the royal family.

But Cumberland! How revolting! As if it could have been anyone else but dear Colonel Garth—as he had been in those days. So tender, so loving, so devoted. She would remember the romance of her youth, forget the disgusting construction people were putting on it in their newspapers.

She would live in her quiet corner of Kensington Palace and perhaps it would be wise for the boy not to come for a while. And after that it would pass . . . perhaps. At least people would cease to talk of it.

"It is time," said the Duchess of Kent to Sir John Conroy, "that we were given apartments away from Kensington Palace. Why should I be expected to live here with the

Princess Sophia—and indeed these rumours shock me deeply
—on one side and the Duke of Sussex on the other and we
know how irregularly he is living with that Buggin woman.
How he can possibly live with a woman with such a name, I
cannot imagine. And under the same roof, *I* am expected to
live with the heiress to the throne."

"My dear Duchess," said Sir John soothingly, "it is iniqui-
tous, I grant you, but I doubt you would be wise to approach
His Majesty at this juncture."

"His Majesty! A fine example he sets. He has insulted me
twice. Once at Victoria's christening and again at Feodora's
wedding."

"Let us do nothing to provoke a third occasion." Sir John's
mouth twisted into that expression which was half a smile,
half a sneer and which so many women, including the
Duchess, found devastatingly attractive.

"At the earliest possible moment I shall demand recogni-
tion for Victoria."

"At the earliest *possible* moment," agreed Sir John.

"Are you sure I am right in not doing so now? This
disgusting scandal . . ."

"Serves us well," murmured Sir John. "Cumberland is in
such ill repute that the nation would rise up in wrath if it
were suggested that Victoria was sent to Windsor while he
was there."

The Duchess began to smile. "That's true," she said.

"So let us not rail against this new scandal which is to our
advantage since it means protection for our Princess. I am
always afraid that His Majesty might send a command that
she be removed to Windsor."

"I should never have permitted it."

"I know. But it would have been difficult if the King had
made it a command and the Parliament had agreed to it."

"I would have taken her out of the country."

"But Your Grace would realize how unwise that would be.
It is imperative that our Princess remains in England.
Heaven alone knows what plot Cumberland might hatch if
she were not here."

The Duchess laid a hand on his arm. "Oh dear, what
should I do without you."

He smiled tenderly. Indeed, she thought, I am relying on
him even more than I do on Leopold. Leopold has changed
lately. It is that Bauer woman. Who would have thought it

of Leopold! And he is tiresome sometimes with all his imaginary ailments.

That was sacrilege of course. One did not criticize Leopold in the Saxe-Coburg family. All the same she did find herself relying more and more on Sir John.

"You can rely on me . . . for ever," he told her. He briskly changed the subject. "Our Princess misses her sister sadly. I was wondering if my own little Victoire might help to comfort her."

"I am sure she does," said the Duchess. His daughter was her godchild—Victoire named after herself and called Victoire so that she should not be confused in the household with Victoria.

"But even more so," persisted Sir John. "Perhaps my daughter could share her dancing lessons."

"She must of course," said the Duchess.

Sir John was well pleased. The two old Baronesses would not be.

Two bundles of German rubbish, he thought. It was time they were neatly packed up and sent off to their native land.

No sooner had the scandal concerning Sophia's child begun to die down than a fresh one arose. This too concerned Cumberland. It was well known that he was having a love affair with the wife of Lord Graves who was one of the King's Lords of the Bedchamber.

As the sins of Cumberland had been so much in the public eye this was given more prominence than it would normally have had and Lord Graves declared he did not believe his wife was being unfaithful to him.

A few days after he had made this announcement he was found in his bed with his throat cut.

He had died, was the report of the newspapers, because of the Duke of Cumberland. And how strange was the manner of his dying. Did their readers remember—it must be nearly twenty years ago—how the Duke's valet had been found in his bed with his throat cut? It was a similar case.

The Duke's valet had had a young and pretty wife; and if Lady Graves could scarcely be so described—she was well into her fifties—the Duke had been reputed to be her lover and he was no longer young.

It was very strange. What was the secret of Lord Graves's death? What was the secret of the Duke's valet? The Duke

had been interested in their wives; they had both been discovered dead in their beds with their throats cut.

It was very, very strange.

This was a hint at murder. It was remembered that the
Duke's wife had had two husbands who had died mysteriously. Royal Dukes might have special names for certain
crimes, but people would draw their own conclusions.

The Duchess of Kent was delighted by the news. She took
Sir John's view now and realized that the more that man's
character was blackened the safer they were from his inter-
ference.

"Why," said Sir John, "if he attempted to force us to hand
over Victoria now the people would tear him apart. We
should have them on our side."

He was right, of course. Späth and Lehzen might try to
poison her mind against him but they would never succeed.
They were a pair of jealous old women. They were devoted,
of course, and she liked to have them with her; she trusted
them; but they were wrong if they thought they were going
to break up her friendship with Sir John.

The Duchess of Cumberland was very uneasy.

"How could this have happened?" she demanded of her
husband.

"How could I know the fool was going to cut his throat?"

"It is certainly very inconvenient of him . . . at such a time
when people are only just stopping to talk of you and
Sophia."

"Let them talk."

"No, Ernest, I do not agree. Let us face the facts. This is
not good for us. You will never get Victoria away from
Kensington now. The Duchess would have the people on her
side. They would never allow their fat little infant to be put
into the hands of a murderer who has committed incest with
his own sister."

"It's all lies."

"It's what people believe that matters in cases like this. For
heaven's sake choose women with sensible husbands in
future. We have to stop these rumours. Why, if it were
possible . . . suppose George died tomorrow, suppose William
really did go mad, suppose Victoria went into a decline . . .
they might be against you even then. You know how ab-
surdly sentimental people can be."

"They like a strong man. They like a mystery. They don't
think any the worse of me for this."

But the Duchess was not so sure.

She was hoping that her son George would bring about the miracle. They must abandon plans for removing Victoria. There would be revolution if anything happened to that child and it was certain that even if they were innocent they would be blamed for it.

The safest plan was a marriage between George and Victoria. Their son would be the Consort and their grandson would be the future King of England.

It was a circuitous way of arriving at an ambition—but it seemed to the Duchess not only the safest but the only way.

Victoria's Vow

SO much was happening and it was infuriating to be only half aware of it. They would insist on calling her a child. There she was in her nursery, never alone, even sleeping in Mamma's room and having Lehzen sit with her until Mamma came to bed, growing up rapidly and knowing things were happening, startling things, exciting things, and yet not being told.

Her only companion of her own age was Victoire Conroy, except when she went to Aunt Adelaide's parties; and she missed almost all of those because they were at Bushy where something disgraceful was going on—or had gone on. Victoria could not believe that Aunt Adelaide had ever behaved disgracefully in her life, although she was doing something at Bushy of which Mamma did not approve.

First her brother Charles had displeased everybody by marrying Maria Klebelsberg, which was apparently not very suitable, but because Charles was the Prince of Leiningen, and the ruler now that his father was dead—and he had died long ago when Charles was young, for how could Mamma have married the Duke of Kent if he had not?—

no one could forbid him. So Charles was one who had married whom he wished.

After his marriage he had visited Feodora in her husband's castle which sounded frightening but which Feodora was now beginning to love. He was very happy, wrote Feodora, and they had talked of their dear little sister and wished she was with them. Feodora's secret was out. She was going to have a baby.

That was very exciting. A baby! It would be like a doll . . . only a living one. And Victoria would be the child's aunt. How very strange to be an aunt!

When she went to Claremont she told Louisa Lewis all about it and they laughed together and Louisa called her Aunt Victoria. Then she was sad talking of how excited the Princess Charlotte had been when she knew she was going to have a child and how the months had led to that great tragedy . . . the greatest of Louisa's life.

Uncle Leopold talked of it too and they wept together. It was his greatest tragedy; but it was very enjoyable weeping with Uncle Leopold over Charlotte. He said his dear little Victoria was his great consolation and it delighted him that she was so tender-hearted.

So waiting for Feodora's baby was a happy time—particularly at Claremont where she and Louisa and Uncle Leopold could indulge in such tearful memories of Charlotte.

And in due course Feodora's baby was born—a little boy who was named Charles Louis William Leopold.

"He is named after you, dearest Uncle," cried Victoria. "That makes him doubly dear to me."

Leopold grudgingly admitted this and was glad it endeared the child to Victoria; but it was clear that he thought Leopold should have been the child's first name.

It was wonderful receiving letters from Feodora. They were all about the baby now. And Victoria thought it would be pleasant to send the child the mug and porringer which she had herself used as a baby.

Feodora was delighted. Her little Charles could not have had a more delightful gift, she wrote; and she was sure that when he was old enough to understand he would love his Aunt Victoria for sending it.

It was very pleasant to be an aunt. She wondered whether in the circumstances she would be too old to play with dolls. She asked Lehzen this and Lehzen, rather reluctantly, agreed that this might be the case.

Victoria sat at the schoolroom table. It was time for the
history lesson and Baroness Lehzen was ready to begin. The
Rev. George Davys had prepared the lesson as he usually did,
for it was he who decided what she should be taught; but he
had left the Palace and it was Lehzen's task to follow his instructions as far as teaching was concerned.

History! She wished it was music or dancing or riding. She
smiled secretly, thinking of how alarmed her attendants were
when she rode with them. She was so daring, they said;
they were always terrified that she would break into a
gallop and take a toss. As if she would! She was an expert
rider.

"Now," said Lehzen, "shall we begin."

She passed the book to Victoria. It was *Howlett's Tables*
and contained the genealogical trees of the royal family of
England. She had seen it many times.

But as Victoria opened the book a piece of paper fell out
of it and on this was a further genealogical tree. She looked
at it cursorily and then saw her own name. Alexandrina Victoria, the only child of Edward of Kent. She stared at it; her
name was in big black letters. The implication was clear. The
King's only daughter Charlotte had died, her baby with her;
Uncle Frederick, Duke of York, was dead without heirs; the
heir to the throne was William, Duke of Clarence, and Aunt
Adelaide would be his Queen. They had no living children,
although some had been born to them. Victoria had seen the
lovely little statue which Aunt Adelaide kept and wept over.
Victoria's own father was dead and he had only one child—
Victoria. That was why her name was in big black letters.
There was Uncle William . . . and after him Victoria.

She looked up and found Lehzen's eyes upon her.

"I have not seen this paper before."

"No, but it is time you realized the significance of it."

"It means that if Uncle William died I should be the
Queen."

Lehzen nodded solemnly.

"I knew that I was in the line of succession," said Victoria
gravely, "but I did not realize until now how likely it is that
I may be the Queen."

Lehzen did not speak but continued to gaze solemnly at
the child.

Then Victoria burst into tears; she was not sure why. Her

feelings were prompted by apprehension, and elation, fear yet pride.

Now she knew why she was never allowed to be alone, why the rest of the family frolicked at Aunt Adelaide's parties and she was not allowed to go. She was important . . . more so than the other children . . . because now it seemed almost certain that one day she might be a Queen.

Lehzen allowed her to weep and after a while she dried her eyes.

"I understand now," she said, "why you have always urged me to study so hard. I am not so *free* as my cousins. I must learn history and English and Latin. Oh, I understand so much now." She put her hand into Lehzen's. "I will be good," she said, as though she was taking an oath of allegiance.

"My dearest Princess," said Lehzen with emotion, "when the day comes you will be a great Queen."

Nothing could be quite the same after that. She no longer played with the dolls. She kept them, though, for she could not bear to part with them; but she stopped her childish conversations with them. She applied herself to her lessons; she was less inclined to indulge in "storms"; all the time she was haunted by a crown and sceptre.

She came to the conclusion that one was much happier if one were not so near the throne—like the two Georges, Cumberland and Cambridge. And yet sometimes it was very exciting to contemplate the future. She thought of Uncle King —so old and ill and who would really be rather repulsive if he were not so charming—and she thought: One is always aware that he is the King. He has royal dignity; he has never lost his regality. That was how it must be with Victoria.

"Queen Victoria." She whispered the words to herself sometimes.

Then she would tell herself: But if Aunt Adelaide had a child—and why should she not because she so loved children and longed for one—Victoria would have to stand back. It was not likely but it was not impossible.

She began to dream of her accession to the throne, of the people lining the streets to see her ride to her coronation. She would look after the dear people. She would be a great Queen.

There was one thing of which she was absolutely sure: I will be good.

All through June the King's death was awaited. He had clung to life for so long; he had been on the point of death for years and always had rallied; but there could be no doubt now.

He lay in his overheated room unconscious of what went on around him; he consumed quantities of cherry brandy; he was almost blind; he suffered from delusions and believed he had won the Battle of Waterloo. Then he would have moments of lucidity when he was his old witty charming self.

But by the beginning of June it was generally believed that the end was near.

Lady Conyngham went through drawers and cupboards; she wanted to miss nothing and now was the last chance to reap the harvest. Once the King was dead her day would be over. She loaded her bags with treasures which she would swear the King had given her, and prepared herself for hasty departure at the appropriate moment.

Cumberland waited. He now had to look to William, for William had managed so far to elude the strait-jacket— thanks to that wise little wife of his. William would be proclaimed King on George's death and Cumberland was determined to see that he was disqualified. He was sure that would not be difficult. William had shown a most unbecoming impatience and he was overexcitable.

Cumberland would get his way, he was sure of it.

But he must be prepared to clear the way to the throne.

So while the old King lay on his deathbed his end was eagerly awaited by those who gazed enviously at his crown.

Victoria in Kensington Palace was told that Uncle King was very ill and there would almost certainly soon be another Uncle King—William instead of George. And Uncle William was very old and often ill and then . . . Victoria.

And on June 25th King George IV died and the Duke of Clarence became William IV.

The Indiscretion of a Baroness

❧ WILLIAM, Duke of Clarence, had arisen early on the morning of Saturday, June 26th, leaving Adelaide in bed. He liked the morning air, he said, and nowhere was it fresher than at Bushy. He was inspecting the flowers when he heard the sound of horses' hoofs and hurrying across the lawn he saw Sir Henry Halford, his brother's doctor, dismounting.

He had no need to ask the news. He saw it in Sir Henry's face. The King was dead.

The wonder of what this meant swept over William. Many times he had anticipated it, but how much more glorious was the realization!

"Your Majesty," began Sir Henry . . . and William did not wait for the rest. He grasped the doctor's hand and shook it, which was a strange thing to have done. But William had never behaved in a conventional manner and the doctor was too excited to notice at the time.

"The Queen must be told," said William, "but I shan't tell her. She's been dreading this. But she must be told."

Sir Henry said he would ask one of her women to waken her.

William went into the house where he was shortly joined by Adelaide who looked more as though she were being told she were a widow than a Queen.

William mutttered something jocularly about Her Majesty but Adelaide gazing at her husband and seeing the flush in his cheeks and the brilliance in his eyes was afraid for him. It was the worst thing that could have happened. While he lived quietly at Bushy with the family she could feel he was safe.

"It's early," said the new King. "We'll go back to bed. I've never yet been to bed with a queen."

72

Sir Henry looked startled but the King insisted and when the Duke of Wellington as Prime Minister arrived to make the official announcement to William that he was the King of England, he found him in bed.

The great Duke of Wellington, who was a less succesful politician than he had been a soldier, cared deeply for the honour of his country. It was, he believed, his great task to guide the King; and there could have been few Kings who needed guidance more. It was not very long ago that William —as Duke of Clarence—had shown how foolishly he could behave when given some authority. Then he had been invested with the office of Lord High Admiral and had brought ridicule on himself and been forced to resgin; how much more dangerous would it be to give him the powers of a King.

And yet King he was, by right of succession. Frederick, Duke of York, Wellington supposed, might have been easier to handle.

Only a short while ago the Duke and Robert Peel had been deploring the state of the country. "A most heartbreaking concern," the latter had called it and due to the conduct of the King and his brothers. Cumberland would have to be watched—a mischief-maker if ever there was one; and when it was considered that the new King had a tendency to his father's malady, it was clear that there were stormy times ahead.

It appalled Wellington that William showed no regret for the passing of his brother, who had always been a good friend to him; William had known this and had been fond of George, but the prospect of being King so overwhelmed him that he lost all sense of decency.

The poor Queen was grieved and doing her utmost to restrain the King.

"William, my dear," she implored, "pray do not be so *overjoyed*. Remember you have lost a dear brother."

"Dear old George! But he had his day. Now I shall wear an admiral's uniform for my first meeting with the Privy Council. An admiral's uniform, eh, Wellington?"

The King frowned at Wellington. He had not been a very good friend at the time of all that trouble over his office of Lord High Admiral. But he was a clever fellow and by God the country owed him something. They'd never forget Waterloo. So it was no use holding that other trouble against him.

He needed Wellington, a good fellow, a fine soldier. A King must trust his ministers.

The FitzClarences were delighted. They were now the sons and daughters of the King. This was going to make a great difference. Lots of honours should come their way.

His daughter Lady Erroll with her husband and their children were in residence at Bushy at the time and they came out to look at him in his admiral's uniform and listen to him rehearsing the declaration.

Wellington felt that never could a King's accession have been received in such a way, but the only member of the household who seemed to be aware of this very odd behaviour was the new Queen.

Wellington was glad when it was time to leave for St. James's with William that they might attend the first Privy Council under the new reign.

On a hot July day George IV was buried. It was some three weeks since his death and during that time William had succeeded in making himself quite popular with his subjects. His complete lack of ceremony endeared him to them; in any case they were prepared to love anyone who was not George IV. He showed a lack of concern for ceremony; he walked about the streets; he would shake any man by the hand, and had a word for everyone. His red weatherbeaten face was unlike that of a King; he lacked the stature of his brother; and the people liked him for it.

It was going to be very different now that he was the King. He was a faithful husband; it was true his wife was by no means beautiful but she had a royal air which was acceptable; and she was fond of him and he of her; and it was not her fault that she had not given him an heir.

He had declared that the royal parks should be opened to the public; they were for everyone to enjoy, he said; the public might wander through the grounds and look in at the windows of Windsor Castle. The Sovereigns belonged to the people; that was William's maxim.

He sent a note to Mrs. Fitzherbert telling her that the late King had been thinking of her at the last and that she was to put her household into mourning for him. This was another popular move. Maria was a respected figure; the late King had been disliked for treating her badly and for the new King to behave as though she were indeed the widow of

George IV appealed to the people's sense of chivalry.

In those first few weeks William could do no wrong.

It was true Adelaide had to remonstrate with him to curb his high spirits. It was unseemly to go to a funeral in such a jocular mood. But there was no subtlety about William; he was overjoyed to have reached his goal and he was not going to pretend otherwise.

And so, amidst rejoicing and a certain amount of frivolity, the remains of George IV were laid to rest in St. George's Chapel at Windsor.

In the late King's apartments his effects were being sorted out. Such a medley of souvenirs had rarely been seen. He had been a great letter-writer and had revelled in his correspondence with numerous women with whom during a long and amorous life he had believed himself to be in love. He had been a hoarder who could never bring himself to destroy anything. There were thousands of letters tied up with ribbons; there were women's gloves and locks of hair, all carefully preserved. He had cared passionately for clothes and had in fact designed many with and without the help of Beau Brummel. It had been impossible for him ever to lose sight of these garments on which he had expended so much loving care. Now they were hanging in good condition and in chronological order in his wardrobes. His servants said that he never forgot one of them and was apt to ask to see some garment which he had not worn for fifty years. With regard to money he was less careful. Among his possessions were found five hundred wallets each containing sums of money the total of which amounted to £10,000.

This strange collection caused some amusement, and was discussed throughout the Castle; and then William began to change everything. He dismissed his brother's French chefs. English cooks were good enough for him, he declared; he would have musicians—English ones—but by no means the number who had served his brother.

George had been a connoisseur of the arts and had filled all his houses with priceless treasure. "What are these?" demanded William. "Cost money, did they? Well, they belong to the people and the people shall have them. They should be put in galleries and museums, and the people should look at them . . . if they wanted to."

He was a man of the people. He was a jolly, unpretentious

old fellow who wanted the people to know that he had their good at heart.

There was no one to grieve for the death of King George, except Maria Fitzherbert who in her household of mourning dreamed of long ago days when the young Prince Charming had met her along the river bank and called her his "Sweet Lass of Richmond Hill."

The Duchess of Kent was in urgent conversation with Sir John Conroy. Surely now Victoria must be proclaimed the heiress to the throne. William might die tomorrow and then . . . It was ridiculous that she, the Duchess of Kent, should be expected to live in obscurity on the bounty of her brother Leopold when she was the mother of the future Queen . . . and not the distant future either. Victoria was eleven years old, a minor. Should there not be some arrangement made in case there was need of a Regency?

This, Sir John agreed, would be a very desirable state of affairs. He wanted to act with some caution, however, for the situation was a delicate one; and the new King was a clumsy man who prided himself on his frankness, which meant of course speaking and acting without consideration for others.

"A buffoon!" said the Duchess. "I always had the utmost contempt for him."

Sir John nodded. That was what he wished. The more the Duchess was estranged from her relations, the better he liked it, for if they decided to befriend her what could his position be? He believed it was most advantageous to him for her to be in conflict with them and it should be Conroy and the Duchess against the royal family.

"The King must realize our Princess's position and the need for a Regency," he temporized.

"Of course he does and I shall see that he is made aware of his duty."

Conroy smiled at her. How magnificent she was in her ambition for her daughter; how single-minded; how completely unaware that by reminding the King of the Regency she was reminding him of his more or less imminent death. Victoria was eleven and in seven years she would be of age. Oh yes, his dear magnificent Duchess was scarcely the most tactful of women.

But let it go. The King would be incensed; the breach between them would widen; and the deeper it was the more the

Duchess must turn to Sir John for guidance and consolation.

He leaned forward and taking her hand drew her gently towards him.

"Well?" she asked.

"I was thinking how beautiful you are in your anger."

Victoria had come into the room with the Baroness Späth a few paces behind her and the Duchess drew back from Conroy a little guiltily, while Victoria, startled, looked from one to the other in dismay.

"Pray," said the Duchess collecting her wits, "do not enter a room so boisterously. And what are you doing here at this hour?"

"I had come to ask, Mamma, if I might sing for the company this afternoon in Aunt Sophia's apartments. Aunt Adelaide will be there with my Cumberland and Cambridge cousins. And as Aunt Augusta will also be there she would regard it as a compliment if I sang one of her songs."

"I think," said the Duchess, "that this might be arranged if you can learn how to enter a room in a fitting manner."

It was strange, thought Victoria; but there was something a little embarrassed in Mamma's attitude; and there was a slyness about Sir John which she did not like at all.

Afterwards she said to Späth: "Mamma was standing very close to Sir John Conroy."

"And pray," said the Baroness, "what do you mean by that?"

"Why should I mean anything other than what I say? Mamma was standing close to Sir John. I believe he was on the point of kissing her."

The Baroness caught her breath with horror and put her hand to her mouth.

"And," went on Victoria, "she immediately began to reprimand me which, I have noticed, is a habit of people when they seek to defend their own conduct."

The Baroness was amazed. Did Victoria realize that she was talking about her own Mamma, she demanded.

Victoria retorted that she was at a loss to understand to whom else the Baroness thought she might be referring.

Indeed, since Victoria had been aware of her position she had become a little imperious; and the death of George IV had, she knew full well, heightened the importance of that position. Strangely enough this had been more apparent in her feelings towards her own mother.

It was a situation which the Baroness thought extremely dangerous and, as soon as Victoria was safe in the hands of Mr. Steward and was deep in the arithmetic lesson, she hurried to the Baroness Lehzen to tell her what had happened.

Lehzen shook her head. She disliked Sir John as much as Baroness Späth did. He had insulted them by insisting that his wife take precedence over them. But what could they do? He was firmly entrenched in the Duchess's household—and affections; and they must try to turn a blind eye to what might be going on. It was always better not to see something that was faintly shocking and there were occasions when ignorance could be so much more comforting than knowledge.

They were both very comfortable at Kensington and they both adored Victoria.

But it was Victoria who had *noticed*, pointed out the distressed Späth.

Lehzen said it was a matter which should never be discussed with the Princess, and left it at that. She was wiser than Späth and determined that she was not going to lose her position, for she could not imagine a life that was not dominated by her beloved Victoria.

Victoire Conroy was a vivacious child with a look of her father. She clearly believed that her father's importance in the household entitled her to very special treatment. The Duchess was after all her godmother and the Princess Victoria her playmate.

The Princess was very imperious and was not very fond of her. A fig for that! thought Victoire. They couldn't get along here without my Papa.

Victoria had said: "I may call you Victoire but you must not call me Victoria. You must address me as Princess or Your Highness."

"But . . ." began Victoire.

"There are no buts about it," declared Victoria, and swept away.

Victoire put out her tongue at the departing figure.

"The airs some people give themselves!" said Victoire to her sister Jane. "Victoria is far too haughty towards us considering what she owes to Papa. The Duchess *depends* on him and is very fond of him—so is the Princess Sophia who colours and twitters everytime she sees him.

Victoire took dancing lessons with the Princess because Papa said it was good for the Princess to have companions of her own age. But Victoria preferred her cousins the two Georges because, as she had remarked to Späth in Victoire's hearing, they were royal. Victoria was becoming very arrogant since the last King died. But Victoire and her sister were going to make sure that she kept her haughtiness for others.

She had spoken to her Papa about it and he laughed. "You're the Duchess's goddaughter," he said. "You have a right to respect in this household; and if that woman Späth— or Lehzen for that matter—insults you, stand up for yourselves."

That was Papa's advice and as Papa ruled the household, Victoire was determined to put it into practice.

Old Späth was sitting knotting—the ridiculous occupation of senile old women, thought Victoire contemptuously. Victoire was angry. She had not been invited to the Princess Sophia's apartments where Victoria was going to show off how well she could sing. Victoire could imagaine the Princess in her white silk dress trimmed with lace and the wide blue satin sash and the little white satin slippers, looking pretty in an insipid sort of way with her plump white arms and her wide blue eyes—and Lehzen would have dressed her fair hair in ringlets.

Victoire was sure that the Princess Sophia would have extended the invitation to her because she would know that to do so would please Papa. She was sure too that the Princess Victoria had deliberately withheld it because now that she was heiress to the throne she felt herself so important that she could go against her mother's wishes. The Princess, who could never completely mask her feelings, had shown quite clearly that she did not like Sir John.

Victoire sat down beside the Baroness Späth.

"What are you knotting?" she asked rudely.

"That is no concern of yours," said the old woman, pursing her lips.

"Do you think I care?"

"Then why ask?"

There was silence. Then Victoire said sullenly: "I wanted to go to the Princess Sophia's party this afternoon."

"Then it's a pity—from your point of view—that you were not invited."

"Was I not invited?"

"You could answer that question better than I."

"I believe I was and that the invitation was withheld."

"You are accusing someone?"

"Victoria may have decided that she did not want me."

"Which might be understandable."

"If I had been invited I should have been *told.*"

"You are acting foolishly, child."

"Why? Because I say I should have gone to the party? Of course Victoria did not want me. She only wants to be with people who are royal. She prefers to have her cousins, the two Georges, all to herself. She likes boys much better than girls."

"How dare you speak so of the Princess!"

"I will speak as I wish."

"You will not criticize the Princess in my hearing."

"My father says we should speak the truth."

"Do not quote your father to me." The Baroness had risen. Her knotting had fallen to her feet; her lips were quivering; she was angry and alarmed. One day there would be a big scandal concerning Sir John Conroy and that was going to be harmful to the dear Duchess and the even more dear Princess Victoria.

"Why not? He is important. He could have you sent back to where you belong, you old German woman. And he will. He says he will."

It was more than the Baroness could endure; she walked away catching the knotting string about her ankle and pulling her work along the floor as she went. Victoire broke into peals of laughter and the Baroness picked up the work, her face scarlet, her lips moving angrily as she tried to extricate herself.

When she had done so she walked away to look for the Baroness Lehzen. She was going to tell her at once what had happened and ask her advice as to what action should be taken because she was sure some action must.

The Baroness Lehzen had accompanied Victoria to the Princess Sophia's apartments and so was not in her room.

How dared that insolent girl say what she had! She was like her father. Oh, why could not the dear Duchess see what vipers she had allowed to enter her household!

She must be made aware . . . Oh, why wasn't calm level-headed Lehzen here.

It was unfortunate for the Baroness that the Duchess of Kent should have chosen to send for her at that time. There was some matter concerning the Princess Victoria she wanted to discuss but the sight of Späth's indignant flushed face drove the matter from her mind.

"What has happened?" she demanded.

"I have just left that . . . that insolent child," spluttered Späth.

"Insolent child?" The Duchess knew very well to whom Späth referred and Späth should know from experience how she disliked anything connected with Sir John Conroy to be disparaged.

"Victoire Conroy. She . . . she dared to criticize the Princess Victoria. She said she preferred the company of *boys* . . ."

"I believe that to be true. Victoria is always talking of those two cousins of hers."

"I could not stand by while that girl made such observations about the Princess."

"You are being foolish again," said the Duchess coldly. She had never let Späth forget how stupidly she behaved over Feodora and Augustus d'Este.

Späth's colour deepened. "I am *not*," she said recklessly. "And there is something I have to say to Your Grace about . . . about yourself and Sir John Conroy."

Späth was too excited to notice the expression on the Duchess's face and to be aware of the ominous silence.

"I do not forget my place . . ." began Späth.

"Do you not?" said the Duchess sarcastically. "You surprise me."

"No, I do not forget it and I speak only out of love for Your Grace and our dear Princess."

"Pray continue."

"The Princess has noticed the . . . er . . . friendship between Your Grace and . . . this man."

"The Princess has long been aware of the friendship between myself and Sir John. Indeed, I hope she feels similarly towards one who has been such a good friend to her and the entire household."

"God forbid!" cried the Baroness.

"My dear Späth," said the Duchess, and her voice showed

clearly that the Baroness was far from being dear to her, "are you mad?"

"I am very anxious," went on the Baroness, "because the Princess has noticed that Sir John Conroy is on very familiar terms with Your Grace."

"How . . . dare you!" cried the Duchess. "Pray go at once to your room. I will deal with your . . . impertinence later."

The trembling Baroness left her. At least, she assured herself, I told her the truth.

The Duchess went at once to Sir John.

"My dearest lady, what has happened?" he asked, looking up from the papers on his table.

"That . . . impertinent old woman . . . That Baroness Späth. Oh dear, and I placed *such* confidence in her. She was a good nurse to Feodora and afterwards to Victoria and now . . . now . . . I will not allow her to remain here. She must go."

Sir John smiled. He would like to be rid of the two old ladies. Lehzen more than Späth, for Späth was an old fool compared with Lehzen.

He rose and taking the Duchess's hands kissed them. "Pray be seated and tell me exactly what happened."

"She was . . . insolent. She said that *Victoria* had noticed that you and I . . ."

"What is this?"

"That Victoria had noticed that you and I were . . . friends."

"This is . . . monstrous."

"I think so too."

"There is only one thing to be done."

Sir John nodded sagely. The old fool had played right into his hands.

The Battle for Lehzen

ADELAIDE was watching the King carefully; she was terrified that his exuberance would overflow and he would do something which would be considered mad. At the moment the people were lenient; he had won their approval by lacking the dignity of George IV—not that he had to cast aside what he had never had—but that royal dignity was indeed lacking and for the moment, the people liked their King. He was an old man with a red weatherbeaten face; and no one could be more homely than the Queen; but somehow they managed to convey that they wished to do their duty.

There was no doubt that William was enjoying his position. He went about among the ordinary people, shaking hands with them and patting children on the head.

When the crowds gathered round him and Adelaide feared for his safety he would cry: "Now, my good people, let me through, let me through. You want to see me and I want to see you. So stand back a bit and give me air."

A very unroyal King! decided the people; but a good and kindly man eager to serve his country.

Adelaide had believed that the stay at the Pavilion would be a rest after all the ceremonies it had been necessary to attend but she was realizing that little respite was to be allowed the King and Queen. It was all very well for George IV to shut himself away from his people; William IV was not going to be allowed to do this. Nor did he wish to. He was still delighted by his office and determined to enjoy it. He was homely; he was bluff; he was the sailor King. He was constantly waving ceremony aside.

"The Queen and I are very quiet people," he would say.

"She sits over her embroidery after dinner and I'll doze and nod a bit."

He had a talent for making the kind of remarks which could be seized on by the press and those who liked to report the eccentricities of the King. For instance when he had asked a guest to attend a ceremony the man replied that he could not do so as he did not possess the required kind of breeches. "Nonsense . . . ceremony . . . stuff!" cried the King. "Let him come without." "Stuff" was one of his favourite words for that etiquette which he wished to sweep away and he applied it to anything of which he did not approve.

Not only was he completely lacking in royal dignity, he was tactless in the extreme. He was constantly telling Adelaide that he did not know what he would do without her and that she was more to him than any beautiful and attractive woman could ever have been. He gave people lifts in his carriage. He shook hands affably like any visiting squire; he told the Freemasons whom he was addressing on one occasion: "Gentlemen, if my love for you equalled my ignorance of everything concerning you, it would indeed be unbounded." He behaved in every way that was unkingly; but all knew that he meant to be kind.

He had made it clear that he would not allow his brother Cumberland to dominate him as he had dominated the late King. Cumberland was deprived of his Gold Stick, told to remove his horses from the Windsor stables because the Queen needed them for her carriage, and at a dinner the King had toasted the country and glaring at his brother had added: "And let those who don't like it leave it."

As Cumberland was at the height of his unpopularity this further endeared William to his people.

He was a blundering old man, but as long as he kept his sanity, the people were pleased with him.

Adelaide, who had become very fond of him since her marriage and suffered from a terrible sense of failure because she had failed to give him an heir, grew more and more nervous. When the people became overexcited she was afraid there would be riots. She had never understood the exuberance of the English; and she was well aware that there was terrible unrest throughout the country. The affairs of France were once more in chaos; what happened in that country could happen in England, so Adelaide believed.

There was one word which was constantly being used in all circles: Reform.

The people throughout the country were dissatisfied with their lot. The differences between the rich and the poor were too great. The harvest had been bad; food was dear and there was no money to buy bread. The silk weavers of Spitalfields were in revolt; the farm labourers of Kent were demanding more money; and the mill hands farther north were restive. Hay-ricks were burned down in the night; barns set on fire. Through the country men were threatening dire consequences if there were not Reform.

All this worried Adelaide.

"Trouble?" said William. "There's always been trouble. My father was nearly assassinated several times."

"But you must take great care."

Dear Adelaide! He wouldn't have changed her for any one of his brother's beauties in their prime.

There was a change of attitude in the FitzClarence children which Adelaide was quick to detect. Now that their father was King they believed all sorts of honours should come their way. They didn't see why they should be left out simply because their father hadn't married their mother and she was an actress. They were the acknowledged sons and daughters of the King.

William had done so much for them and he loved them all dearly, and Adelaide thought them ungrateful. She was glad—and so was William—that the dear little grandchildren were too young to understand the greatness which had descended on their grandpapa.

So at Brighton she had hoped for a little respite from the glare of publicity. As if this could be found at that most glittering of towns! Brighton welcomed its new sovereign as it had always welcomed the late one, to whom it must for ever be grateful for making it what it was—rich, fashionable, elegant Brighton in place of Little Brighthelmstone which had nothing to recommend it but a little fishing.

The Pavilion—home of the late King's most brilliant entertainments—was scarcely the place in which to relax. But they would rest here, said William. They would have no reclining on sofas to listen to music like so many Eastern worthies. There would be no brilliant banquets with people vying with each other to show off their silks and satins and brocades. A homely atmosphere should be brought into the Pavilion.

So the King chatted freely with his guests; and he break-fasted with his wife precisely every morning at nine—no lying abed all through the day as his brother had done—and Adelaide herself made the tea at one end of the table while one of her maids of honour made coffee at the other end.

Then they chatted for a while and the King went off to receive some of his ministers who had come to see him, or he would take a drive with the Queen. In the afternoons he sometimes walked out alone. He liked to do this without attendants, and the children of the town, recognizing him, would run up and call: "Hello, King!" which amused him; and he would very often take them into one of the shops and buy sweets for them.

He was a most unusual monarch, but a source of amuse-ment to the people; and there was nothing they liked better than to be amused.

As for the ceremonies and elegance of the last reign— "Stuff!" said the King.

But in spite of his popularity those uneasy murmurs were rumbling through the country. There would have to be Re-form.

When the royal pair could stay no longer in Brighton they returned to St. James's, and Adelaide pointed out to the King that it would be necessary for him to see more of Victoria now. They must not forget that she was heiress to the throne.

"We might supplant her even yet, eh?"

"Ah, if that were possible! But I greatly fear we shall never have a child. It is some fault in me."

"Now, now, you don't want to fret yourself. There's this little girl at Kensington. Nice little creature. Don't like her mother, though. My God, what a handful of a woman. And to think I might have had her! They gave her to Edward be-cause she had to be wooed and they throught I'd make a mess of the wooing. So they gave me you, Adelaide . . . who had no choice. So you see we had no choice, either of us."

"So we should be grateful that we were not displeased."

"So you weren't displeased, eh?"

"I thank God every night for my good husband."

His eyes filled with tears. "And I for my good wife. Couldn't have a better. You could give me all the beauties in the land . . ."

That reminded him of those days when having deserted Dorothy Jordan he had sought to marry and been flouted by the heiresses he had chosen except Miss Wykeham, who had accepted him only to learn that her hopes of becoming Duchess of Clarence were dashed as his family rejected her. He smiled. What a scene there had been at the time with George—the Regent then—and his mother, Queen Charlotte, explaining why he couldn't have Miss Wykeham for all her money and must take the German Princess Adelaide instead.

He went on thinking aloud—a habit to which Adelaide had become accustomed. "Should do something for Miss Wykeham. She hoped to marry me. But they wouldn't have it. She was the only one who agreed to marry me. Yes, should do something for her. Give her a peerage, eh?"

"Yes," said Adelaide, "give her a peerage, but we must see something of Victoria now. She ought to appear at Court."

"Could have seen more of her years ago but for that stuck-up mother of hers. She won't let Victoria mix with my children! By God, does she realize that my children are the children of the King!"

"She will now," said Adelaide soothingly. "But I think I shall take the first opportunity of calling at Kensington Palace. I'll go and see Sophia first. She will know what is happening in the Kent apartments. But Victoria must be present at the next Drawing-Room."

"You go, my dear. And tell that woman that her daughter will be *commanded* to come to Court no matter who is there. It's for the King to decide who shall or who shall not come to his Court."

"Yes," said Adelaide, "I will go to Kensington."

The Princess Sophia laid aside her netting to embrace Adelaide.

"It is so good of you to come, my dear. There must be so much to do. How is the King?"

"He is very well, thank you."

"I'm glad, I'm glad. William was always a little excitable."

Sophia was looking sideways at her sister-in-law. Oh dear, thought Adelaide, people who lived lonely uneventful lives were avid for every bit of gossip; and if it were not good news they seemed to enjoy it more.

What had Sophia heard about William's unbalanced state?

"Oh, he is becoming accustomed to being the King now," said Adelaide. "At first it is a little bewildering."

"And he has the Duke to help him."

"Oh yes, the King relies on Wellington."

"You have heard the news from there." Sophia nodded towards the wall in the direction of the Kent apartments.

"News?"

"Späth is going."

"The Baroness Späth . . . to leave!"

"Oh yes, she is being sent to Feodora. She will be *so* useful in the nursery there, so says the Duchess."

"But surely she is needed here."

Princess Sophia lifted her shoulders. She was not going to mention the real reason for the dismissal of Späth. She felt it was in some way disloyal to Sir John; and in any case she did not like to think of his being on familiar terms with the Duchess.

"They say Lehzen will be going next."

"Lehzen. They could not lose her. Where would they find another like her?"

"We don't want another like her. She makes too much of the child. Victoria has too much sense of her own importance."

"Poor child, I fear it is a great responsibility for her. And she is so young."

"She is watched all the time. If it isn't her mother, it's Lehzen."

"I always believed Lehzen was devoted to the child."

Sophia laughed. "You know there have always been complaints about the Germans surrounding the Princess. I think the people would like to see some English women there."

"So Späth is going because she is to be replaced by some Englishwoman?"

"That I can't say," replied Sophia, "but it may well be the case."

She wondered whether Adelaide would hear the rumour about Sir John and the Duchess. At least she had given no hint of it.

"We shall expect to see Victoria more often now," went on Adelaide. "It is time she came out of seclusion."

"Ha! You'll have to see what her Mamma has to say about that." Sophia went on to ask after George Cambridge and Adelaide, always ready to talk of the children, settled down to a long discussion about them.

Then she went to see the Duchess of Kent.

The Duchess greeted the Queen not without some con-
descension. Adelaide might be the Queen, but she was only
Queen Consort, whereas Victoria Duchess of Kent was the
mother of the future Queen.

After the first pleasantries were exchanged Adelaide asked
after Victoria and learned that she was very well.

"That is good. She is always in such blooming health, and
what vitality she has! Our little Victoria is a credit to you."

The Duchess radiated momentary contentment. Victoria
was indeed well, indeed she was a credit; and so she should
be. Nothing had been spared in Victoria's upbringing. When
the time came she would make a perfect Queen.

"The King and I have been saying that we should see
more of her at Court."

The Duchess's eyes had narrowed slightly.

"She is young yet."

"But she is eleven years old; soon she will be twelve. It is
quite time that she made a few appearances. The people
expect it. Have you forgotten that she is heiress presumptive
to the throne?"

Heiress presumptive! What a horrible title. It reminded
one so clearly that something could go wrong. And by wrong
the Duchess meant Adelaide might have a child. What a
dreadful possibility! This woman—this Queen—was not
old; she could still bear a child; and the Duchess could be
sure that she was making every attempt to do so. What if
she did? She had had several attempts. It was true they had
failed but what if there should be another attempt and that
be successful? Heiress Presumptive! No, Heiress Apparent
was so much better. And how much better still: the Queen.
But this woman's wretched husband had to die first and on
no account must Adelaide be pregnant.

"I have certainly not forgotten," said the Duchess coldly.
"It is for this reason that I have had to *protect* my daughter
for so long."

"Well, I trust now that she is growing up we shall see
more of her. The King would like to see her at Bushy."

"If His Majesty wishes to see her, he knows what he must
do!"

Adelaide was amazed that the Duchess could speak so of
the King. No wonder William disliked her.

"I . . . don't fully understand," said Adelaide hesitatantly.

"His Majesty is surrounded by his bastards at Bushy. I

think it would be extremely unsuitable for the . . . er . . . Heiress Presumptive . . . to mix with them."

"They are the King's own children, and he as King has them living with him *en famille*."

"I should never allow Victoria to come into contact with these people."

"But the King wishes to see more of her and as he has no intention of dismissing his own family, it is almost certain that she will."

"I cannot allow it." The Duchess was imperious. Any observer would have thought that she was the Queen, Adelaide the Duchess. She began to walk about the apartment, her bracelets jingling, her impressive bosom heaving, so that the jewels with which she loved to adorn herself glittered in fiery defiance. "Nor," she went on, "do I think that I should be expected to live in these apartments which are entirely inadequate for the Heiress to the throne. I am living under the same roof as that Buggin woman. Oh, I know she has rented Niddry Lodge on Camden Hill there, but she is more often in the apartments of the Duke of Sussex. Buggin! My daughter is expected to live at close quarters with a woman named Buggin."

"She is hardly responsible for her name."

"She is entirely responsible. She married it! As the daughter of the Earl of Arran she should have known better."

"Augustus seems to be delighted with her."

"Augustus has no right to be."

"Perhaps he will marry her now that Augusta is dead. He swore that he couldn't, you know, while he had a wife living, and although Augusta was not recognized as his wife he always regarded himself as married to her, even after they separated. I think it rather noble of him."

The Duchess looked with scorn at Adelaide. How *mild* she was! She had no jealousy of herself which the Duchess could not understand when what Adelaide desired above all else was a child, and she, the Duchess, had her healthy Victoria, Heiress Presumptive to the throne.

"Noble!" snorted the Duchess. "Living with the Buggin woman, which is what he is doing. It's most irregular. But what I find so disturbing is that he should be doing so under the same roof as Victoria."

Oh dear, thought Adelaide. The Duchess of Kent was in a truculent mood. She had better leave her and decide later what should be done. She must be careful not to tell William too much. He was always annoyed with the Duchess; and indeed the woman did give herself airs. But if he knew she was going to set herself up in deliberate defiance he would become very excitable, which was just the state he must most carefully avoid.

When the Queen had gone the Duchess sat at her table and wrote to the Duke of Wellington.

Now that King George IV was dead and his brother had become King William IV, this meant that the Princess Victoria was heiress to the throne (She would not use that *horrible* word Presumptive.) She believed that it was quite *unsuitable* for the heiress to the throne to be living in comparative *penury*. She believed that an income should immediately be settled on her, and that her mother should become the Dowager Princess of Wales.

When she had written the letter she took it to Sir John and showed it to him.

He smiled. His tempestuous Duchess was indeed a handful, but he liked her for it; and as long as he could guide her, he had no objection to her arrogance towards others.

The request was absurd, he knew. Her husband, the Duke of Kent, had never been the Prince of Wales and so it would be quite irregular to bestow a title on her to which she had no right.

He imagined the Duke's face when he received such a demand.

Should he advise her to send it? Why not? It would estrange her farther than ever from the King, and Conroy's one fear was that the Duchess would become friendly with her late husband's family. If she did so, they might turn her from Sir John. It was bad enough to have Leopold as a rival, for while Leopold was so close to her, Conroy could never have the complete control he longed for. He always had to be wary of Leopold. But he was determined that no other members of the family should attempt to oust him from his position.

"It is as well to let the King know through Wellington that you are conscious of your position," he said; so the note was sent.

When Wellington received the Duchess's letter he said:

"The insanity in the royal family has spread to the Duchess. She is certainly mad to think for one moment that such a possibility could be considered."

"Madam," he wrote, "your request is not admissible."

When the Duchess received his cold reply she was furious. She went with it at once to Conroy.

"This man Wellington gives himself airs. Because he won a battle he thinks he can rule the country. Who is he? Arthur Wellesley! He thinks because he *was present* at the Battle of Waterloo that entitles him to insult me. It was very likely Blücher who was responsible for that victory. And because of it, he thinks he can *command* us all. And what of his relationship with Mrs. Arbuthnot? I have heard that he neglects his Duchess shamefully for that woman. The Duchess of Wellington may be a fool but it is nothing to his credit that he should treat her as though she does not exist. And this is the man who dares tell me I have no right to the title of Dowager Princess of Wales."

Sir John let her run on. Let her start a feud with Wellington; the more trouble she had with other people, the more friendly she would be towards her dear Comptroller of her Household.

But in due course the Duchess admitted that there had been no hope of receiving that title. Yet, Sir John assured her, it was as well to let them know that she was aware of the dignities for her position as mother to the Heiress of the throne. Presumptive? No! Apparent! Victoria was going to be Queen.

Very soon after the Duchess was in a state of elation. The Lord Chancellor, Lord Lyndhurst, presented a Bill in Parliament that should create the Duchess of Kent Regent in the event of the King's dying and her daughter's ascending the throne as a minor.

The Duchess was delighted. Wellinton might have treated her without due respect; Lord Grey might have referred to her as a tiresome devil; but Lord Lyndhurst had put her case to Parliament and Parliament had seen the reason in it.

Nor was Lord Lyndhurst the only one, for the Bill was passed. The Duchess would be Regent of England; Parliament had added £10,000 to her income, to be used for the education and household of the Princess Victoria.

This was triumph.

The Duchess summoned Victoria to tell her what had happened.

"We must never forget your position," she told Victoria. "The death of your Uncle George has brought you right up to the throne. And when your Uncle William dies, as you won't be old enough to govern, I shall be the Regent."

"But, Mamma, suppose I *am* old enough before Uncle William dies."

"Victoria, you say the most surprising things."

"Is it surprising? People do live longer than is often thought. There was Uncle George. His death was expected long before it came."

The Duchess looked pained. Victoria was beginning to be too self-assertive. "When William dies," she insisted, "I shall be Regent."

Victoria felt a little indignant. The idea of the Duchess as Regent was not very pleasant to her. As a daughter she had had to do exactly as Mamma said; how disconcerting if, as Queen, she should find herself in the same dilemma!

But once she was eighteen she would be of age. That day was a long way ahead. Seven years. She secretly hoped that Uncle William would not die before that time.

The Duchess dismissed her. She gave herself the airs of a Regent already.

Victoria wept when she said good-bye to Baroness Späth. "Darling Späth. I shall miss you so."

Poor Späth dabbed at her eyes and embraced the Princess. "It breaks my heart to leave you."

"But you will be with dearest Feodora," said Victoria, because she felt that heartbroken as she was she must at all costs comfort poor Späth.

"Ah, yes, but my heart will be with you."

"You'll love the little babies. Imagine Feodora with two babies now. I know she loves them dearly; she shows it in her *dear* letters. Little Charles is *such* a handful now and you will be so useful to her."

"I daresay she is surrounded by useful people."

"But she always had a special feeling for you; besides she will be able to talk to you of me, which I am sure is what she will very much enjoy."

"My dearest Princess, make sure that the Baroness Lehzen is not sent away."

"Lehzen!" cried Victoria in horror.

"It may be that those who decided to be rid of me may wish to see her out of the way, too."

At the thought of losing Lehzen Victoria felt sick with horror. Dear Späth was bad enough, but the old Baroness was a bit of a fool though a dear one. But Lehzen was as close to Victoria as her own mother—oh much closer than that if the truth must be known. Lehzen was second only to Uncle Leopold.

She said firmly: "You may be sure that I should make such a storm that they would not dare send her away."

Späth took her last farewell and set out on her sad journey, back to her native land, and to try to find solace for the loss of Victoria in Feodora and her babies.

Uncle Leopold called at Kensington to take his farewell, he said, of his beloved niece.

Victoria had found it hard to believe when she had heard that he was going to leave England. He came to tell her himself that fate had cruelly decided to separate them.

He embraced her and laid his cheek against hers; she was too deeply moved for tears. She looked into his beautiful face with the utmost love and admiration.

"You see," he explained, "the people of Belgium have separated from Holland. They need a King; and they believe that no one will fill that role but me."

"But it means your living in Belgium, Uncle Leopold!"

"Alas, exactly so. I could not be the King of a country and not live in it."

She saw that; she saw too the gleam in Uncle Leopold's eyes at the prospect of kingship, and she knew at once how much more *suitable* it would be for Uncle Leopold to be a King rather than the Prince Consort of a wife who though she would have been Queen had she lived was long since dead.

Oh yes, she must accept this sorrow. Uncle Leopold could not forgo his crown even for her.

"I shall always be with you . . . in spirit," he told her. "I shall write to you very very often. I have told your mother that I shall be constantly in touch. Your affairs will continue to be those nearest my heart. Nothing . . . no one could ever supplant you."

She wept; she embraced him and told him she loved him; then she said good-bye.

"But it is not good-bye," said Uncle Leopold. "We are too close, my darling, ever to say good-bye. You will be with me in my thoughts; and I shall follow everything you do."

"No," said Victoria sturdily, "it is not good-bye. It could not be because if it were I would be too unhappy to bear my sorrow."

Sir John was elated. The Baroness Späth had been removed through her own folly and his ingeniousness; even better, benevolent fate had removed Leopold. The new King of the Belgians would of course continue to direct affairs but how different to do so from Brussels than from Claremont. There would be no more Wednesday afternoons when he pried too closely into the Duchess's affairs for the comfort of Sir John Conroy. The field was clear now for Sir John—as far as the Duchess was concerned.

They must not ignore Victoria, of course; and she was too much under the spell of her German governess. Lehzen gave herself too many airs. Stupid old woman continually munching her caraway seeds and, he was sure, antagonizing Victoria against him.

He came unceremoniously into the Duchess's drawing-room, where she was sitting at her table frowning over some papers.

"My dear Duchess, you are bothered."

"Oh these tiresome papers! Why do they send them?"

"You must allow me to deal with them. They are not important enough for you to bother your head over."

He looked very handsome with his finely chiselled features and that amused expression which was so often in his eyes. So tall, such a commanding figure. Dear Sir John!

"I wanted to talk to you about something of far greater moment."

"Come and sit near me."

He drew up a chair and leaning an elbow elegantly on the table, smiled admiringly into her face.

"I am disturbed about the Baroness Lehzen."

"Indeed."

"She has become too self-important since the departure of her crony."

"I fear so."

"And I believe she is influencing Victoria far too much."

"Victoria has always had a great affection for her."

"All very well when she was a child. But now she is nearly twelve. She has her newly appointed governess. What need of Lehzen?"

"The Duchess of Northumberland is her nominal governess only. She will not perform Lehzen's old tasks."

"That's so. Lehzen is a very good governess . . . for the nursery. I am sure the Princess Feodora would find her most useful in the bringing up of her children."

The Duchess looked surprised. "You mean that we should send Lehzen away?"

"I mean that certain changes should be made in Victoria's household. We want the world to realize that she is no longer a child, and the best way in which we can do this is by removing her nursery governesss."

"Lehzen would not like to hear herself so described."

"I fear there is a great deal that Lehzen does not like about the household. She does not relish these changes. In fact she is trying to poison the Princess's mind against *us*."

"Can that be so?"

"You have noticed the difference in the Princess's attitude lately."

The Duchess admitted that she had.

"And who do you think is responsible?"

"You really think it is Lehzen?"

"I know it is, my dear Duchess."

"Then," said the Duchess, "Lehzen must go."

Lehzen said: "They are trying to part us." She corrected herself. "That man is trying to part us."

Victoria's blue eyes were blazing. "They never shall."

"*He* has sent poor Spath away."

Victoria threw her arms about Lehzen. "They shall never send you away," she declared.

Lehzen noticed the use of the word "they." So Victoria included her mother in the conspiracy. What, wondered Lehzen, did Victoria know of the relationship between her mother and the Comptroller of the Household? Perhaps a great deal, for her dislike of the man grew greater every day; and sometimes Lehzen felt the Princess included her mother in her dislike.

"Don't worry, dear Lehzen," she went on. "They shall never part us."

"I should be terrified if they did."

"Never fear. They shall not."

Victoria looked defiantly from her mother to Sir John Conroy.

"I know what you are trying to say," she told them coolly. "You want to tell me that it would be advisable for the Baroness Lehzen to leave us and go back to Germany to join Feodora and poor Späth. I must make it clear that that is something I do not wish."

"*You* do not wish?" said her mother.

"That is what I said. *I* do not wish it."

For all the world, said the Duchess afterwards to Sir John, as though she were the Queen already.

They were so struck by her defiance that they were momentarily speechless; and that gave Victoria her chance.

"If the Baroness Lehzen received orders to leave my household," went on Victoria, "I should not let her go. I should go to the Queen and beg her to tell the King exactly what I felt. I know she would do so; and I know that His Majesty would grant my wish. The Queen has told me that she understands *exactly* how I feel about losing dear Späth and she was most sorry for me."

"The King does not control Kensington Palace," said the Duchess, her colour rising.

"I was of the opinion that the King ruled his kingdom, and as Kensington Palace is part of that kingdom I cannot see that it should be oustide his rule."

"Oh," said the Duchess, "so we are having a little storm, are we?"

"A storm, yes, Mamma," replied Victoria, "but it will not be a little one if any attempt is made to part me from the Baroness Lehzen."

With that she swept out of the room.

The Duchess stared after her in fury; but Sir John merely smiled.

"Her Majesty is in a regal mood today."

"The impertinence . . ." cried the Duchess. "I shall send for her. She will be severely taken to task. I . . ."

He laid a hand on her arm.

"She is no longer a child."

"She is twelve years old."

"She has been made aware of her destiny. We shall have to be careful now."

"Careful . . . of my own daughter!"

"The Queen-to-be! And she is shrewd too. She would have Adelaide on her side and Adelaide would bring in William. I am convinced that we should receive a royal command to keep Lehzen in the household."

"This is *my* household," spluttered the Duchess.

"Yes . . . yes . . . it's true. But William could issue an order. And then where should we be? Our best plan is to be astonished that she took us so seriously. We had no real intention of sending Lehzen away. It was a complete misunderstanding." The Duchess stared in amazement at Sir John, but he only smiled at her tenderly.

"You will see that this is the wise course to take," he said.

After a little persuasion she came round to his view as she always did.

Lehzen stayed in the household.

The Duchess and Sir John had requested the presence of Victoria in the Duchess's drawing-room. There was a subtle difference in their attitude towards her since the Lehzen affair. Victoria, always frank, was unable to hide a vague antipathy towards her mother and a decided one towards Sir John.

"She will grow out of it," said Sir John; and implored the Duchess not to show that she was aware of it.

"Sometimes I think she forgets that I am her mother," said the Duchess indignantly. "She is more devoted to Lehzen and her affection for Leopold is positively sickening at times. And yet towards me . . ."

"She is going through a certain phase," Sir John assured her.

"I am not sure that *I* am going to allow her tantrums."

"I am sure you will know exactly how to deal with them," he said smiling fondly.

And now there was this matter of changing her name.

"It was the late King's fault," said the Duchess. "I wanted her christened Georgiana. I even mentioned Elizabeth. He would have none of it. He said she was to be named after me."

"She couldn't have had a more charming name."

"She needed a *Queen's* name. And now they want her to have it."

Victoria entered the room. There was a faintly wary look in her eyes. She was never at ease when she was alone with her mother and Sir John.

The Duchess held out her cheek to be kissed; and Victoria dutifully kissed it. The Duchess overawed her and so in a way did Sir John. It was only when she had to fight for some worthy cause that she could stand against them.

"My dear child," said the Duchess, "pray sit down. You know that you are now accepted as the heiress to the throne."

"The heiress presumptive, Mamma," corrected Victoria.

"Oh, why harp on that horrible word."

"Do you mean 'presumptive'?" asked Victoria "It is a very important word. It means . . ."

"I think we know what it means, don't we, Sir John?"

Sir John assured Victoria that he did; and the Duchess continued. "Now that you are accepted as the heiress to the throne, two Members of Parliament, Sir Robert Inglis and Sir Matthew White Ridley, have suggested you change your name."

"Whatever for?"

"Because, my dear, when you are Queen the people will wish you to have a queenly name. There has never been a Victoria who was Queen of England."

"Then, if I am Queen, there will be one."

"They suggest that you change your name to Elizabeth."

"Elizabeth. I should hate to do that."

"Perhaps you would, but the people would like it. Elizabeth was a great Queen; she would be known as Elizabeth I and you would be Elizabeth II."

"I refuse."

"Another storm?"

"Yes, another storm."

"We seem to be enduring some very stormy weather," said Sir John facetiously.

"I shall inform these gentlemen that I shall not change my name. Elizabeth! I would never be Elizabeth."

"Why not? Elizabeth was a great Queen."

"*I* do not admire her."

"Others do."

"But they are not expected to take her name."

"If the Parliament decide that it is a good thing for you to change your name . . ."

"They must be told that I refuse to do so."

"You would do well to remember that you are very young. You are in great need of guidance."

"I know that, Mamma, and I trust that when the time comes I shall receive that guidance. But this is something I know in my heart to be wrong. I will not be Elizabeth II. If I am to be Queen I shall be Victoria. It is my name and I refuse to have another."

Sir John looked at the Duchess as to say: "Very well. It is not an important matter."

"I have a letter here from your Uncle Leopold."

Victoria's face lit up with pleasure. "May I read it, Mamma?"

"You may. He thinks you should see something of the country. You should know something of the people you will one day govern. He believes that a series of little trips would enhance your popularity with the people and teach you a great deal."

"Are you going to object to that?" Sir John asked, his voice faintly tinged with sarcasm.

"Oh, indeed no. I'm sure Uncle Leopold is right."

"It is more important than the name," Sir John told the Duchess after Victoria had left them. "It is not a bad thing for her to refuse to change. The people know her as Victoria and they will think of her as that. Besides, they will tell themselves they don't want another Queen Bess; they want a Queen who is herself."

Meanwhile Victoria took the dolls from the drawer in which she kept them. She had not played with them for a long time.

There was a figure in stiff farthingale and ruff. "Certainly I shall not take your name," said Victoria sternly. "It would be as though you had laid a spell on me. And that, as you know. I should never allow. I am myself. And if dear Aunt Adelaide does not have a child and I become a Queen, then I shall be Victoria."

The King's Drawing-Room

❧ HOW pleasant it was to go to Ramsgate. She missed Uncle Leopold because the last time she had visited the place he had been with her. They used to walk along by the sea together, he holding her hand, and the people scarcely noticing them, while he told her about dear Charlotte and how he had loved her and had had to control her—and how grateful she was to be controlled. ("As you must be, my darling." "Oh yes, yes, dearest Uncle. I am sure you know best.")

And now Uncle Leopold was in Belgium being a King and there were only his letters which she looked for, and they came regularly; she treasured every one and read them again and again. Perhaps, she told herself, one day he will come and see me.

In the meantime, here she was at Ramsgate without him, but with dear Lehzen and her new governess the Duchess of Northumberland, who interfered very little, and Mamma and Sir John and the rest of the houshold.

She wrote to Feodora and Uncle Leopold and told them all about it. What a pleasure it was to write. It makes one's experiences so much more vivid, she told Lehzen; and Lehzen said it was a very good exercise.

Life was exciting. She was growing up. There was a great deal of talk about what she should do. When they returned to Kensington she might go to the opera. Uncle William had hinted that he wished her to make public appearances. Perhaps she would be allowed to go to some of Aunt Adelaide's parties, and share in the fun which her cousins enjoyed.

In the meantime Mamma gave orders that the Royal Standard should be flown over the house in which they were staying.

"Is that right, Lehzen?" asked Victoria. "I thought the

Royal Standard only flew over the Sovereign's residence."

"That is true. But your Mamma regards you as the Sovereign and therefore has given this order."

Victoria frowned. "I don't think Uncle William will be very pleased when he hears of it. Mamma should not have done it."

Oh dear, there were so many things which Mamma did and which she really had no right to do.

At precisely a quarter to eight the King's valet knocked at the door of the bedroom William shared with Adelaide.

The King sighed, stretched his legs and remembered the irritating thoughts on which he had gone to sleep the previous night. That woman. She would have to be stopped. The idea of flying the Royal Standard over the house in Ramsgate! It was as though she had killed him off and buried him already.

It would not do. And she should be told so.

He allowed himself five minutes before he rose. He looked over at the Queen's bed; Adelaide was still sleeping. They did not share a bed nowadays, although they slept in the same room.

"Work to be done," he said to himself; and getting out of bed put on his flannel dressing-gown.

In his dressing-room his valet was waiting for him.

"Good morning, Your Majesty."

The King nodded. He looked about him slyly, knowing what was expected of him.

"No visitors this morning, Jemmett?"

"Well, Sir, not that I've seen."

"Better begin, eh, without them."

"If that is Your Majesty's wish, Sir."

The King sat down and winked at Jemmett, who began to fix the towel about his neck.

There was a sudden whispering of "No . . . let me. It's my turn." "You said . . ." All of which William pretended not to notice. Then a pair of small hands was put over his eyes; someone was standing on the chair Jemmett had discreetly placed at the appropriate spot.

"Guess who? Guess who?"

"My goodness me!" cried the King. "What is this? What is this, eh?" As though he did not know and that it did not happen every morning in the King's dressing-room.

"Guess who, Grandpapa."

"Then let me see. It is George."

"No, it is *not*."

"Then it is Adelaide . . ."

"No . . . no . . . *no*."

And he would go through the names of the grandchildren until he said the one expected of him; and knowing who it was he always left that one till last.

That little game over, the children came to stand round the silver ewer which Jemmett was placing on the table in front of the King.

"Now you've got to bend your head over . . . hasn't he, Jemmett?"

"It's true," Jemmett agreed.

"And whish . . . over it goes all over Grandpapa's poor old head."

"It smells nice though."

"Oh yes, it smells *lovely*."

"I shall have first smell."

"No, me . . ."

The King's eyes filled with tears as he watched them—his dear dear grandchildren who enlivened his days and made him forget the minor irritations of adult life: the growing cupidity of his children—the parents of these little ones; the arrogance of that Kensington woman; the inability of Adelaide to bear a child; and worst of all the growing unrest in the country and the continual cry for Reform.

Intent eyes watched him; little pink faces glowed with anticipation. One would have thought it was the first time they had ever seen his valet wash him. Dorothy's grandchildren! he thought. How proud she would be to see them now! So lively and healthy, so much a part of the royal household. Adelaide loved them no less than he did, bless her.

He bent his head over the bowl and there were squeals of delight as the rose water was poured over his head. Jemmett rubbed the liquid into his hair and over his face and then dried it vigorously.

"There," said William. "Now I am a clean old man."

"Grandpapa is a clean old man," cried the children.

"Where's my coat, Jemmett?" asked the King.

He was dressed while the children looked on. Then he sat down and one by one they came up and gave him a smacking kiss.

When the last kiss had been exchanged, the King rose.

"I think it is time we went to breakfast."

"Queeny will be waiting," one of the children said.

"Then let us waste no more time. I am hungry if you are not."

"Oh we are, Grandpapa."

They jostled each other for the possession of a hand and clusterd round him they went in to breakfast.

The Queen, seated at one end of the breakfast table, received a good morning kiss from each of the children.

"Just a dish of coffee, William?" she asked.

"Just that."

"And the usual two fingers of bread. My dear William, you do not eat enough."

The children had seated themselves at the table; at the other end, opposite Adelaide, one of the maids of honour was making the tea.

"Did you sleep well?" asked Adelaide.

The King nodded. "But I had that woman on my mind."

The children were listening intently, so Adelaide made the usual "not before them" sign which William constantly provoked.

"Grandpapa doesn't eat enough," said young Adelaide.

"My father used to say that people ate too much and there was a tendency in the family to run to fat," said the King.

"Run to fat." Some of the little ones were bewildered. "How do you *run* to fat, Grandpapa?"

"Now you have some explaining to do," said Adelaide, glad that the conversation had turned from William's father, who in himself was a dangerous subject. Soon these little ones would be learning why they were not always received at certain functions, why the difficult Duchess of Kent would not allow her daughter to mix with them. There was so many secrets in the family.

But William was happy while the children were with him; he could throw himself into playing games with them, amusing them, being one of them. If only, sighed Adelaide, we had had children. If only we could live the lives of simple people.

But very soon some of the King's ministers would be arriving and State business would begin, and there was all this dreadful trouble in the country. Adelaide was often fearful when she contemplated what had happened in France. Oh dear, if there should be revolution here!

But William was popular, or he had been in the first weeks of his accession. The people's mood changed quickly, though.

Dear William! He was doing his utmost to be a good King and he did enjoy the role. There was no doubt about that. Even when he had to sign countless papers—a monarch's less majestic task—he enjoyed it. And what a stack of papers his brother had left unsigned! She would never forget the sight of poor William spending his evenings trying to catch up with the unsigned documents, and how she and the Princess Augusta had had to bathe and massage his poor fingers because they grew so stiff with holding the pen. How much happier he would have been playing a game of Pope Joan!

Now the nurses were coming in to remove the grandchildren who set up wails of protest at being removed, much to William's secret delight.

"Later we'll have a game," he said.

"Promise, Grandpapa. Promise!"

And the King gave his solemn promise.

"Rascals," said the King indulgently, smiling at Adelaide. "They adore you."

"You too, my dear. You've been good to them, Adelaide."

The newspapers were brought in. This was an uneasy hour. Who could know what he was going to find? He sat growling over them. Now and then an exclamation would break from him. "Stuff!" "Damned lie!"

Adelaide was glad when the Duke of Wellington arrived.

George FitzClarence, William's eldest son, looked in to join them at luncheon. The King was proud of his handsome first-born. George was now interesting himself in politics having retired two years ago from the Army as lieutenant-colonel. Adelaide felt rather uneasy. The "children" as she called them had changed since William had become King. In the old days when she had first married they had been as her own children; she had nursed this very George during her honeymoon when he had broken his leg and William had brought him to her. They had been great friends, but now George and his brothers and sisters had become rather sullen, resenting the fact that they were not legitimate. The Duchess of Kent was responsible for a great deal of this. She had given instructions that Victoria was not to come into contact with the FitzClarences. It was all very silly—and worse, it made trouble. Adelaide hated trouble.

It was brewing now, she could see by George's expression. Oh dear, he was going to upset William, but the King cheerfully eating his two cutlets and disposing of his two glasses of sherry was as yet unaware of it.

Luncheon over William decided that he would take a walk in the gardens and that George should accompany him. This suited George for it would give him an opportunity of saying what he wanted to.

As soon as they were alone, George said: "It's ridiculous, Father, that you as the King should have an untitled eldest son."

William sighed. "My dear George, I have looked after you children well . . . as your mother would have wished. You shall have honours, in time. These things have to be arranged."

"That's an old story," said George rudely—since William had become King he and his brothers had delighted in being rude to the old man. "It's easy enough if you want to."

"I've looked after you all. And I shan't forget you."

"I want a title. I should be an Earl. I am the King's son."

"I tell you you'll have to wait."

"I don't feel inclined to wait. I've waited long enough."

"By God," cried the King. "The Crown hasn't been mine for a year yet."

"It doesn't take a year to recognize your son."

"When have I failed to accept you as my son?"

"As your bastard . . . perhaps."

"My dear George, that's exactly what you are."

George strode off in a fury. William looked after him with the tears starting to his eyes.

He could not bear to quarrel with his children. He would have to see what could be done to satisfy George.

"You must never forget your position," said the Duchess of Kent. "The King and Queen are apt to act in the homeliest way; and this may have its effect on you. However *they* behave, *you* must always remember who you are."

"Yes, Mamma," said Victoria.

"Now this is one of your *first* public appearances. Don't forget that everyone will be watching you."

"Yes, Mamma."

"We have to uphold our dignity, you realize that, I hope."

Victoria did realize this.

"You will stand on the *left* of the Queen, and you must never forget that you are the heiress to the throne."

"I should not be allowed to if I wished it," said Victoria with some irony.

Driving to St. James's was pleasant, although the people did not notice her as Mamma wished. She would have liked them to shout: "God save the Queen-to-be." Mamma seemed to forget that it was possible for Aunt Adelaide to have a child. And if she did? Victoria sometimes thought that it might be rather pleasant to be like the Georges, Cumberland and Cambridge, and not have to be constantly watched and primed.

It was very grand at the Drawing-Room. The King couldn't look anything else but a weatherbeaten jolly old gentleman and all the silks and satins and jewels couldn't make Aunt Adelaide into a beautiful Queen; but Victoria standing on the Queen's left looking very young in her white silk dress with her pearl necklace and the diamond clasp in her hair attracted some attention. There was something so fresh and young about her which was very appealing.

Aunt Adelaide whispered to her that it was a bit of an ordeal but it would soon be over and she was behaving charmingly so that all the people would love her.

Dear Aunt Adelaide, who was also so kind and sympathetic towards the young, and showed no resentment at all because her own little Elizabeth had not lived to stand in the place where Victoria now stood today. Sometimes Victoria even now felt a desire to cling to Aunt Adelaide and talk to her as she could not talk to her own mother—not even to Lehzen. The Duchess was too ambitious; Lehzen just a little stern; as for Uncle Leopold he was too perfect and therefore somewhat remote. But Aunt Adelaide with her plain face and her nose that was a little pink at the tip and the rather spotty complexion seemed to shine with a motherliness which offered infinite comfort—even to a little girl whose mother had been rude to her.

"You are managing splendidly," whispered Aunt Adelaide.

"Oh, *dear* Aunt Adelaide, I love you so much."

Aunt Adelaide's eyes filled with tears; and Mamma was watching. "Don't be too friendly with the King and Queen," had been Mamma's injunctions, "otherwise they will try to *impose*. There is no need to feel that you must *placate* them.

Nothing can alter the fact that you are the heiress to the throne."

But she wanted to be friendly with them because they were such friendly people. Oh dear, she wished she did not feel so *uncertain*. Obeying Mamma had become a habit. It was usually easier in the end to do as she wished, rather than make storms.

Mamma was watching her now; she had seen the exchange between her daughter and Aunt Adelaide, and was displeased.

Family quarrels are so tiresome, thought Victoria. And surely the Queen-to-be should be able to decide on whom she will bestow her friendship.

The King was smiling at her, but Mamma was watching and she met his smile stonily. William reddened a little and turned away.

Oh dear, thought Victoria, is the King angry? He is a nice kind old man really and my uncle. Why should I have to be unpleasant to him? I won't do it. I'll smile at him next time.

But the King did not look her way again.

When the Drawing-Room was over the royal party remained to talk together, and Victoria found herself sitting between her two cousins George Cumberland and George Cambridge.

They were both eyeing her with approval. She knew she looked quite pretty with her cheeks flushed and her eyes exceptionally blue which they always were when she was excited. The two boys were definitely interested in her and it was pleasant to bask in masculine admiration.

"I wonder you never come to the Queen's parties," said Cumberland.

"You miss a great deal of fun," added Cambridge.

"I know," sighed Victoria. "But my Mamma does not think I should."

"Why ever not?" demanded Cambridge.

"There is some reason."

"There must be a reason," put in Cumberland. "Nothing happens without reason, does it?"

"But what can it be?" asked Cambridge.

"That is something I should like to know," said Victoria.

"The house is always full of FitzClarence children," George Cambridge told her.

He could not take his eyes from Victoria because he had heard the King say to the Queen that he thought it might not be a bad idea to arrange a match between them. Imagine this little girl, his wife. And she would be Queen of England if the King and Queen did not have a child. George Cambridge imagined that would be rather pleasant, because the Queen's husband would really be the King and living with Uncle William made him feel that life as King could be very enjoyable.

He must not mention this to Victoria now. It was obviously something of which one did not speak, but it was very pleasant to contemplate the prospect.

He wanted to discover more about Victoria; so did George Cumberland. His parents were constantly speaking of her.

"You must be very lonely at Kensington," said Cumberland.

Victoria considered this. "Well they never allow me to be alone. So I suppose I am not lonely."

"Do you never meet any young people?"

"Only Victoire and Jane Conroy." Her mouth tightened at the mention of that man's name.

"You ought to meet your cousins."

"I am meeting them now."

"And this cousin is enjoying the encounter very much," said Cumberland.

Victoria glowed with pleasure. How exciting was the company of the other sex. Now she considered it she rarely met anyone but women. There were her tutors of course and that man—but she didn't count those. It would be different now that she was growing up.

"And so is this one," added Cambridge determined to be as gallant as his cousin. "But you would have enjoyed Aunt Adelaide's parties. Aunt Adelaide is a darling."

Victoria could heartily agree with that.

"I have lived with her and the King now for a long time, and as I can't be with my own parents there is no one I would rather be with. She says I am like a son to her."

"Oh, you are the favourite," said Cumberland.

"I don't think Aunt Adelaide has any favourites. She is fond of all the children. Those swarms of grandchildren . . . the King's I mean, are always at Bushy or wherever they are. They call her Queeny. Some of the young ones are rather silly."

"Do you miss your parents?" asked Victoria. "They are in Hanover, I believe."

"Yes. My mother writes to me every day."

"She must love you dearly."

"She said that a day when she has not written to me is a lost day."

"How sad that you must be parted."

"I had to come over here to be educated. It was necessary for me to be educated here."

Victoria wondered why, but Cumberland had been kept out of the conversation too long and he wanted his young cousin's attention. How truly delightful, she thought, to have them both vying for her notice. This was proving a very happy occasion.

"Aunt Adelaide's party last Christmas at the Pavilion was wonderful," he told her. "She put a great fir tree in the Dragon Room. She says they do it at Christmas time in Germany, and on the tree are hung presents. It's such fun. Names are on the presents and there is something for everyone. Then we had music and dancing and games. The King played with us. Of course there were too many *little* FitzClarences and Aunt Adelaide always sees that *they* are not left out."

"Oh, how I should have *loved* to be there."

"I can't think why you weren't. All the rest of the family seemed to be—and you are one of the family."

"Oh yes," said Victoria happily, "I am one of the family."

So they chatted and it was so pleasant that Victoria did not notice how time was passing and she was sad when it was time to go back to Kensington.

Mamma was grim as they drove back.

"I do not think you behaved with absolute decorum. And what were you whispering about to the Queen? And then laughing and giggling with those two boys. What were they saying? And do they have *hopes* . . . because if they have they can forget about them . . . and so can their ambitious parents, because neither of those two boys will have a chance."

What was Mamma talking about? Victoria, listening to the clop-clop of the horses' hoofs, was gently rocked by the movement of the carriage. She was thinking of a wonderful party in the Dragon Room at the Pavilion; a green fir tree reaching almost to the ceiling—loaded with presents.

And I was not there, she thought.

She pictured herself seated there, with a George on either side, admiring, attentive. And why was she not there? It was very odd that she should not be. Why should she be shut away in Kensington Palace with only the daughters of

That Man as companions, when she could enjoy the admiring society of boy cousins like the two Georges?

The reason she decided was Mamma. Mamma was ruling her life and shutting her off from such pleasures.

She was beginning to feel very resentful towards Mamma.

The Duchess of Cumberland wanted to hear what her son had thought of Victoria.

"She's a pleasant girl," he told her.

"Rather homely to look at I believe."

"No, I think she is pretty."

"I have heard that she is fat and inclined to be plain and vulgar-looking."

"It's not true," said George Cumberland with some heat.

The Duchess's face softened as she looked at him. He was her adored son who aroused in her a tenderness she had not known she possessed. He was good-looking—tall for his age and he had a sweet nature.

Odd, she often thought, that Ernest and I should be blessed with such a son, so different from a pair of old sinners such as we are.

"Well, I'm glad you like her, darling."

"I like her very much. She is fresh and excited about things and very . . . innocent."

"Ha! Poor child, she does not have a very good time guarded by the old dragons of Kensington."

"It's a shame that she can't enjoy Aunt Adelaide's parties."

"It's all due to that wicked old mother of hers."

"Is she wicked?"

"No. She's just an arrogant old fool. If she's not careful she will lose Victoria when the child grows up. Ah, that will be the time. George dear, how would you like to marry her?"

"Marry Victoria! When?"

That made her laugh. "You are too impetuous, my darling. It wouldn't be for years. And don't mention it for her dear Mamma will do her utmost to prevent it. But it is what your father and I would like. And if you liked it too, well that would be pleasant, wouldn't it?"

"You mean it is one of your plans."

"Something for the future. Don't speak of it. Just get to know Victoria whenever possible."

"How is it possible? She is always shut away."

"That won't last. The King has given orders that she is to be seen with him in public."

"Will her mother allow it?"

"I grant you that woman has effrontery enough to disobey the King, but I think even she will see that Victoria has to emerge a little. So . . . you will have a chance to know your charming cousin."

"I think she *is* charming."

"So the thought of a match is not displeasing to you."

"No, but I think it is rather early to be thinking of it. We are only twelve years old."

"Which shows how I take you into my confidence, my wise little son. Don't mention this to anyone. But do try to like Victoria. It would be so pleasant if you did."

"I should not have to try. It is something I should do without effort."

"I have a feeling you will always be a credit to us, George, my darling."

"I hope so, Mamma."

"Are you going now?"

"To my tutor," he said. "It's time."

"*Au revoir*, my love." She kissed him, and when he had gone she smiled. We don't deserve him, either of us, she thought.

When the Duke came in she was still thinking of young George and she began to speak of him at once.

"He's met Victoria and is quite taken with the child."

"I'm glad to hear it."

"There must be a match between them."

The Duke nodded and she laughed. "I know you want the throne for yourself and for him to follow. But how can it be while our plump pigeon lives? We shall have to reconcile ourselves, Ernest. It'll be Hanover for you. You'll be a King and I'll be a Queen. We'll just have to accept Hanover in place of England; and if our George is the young Queen's Consort I don't think we shall have come out of it too badly."

He was still frowning and she went on: "It's no use your thinking about the English crown, Ernest. It's impossible. If anything happened to Victoria I do believe they would never have you. That Graves affair did you no good and all that scandal about Sophia. Hanover will be best for us . . . with George in control over here, because he will be, you know. He is such a darling that she will adore him and he will have his way through the sweetness of his character because she will want to please him in every way."

"You think everyone adores your son in the same way that you do."

"And I think you have a fondness for our son, eh, Ernest?"

"He's a boy to be proud of."

"He's so *good*. That's what amazes me."

The Duke was not going to admit that he shared the Duchess's fondness but his was almost as great as hers. They had wanted this son; they had him; and he delighted them both.

"You know." he said, "that that fool William will try to marry Victoria to Cambridge."

"I'm sure he's the favourite."

"He'd want it just to spite me."

"Well, you have not exactly been a friend of his, my darling. You did try to fit him into a strait-jacket."

"And it would have been a perfect fit."

"You'll never forgive him for not listening to you and taking you into his confidence when George died."

"William's always been an oaf and I certainly don't forgive the way he insulted me by telling me to take my horses out of the Windsor stables to make way for Adelaide's carriage."

"And for depriving you of your Gold Stick."

"What a King!"

"Yet the people seem to like him."

"At the moment. They so hated George they're ready to like anyone after him."

"I admit you would make a more kingly King."

"And you a more queenly Queen than our spotted Majesty."

"Poor Adelaide! Our George is devoted to her."

"All the children are. She should have been a nursery governess, not a Queen."

"Mrs. Fitzherbert is very friendly. Of course he was gracious to her and behaves as though she is George's widow." She looked at her husband slyly. "I know your new plan; you are going to put it about that Mrs. Fitz is persuading the King to become a Catholic."

"The people would never have a Catholic monarch."

The Duchess laughed. "You try so hard, dear Ernest. If he won't be forced into a strait-jacket the Catholic Faith will do as well."

"Are you on my side or not?"

"I'm on your side, but I am perhaps a little more realistic. I have decided that the crown of Hanover will do very nicely, with George as Victoria's husband."

"It may well be what we have to accept."

"Ah, so you are coming round to that view, eh?"

"I have always seen it as second prize, but that does not mean I would not try for the first."

They were laughing together. They had always worked together; and although she might deplore his involvement in scandal, and although his violent rages might alarm even her at times, there was a bond between them which nothing but death could break.

On the Brink of Revolution

THE KING was angry. His children were demanding titles and honours; they were growing more and more arrogant, showing clearly that their pride in their father's rank was greater than their love for him, and this hurt his sentimental heart. He was going to raise George to the peerage. He was after all his eldest son; and as soon as it could be arranged he should be the Earl of Munster—one of his own titles—and Baron Tewkesbury. That should satisfy him; but when he thought of the little George who used to ride on his knee and play fisticuffs with him in the gardens of Bushy he was bitterly disappointed. Young Victoria had given him a sour look at the Queen's Drawing-Room and he had not liked that at all. He had told Adelaide about it and she had soothed him by telling him it was not the little girl's fault. Victoria was an extremely affectionate child, and the manner in which she was brought up in Kensington was really very sad. She had probably been forbidden to smile at the King.

"What stuff is this? growled William. "I'll be having an open quarrel with that woman before long, you see."

The Queen sincerely hoped not. There was enough trouble in the country without having it in the family as well.

And how right she was! That was the main source of anxiety. The trouble in the country. Everywhere one turned there was talk of Reform. Lord John Russell, one of the leading Whigs, had brought forward the Reform Bill and there was great controversy throughout the country because of this. The differences between rich and poor were great; farm labourers were expected to exist on less than threepence a day; the mill workers were in revolt; the silk weavers of Spitalfields were ready to riot. Every day there was evidence of unrest. Reform was needed and the people saw in the Bill the hope of better times, for although it was concerned with Parliamentary Reform it was believed that this was at the root of the terrible conditions. There were fifty-six boroughs in England comprising less than two thousand people; there were at least thirty others almost as small which were sending a member to Westminster. Only a small and wealthy section of the country was able to use the vote. It was a monstrous state of affairs. The working classes depended on the good graces of their employers who were in complete control. It was small wonder that people were toiling for wages which kept them only sufficiently above starvation that they might continue to work.

"Reform! Reform!" cried the hungry farm labourers; and every trade all over the country was taking up the cry.

So when Lord John Russell on behalf of the Whigs introduced the Reform Bill which was to disenfranchise the "rotten" boroughs and give more people the power to vote, he was looked upon as a hero by the people. They were not going to let this chance escape them. The Reform Bill was going to become law no matter what opposition was set up against it.

William was not inclined to let political matters worry him overmuch. He liked to make speeches and did so on every possible occasion. Wellington had in fact expressed the view that while the King was eager to do his duty and did in fact attend to business with an expedition which was rare in recent monarchs, he would undo quite a lot of the advantages by making too many speeches in which he betrayed himself as a somewhat choleric, sentimental and a not very capable old gentleman.

There had been trouble in France. Charles X had been forced to abdicate. The terrible days of the great revolution were recalled through this lesser one, and what was happening abroad was talked of in the streets of England. Adelaide was worried. She told William that she dreamed about Marie Antoinette and the terrible fate which had befallen her.

"The English wouldn't behave like that," said William stoutly, but she did not believe him, and William couldn't help but be affected by her fears. He said he wished that fellow Russell and the whole Whig party further when they'd brought up this business of Reform.

"If this Bill is passed it may well be the end of the Monarchy," Adelaide had said. She had got that from Lord Howe, her Chamberlain, of whose opinions she thought so highly.

"Stuff!" said the King; but even he was uneasy.

Wellington was in command and he could trust Wellington. The victor of Waterloo could not be wrong. "Wellington will pull us through this bit of trouble as he did that other," said William. "There was a time when the people of this country were more afraid of Napoleon than they ever were of Reform. And then . . . Waterloo! Trust Wellington."

Wellington was at heart a soldier. After Waterloo he had been cheered wherever he went; his name was spoken of in hushed whispers, and he could not believe that the great victory of Waterloo would ever be forgotten. The war at an end he had turned to politics where he looked for the same success as he had enjoyed on the battlefield. The great general had become the great Tory leader.

Politics was a more tricky game even than war, and Wellington could not believe that the people would cease to regard him with awe and respect. In his home his Duchess, whom he had married out of chivalry and of whom he had long since tired, thought him a genius; his sons admired him; the charming Mrs. Arbuthnot was his great friend. He saw himself as one of the great leaders of the day and he could not conceive that anyone should see him otherwise.

He was against Reform. He did not believe that the poor and uneducated should have an opportunity of expressing their opinions through the vote; he believed that the present method of sending members to Parliament was the best that could be contrived.

When Parliament met he stood up and gave his views.

"The system that is in being today," he said, "deserves the confidence of the country. As long as I hold office I shall oppose Reform. If the disenfranchisement were admitted it would soon be pushed to lengths which would deprive the upper classes of the political influence which they derive from their property, and possibly eventually of the property itself."

These were his views; he had never been a man to prevaricate.

He had no doubt that now he had spoken the people would see reason and agree that no change in the parliamentary system was necessary. There should be no Reform.

Apart from Wellington, no one was surprised by the effect his speech had on the people. Wellington had become the most unpopular man in England. The Tories were against Reform. Therefore the Tories must go. Wellington was eager to keep the poor poor, was he, for the sake of the rich? Then Wellington was no friend of the people. There were riots all over London. People were complaining bitterly about the Peelers, that body of men whom Sir Robert Peel had inaugurated in 1822 and who walked the streets keeping law and order. What next? they demanded. The Bobbies or Peelers prevented them from causing a disturbance, and the Duke of Wellington was preventing their having the vote. And what of the King? He had walked the streets and been mighty friendly with the people—but what was he doing for them now?

Stones were thrown at carriages; crowds collected and the wrongs of the people were discussed; the mob was always ready for the excuse to make trouble.

"This could mean revolution," Lord Howe told the Queen.

Wellington's speech on that November day had certainly changed the situation. It had become truly threatening. The Lord Mayor had invited the King and Queen to his yearly banquet on the ninth and of course the Duke of Wellington, as the King's chief minister, would be present.

Everyone was waiting for the Lord Mayor's banquet; they felt that it would be a climax and there was a brooding silence in the streets. Rumour was everywhere. This would be the end of Wellington. He would ride to the banquet at his peril.

Wellington called to see the King.

"My dear fellow, my dear fellow," cried William. "What is all this *stuff?*"

"The people are in an ugly mood," said Wellington. "They did not like what I said the other day."

"They did not and they are working up to something, so they tell me. You should ride in my carriage to the banquet, my dear Duke. You'll be safe with me."

The Duke did not think so.

They were taking wagers throughout the Court. Would the King go to the Lord Mayor's banquet or would the whole thing be cancelled? What was the wise thing to do? The King would not wish to appear a coward—and yet this was how riots started and riots could spill over into revolutions.

Adolphus FitzClarence was certain his father would go.

"The old fellow's not a coward," he assured his friends. "I'd take a bet on it that he'll go."

"A hundred pounds," was the offer.

"A hundred pounds let it be," said Adolphus.

Wellington was no coward either. He was ready to face an army in the course of duty but he hated to lose his dignity. He was a handsome man—of a fine stature. He was five feet nine inches tall; and his aquiline nose was his most distinctive feature—that and his keen grey eyes. He was always immaculate; he could not bear to be other than well dressed. The idea of what might happen in the streets appalled him. The thought of his garments being spattered with mud was nauseating. It might even be worse. Who knew what the mob could be led to do? He had been shocked that the people could so far forget Waterloo as to threaten him; now he was remembering that though they might cry "Hosanna!" one week it could be "Crucify him!" the next.

As a successful soldier he believed in the theory that discretion is the better part of valour, so he went to see the Lord Mayor and they decided that for the good of the City of London it would be better to cancel the banquet.

The Queen talked of these matters to her Chamberlain. Richard, Earl Howe, was one of the most handsome men at Court, and from the moment he had entered Adelaide's household she had been aware of his special qualities. His attitude towards her had been one of great chivalry and admiration and Adelaide found that in his company she became animated and when she saw her reflection at such times she was amazed at the change in her face. If she did not look pretty or beautiful, at least she looked alive and not without attraction. He had such a flexible mind, she thought; he never raved and ranted; he was always completely tactful. She did not realize for some time that she was comparing him with the King.

She was always exhilarated by his company and he seemed to be by hers, but she never allowed herself to examine too closely her feelings for him. He was her Chamberlain and her friend; the King enjoyed his company too. Earl Howe was married and Lady Howe was a woman of great beauty who, before her marriage, had been one of the toasts of the town but she was rather eccentric and caused her husband some embarrassment. Adelaide would never forget the occasion recently when she had been driving with her Chamberlain and his wife. Lady Howe was seated next to her in the carriage and Earl Howe opposite when Lady Howe had said she was tired and put her feet on her husband's knee. He looked so taken aback and had given her such a look that she had replied: "What do you mean by making signs at me?" Then she had laughed and, adding that her feet were hot, rested them on the window ledge so that they were half out of the window.

Adelaide wondered why Lady Howe had behaved so in her presence and the thought did give her some uneasiness; she knew that she had become very unpopular since the Reform Bill had been brought into the house. To some extent the King too had lost his popularity—but not entirely. The people were still fond of their bumbling old sailor and since they must blame someone they blamed the Queen. The Queen, they said, was the one who was advising the King to oppose the Bill. And why? Because Earl Howe opposed it and the Queen listened more to her Chamberlain than to anyone else.

Adelaide refused at first to believe that people were whispering about her and Earl Howe but when she was forced to accept this she suspected the FitzClarences of spreading the gossip and was very unhappy by the way in which they had changed towards her. They had been such friends when William had been merely Duke of Clarence, but it seemed that they could not endure the fact that she was legitimately accepted into the royal circle and they were not. They were called the "bastidry," which infuriated them, and because their treatment of the King was common knowledge, some wit referred to them as the King's *un*natural children.

Earl Howe was saying that he was pleased the Lord Mayor's banquet had been cancelled.

"I should not have cared for Your Majesty to ride through the streets with the people in their present mood."

"That Bill. How I wish it had never been thought of."

Earl Howe looked grave. "If it ever became law I believe that would be the end of the Monarchy."

"You are not the only one who thinks so. I believe that the Duke of Wellington is of the same opinion."

"I shall vote against it. If by some chance it got through the Commons it would never get through the Lords."

"It will not get through the Commons. Wellington will not allow it."

"And Your Majesty will make sure that the King refuses to give his consent even if it should."

It was flattery, the implied suggestion that she carried great influence with the King. It was not really true, although she had to admit that William had always been good to her and treated her with respect; but it was Wellington on whom he relied.

This was perhaps why she enjoyed Lord Howe's company so much. He made her feel wise . . . and yes, she had to admit it, an extremely attractive woman. For the first time in her life she was enjoying masculine admiration, and when it came from one of the most handsome and attractive men at Court how could she help being flattered.

There was to be a small dinner party at Clarence House. The Queen was dressed in white silk which fitted her beautifully. She wore a few diamond ornaments but she never overloaded herself with jewels and feathers as the Duchess of Kent did.

When she went to the drawing-room William was already there, seated in a chair waiting to receive his guests. He never behaved like a King and although he was courteous to the ladies, people laughed at his lack of regality. He had been jeered at for offering people lifts in his carriage and going to the door of Clarence House or even St. James's to wave goodbye—acts which while they endeared him to those who received them, were noted and laughed at.

"He'll never be the King his brother was!" was the comment; and although the most unpopular of monarchs had been George IV, there was a note of nostalgia in the words.

"That's a nice dress," he said. "Why, you look quite pretty tonight, Adelaide."

"I'm glad you like it," she said. "It's made of English silk. I shall tell the ladies tonight that every bit of it was made in England and that I consider our own silk equal . . . if not better than . . . the French. It would be much more helpful to these people who are so dissatisfied if more work came their way, and surely it would if we bought less abroad."

"You're right . . . damned right."

"Well, I shall tell them tonight."

William said, "I hope they'll soon be forgetting all this *stuff*."

Adolphus FitzClarence arrived, bursting into the drawing-room with the studied lack of ceremony affected by all the FitzClarence family.

"Lots of people in the streets," he said. "You'd think something was going on."

"Oh." Adelaide laid her hand to her heart.

"Crowds shouting. Banners." He grinned at the Queen. "They don't seem very fond of you."

"They blame me," said Adelaide. "As if I had anything to do with it!"

"The people always have to have something to shout about," growled William.

"By the way, Father," said Adolphus, "will you let me have a hundred pounds?"

"What?" cried the King, growing red in the face.

Adolphus laughed. "It's to settle a debt. I bet you'd ride to the Lord Mayor's banquet; and you see, Father, you let me down and didn't go. So . . . I owe one hundred pounds."

"Gambling!" said the King.

"Now, Papa, you don't expect a shilling at Pope Joan to suit us all."

The King laughed. How he loved those children! thought Adelaide. They could behave as badly as possible and he would forgive them. Whenever she saw him with Dorothy Jordan's brood she longed more than ever for a family of her very own; and now she tried not to think of that cold little stone figure carved on a couch—the effigy of her child who had once been warm flesh and blood in her arms and the delight of her life.

There was another arrival. This time it was Frederick Fitz-Clarence bursting in just as his brother had.

"The Government's been defeated in the Commons," he said. "This means Wellington's out. The Whigs will be in and that means . . . the Bill."

"Oh God help us," said the Queen. "It will be the end of everything."

"Stuff!" said the King; but he too was uneasy.

The guests would be arriving at any moment. They must behave as though they were not in the least perturbed. William was not seriously so. His father had been shot at several times and so had his brother. He was not afraid of assassination; this indifference to danger was a family characteristic. They'd all had it, except perhaps George; and he used to say he was too civilized to be indifferent to violent and undignified death. Poor George! He had died in a far more sorry state than if he had been carried off by a bullet in his carriage or in the box at the opera.

No, William was not seriously perturbed. Wellington might have been defeated in the House but there would be a way out of it.

No one mentioned the Reform Bill at dinner; they knew it irritated the King. Instead he talked of the old days at sea and how he had been best man at Nelson's wedding. Then he showed them how Nelson had won the Battle of Trafalgar and they were all very bored.

Dear William, thought Adelaide. I believe he is the most boring man at Court. How different from Earl Howe!

The dinner over they left the table and retired to the drawing-room where they sat and talked. The King dozed and snored faintly and everyone pretended not to notice.

He awoke with a start and looking at Lady Grey who was sitting next to him he said: "Exactly so, M'am! Exactly so!" at which everyone was amazed for Lady Grey had not spoken for the last ten minutes.

The King then went to sleep again for a while, and when he awoke he said: "Well, well, I'll not delay you from your beds. And I'll go to mine. Come, my Queen."

As everyone had to admit, it was scarcely Royal behaviour.

The next day Wellington resigned and William had no recourse but to send for Earl Grey. There was great rejoicing throughout London. The Whigs would bring in the Reform Bill and the hope of every undernourished farm labourer, every worker in the towns was that the passing of the Reform Bill would bring justice to them and their kind.

Everyone was waiting now for the debate on the Bill. The King, never very stable, became ill suddenly and the Queen was terrified that his malady would be similar to his father's. Cumberland was watchful. If William went mad, Victoria would be Queen. There were great possibilities. A country on the verge of revolution, a little girl Queen, a mother as Regent who had not exactly endeared herself to the people; and the next heir a strong man, who might have an evil reputation but who could be trusted to be a firm ruler.

Commentators were saying that this could be the end of the Monarchy in England. Riots were occurring every day. "Reform! Reform!" shouted the City apprentices without knowing what the word meant.

Adelaide had never been so frightened; she discussed matters continuously with Earl Howe. Wellington must come back to power, she said. It was their only way of preventing this Bill's becoming law and she was certain that if it did it would mean the end of the Monarchy.

Her support for Wellington became known and the people were enraged against her. Those chose her as the scapegoat. She was a dowdy old German *hausfrau*, they said. She was an extravagant woman who was spending the country's money on adornments; she was arrogant; she was homely; and she was the mistress of Lord Howe.

She should take care.

"A foreigner is not a very competent judge of English liberties, and politics are not the proper field for female enterprise and exertion," said an observer in *The Times*.

She was constantly compared with Marie Antoinette.

"I bid the Queen of England remember that in consequence of the opposition of the ill-fated woman to the wishes of France, a fairer head than ever graced the shoulders of Adelaide, Queen of England, rolled on the scaffold."

"They hate me," she cried. "They hate me because I am a foreigner."

The King recovered. She felt happier when he was well. He made less of these matters than she did.

"Lot of stuff," he said. "It'll pass."

When they went to the play they were received in the

theatre by silence but when they drove home mud was thrown at their carriage and a stone broke the window.

Adelaide was trembling and William was red with fury.

"This is an inconvenience," he shouted. "If people are going to throw stones through the windows of my coach it will constantly have to be repaired and I'm always going somewhere."

The uneasy weeks went on. There was undoubtedly revolution in the air. And in due course the Reform Bill was passed through the Commons and was rejected by the Lords.

The Duchess of Kent and her Comptroller were watching events with great attention.

The Duchess's great fear was Adelaide's friendship with Earl Howe.

"For," as she whispered to Sir John, "what if she should have a child by that man? What fearful complications! What a terrible thing!"

"I'm sure she will never do that. She is far too prim."

"Of course if she did become pregnant *I* should want to be very sure who was the father."

Lights of cupidity were in the Duchess's eyes. Suppose the dreaded event should come to pass. Suppose Adelaide was with child. She would swear that it was Earl Howe's. There would be a revolution. There would have to be. It would be the only way to get Victoria where she belonged . . . on the throne.

Sir John smiled at her indulgently. "Don't let us face this terrible fact until it has happened," he said. "I am convinced that it never will."

"Dear Sir John, such a comfort. But I do declare I shall have to make the King see reason. I believe he thinks of nothing but how to mortify me."

"He may well be equally concerned with the trouble over the Reform Bill," suggested Sir John with that irony that always passed over the Duchess's ornate head.

"And serve him right. I hear they threw mud at his carriage. He is really most unpopular. And can you wonder at it. A foolish old man. And they *hate* Adelaide. She becomes more and more unpopular."

Sir John said that the people did not like German ladies and the Duchess agreed, seeming to forget that she was one.

"And now that Buggin person. Because she changes her name to Underwood does that alter the fact that she is a Buggin?"

"She was an Underwood before her marriage."

"But she is a Buggin now; and even though the Duke of Sussex has gone through a ceremony of marriage with her that does not make her his wife. She will never be accepted. Victoria will never receive her. I shall see to that. And I am expected to live at Kensington Palace under the same roof with a Buggin!"

"The Duke I have heard dotes on her and likes to smother her with jewels."

"Then she must look like a decorated barrel. She is so short and fat. I wonder what he sees in her?"

"I was going to suggest," said Sir John, tactfully changing the subject, "that since the Princess is so refreshed by sea breezes we take a little trip to the sea."

"What an excellent idea. I should enjoy to get away from Kensington for a while. People talk of nothing here but reform. And the people in the streets are getting so disgusting. So many dirty people standing about and they come too close to the Palace to please me."

"Then let us take a little trip. It is as well for the Princess to be seen about the country. She should travel like the heiress to the throne. And whatever objections there are the royal standard should fly over her residence and the guns give the royal salute."

The Duchess nodded.

Trust Sir John to soothe her.

As the Reform Bill had been passed through the Commons—though it still had to go through the Lords—William decided that his coronation should take place.

The people were always beguiled by ceremonies; and it would be a change to have a bit of pageantry in the streets. They might well find it much more to their taste than a lot of sordid riots. Earl Grey applauded this decision; he felt it would do a great deal of good in conjunction with the fact that the Bill's passing through the Commons had put the people in a good mood.

"Mind you," said the King, "I don't care for too much ceremony, I don't want any Bishops kissing me, and I think that we don't want to spend too much money on the business."

"If it is going to please the people it should be done in appropriate style, Sir."

"I'll not have money wasted," said the King.

The people were of course delighted at the prospect of a coronation. The disgruntled Tories said that it was a great mistake to try to economize on this, and they would not wish to attend a coronation which was tawdry and over which there had been obvious economy.

"All right, all right," said the King. "And what do they propose to do about it?"

Wellington told him that his colleagues would not attend unless a required amount of money was lavished on the necessary details.

"By God," cried the King. "So they'll stay away, eh? That's good news. It'll avoid the crush."

There was no way of making a King of William.

Then came trouble from the Duchess of Kent.

She wrote to the King to say that she was delighted to hear he had at last agreed to be crowned. He would, of course, wish Victoria to take her rightful *place* immediately behind him.

When William received this letter he was furious. He went into Adelaide's sanctum where she was enjoying a pleasant *tête-à-tête* with Earl Howe.

"That woman!" he cried. "That damned woman!"

"Is it the Duchess of Kent?" asked Adelaide.

"Is it the Duchess of Kent! Of course it is that damned irritating woman."

"What is the trouble now?" asked Adelaide.

"She's giving me instructions about the coronation. Her daughter is to walk immediately behind me, to show everyone that she is second only to the King. Did you ever hear such . . . such . . . impertinence."

"William, my dear, I beg of you to sit down," said the Queen. "The Duchess is merely being her tiresome self."

"And if she thinks I'm going to have that . . . that chit . . ."

"She is only a child. *She* should not be blamed."

"I don't blame her. Nice little thing. But that doesn't mean I'm going to let her mother poke her interfering finger into royal affairs. Certainly not, I say. Certainly she shall not walk immediately behind me. Every brother and sister of mine—and I'm not exactly short of them—shall take precedence over Victoria."

"Is that right . . ." began Adelaide. "I mean is that the way to treat the heiress presumptive to the throne?"

"It's the way I am treating her," said the King. His lips were stubborn. "That child will come to the coronation and walk where she is told."

"Oh, it is monstrous!" cried the Duchess. "If I were not so *angry* I should faint with fury."

"Pray do not do that," said Sir John. "We need all our wits to deal with this situation."

"Victoria shall not be *exposed* to indignity, which she would be if she followed those stupid old aunts and uncles of hers."

"She must not do it."

"Then how . . . ?"

Sir John smiled, delighted that once again the Duchess was at loggerheads with her family. The more isolated she was, the more power for Sir John. As it was he was almost constantly in her company; his home was Kensington Palace, and to give respectability to the situation, Lady Conroy and the children were there also. His daughters Jane and Victoire were the companions of the Princess Victoria and he endeavoured to arrange that she saw as little as possible of the young people of her own family. The fact that the King had said she must make more public appearances had worried him; he had had visions of Victoria's affection for the Queen —which was already considerable—being a real stumbling block. So he welcomed controversies such as this and encouraged the Duchess in her truculent attitude.

"If the King will not give her her rightful place," said Sir John, "she must refuse to attend the coronation."

"The heiress to the throne not present at the coronation!"

"If it is regrettably necessary, yes. The people will notice her absence and they will blame the King for it. Moreover, the King wishes Victoria to be under the charge of his sisters and not to walk with you, which is significant."

"Significant," cried the Duchess.

"It means that on this important occasion he is taking your daughter from your care. Don't you see what meaning people will attach to this?"

"I do indeed and my mind is made up. Victoria shall *not* attend the coronation."

"I should write and tell His Majesty that you believe you

should stay in the Isle of Wight as to leave it now might be detrimental to your daughter's health."

The Duchess nodded sagely.

"This will show the old fool," she said.

"Let her stay away," growled the King. "I tell you this, Adelaide: my great hope is that I live long enough to prevent that woman ever becoming Regent."

"Of course you will. There are many years left to you."

William's eyes glinted. "God help the country if she was ever Regent. I'm going to live long enough to see Victoria stand alone."

"You will if you take care of yourself."

He smiled at her, his eyes glazed with sudden sentiment. "You're a good woman, Adelaide. I'm glad I was able to make a Queen of you."

"It's enough that you are a very good husband to me."

William was pleased. Momentarily he had forgotten that maddening sister-in-law of his.

It was not a very bright September morning but the crowds were already lining the streets. They chatted about the odd but not unlovable ways of the King; some muttered a little about the Queen—why must we always bring these German women into the country?—but after all it was Coronation Day and the Reform Bill had passed through the Commons and better times they believed lay ahead, so for this day they were prepared to forget their grievances.

When the King and Queen drove past on the way to Westminster Abbey a cheer went up for them. William wore his Admiral's uniform and looked exactly like a weatherbeaten sailor which amused the crowd; and the Queen looked almost beautiful in gold gauze over white satin.

"Good old William," the cry went up, and although no one cheered Adelaide there were no hostile shouts.

But where was the Princess Victoria? One of the most delightful sights at such functions was usually provided by the children and the little heiress to the throne was very popular. Her absence was immediately noticed and whispered about.

"They say that the Duchess and the King hate each other."

"They say the Duchess won't bring Victoria to Court because she is afraid of Cumberland."

Rumours multiplied; there were always quarrels in the royal family.

Meanwhile the King and Queen had reached the Abbey and the Archbishop was presiding over the ceremony of crowning them. William who looked upon all such occasions as "stuff" showed his impatience with the ceremony and so robbed it of much of its dignity; but Adelaide behaved with charming grace and many present commented on the fact that although she might not be the most beautiful of Queens she was kindly, gracious and peace-loving.

During the ceremony the rain pelted down and the wind howled along the river; however, when the royal pair emerged the rain stopped and the sun shone, so they were able to ride back in comfort through the streets to St. James's.

The people cheered. He was not such a bad old King, they decided, and if he was ready to put up with his spotted wife they would too.

William was grumbling all the way back about Victoria's absence. It had been noticed; it had been commented on.

"It's time," he said, "that someone taught that woman a lesson."

Soon after the coronation Adelaide went to Brighton with her niece Louise of Saxe-Weimer, the daughter of her sister Ida, for whom the Queen had very special love among her family of other people's children because Louise was a cripple. Adelaide had had this child in her care for most of her life and this made her seem like her own daughter, just as George Cambridge was like her own son.

But Louise was growing weaker as the years passed and this saddened her. Louise's mother was now paying a visit to England and to her Adelaide was able to talk of her anxieties —the state to which the country had been reduced and her fears (quoting Earl Howe) that if this dreaded Reform Bill was passed it would be the beginning of the end for the Monarchy.

Ida listened sympathetically and admitted that she was glad to be the wife of a man who was not the ruler of a great country. She was not rich and not really very important but she would not wish for Adelaide's anxieties.

"I had the Crown and was barren," said Adelaide. "But I

have been happier than I would have believed I could possibly be . . . without children."

"You have other people's," said Ida. "And how is the little girl at Kensington?"

"We scarcely ever see her although William has expressly told her mother that as heiress to the throne she must appear with him in public."

"The Saxe-Coburgs give themselves such airs. Though why they should, I can't imagine. There was all that scandal about Louise of Saxe-Coburg. They kept very quiet about that. And I believe they are hoping that Victoria will marry one of the two boys—Ernest or Albert."

"William has decided that she shall have George Cambridge. He is already rather taken with her."

"He's a diplomat already, then."

"I don't think he thinks of her position so much. She is not without charm, you know. Such a dignified young lady. I declare that it is not right that she should be shut away there in Kensington and scarcely ever allowed any fun."

"Oh, that Saxe-Coburg woman!"

"She really is trying and William is becoming incensed at the very mention of her name."

"I dare say the Cumberlands are hoping that their George will win the prize."

Adelaide laughed. "He is a delightful boy, too. It surprises me that . . ." She stopped. She had rarely been heard to make a malicious comment even about her enemies.

"Surprise you that such parents could have such a son?" said the forthright Ida.

"Well, it is a little odd. And he *is* a charming boy. Of course if Victoria loved him I daresay there would be no objection; but we are hoping it will be his cousin."

"Your special protégé. Oh, Adelaide, how long it seems when we were together in Saxe-Meiningen wondering what would happen to us and who our husbands would be."

"And when the Duke of Saxe-Weimer came riding to the castle to seek his bride who was supposed to be the elder sister no one was very surprised—certainly not that elder sister—that he chose the younger."

"You were always the sweetest and most modest of sisters. The Duke of Saxe-Weimer was stupid. He would have been so much wiser to have chosen you."

At which Adelaide laughed and began to talk of the baths which she thought might be beneficial for Louise. She would take her to them the next day.

"I believe," said Ida, "that if I wanted to take her back with me you would refuse to let me do so."

"I would have Louise choose where she wishes to be."

"And you know where that is," laughed Ida.

It was true that Adelaide knew, and she could not help being pleased. She was born to be a mother, for her fiercest inclination was to care for children. How happy she would have been with a nursery full of them. Instead of which she had had to make do with a family of stepchildren, all of whom were now proving to be rather ungrateful. But she did have William's grandchildren and like all young people they were devoted to her. In addition there was George Cambridge and Louise . . . and George Cumberland too who was constantly visiting her—and it would have been the same with Victoria if the Duchess had permitted it.

She smiled thinking of them. They took her mind off other matters; and this was a few days respite in Brighton with her dear sister, when they could talk of the days of their youth during which they had been so happy together.

It took her away from the stark reality of the uneasy days through which they were living. Revolution was a fact on the Continent and a possibility in England. Her dreams were haunted by memories of riding through the streets in her carriage and the faces of the mob leering in at her. She dreamed of the mud spattering the windows, of the stones that broke the glass. She heard their comments: "Go back to Germany, dowdy *hausfrau*." She knew that they called her the "frow,' and they whispered unpleasant things about her and Earl Howe.

She must enjoy these days in Brighton before returning to London where everyone would be thinking of and talking about the Reform Bill.

London was seething with rage. Although a strong majority had passed the Bill through the Commons, the Lords rejected it by a majority of forty-one.

Earl Grey came to see William.

"If the Bill is not passed, Your Majesty," he said, "there will be a revolution."

"Bills have to pass through the Commons *and* the Lords and receive my signature before they become law."

"This one *must* become law," insisted Grey.

"And how do you propose it should?"

"Your Majesty must create new peers who will support it."

"I'll be damned if I will," said the King. "I'm against that measure in any case. They'll have to forget about reform."

"That is something I fear they will never do, Sir. The people are intent on reform and reform they'll have."

"But if the Bill is thrown out . . ."

"By the Lords, Sir? The Commons have passed it. Something will have to be done, and I think it would be wise if Earl Howe were dismissed from his post of Chamberlain to the Queen."

"Howe dismissed? The Queen will never hear of it."

"Nevertheless, Sir, perhaps she should be persuaded to relinquish him."

"Why so? Why so?"

"He voted against the Bill."

"So did many others. A majority of others voted against it."

"But owing to Earl Howe's position in the Queen's household and the fact that he is on friendly terms with . . . er . . . Your Majesties . . ."

William was obtuse. He did not understand the reference.

Earl Grey saw that it was no use pursuing it and went back to report to his Cabinet that he had made no progress with the King.

Earl Grey discussed the King's obstinacy with his fellow-ministers.

"He refuses to see the implications about Howe. He refuses to create new peers. If the Lords are adamant the Bill will be thrown out. I have to make them see that this will mean revolution."

The Cabinet insisted on the dismissal of Howe. Secrets which Grey discussed with the King were leaking out to the Tories; Howe was an ardent Tory and a sworn enemy of the Bill. The likeliest leakage would come through the Queen and as the Queen was on such terms of . . . er . . . intimacy with Earl Howe and the King was notoriously outspoken and completely lacked finesse, it seemed that Howe was the informer. No sooner had Grey discussed some matter with the King than Wellington was aware of it. The dribble of information into the opposite camp must be stemmed—and the dismissal of Howe would bring this about.

It was not difficult to work up public feeling against Earl Howe. The Queen was already loathed because she was blamed for persuading William against Reform. There were scurrilous paragraphs in the press about her. There had been criticisms for some time of her "spotted Majesty," an unkind reference to her blotchy complexion; she had been accused both of dowdiness and extravagance; of Machiavellian craft and crass stupidity. But now there was Earl Howe.

There were cartoons of the Queen in the arms of her Chamberlain. In one they were embracing behind William's back. In another they were kissing and a balloon coming from the Queen's mouth enclosed the words, "Come this way, Silly Billy."

There would be riots if something was not done. Grey decided something must be done and quickly; and if the King would not dismiss Howe, then Howe must resign.

He sent for Howe. He bade him be seated at his table across which he passed the cuttings from the newspapers.

"You will see, my lord," said Earl Grey, "that it is imperative for you to resign from the Queen's service without delay."

Adelaide, returned from a ride, was about to change her costume when she received an urgent message from Earl Howe. When she said she would see him later, the messenger returned immediately and said that as the matter was of the utmost importance would she please see him at once.

Somewhat agitated, she received him.

"Something terrible has happened," she said. "Tell me quickly."

He told her. "And I have come to return my keys to you."

"I shall not accept your resignation."

He smiled at her affectionately. "The Prime Minister has made it very clear that I must go."

"But the Prime Minister does not manage my household."

"Your Majesty will see that in the circumstances I must resign. You, more than the King, are aware of what is going on in the streets. At times like this the people look for a scapegoat."

"And they have chosen you."

"If they had I should not be so alarmed. I would refuse to resign. I believe they have chosen Your Majesty."

She stared at him in horror.

"And for that reason," he said, "there have been many disgusting cartoons."

She understood.

"But to insist on your resignation . . . it is an insult."

"It is one we must accept. It is necessary for your safety. That is why I must insist on handing you the keys."

She felt sick and ill. Reform or Revolution. That was what Grey thought. But Adelaide believed that Reform *was* Revolution.

She sat down in her chair.

"You are feeling faint?" asked Howe, kneeling beside her.

She shook her head. "Please do not stay. If you were to be seen . . . what construction would they put on that? Please . . . send my women to me."

He stood up and before he went he laid the keys on the table.

The mood of the people grew more ugly. The windows of Apsley House were broken by the mob. Anyone who opposed the Bill was the enemy of the People. Effigies of the Queen were burned in public places, but the people still retained an affection for the King who continued to be represented as a foolish old man led astray by his scheming Queen. "Oh, I'm a poor weak old man," he was reputed to say in the cartoons. "They know I'm not able to do anything."

Earl Grey came to the King. The Bill must be passed through the Lords. If the King would not create new peers who would support it, the Whig Ministry must resign.

"Resign, then," said the King.

William sent for the Duke of Wellington and asked him to form a government. There was a menacing lull in the streets. If Wellington was at the helm with his Tories this would mean disaster for the Bill, and the people would not see the Bill thrown out. They had become obsessed by the Bill; they looked upon it as a magic formula and believed that once it was passed Utopia would be established in England; everything they had hoped for would come to pass.

It was said that young ladies imagined they would be at once married . . . when the Bill was passed; schoolboys believed that grammar would be abolished; poets believed that the public would clamour for their works; soldiers would receive double their pay; and the price of pies and cakes would be halved . . . all that was needed to bring about this miracle was that the Bill should become law.

The Bill was discussed in every tavern by many who did not understand a word of it. To them it was merely the key to paradise on Earth.

If Wellington formed a new Tory government opposed to the Bill it would be the sign for the mob to march. There was not a politician who did not know this, and Wellington's plan was to bring in a new Bill—a Reform Bill, yes, but a modified one. Even this would not do; and because there was not a man among them who did not realize that a change of government at that time would mean that the people would rise, it was impossible for Wellington to form a government.

The Bill must be passed; and since the King would not create the necessary peers to pass it through the Lords, those peers who would not vote for it must abstain from voting at all. It was the only way to pass the Bill.

So . . . with London ready to rise and destroy the existing régime which would not bring about reform, the Bill was again presented. Breathlessly people waited for the result. In the House of Lords it was put to the vote. As the members of that House were aware of what would happen if the Bill was rejected, the Tory benches were half empty. So those who opposed, refrained from voting and on June 4th of that year 1832 the Reform Bill was passed.

Adelaide was terrified, expecting revolution at any moment. The King tried to soothe her. "Devil take them all," he said. "By God, if I hear the word Reform again I shall never speak to the man who says it."

He refused to give his assent in person, which was foolish as this was only a matter of form, and royal confirmation was given by the commission.

London was jubilant; there were carousing in the streets and bonfires at every corner.

Reform was coming. Now all they had to do was wait for the miracle.

The King had refused his personal assent. Then the King was no friend of the people. It was not his fault at all; it was that German Queen of his. She was the real villainess. But Billy should be taught a lesson.

When William drove through the streets on his way to dis-

solve Parliament, the people refused to take off their hats;
they came close to his coach and jeered at him. Silly Billy,
who did what his wicked wife told him. He had been against
Reform.

William was unperturbed. He had faced death during his
life at sea and he lacked the imagination to worry about the
harm an angry mob might do to him.

He was annoyed by these people who no longer loved him.
They were threatening him; they would start throwing stones
in a moment. Adelaide seated beside him was trembling. Poor
Adelaide, she didn't understand these people. They wouldn't
really harm him; they were just an ill-mannered crowd.

To show his contempt for them he leaned out of the window and spat at them.

This unkingly act had such an effect on the crowd that it
fell back in amazement. A king to spit on his subjects! The
mob could spit; it was a common habit of the lower orders,
but for a king to do so . . . was unheard of.

They could think of nothing to say or do; and then a
voice was distinctly heard to say: "George IV would never
have done that. George IV always remembered that he was a
king."

And by that time the royal coach had driven by.

The King was on his way to dissolve Parliament. And
what did it matter? The Reform Bill was passed.

An Accident at Kew

❧ THE Duchess of Kent was discussing with Sir John
Conroy the new arrival to her household.

"Of very good family," she said. "The eldest daughter of
the first Marquis of Hastings and second Earl of Moira."
The Duchess was knowledgeable about the family connections
of those who served her, as she assured herself, one needed to

be when these people would live under the same roof as the future Queen. "The Marquis you know made quite a name for himself in the Army and he was a friend of the late King. So I think Flora will be quite *suitable*."

Sir John Conroy agreed with the Duchess that this was so.

"And since it is the King's wish that Victoria should meet more people, I do not see why this should not be achieved in her own household."

"There is no reason at all."

"Lady Flora is not exactly young. She is twenty-six years of age and *serious*."

"And an excellent addition to the household!"

"She knows that although she is a member of my retinue her main duty is to accompany Victoria."

"And how does Victoria like her?"

"You know the child. She is overflowing with affection. She really must practise a little restraint."

"She does not overflow for all," said Sir John, smiling not very pleasantly as he recalled the Princess's coolness towards himself. The Duchess sighed. She understood. Victoria could be difficult. She, too, was aware of her daughter's coldness not only towards Sir John. Sometimes she could believe that the child was critical of her own Mamma—but this, of course, could not be possible. The Duchess felt sure that Victoria must love and admire her unquestioning.

"I cannot think where she gets her ideas," she said vaguely.

"The Princess is aware of her destiny," replied Sir John. "So I suppose a little arrogance must be forgiven now and then."

"But not in her own home," declared the Duchess. "She must be guided and I believe that Lady Flora will have a good influence."

"A mild one, at any rate," said Sir John. "As usual, my dearest Duchess has chosen wisely."

"I will send for Victoria and ask how she likes her new companion."

Victoria came and immediately felt embarrassed as she always did when in the presence of her mother and Sir John.

"Oh, Victoria. Do stand up straight, child. You will be like the Princess Charlotte if you do not. She had to have one pocket loaded with heavy stones to stop her from being lop-sided. How would you like that?"

"I daresay it would be no worse, Mamma, than having a

piece of holly tied around one's neck to make one hold one's chin up."

"Aha!" said the Duchess. "You should be grateful, should she not, Sir John, to have a Mamma who cared so much for you to walk straight that she devised such plans."

Victoria touched her chin recalling the jabs she had received from the branches of holly. She would never see the plant without remembering that particular discipline of her youth.

Yes, thought the Duchess, Victoria was becoming a little arrogant. She would have to be persuaded to be otherwise. It was difficult to remind her that she would soon be a Queen at one moment and then the next to teach her to be humble.

What a task! sighed the Duchess inwardly; and then remembered that she had dear Sir John to help her.

"Victoria, I trust you will find the company of Lady Flora congenial. She is of very good family and suited to her new post. *I* have made sure of that."

"Yes, Mamma, I do like Lady Flora."

The Duchess folded her hands together and with the pious expression of one who has done her duty added: "Perhaps that will satisfy His Majesty." She spoke the title with a touch of contempt which was of course not directed towards that but to the man who now bore it.

Victoria was thinking that Lady Flora was friendly enough and pleasant in her way, but *old*. Why could she not have young people about her, and of the opposite sex at that? They were so much more interesting, she thought. She fancied she liked a little flirtation. And what boys did she ever see other than Sir John's young sons? And the only companions of her own age were Victoire and Jane Conroy.

There is too much Conroy in this household, she thought.

"Sir John believes you should undertake some journeys," the Duchess was saying.

"Journeys, Mamma?"

"That you should travel a little."

"To the sea?" Victoria's eyes began to sparkle. How she loved the sea!

"The sea and the countryside as well. It is fitting that you should know something of the kingdom you are to rule."

"Oh, Mamma, I should enjoy these journeys."

The Duchess smiled. "You must not think of them as pleasure only, although I am convinced that you will derive some enjoyment from them. You will know that you are doing your duty, and that is always—or should be—a source of pleasure. Sir John and I have decided that you shall pay a round of visits. We are now deciding when you shall start and where you shall go."

"Oh, Mamma, who will come with me?"

"You need not fear that I and Sir John will not accompany you."

Victoria tried to compose her features so that she did not show her disappointment. Journeys had sounded so exciting. She had pictured herself visiting the King and the Queen, and perhaps sharing in Aunt Adelaide's parties. But it was to be different from that. She was to travel with Mamma and Sir John, which meant of course that they would not be visiting the King and Queen.

"You will hear more of this later," said the Duchess. "In the meantime I have a present for you."

"Oh, Mamma, how exciting!"

"I hope you will appreciate it."

The Duchess went to a table and picked up a leather-bound book.

"Thank you, Mamma."

"Open it," commanded the Duchess.

Victoria did so and looked at the blank pages in some astonishment.

"It is a Journal," said the Duchess. "You must write your impressions in it. I shall wish to see it at regular intervals so you will have to write your best. I am sure you will find it a rewarding exercise both at the time and in the future."

Victoria was pink with pleasure. Yes, she would enjoy a Journal. What fun to write in it what she felt. Perhaps she could do some sketches in it. She did enjoy sketching and was really rather good. No, it would be for writing only. Oh dear, Mamma would have to see it, which would mean she would have to be careful of what she wrote.

"You may take it away now," said the Duchess, "and start writing your impressions on the day we leave. Very soon we shall have news for you."

Victoria went from the room. Lehzen was waiting outside for her. They would never allow her to be alone even in the apartments. I'm nothing but a prisoner, thought Victoria resentfully, as she had done a hundred times before.

She told Lehzen about the Journal and Lehzen of course thought it would be an excellent exercise.

In the schoolroom Victoire Conroy was sitting on the floor

blowing bubbles. Victoria caught a beautiful one which reflected the windows in a lovely reddish blue light.

"I want to blow bubbles," she cried.

She took her clay pipe and sat down with Victoire.

Lovely soap bubbles, riding up to the ceiling, some reaching it only to burst when they touched it, others fading out before. She laughed with pleasure, vying with Victoire to blow the biggest and send them off farther than hers.

She dreamed as she always did when she blew bubbles; perhaps that was why she liked doing it. She saw herself growing up, sitting with the young Georges, being flattered by them, dancing with them, and both of them trying so hard to please her.

But of course Mamma would not allow her to see them. She had cousins but she must not play with them; she was going to be a Queen but she was a prisoner; she was going on journeys but her jailers would be with her; she had a Journal in which she could write everything she felt, but Mamma would see it.

It will not always be so, she thought; then she exclaimed with joy. She had blown the biggest and most beautiful of bubbles. It rose and fell and went sailing round the room. Victoire had stopped to watch it. There never was such a bubble; and then suddenly it exploded in mid-air and was gone.

The Queen called on the Duchess of Cumberland.

It was typical of the King and Queen that they called on their relatives and rarely summoned them regally as other monarchs had done. Imagine George IV calling on them! thought the Duchess of Cumberland. William and Adelaide had little dignity.

"How delightful of you to come," said Frederica. "You must have known that I needed cheering up."

Adelaide smiled. She knew it well enough. She had learned what it meant to have the scandal sheets directed against one.

"And," went on Frederica, "I feel better already. But pray tell me, how is the King?"

Adelaide had seated herself comfortably on a sofa as she said: "Oh, not very well. His asthma is troubling him and his hay fever is starting again."

"Poor William. I feel for His Majesty."

"It is tiresome . . . with all his duties."

She spoke, thought Frederica, like a humble housewife. How ironical that she should be the Queen. Obviously she cared little for the title and would have been happier as plain Duchess of Clarence for the rest of her life. Being fairy godmother to countless children pleased her more than anything else.

"The children are at Kew," said Adelaide. "The children" were never long out of her conversation. "They enjoy it there so much. The boys can play their wild games in the gardens and the little ones can have plenty of fresh country air."

"And you will soon be with them, I daresay."

"The King and I go to Kew tomorrow."

"How the old King and Queen used to love Kew!"

"William says they always referred to it as 'dear little Kew.' I must say I think that is very apt."

"And my boy is behaving well."

"Admirably," said Adelaide. "A dear boy! How proud you must be of him!"

Frederica admitted this was so. "His father is, too."

"But of course. What a great comfort!" Adelaide spoke wistfully.

How amusing, thought Frederica, if Adelaide was with child after all. No, it was not really amusing. Ernest would be furious, because if it were the case their son's marriage to Victoria would be of little significance. And William was unwell. If William died and Victoria was Queen, the Duchess of Kent would be Regent. That would never do, and what chance had Ernest now of getting in and taking the throne? The people would never let that happen. Circumstances changed one's desires. At one time Ernest—and she with him—had wanted William put away as insane, but not now. The Duchess of Kent's regency would be far worse than William's rule. For that woman would never permit a marriage between Victoria and the Cumberlands' son, George.

"Our George really is a bright boy," went on Frederica. "I know all parents think that of their children but I don't believe Ernest and I are deceiving ourselves."

"Indeed you are not," Adelaide declared warmly. "He is a bright and charming boy. As you know, I love him well. It would be impossssible not to."

"And he loves you. You should hear him talk of the perfections of his Aunt Adelaide. Sometimes he calls you Queeny as the little ones do."

Adelaide smiled. "The darlings!" she said.

"And Victoria . . . she is never there," said Frederica.

"Never. Such a pity. Poor child. They are bringing her up so strictly. I believe she rarely has any fun."

"She should be meeting her cousins."

"That's what William says. But to tell the truth I rarely broach the subject of Victoria to him. It upsets him."

"And George Cambridge is well."

"Very well and happy I'm glad to say." Adelaide's expression softened even further. Young Cambridge was the favourite . . . he and little crippled Louise. They were the Queen's special charges because they were always with her, the parents of both those children being overseas.

And how, wondered Frederica, are we going to oust Cambridge from first place? That will be difficult. The only one who could do it would be Victoria herself. Surely she must prefer her cousin Cumberland. Was there some way of bringing their son to Victoria without young Cambridge's being there?

That was something which could not be discussed with Adelaide.

"The two boys are the best of friends . . . your George and mine," said Adelaide.

Her George! Oh dear! She would try to marry Victoria to Cambridge and the King would do the same. She and Ernest would have to think of something.

"Such a good boy! He writes to his mother regularly. Poor Augusta! I fear it is a sad wrench to part with him. I do not know how she does it. I tell her that her loss is my gain . . . but *how* I feel for her!"

Adelaide would run on for hours about her precious children if allowed to but Frederica found it particularly galling to listen to an account of the virtues of George Cambridge, her son's chief rival for the hand of Victoria.

"I know," she said, "that you came to comfort me. Dear Adelaide, you are such a good soul. But there is no need to remain silent about all these distressing matters. They are uppermost in our minds, we both know."

"My dear Frederica, I too have suffered from these wicked scribblers."

"They delight in taunting us. That affair took place eight years ago. It is wicked of them to revive it now."

Frederica was referring to a recent pamphlet printed by a certain Joseph Phillips which had revived that long-ago scandal concerning the Duke of Cumberland and his valet Sellis. Sellis had been found in his room in the Duke's apartment at St. James's with his throat cut; the Duke had been badly wounded. The Duke's story had been that the valet had attacked him and then cut his own throat because he feared the consequences. "He went mad suddenly," was the Duke's verdict, but as Sellis had a pretty wife and the Duke's reputation was quite evil then as now the general opinion had been that the Duke had been discovered in the woman's bed by her husband who had understandably remonstrated. The Duke had then murdered Sellis and inflicted a wound on himself to attempt to make good his version of the affair. This had happened more than twenty years before; but the Duke had become very unpopular during the agitation over the Reform Bill because he had been one of its most enthusiastic opponents. Then of course there had recently been the charge of incest with his sister Sophia which had been brought up against him, in addition to which there was the suicide of Lord Graves, with whose wife the Duke was conducting an affair. No member of the royal family had a more sinister reputation than the Duke of Cumberland; but never had the people been so much against him as when he opposed the Reform Bill.

Cumberland, angry that Phillips should have dared print this pamphlet particularly at such a time when, with the help of the Orange Lodges, he hoped to be the King of England, prosecuted Phillips who had just been found guilty and sentenced to six months imprisonment.

"At least," soothed Adelaide, "the man was found guilty."

"Yes, yes," said Frederica, a little impatiently, "but people forget that the man was sentenced and they go on thinking Ernest a murderer."

"They cannot do that." But Adelaide spoke half-heartedly. She was remembering how she had once feared that Ernest was planning some harm to little Victoria. She had herself spoken to the Duchess of Kent and begged her to be careful not to let the child out of her sight.

It was hard to think of dear George being the son of a murderer. He was such a delightful boy and she loved him dearly, nearly as much as George Cambridge.

Frederica sighed. "We must resign ourselves to being targets for the wits," she said. "But there are some who are determined to blacken Ernest's name."

To blacken it? thought Adelaide. That would be difficult.

It was really as black as possible already.

"Brougham," went on Frederica, "insulted him in the Lords the other day."

"Is that so?"

"I'm afraid it is. He referred to him—and Ernest was present at the time—as 'the Illustrious Duke—illustrious only by courtesy.' "

"And what will Ernest do about that?"

"What can he do? He can't prosecute Lord Brougham. But he'll remember it if ever . . ."

Oh dear, she was being led away by Adelaide's sympathy.

"It is so distressing," she finished on a pathetic note.

"My dear Frederica! And my purpose in coming here was to comfort you! Let us talk of happier things. Shall I tell you about the children's ball I am planning?"

"Please do. And will Victoria be there?"

"She shall be invited."

"I'll tell you a secret. My George is very taken with her."

"So is mine . . . dear Cambridge! He could talk of nothing else after their meeting. She is a charming creature. Oh, how I wish her mother would be less tiresome. In fact, I believe the King will be firm and insist on her coming out of retirement. It is ridiculous . . . the heiress to the throne!"

"Quite!" agreed Frederica.

She was wondering whether to speak to her son. He was something of an idealist. She could imagine his saying: "Well, if she prefers Cambridge, she must marry him." How did we produce such a son . . . such an intelligent, charming, *good* boy? But he was not really very ambitious. Doubtless he would be happier so. And I want his happiness above all things, thought Frederica, but I want him to rule England as well.

When Adelaide left she was turning over in her mind how she could bring Victoria and her son together. If only she could ask Victoria to visit her. As if that would be allowed! Well, that was Ernest's fault. He had at one time had rather wicked ideas about her and as he had been too indiscreet and not clever enough people had got wind of his intentions. No, little Victoria would never be allowed to escape her watch-dogs. And to come to the wicked Cumberlands! That was a joke!

Never mind; she would discuss this with Ernest and they would think of something. She would not despair. Her plan now was to see Ernest King of Hanover and George consort of Victoria.

If that happens I shall be content, she told herself.

She was musing on this when a messenger came from Clarence House. It was from the Queen. She was setting out for Kew immediately and she believed that the Duchess might wish to come with her. There had been an accident in the gardens. George Cumberland had been hurt.

The Duchess set out at once.

Adelaide comforted her. The reports had been exaggerated she was sure. They would find this so when they reached Kew. Frederica must not imagine the worst.

Adelaide's message had not been very clear. All she knew was that there had been an accident.

"A . . . serious accident?" whispered Frederica.

Adelaide put an arm about her. "I beg of you . . . don't despair. Wait and see. I *know* he is going to be all right."

So on that anxious journey down to Kew, the Queen comforted the Duchess of Cumberland, and when they arrived Frederica was taken straight to the room in which her son lay. His head was bandaged so that she could not recognize him. She took his hand and sank down by the bedside.

"Your Grace," said the doctors, "His Highness will live. You need have no fear of that."

She wept quietly and meanwhile the Queen had called the doctors aside.

"Pray tell me the worst," she said. "I want the truth."

"Your Majesty, His Highness is in no danger of death."

"Then . . ."

One doctor looked at the other who said, "We fear that he has damaged his eyes so badly that blindness may result."

The Queen felt as though she would faint.

"Pray," she said, "do not tell the Duchess yet. It must be broken gently . . . gradually. Leave this to me."

And they were content to do this.

Royal Progress

VICTORIA, waking at half past seven, sat up in bed and looked about the strange room wondering where she was. Then she remembered. Chatsworth! They had arrived here on the previous night and it had been dark so that she had been unable to see the house. The Duke of Devonshire had welcomed them at the door and been very respectful to Mamma and herself, declaring that he was honoured to receive them. These receptions always delighted Mamma and put her into a good temper; and if their hosts and hostesses were especially welcoming to Sir John Conroy, Mamma was even more pleased.

There was no doubt about it that she enjoyed travel. They had been moving from one place to another since August. How excited she had been on that day when they had left Kensington Palace and taken the new road to Regent's Park, through such pretty country! Such good progress they had made, leaving the Palace at six minutes past seven and arriving at Barnet, where they changed horses, at twenty minutes to nine. She could be precise about the details because she had written it all down in her Journal.

How right Mamma had been about the pleasures of a Journal! One could recall what had happened so vividly. Of course, she must always remember that Mamma would read her Journal and that meant that she could not write *exactly* what she felt. In fact she was not always sure what she did feel—about Sir John for one thing. But if she could have written down these vague doubts it would have been rather exciting.

But there were so many things one must not do—far more it seemed than those one could. So it was best to enjoy what one was allowed to and keep the rest for the days when she would be free.

And now here she was on this sunny October day lying in bed in Chatsworth. The door was open and Mamma was sleeping in the room beyond. There was no escape. "Chatsworth is a very fine mansion," Mamma had said when they drove towards it; she was looking forward to seeing it in detail. Last night she and Lehzen had dined alone in this room while Mamma was entertained at a grand dinner which Victoria was considered too young to attend. Oh dear, it would not always be so!

What a great deal of England she was seeing! Of course she already knew Ramsgate very well and she had been to Brighton; but this was different; this was traveling all over England which, Mamma had said, "will one day be yours."

So fascinating, she thought. I have been very much *amused*.

They had journeyed right up to the Midlands and seen the Black Country—where everything indeed did look black. She had been rather worried about some of the poor ragged children, but Mamma had said that they were *necessary*. She wondered why, but one did not argue with Mamma. They had been received in great houses wherever they went; some of the castles had been a little draughty, but there had always been fires in her room. Everyone seemed anxious to placate her, even though Mamma insisted that she was only a child and in great need of guidance.

Wales had been exciting—particularly when she had explored the ruins of Carnarvon Castle and a royal salute had been fired. In fact royal salutes were fired everywhere and this seemed to make Mamma very pleased, while Sir John had that strange rather mischievous twinkle in his eyes which she had begun to notice.

She heard him say to Mamma: "This will give His Majesty the greatest pleasure when he hears of it," and she knew by the tone of his voice that he meant exactly the opposite—which was to say the least deceitful—and deceit was a trait which Victoria particularly disliked.

Then they had gone on board the *Emerald* which was lying off-shore. And how she loved the ship! They had just heard that Uncle Leopold had married. Mamma said it was a Good Thing, but she was not quite sure in her mind of this. She and Uncle Leopold had loved each other fondly, and she had always believed that she had been his dearest; but if he had a wife could this be so? There again, that was something one could not write in one's Journal. "Your welfare is the nearest thing to my heart," Uncle Leopold had said many times. But how could that be if he had a wife? Of course she was only a little girl—thirteen years old and Uncle Leopold was a man who had already been married. It was quite impossible that she could marry Uncle Leopold, but if she could have . . . It was something which it was absurd to think of and which she would never write in her Journal, but she had to admit that she did love him more than anyone else in the world and that was how one should feel about one's husband. And now he had a wife . . . a new wife to take the place of that hoyden Princess Charlotte who was long since dead but who lived on in dear Louisa Lewis's memory in haunted Claremont.

"It's a good marriage," Mamma had said. "I believe Louise to be the favourite daughter of the King of France."

Oh yes, it appeared to be a very good marriage. Louise of Orleans, daughter of Louis Philippe. She would be the Queen of the Belgians now. And Victoria hoped she would be worthy of dearest Uncle Leopold—although she gravely doubted that anyone could be that.

That was August 9th; and she would always remember it as Uncle Leopold's wedding day.

Her feelings had changed little, for she and her uncle still exchanged loving letters. She was longing to meet her new Aunt and she felt that she was going to love her because Uncle Leopold did.

Well, they had travelled through Wales and been much fêted, but her pleasure had been marred by the sad news about George Cumberland. Poor George! There were grave fears that he would go blind and his Mamma was frantic about it and was talking about taking him to Germany for an operation.

"How I should love to go and see him," she had said. "I should like to tell him that I am thinking of him. I should like to send him flowers every day which I would pick myself."

"What nonsense!" Mamma had said. "My dear child, don't you realize yet that everything you do is significant. As the future Queen you cannot send flowers to boys. In any case it would only arouse hopes which could never come to anything."

"I only want him to know how sorry I am, Mamma, about his eyes."

"It's a judgment," said Mamma piously, and obscurely as far as Victoria was concerned.

But she did think of poor George Cumberland often, and she would shut her eyes and wonder what it was like not to be able to see at all.

It was now eight o'clock and time to get up. So she did and by nine she was seated at a table in a room overlooking the park where she breakfasted in the company of Lehzen. She studied the room, for she would have to describe it in her Journal. She wished she could make a sketch of it, but Lehzen sitting there with that rather anxious look on her face would be far more interesting to sketch than any room. Why was Lehzen anxious? Was she worried about something Victoria had done, or was it Mamma and Sir John—for she was sure Lehzen did worry about them—or was it because of the royal salutes and all the ceremonies which Mamma and Sir John insisted on and of which the King had expressed his disapproval?

She studied the ceiling painted with figures to represent some mythology, she did not know which, nor would she ask Lehzen for it would only provoke a lecture. The things she really wanted to know were not told her. So she remarked that it was a splendid room and it was a magnificent carpet and the waterfall she could see in the grounds was very lovely. All of which seemed the right sort of conversation to satisfy Lehzen.

"It is a very fine house," she said.

"It is reckoned one of the finest in the country," remarked Lehzen.

"Finer than Kensington Palace," commented Victoria.

"Later in the morning you will be taken on a tour of the house. Lord and Lady Cavendish are making up a party."

"That," said Victoria, "will amuse me very much."

And it did and gave her plenty to write about in the Journal; and when they were in the grounds the Duke of Devonshire, who was walking beside her, said: "I wonder whether Your Highness would honour us by planting a tree in the grounds."

"Oh, I should like that."

"I will ask her Grace if you may do so."

"But I *will* do so."

Oh dear, what had made her say that! She was pink with mortification, for what if Mamma should say "No" and she had to break her word.

But Mamma was already approaching, accompanied by Lord and Lady Cavendish. "Victoria," she said, "you are to plant an oak and I a Spanish chestnut." So it was all right.

They planted their trees and she wondered what the world would be like when hers became a great tree; and what fun it would be to come to Chatsworth now and then and examine its progress.

Mamma was in a good mood because she too had planted a tree. Victoria had noticed that although Mamma wanted all possible honours for her daughter she was always a little cross if they were not extended to herself. What Mamma really wanted was Uncle William to die so that Victoria could be a Queen who had no authority. Then Mamma could be Regent. Oh dear, she was becoming *very* critical of Mamma who, as she was so fond of telling her, had done everything for her.

After luncheon there was a visit to Haddon Hall—a fascinating old house which dated back to the twelfth century; and afterwards they returned to Chatsworth where the Devonshires and their friends had devised a charade for the royal visitors.

Lehzen said: "The Duchess tells me that you may be allowed to sit up for the charade."

"Oh, that will be wonderful!"

"It is really," went on Lehzen, "not to disappoint the Devonshires."

"It makes me very happy to know that they would be disappointed if I were not there."

"It is not to be taken as a precedent," Lehzen warned.

No! thought Victoria. But I am getting older and when I am of age I shall not be told when I must go to bed either by Lehzen, Sir John Conroy or even Mamma.

It was ten o'clock when the charade began. Victoria was seated beside Mamma and chairs were all round them. Most of the candles were put out and the few remaining ones gave only a glimmer of light. Victoria was very excited. She looked at Victoire Conroy who always shared everything and on this occasion she was glad because they would be able to discuss the charade together afterwards.

"It is to be in three syllables," said Mamma, "and there will be four acts. In the last, you must listen for the whole word."

"I shall, Mamma."

This, she thought, is the sort of party Aunt Adelaide gives.

How I should love to go to them. And once again the resentment towards Mamma was making itself felt. But she must give her entire attention to the charade if she were going to discover the word.

The first act was a scene from *Bluebeard*. How exciting! And then there was one depicting a scene at the Nile, and after that a scene from *Tom Thumb*. Best of all was the last act in which Queen Elizabeth figured with the Earl of Leicester and Amy Robsart. Victoria was excited because she guessed the word which was Kenilworth; and there they were in costumes similar to those her dolls had worn. She became so excited that the Duchess laid a restraining hand on her arm.

"Pray, child, you forget yourself," she whispered in a shocked voice; and for a moment that resentment flared up again.

Mamma disapproved. Victoria would hear more of this, and she would have to be taught to remember her dignity in all circumstances.

Victoria noticed with glee that it was nearly twelve o'clock before she went to bed.

After Chatsworth there were many other country houses to be visited, but the weather was changing. Autumn had come and soon travelling would be impossible. Already they had suffered from heavy rainfall and there had been too much mud on the road. They had now turned southwards and were on the return journey.

They drove through Woodstock and Oxford, where they stayed with the Earl and Countess of Abingdon in their lovely residence, Wytham Abbey. Of course they must visit Oxford and the colleges, and Mamma took most of the honours, although one great one came to Sir John who was made a Doctor of Civil Law. But everyone was delighted to see them and Victoria was very interested in Queen Elizabeth's Latin exercise book which she had used, Lehzen pointed out, when she was thirteen years old.

It was very absorbing, but Victoria's feelings were mixed as they came closer to London. It would be pleasant to be home again, she mused. Perhaps now that she was so travelled she would be allowed to go out more often; perhaps the next time the Queen invited her she would be permitted to accept the invitation. Thirteen was no longer so young.

And on a misty November day they came riding into Kensington. The Palace looked just the same as ever and the mist which hung about the trees in the park touched with a blue haziness moved her deeply. It was good to be home.

Lord Liverpool was there waiting to receive them and the Duchess said they should all dine together, including Victoria, which they did.

Almost before dinner was over the Princess Sophia left her apartments in the Palace to call. She embraced Victoria almost nervously. She seemed to have grown much older since they had been away. Ever since the resuscitated scandal about her illegitimate son had been the talk of the town she had grown furtive, as though she were wondering what would happen next.

She whispered to the Duchess that she had come to warn her.

"Warn me!" cried the Duchess imperiously. The last months of travel when she had demanded and received so many honours had made her more arrogant than ever.

"His Majesty," whispered Sophia. "William . . ."

"What of the King?"

"He is not very pleased. He has said so often that you had no right to travel as though Victoria were already the Queen. He said he would have you remember that there is a King on the throne and the honours you insisted on are for the Sovereign alone."

"If," said the Duchess, her eyes flashing, her feathers shaking. "I were to borrow His Majesty's own inelegant method of expressing himself I should say 'Stuff!' "

Victoria was listening. Oh dear, so the King was angry. Mamma was wrong really. She had known that they should never have been treated as though they were the most important people in the country. Even Uncle William who, she secretly believed, was a very kind man indeed, would be angry.

"I think Victoria is tired," said the Duchess.

"Oh no, Mamma, I . . ."

"You are longing for your bed, I know."

"Indeed not, Mamma. Why, at Chatsworth I was up until nearly twelve. Do you remember . . . the night of the charade . . ."

"This," said the Duchess, "is not Chatsworth." She signed to one of her women. "Pray send for Lehzen."

Lehzen arrived. She must have been waiting outside. She was never far away from Victoria.

"Pray conduct the Princess to her room," said the Duchess. "It has been such a long, tiring day."

Victoria said good night to Lord Liverpool, the Conroy girls and their father and to the Princess Sophia.

The Princess kissed her warmly. "Don't you worry," she whispered. "The King will not blame *you.*"

"I know, Aunt Sophia," she whispered back and then was ashamed because it was as though she were in a conspiracy against Mamma.

When she was in her bed she saw that it was only a quarter to nine.

She lay still watching Lehzen working on her sewing close to the candelabrum.

She felt angry. I am so tired of being treated ilke a child, she told herself. But let them wait . . .

Almost as soon as they reached home Christmas was with them and there was the excitement of buying and making Christmas presents and all the secrecy that went with it. Victoria was making a white bag for the Duchess under Lehzen's guidance and it added a thrill to the days to have to thrust it out of sight whenever her mother approached. For Lehzen she was making a pincushion in white and gold which was very very pretty; and she had bought a pin with two hearts attached to it with which to ornament it. She knew that Lehzen would love it because the hearts were symbolic—hers and Lehzen's. She believed she loved her dear Lehzen best in the world next to Uncle Leopold and of course . . . Mamma. She believed she would love Aunt Adelaide if she were allowed to see her. Oh dear, now she was feeling angry again which one must not do at Christmas time.

Sir John, however, was behaving in a much more likeable way. For instance, a few days before Christmas Eve he came into the room where she was sewing with Lehzen and Flora Hastings looking excited and conspiratorial.

"I want to share a secret with you," he told Victoria; and she could not help being excited at the thought of sharing a secret—even with Sir John.

He was carrying a little basket. "It is a present," he told her, "for the Duchess." And lifting the lid he disclosed a little dog.

Victoria cried out with pleasure. She loved animals and in particular dogs and horses.

"But he is beautiful," she cried.

"*She*," corrected Sir John, "is a present for the Duchess."

"Mamma will be delighted."

"I thought she would be. But I have to keep the little creature in hiding until Christmas Eve and I thought I would tell you of her existence just in case you discovered it. So . . ." Sir John put his fingers to his lips.

Victoria, with a laugh, did the same.

"What is her name?"

"She hasn't got one at the moment. Doubtless the Duchess will give her one."

"Oh, but you should say 'This is . . .' whatever her name is. Everyone should have a name and the poor little mite can't be nameless until Christmas."

"The Princess has spoken," said Sir John, raising his eyes to the ceiling with one of those expressions Victoria disliked; but she was too excited about the dog to notice it now.

She thought: How I should love the darling to be named after me! But of course Mamma would never allow that because it would be undignified. She looked at Lehzen. Louise. No, that was not very suitable for a dog. But Flora . . .

"I think Flora should be her name. You would not mind, Lady Flora, if this dear little dog had the same name as you?"

Lady Flora, the most acquiescent of ladies, said that she would have no objection.

"I name you . . . Flora," said Sir John in sepulchral tones like a Bishop at the christening of a royal infant which made Victoria laugh out loud. Sir John was studying her closely and looking rather pleased with himself.

When he had gone and Lehzen was restored to that equanimity which the presence of Sir John always seemed to destroy, Victoria said: "I have an idea. Besides her bag Mamma shall have a collar and a steel chain for Flora."

Christmas Eve was the day for giving presents and the Duchess, like the Queen, liked to practise the German custom of decorating the rooms with fir trees. Victoria had found it difficult to get through the day because presents were given in the evening after dinner which as usual was taken with the Conroy family.

Afterwards the Duchess took them all to her drawing-room

and there Victoria cried out with pleasure. There were two big tables and one or two little ones on all of which were fir trees hung with lighted candles and little sweetmeat favours in the form of animals and hearts and all kinds of shapes, and which Victoria knew to be delicious; and best of all piled under the trees were the presents. One of the big tables was entirely Victoria's, the other was for the Conroy family.

What joy! thought Victoria. Mamma's presents must be opened first. A lovely cloak lined with fur and a pink satin dress.

"Oh, Mamma, but how lovely!"

The Duchess allowed herself to be embraced and forgot to remind Victoria of her rank in the excitement of the moment. And that was not all. Mamma had worked with her own hands a lovely pink bag the same colour as the dress; and there was an opal brooch and ear-rings.

"What lovely . . . *lovely* presents."

"Open the others," said Mamma. She did. Lehzen's first because dear Lehzen was there and she was determined to love whatever Lehzen gave her. A music book! "Oh, Lehzen, *just* what I wanted." More embraces and emotion. The tears come too easily, thought the Duchess. That must be curbed. Just like her father's side of the family.

The Princess Sophia had embroidered a dress for her and from Aunt Mary Gloucester there were amethyst ear-rings; Sir John gave her a lovely silver brush and Victoire a white bag which she herself had made.

What lovely presents—and she knew that there would be more to come. But perhaps watching the other people open theirs was equally delightful.

And Mamma was kissing little Flora and loving her already and lifting her grateful eyes to Sir John.

Anyone would love Flora, thought Victoria; but perhaps Mamma would love her especially because she was a present from Sir John?

What a happy time was Christmas—more exciting really than travelling. And when Christmas was over, she thought, it will soon be the New Year, and in May she would have another birthday.

She was growing up.

A Birthday Ball

   THE QUEEN sat beside the bedside of her niece Louise, Princess of Saxe-Weimar, and tried to persuade herself that the child was not dying.

This was the girl whom she had looked on as her own, who had done so much to comfort her when she had despaired of having children. Of all the young people whom she had gathered about her it was Louise and George Cambridge who had seemed most like her own; they had lived with her; she had mothered them both because their parents were far away; she still had George, but how long would Louise remain with her?

She had spoken to the doctors, begging them to tell her the truth, so she knew the worst. It was to be expected, they warned her. Louise had always been an invalid and now the end was in sight.

"My dear child," whispered Adelaide; and Louise could only look at her with loving eyes mutely thanking her for all the kindness she had received from her.

"Is there anything you want, darling?"

Louise's lips moved and Adelaide bent over her. "Only that you stay near me, Aunt Adelaide."

"I shall be here, my dearest."

Louise smiled serenely and Adelaide sat silent while the tears gathered in her eyes and began to brim over.

She was buried at Windsor and Adelaide wrote sorrowfully to her sister Ida; but Ida had her own busy life and other children to comfort her. In any case Louise had always been more Adelaide's child than Ida's.

There was no point in brooding over the death of this

dear child. There were the living to think of and Adelaide went to see the Duchess of Cumberland who was facing another tragedy.

"Oh, my dear Frederica, how is dearest George?" she asked.

Frederica shook her head. "His sight seems to grow more dim each day."

"And George himself?"

"It seems so strange but he bears it all with such fortitude. *He* comforts *me*, Adelaide."

"Dear child!"

"Yes, he bids me not to fret. He says his sight will come back."

"That this should have happened," sighed Adelaide. "It seems such a short time ago that he was playing with Louise. He was always so gentle with her . . . more gentle, I think, than any of the others, though my dear George is such a good, kind boy."

"He was too good," said Frederica almost angrily.

"And Ernest? How is Ernest taking it?"

"As he takes everything. He believes the boy will recover his sight."

"And the doctors?"

"You know what doctors are. But, Adelaide, I am thinking of taking him to see Baron Graefe. I believe him to be the best eye specialist in the world. You know he operated on Ernest most successfully. I am sure he could do something for George."

"My dear Frederica, how I hope so!"

"And you, my poor Adelaide, have suffered a great loss."

"I knew it had to come. There was really no hope for my poor Louise. Yet she used to be so happy."

"You have a gift for making the children happy, Adelaide. George will want to see you before you go."

So Adelaide spent an hour with George who laughed with her and behaved as though he was not disturbed by this terrible tragedy which had overtaken him.

"He is an example to us all," said Frederica, strangely subdued, unlike herself, thought Adelaide.

There were further troubles. The FitzClarence children were becoming more and more arrogant. They were rude to Adelaide and did not hesitate to speak ther minds to the King. William was unhappy. Frederick as well as George had declared he would resign from the post recently bestowed upon him by the King—because he was not paid enough.

The papers noted these quarrels between William and his *un*natural children and William pretended that there was no quarrel at all.

He was becoming too excitable again and Adelaide was afraid people would notice. He would suddenly start one of his tirades without warning. At breakfast he would often appear his amiable self, and having entertained the young children at his ablutions, he would joke with the family in the old way; but when he settled down to the papers he would mutter to himself, and sometimes the muttering would grow into a shout.

Something would happen to remind him of Victoria. "Royal progress, that's what it is. I'm going to put a stop to this. Parading about the country. I believe that woman believes I'm where she's been longing for me to be these last few years—in my coffin. Well, I'm not. I'm here on the throne . . . and that's where I'm going to stay. And by God, I'm going to live until Victoria's old enough to take over. I'm not going to let that Kent woman have her heart's desire. For make no mistake about it. That's what she wants. Royal parades! Royal salutes! That girl is not Queen yet. Nor is she going to be until she can stand without her mother."

He would go on and on until Adelaide could think of something to distract him; and she was always afraid that by doing so she would lead him to a subject as irritating to him as that of the Duchess of Kent and her daughter.

He was at present raging against the Chapter of St. Paul's because they had refused to allow a statue of Dorothy Jordan to be placed in the Cathedral.

"Why? I wanted to know. Eh, why? Why shouldn't the mother of my children have a statue in my Cathedral, eh? Because she was an actress? Because the union didn't have the benefit of clergy? The insolent dogs. By God, am I the King of this realm or not?"

Then his eyes would fill with tears and he would tell Adelaide of the virtues of Dorothy, his eyes glistening with emotion. The happy years . . . oh, the happy years at Bushy when she was working in her parts and the children were being born. "What a woman she was, Adelaide! What a woman!"

It did not occur to him that his wife might not wish to hear of the perfections of his mistress; nor did Adelaide point this out to him. She was only eager that he should remain calm, accept the Chapter's verdict and forget that he had wanted a statue of Dorothy in the Cathedral.

"It will be Victoria's fourteenth birthday in May," she said. "I think we should give a ball for her."

"And what will Madam Kent have to say to that? She seems to think the chit is contaminated by being near us."

"I think she is only eager that Victoria shall have the respect due to her position."

"Her position! That woman believes she is Queen already. She has to be made to see that's not the case."

"We will make it perfectly clear," soothed Adelaide. "But I think, don't you, that her fourteenth birthday—which is a kind of landmark—should be celebrated at St. James's."

"I suppose you're right." He gave her one of his affectionate smiles. "You usually are."

And talking of the party—for he loved to arrange such entertainments within the family—he grew calmer and forgot his grievance against the Chapter.

While they were talking a messenger arrived from Kensington Palace. The Duchess of Kent begged the honour of entertaining the King and Queen for dinner.

Adelaide watched the King fearfully. He was in no mood for friendship with his sister-in-law.

"Damned woman," he growled.

"But I think we should accept, William," said Adelaide. And as he knew she was usually right, he agreed.

The year so far had been a happy one for Victoria. After his success with Flora, the dog—and the Duchess had declared she could not have had a present that pleased her more, although whether this was due to the present or the donor was debatable—Sir John decided to repeat his success.

Early in January he gave her another dog—a King Charles's spaniel whom they had named Dash. Although he was the Duchess's dog and she adored him—as she must any present of Sir John's—he followed Victoria everywhere and seemed to have made up his mind that he belonged to her. In a very short time she was devoted to dear little Dashy and Sir John and her mother were not displeased because anything that made her feel more kindly towards Sir John was to be welcomed; and the dog had certainly done this.

So with Dash always at her heels or lying curled up on her

lap and with her dear horse Rosy whom she herself fed and loved to exercise, she was happy. Moreover, now that she was growing up and the King had said he wished her to appear in public she was visiting the opera and the ballet quite frequently. She and the Duchess would be accompanied by Sir John—and Lady Conroy often came with Victoire and Jane and Lady Flora Hastings and others of the household. How Victoria loved to go to the theatre. It was so enchanting, she told Lady Flora, when the curtain rose on the colourful scene and those clever performers came on to the stage.

In the Journal she wrote long accounts of what she had seen, describing the dresses and performances in detail to show to the Duchess who demanded to see the Journal every now and then without warning, so that it was necessary to keep it up to date.

Then there was her sketching. She was really rather good at it, and she loved to sketch people most of all. She had done a beautiiful one of Lehzen which her art master said showed great promise.

The days passed quickly, with lessons which were becoming more and more interesting and Rosy to exercise and look after because she did not care to leave dear Rosy to anyone else and with Dash always ready for a game. There was dear Uncle Leopold to write to; his letters came regularly to her and she was longing to meet her *dear* new Aunt Louise. "I love her already," she wrote.

Sometimes when they went to the opera they arrived back at Kensington Palace quite late. It always amused her to write in her Journal that she did not get to bed until midnight. That made her feel very grown up.

"Nearly fourteen," she whispered to Dash. "That will be a turning point."

The Duchess came into the schoilroom to find Victoria on the floor playing with Dash. The Duchess smiled tolerantly.

"He *is* such a dear little dog."

"Oh, Mamma, he is the *best* dog in the world."

Ordinarily the Duchess would have warned her about exaggeration; but this time she said: "I really do believe he is." She smirked slightly. "We are to be honoured. Their Majesties are dining with us."

"Oh!" Victoria's face was bright with pleasure. "That will be lovely, Mamma. When . . ."

"Next Wednesday, but you will not be there, my child. I

hardly think you have reached the age to be present at a dinner party."

"I see."

"Now there is no need to be sullen. It will come all in good time."

"Yes, Mamma."

"I think, though, that you may meet the company afterwards."

Victoria was silent. "Still sullen?" asked the Duchess.

"No, Mamma. I was thinking that very soon I shall be old enough to have my own dinner parties. Then I shall be quite grown up. It is really only four years."

Only four years! thought the Duchess uneasily. She must be made to see that even when she was eighteen she would need guidance.

She would speak to Sir John about the change in Victoria's attitude lately.

A very unpleasant rumour was going round the Court. The King with his usual bonhomie had been unbecomingly jocular with one of the Queen's ladies and when she went home to spend a few weeks with her family it was said that she had gone away to have the King's child.

When this reached Adelaide's ears she was angry because she knew that there was no truth in this statement. With all his shortcomings William was a faithful husband and although his attitude towards the ladies of the Court was at times flirtatious, he had never broken his marriage vows.

She immediately commanded the young woman to return to Court and when she came it was clear she could not possibly have had a child, so the story was shown to be an absurd lie and Adelaide made a point of having the girl constantly in attendance on her in case the rumour should start up again. By acting promptly she settled that matter; but it depressed her to consider how easily rumours could start and she realized that she must be constantly on the alert. She was conscious that there were forces at work to discredit William; and she knew that the Duke of Cumberland was one of the chief movers in these schemes, and although this did not change her attitude towards Frederica and the poor afflicted George, she was determined to be wary.

She developed a cough which she could not shake off and on the night of the dinner party at Kensington Palace she felt feverish and really ill. Had she been going somewhere other than the apartments of the Duchess of Kent she felt she might have been equal to the occasion, but when she considered the possibility of conflict between the King and his sister-in-law she felt too weak to deal with them.

She was lying on her bed when the King came in to see how she was.

"You look sick, Adelaide," he said anxiously.

"I am just a little tired," she answered. "I don't feel well enough to go to Kensington."

"Then we'll not go."

"William, you must go. The Duchess would take it as a personal insult if you did not."

"Let her. It's time she was insulted."

"But, William, it would not be good."

"It would do her the world of good. The insolent old bitch."

"William."

"Rough sailor's talk, my dear. You should be used to that by now."

"William, I beg of you to go tonight. You sometimes forget that you are the King."

That was the right note. He liked to be reminded of his kingship.

"If you don't honour the company with your presence it will be the talk of the town, for everyone knows of your feelings towards the Duchess. Go, and try not to be irritated by her. Those miserable papers exaggerate everything. I should like to hear how Victoria is getting on."

"That child should be seen with us. The people expect it."

"Therefore it is wise to have friendly relations between us all."

"You're asking for a miracle."

"Kings often make miracles."

He was in a good temper. "Very well, I'll go. But you shall stay here and rest. I'll not have you running any risks with that fever."

The Duchess was excited. This was going to be one of the grandest parties she had ever given.

"And to think," she said to Sir John, "that our guest of honour is that old buffoon."

Sir John reminded his dear Duchess that the old buffoon was at least the King.

"I am sure," said Sir John, "that the evening will be a successful one, for with your usual wisdom you will hold your feelings in check and not allow His Majesty to irritate you."

"I shall have my eyes on Cumberland. He is the one I have always feared. I *despise* William, but Cumberland has often alarmed me. You know how he set rumours in progress concerning Victoria's health. I'm sure he meant to murder her."

"Yes, we'll have to be watchful of Cumberland. The fact that his Duchess has become more gentle lately and the boy is going blind doesn't change him."

"Indeed no. But how could he hope for his son to marry Victoria now? That has been a lesson to him."

The Duchess raised her eyes piously as though thanking God for the lesson which the Cumberlands had had to learn through the affliction of their son. Victoria was not for George Cumberland. How could she marry a blind man? And she was not for George Cambridge either. The Duchess had her eyes on her own relations in dear Saxe-Coburg.

"And I think," she said, "that Victoria may come down to meet the company after dinner."

"Have you made this clear to her?"

"I have. She is just a little . . . sullen. I am growing more and more of the opinion that the older she grows the more correction she may need."

Sir John replied that this was the case with most people; but the Duchess need have no fear. Between they they would show their beloved Princess which way she should go.

To dine with Lehzen simply in her own room was certainly rather annoying when there was such a dinner party going on in the large saloon.

"Lehzen," she said, "how I should love to be there sitting beside Uncle William. He is really a very nice old uncle and the Queen is always so kind to me."

"In time you will be giving dinner parties of your own."

"Oh yes, of course. That will be the greatest fun. *I* shall decide who the guests will be. Suppose this were my dinner party it would be a little different, I do assure you. I should have the King and dear Aunt Adelaide and George Cambridge and poor poor George Cumberland. Oh, Lehzen, I could weep to think of him. I suppose I should have to have Victoire and Jane Conroy. Have you noticed, Lehzen, how they are always everywhere?"

"I have noticed," said Lehzen primly.

"I shall not have so many Conroys round me when I have my say—although the little boys are sweet. I quite like Edward, Stephen and Henry—and I suppose I am so used to Victoire and Jane that I don't notice them. They really do seem like members of my own family. You must admit that, Lehzen."

Lehzen did admit it, in a somewhat aggrieved way which Victoria was quick to note.

"Oh, listen. The guests are arriving. Be quiet, Dashy. Dear, sweet, darling Dashy, he wants to protect me. There is no need really. It is only Mamma's guests."

"Perhaps he has his reasons for barking at them," said Lehzen obscurely. "I hear the Duke of Cumberland is to be of the company tonight."

"Uncle Ernest is really rather frightening I admit," said Victoria with a happy shiver. "It is because he has lost an eye, although it was lost most nobly, Lehzen, and he should therefore be honoured for it. Eyes! Is it not strange, Lehzen, that poor George has hurt his eyes when his Papa lost one of his at the battle of Tournay?"

Lehzen said it was not for them to question the ways of God.

"But we are surely allowed to comment on the strangeness of them," said Victoria sternly.

Lady Flora Hastings had come in. The Duchess wished the Princess to join the company after dinner. So Baroness Lehzen was to prepare her.

"So I am to be part of the ceremony after all. Hurry, Lehzen. What shall I wear, Flora? Which dress do you think is most suitable for me to wear to meet the King and Queen?"

"The Queen is not there," said Lady Flora. "She is indisposed."

"Oh, poor, *poor* Aunt Adelaide. *She* was the one I most wanted to see. I wanted to *tell* her how sorry I was about poor Louise and to ask her if there is any news of George Cumberland. And I was hoping too that she might ask me to one of her parties. Since she had come to one of ours, Mamma could hardly refuse to let me go, could she?"

"Come," said Lehzen. "I'll dress your hair. I think the King likes ringlets."

"Tell me who are present," said Victoria while her hair was being dressed. "I must have a list of the guests for my Journal."

"All the nobility," said Flora, "including the Archbishop of Canterbury."

"I shall discover for myself," said Victoria, "when I go to the saloon. Then I shall be able to list them in my Journal. I daresay I shall stay up late tonight."

How pleasant it was in the saloon with the band of the Grenadier Guards playing stirring tunes.

All eyes were on Victoria. She knew some of the guests—the Earl of Liverpool, for instance, and the Earl and Countess Grey, and the Dukes of Norfolk and Devonshire.

And there was the King, old, with a very old red face, looking less like a King than any of the others so it was well that she knew him, for she would never have believed he was the Sovereign otherwise.

His eyes were soft as she curtsied before him. She looked very young and fresh with her hair in ringlets and the wide blue sash on her white silk dress.

"Well, my dear," said the King, taking her hand and pulling her towards him, "you're a pretty sight." And he kissed her in a very unkingly fashion. "Now, you sit here beside your Uncle William and tell him what you've been up to."

What expressions he used! She was sure Mamma would be very shocked; but she did not care. She *liked* Uncle William.

"I am so sorry, Your Majesty." she said, "that the Queen is unable to be present."

"I had to stop her coming. She was looking peaky. So she's tucked up safe in bed."

"I do hope, Sir, that she is not really ill."

"Now, I'm your Uncle William, my dear. That's what I like you to call me."

She laughed. "I like it too, Uncle William."

"Then we'll please ourselves, eh? We won't bother ourselves with what the company expects."

What a strange King! But very agreeable, she decided.

"That will be very *interesting*, Uncle William."

"Now, your Aunt Adelaide wants to know why we never see you. She's always saying: 'Victoria should be here.' "

"Oh, Uncle William, how I should love to come and see

Aunt Adelaide. The Georges—it's what I call my two cousins—say that she gives the loveliest parties."

"And you should be there, my dear, and you *shall*." The King had raised his voice and Victoria noticed that Sir John —who naturally was there—looked alarmed.

Victoria whispered: "Do tell Aunt Adelaide that I should love to come."

The King entered into the conspiratorial mood and whispered back: "I'll tell you something. Your Aunt is planning a grand ball to celebrate your next birthday."

"And shall I be there?"

The King laughed aloud. "No good having a ball if the guest of honour is not present."

"So I'm to be the guest of honour. Oh, dear *Uncle* William."

"Well, you're a good girl. Not your fault . . . though you did give me some black looks, I remember."

"Oh, dear Uncle William, I did not mean them to be black."

"Knew you didn't. It was that . . ."

She waited for the King to go on but he did not. Instead of which he took her hand and patted it. He was so friendly that she told him about Dash.

"He was really given to Mamma by Sir John." The King's eyes narrowed. Oh dear, thought Victoria, he does not like Sir John. She went on quickly: "But he seems to have become *my* dog."

"Don't blame him," said the King. "Don't blame him at all. Sensible little dog."

"He is the most sensible little dog in the world, Uncle. But perhaps I shouldn't say that because I have not really known all the dogs in the world, have I? But he is the most sensible dog I have ever known. The other evening after dinner I dressed him in a red jacket and blue trousers. He looked so sweet. He did not mind in the least."

"Sensible little dog for a sensible little girl."

The Duchess of Kent came forward.

"Now Victoria, you must not tire His Majesty with your childish chatter."

"The Princess's chatter does not tire me, Madam," said the King, "as much as that of some other people."

The Duchess laughed—not very pleasantly, thought Victoria, who knew that laugh well, but, she hoped, perhaps the King did not. However, even Mamma could not order the

King to stop talking to her if he did not wish to, so he went on asking her about Dash and Rosy and telling her about the ball Queen Adelaide was planning for her next birthday.

It was such a pleasant evening, and she did love the King, who might not look as one would expect a King to look but made a very *cosy* kind old uncle.

She gleefully noted that it was eleven o'clock before she went to bed.

Adelaide was better and well enough to accompany the King to the private view of the annual Royal Academy exhibitions of paintings.

"Not much in my line," said William. "More like George's. The paintings he had there at the Pavilion and Carlton House! Worth a fortune, they tell me. Can't think why. If people are fools enough to pay these artist fellows . . . Well, I gave them back to the nation, didn't I? The nation's welcome to 'em."

Adelaide looked a little anxious. He was in one of his ranting moods and they were becoming more frequent. He would take up a subject and go on and on as though he were addressing the House of Lords. In fact he was making too many speeches on every occasion. If he was at a dinner party she would be unable to stop his getting to his feet and addressing the company in one of his long boring speeches, but when he did not bore his audiences that was far worse because he would probably then talk in the most outrageous manner about one of his aversions in such terms that the papers would be full of it next day.

She must stop his working himself up about artists on this occasion when they were going to visit an exhibition of artists' work.

When they arrived at Somerset House where the Exhibition was held, William was not in a very good mood. His face was a deeper tinge of red and he had talked excitedly to Adelaide on the way about various aspects of his capital city as he drove through it. The people no longer received him with acclaim and although they did not abuse him since the Reform Bill was passed, they displayed an indifference which he did not like.

"Pictures," he said. "Nowadays some of the fellows think they can paint . . . George was a one for pictures. He reckoned he knew something about them."

"Your brother was a very artistic man, William," said Adelaide.

"Oh yes, old George, he was the clever one of the family. He could look at an unknown artist's work and say, 'That's good.' He did a lot for 'em. Not that they were grateful. Who ever is grateful to kings?"

Oh dear, thought Adelaide, she must change the subject. The ingratitude of the people was a dangerous one.

"I hear some of the portraits are good. Lady Grey was telling me that one of Admiral Napier was especially so."

"*Captain* Napier!" growled William. "And why do we want a picture of that fellow on show, I want to know."

"Because, I suppose, it's rather a fine picture."

"Fine picture of a knave! He calls himself Admiral. Admiral of what? Of the Portuguese Navy? He proved himself not good enough for ours. By God, you forget I'm a sailor, Adelaide. I'm an Admiral myself. Lord High Admiral for a time . . . but that didn't please them either. So this fellow becomes Admiral in the Portuguese Navy . . . and we make a fine picture of him and people here are expected to go and admire him. Captain Napier, I say! By God, I've no admiration for that fellow, I can tell you. But there are envious people in the Navy, Adelaide. You know what it was like when I tried to bring about reforms. You know what happened. That fellow Cockburn with his Board of Admiralty. Tried to tell me what to do. And Wellington . . . well, I was surprised at Wellington. I thought he was a man of good sense. Waterloo . . . Fine . . . fine . . . Great victory. And George, he was on their side too. 'Resign,' said George. 'The only thing you can do, old fellow. Resign. Love you as a brother but can't stand out against the Admiralty Board. Have to give way.' "

"Oh, William, that is long ago."

"Maybe, maybe, but I don't forget."

She listened to his voice without taking in the words and she asked herself: Is this how his father used to talk? She had never heard him. When she had come to England George III had been shut away from the world. Poor sad, mad King. But was William growing more and more like his father?

She was relieved when they arrived at Somerset House where the President was waiting to receive them.

"I trust Your Gracious Majesty will find plenty of interest in the Exhibition," said the President. "We are honoured and delighted that you have favoured us with a visit."

William beamed, his good temper restored.

But it was almost as though a mischievous sprite was at the President's elbow, thought Adelaide. Why did he have to lead them to that particular picture?

"A very fine work, Sir. One of the best in the Exhibition. A portrait of Admiral Napier."

For a few seconds the King was speechless. Then the storm broke.

"*Admiral* Napier. Oh no, sir. *Captain* Napier. And may Captain Napier be damned and you with him, sir. And if the Queen were not here with me, sir, I should kick you downstairs."

The King had spoken so loudly that everyone present heard each word clearly. The President could not understand what he had done to offend the King; and whatever his offence he certainly did not expect to be kicked downstairs.

The King's face had grown scarlet. He addressed the company on the shortcomings of *Captain* Napier and the President of the Royal Academy who had allowed a picture of the *knave* to be put on show.

His audience averted their eyes; if it were possible they would have slipped away.

Adelaide stood by shocked and trembling.

Everyone was thinking: This is George III all over again. The King is going mad.

Victoria awoke on May 24th in the year 1833 and said to herself: "My fourteenth birthday! How *very* old!"

As it was only half past five it was not time to get up yet, so she lay thinking about the day before her and wondering what her presents would be and what difference being fourteen would make. There would be letters as well, and surely one from dear Uncle Leopold and perhaps from Aunt Louise. And then the ball that the King and Queen were giving at St. James's for her. What fun that would be and Mamma could not prevent her going to it since it was her ball. A Juvenile Ball Aunt Adelaide had called it. But most important of all was the fact that she was fourteen years old—surely a milestone. Although she was not yet of age—there were another four years to go before that happy day—fourteen was no longer very young; and surely people could not continue to treat her as a child.

It was pleasant to lie in bed brooding. Mamma was not yet awake. Oh, how humiliating to have to sleep in one's mother's room. And when Mamma was not there Lehzen was.

The first thing I shall do when I am of age is *Be Alone,* she assured herself.

And then she went on to think of the presents which would be hers. Mamma had been working rather secretly on something for the past weeks. She suspected it was a bag; in fact one or two people in the household had been hastily putting their work away when Victoria appeared.

It was very pleasant lying there speculating on the future—both immediate and distant—until it was time to get up.

After breakfast the Duchess took her to the table which had been laid out with her gifts and she cried out in pleasure as she discovered the bracelet and ornament of topaz and turquoise besides the lovely bag Mamma had worked for her. There were dresses and handkerchiefs and books. The Duchess certainly did give the most delightful presents. Dear Lehzen's gift was a china basket and a little china figure. "Oh, dearest Lehzen, they are exquisite!" cried Victoria. No one had forgotten. Sir John had taken great pains to have a picture of Dash painted for her.

"Oh, but it is lovely, and so like darling Dashy." Sir John was pleased.

The Conroy children—all five of them—Jane, Victoire, Edward, Stephen and Henry—were eagerly watching while she unwrapped their joint offering. It proved to be an enamel watch chain.

"Papa said it would please you," announced Henry, as though that settled the matter. Indeed, thought Victoria, Papa Conroy was a *god* in this household. But there must be no discordant notes on a birthday—especially a fourteenth birthday.

It was no ordinary day. There were many calls during the morning, for it seemed that everyone must come to pay tribute to Victoria on her birthday.

Poor Aunt Sophia toddled along with the bag she had made herself.

What a lot of bags I have! thought Victoria, but one must be pleased however many there were, especially when they had been so beautifully worked.

"You are growing old, my dear." Aunt Sophie held her fast in her elderly embrace, from which Victoria longed to escape. "Enjoy yourself while you are young. It is not always easy when you grow old."

Poor old Aunt Sophia! She was so often alone in her apartments and sat there peering at her embroidery and netting her purses. But she must like her lonely apartments because she had chosen them. There were whispers about a certain visitor . . . a man who was connected with her past. People did not realize that Victoria had a pair of ears and that she liked to use them.

The Duchess of Cumberland called and Victoria immediately asked after poor dear George.

"I am planning to take him to Germany," the Duchess told her. "There is a very good man there who will do something for him."

"Oh, I hope so."

"He will," said the Duchess almost angrily. Poor sad Aunt Frederica who must deceive herself into thinking that her son would regain his sight!

"He asked me to tell you that he hoped you would have a happy birthday."

"Oh, do please thank him."

"I have a gift for you from him."

"That is lovely."

"See it before you pass judgment," said Frederica with a laugh.

Tears came into Victoria's eyes as she looked at the turquoise pin which was George Cumberland's present to her.

"He says he hopes you will like it."

"Pray tell him, dear Aunt, that I love it, and every time I wear it, which shall be often, I shall think of him."

"That will be a great comfort to him."

"Dear, dear George. Oh, I do hope this German will be able to make him well again."

"He will," said Aunt Frederica with a return of her old fierceness. "Now look at the present from myself and your Uncle Ernest," she went on. It was a bracelet in turquoise to match George's pin.

When she had exclaimed her pleasure she must leave the Duchess and turn to others to receive presents and give thanks. So many things, she thought. I must list them all and leave nothing out of my Journal, because Mamma is sure to have a list and will say I am ungrateful if I forget one.

All day long visitors called, and dinner was early that day

so that there might be plenty of time to prepare for the ball at St. James's.

The Queen was smiling at the young people. Tonight she was going to forget her anxieties about William, who was in good spirits too, though rather annoyed that Sir John Conroy had come with the party from Kensington Palace.

"Why does that fellow always have to be there?" he demanded of Adelaide. "Behaves as though he's Victoria's stepfather."

Adelaide did not say that that was what he assuredly felt himself to be because it would only disturb William. But she did wish the Duchess of Kent would have the sense to keep Sir John out of the King's sight. But it was becoming clearer and clearer that the Duchess had no intention of placating the King.

But the sight of the excited Princess restored William's good humour. She was wearing the diamond ear-rings which he had sent to Kensington Palace for her and which were his own special present as well as the brooch of turquoise and gold which Adelaide had given her.

She came into his closet next to the ballroom and embraced him.

"It is so nice to see you, Uncle, *privately* like this. It means I can give you a really big hug."

William's eyes filled with tears. A charming girl. Adelaide had always said so and he could trust Adelaide to be right. The only thing wrong with Victoria was that mother of hers.

"The ear-rings are quite *beautiful*."

"So you like them, eh? And that's a nice brooch you're wearing. Turquoise, is it?" He was looking sly. He knew it was Aunt Adelaide's gift.

"Yes, Uncle. It it not beautiful?"

"Your Aunt Adelaide always knows what you young people like. Now it's time we went into the ballroom. We have to open it together, you know."

It was very pleasant going into the ballroom, hand in hand with the King; and even the Duchess was pleased. The Queen had taken the precaution of asking Victoria's dancing mistress Madame Bourdin to the ball so that she could supervise the dancing.

As soon as they were in the ballroom the Queen came up with George Cambridge.

"I think it would be an excellent idea if you two danced the first dance."

George Cambridge said he thought so too and taking Victoria's hand led her on to the floor. Flushed and happy Victoria was aware of Mamma's eyes on her; the Duchess was none too pleased; she did not want the King and Queen to imagine that they could pair off Victoria with her cousin. However, Victoria did not care; she gave herself up to the pleasure of the dance which she enjoyed so much.

"So here you are," said George, "at one of Aunt Adelaide's parties at last. I'm so glad you came."

"But of course I came. It is *my* birthday. You must know that because you gave me that lovely lily-of-the-valley brooch. Do you realize I'm fourteen?"

"I did, because we are almost the same age."

"We are getting so *old*," said Victoria gleefully. Then she added sadly: "The last time I saw you George Cumberland was there."

"He's going blind, they say."

"But he will recover. He is going to Germany to a doctor there."

They were silent for a second or so but it was too happy an occasion for sadness and Madame Bourdin was watching them to make sure that they danced the steps correctly.

"Soon," said Victoria, "it will not be a children's ball but a grown-up one."

"I shall claim the first dance at your first grown-up ball."

Victoria laughed. What fun it was to have a young and handsome cousin like George Cambridge. Poor George Cumberland was sadly afflicted, but there were other cousins in Germany. Mamma had spoken of them occasionally.

The dance was at an end and she must not dance all the time with the same partner. The Queen brought to her those young gentlemen who had been selected for the honour of dancing with her and so the time passed until it was time for supper and the Queen took her to the King who led her to the supper room. There she sat between the King and the Queen and everyone drank to her health and wished her long life and happiness, which was very affecting.

Then she went back to the ballroom to dance once more; it was such a happy ball she wished it would never come to an end. She noted gleefully that it was midnight and still she was dancing.

But a few minutes later the ball was over and she was in

the carriage driving back to Kensington. The Duchess sat beside her and Victoria closed her eyes and pretended to be sleepy because she was afraid that Mamma would talk disparagingly about the King and Queen and so spoil it all. She did not want to hear anything against anyone on that night. It was all so perfect and she wanted it to remain so.

The next day she wrote an account of it in her Journal which she finished with the words: "I was *very* much amused."

The Cousins from Württemberg

THERE was a great deal of excitement in Kensington Palace that June because two of Victoria's cousins, Alexander and Ernest, the Princes of Württemberg, who were the sons of the Duchess's sister, were to visit England.

"Of course," said the Duchess to Sir John, "there will be speculation at St. James's."

"Naturally, and with good reason," he replied.

"I should certainly want Victoria to marry someone from *my* side of the family."

"Most certainly," agreed Sir John.

"And these dear boys are charming. It will be interesting to watch Victoria's reactions."

"She is inclined to react favourably to some members of her opposite sex."

"I certainly do not like her fondness for George Cambridge."

"And you can be sure Their Majesties are delighted by it."

"They will be shown," said the Duchess haughtily.

She sent for Victoria to prime her about the visiting cousins.

"You will want to be very hospitable to your cousins," she said. "And I am sure you will be on your best behaviour."

Victoria was silent. Did Mamma think she was a child, who did not know how to behave with visiting relatives?

"I have planned some excursions for your cousins. They will naturally want to see as much of England as they can . . . and of us."

"Why yes, Mamma, I suppose that is why they are coming."

"They are coming, my dear, because I have invited them."

"But of course, Mamma."

The Duchess was becoming more and more uneasy about Victoria. Fortunately four more years must elapse before she was of age.

The day of arrival was a Sunday and Victoria was overcome with impatience to see the cousins. She chatted to Lehzen about them. They were quite old . . . that was older than the Georges. They would be different, too, for the Georges were being brought up to be very English and the Württemberg cousins would be very German. It was most exciting to have male cousins. There were two others whom Mamma mentioned now and then—the sons of her brother, the Duke of Saxe-Coburg-Gotha—Ernest and Albert. She hoped to meet them too one day.

"You will," said Lehzen.

"Oh, I do hope so. But in the meantime we have these *dear* cousins from Württemberg."

The day went on much as usual. She found it hard to concentrate on prayers, which was such a pity, for the Rev. Mr. Pittman—who subsidized for the poor Dean whose little daughter had died of scarlet fever so that the poor man was too overcome to take prayers—gave an excellent sermon, his text being "Lord, teach us to pray." She had trained herself to remember such details, for Mamma expected to see them all recorded in her Journal, which she admitted to herself, was very good training for her.

At three o'clock in the afternoon the cousins arrived, and from the moment she saw them she was enchanted with them. They were so tall and handsome and vied with each other to charm their little cousin. The Duchess was delighted with them, too, and she took them into her drawing-room and asked all sorts of questions about the family, which Victoria found most interesting. Later they went for a drive in the park and were back at the Palace in time for dinner.

Victoria confided to Lehzen that night that she was fond of them already.

"I am very pleased to hear it," said Lehzen. "And I am sure they are ready to be fond of you . . . very fond."

It was so pleasant to be admired.

"They are *extremely* tall," said Victoria with a laugh. "And Alexander is very handsome."

"So you prefer Alexander?"

"Well, Ernest has a very *kind* expression; but I think they are both *extremely* amiable."

Lehzen looked more pleased than ever and Victoria added that she thought she was going to be very much amused.

"So," said William to Adelaide, "that woman has brought her relations over. Those two young men! You know what this is for, eh?"

"I suppose she feels she wants to look around for a husband. Victoria is fourteen now. She may well be married in four years' time."

"She'll have to have my consent," said the King grimly. "And Victoria is to have George."

The Queen sighed. "I hope so. But I daresay if Victoria wanted someone else you would not be the one to withhold your consent."

"That's what that woman knows, Adelaide. She wants to lead the child not where she wants to go but what suits my lady Duchess best, and I won't have it. I want the child to be happy, as you know. But that woman would force her into a marriage whether she wished it or not."

"Perhaps you would like to have a look at these young men."

"I should."

"Then I will give a ball for them and we will invite the entire Kensington party."

"You do that, Adelaide; and I shall let that woman know that she is not going to bring one of her miserable nephews over here to be the consort of the Queen of England."

When the Duchess received the invitation to St. James's she was furious.

"You know what this means," she cried to Sir John. "They want to look them over. I should not be surprised if that old buffoon isn't planning some discourtesy to my nephews."

"He suspects, of course, that you have asked them here as possible suitors for Victoria."

"Then he suspects rightly."

"You will have to go carefully. Remember that his consent would have to be given. There is that Royal Marriage Bill to consider."

"Marriage for Victoria is some years away."

"That's true. But he and the Queen want her to take young Cambridge. That's why they want to see Victoria and the Princes together."

"Impertinence!" said the Duchess.

"But you will accept the invitation. It is, after all, in the nature of a royal command."

"I shall accept, but there shall be no nonsense. If he behaves indecorously I shall simply retire and take my party with me."

"A ball at St. James's" Victoria was excited. "You will love it," she told the cousins. "The Queen gives such *wonderful* balls. She thinks of *everything* to please her guests. She gave me such a beautiful ball for my birthday."

The amiable cousins said they were greatly looking forward to meeting their Majesties.

It was a ceremonial occasion and the King and Queen seated on gilt chairs received their guests under a canopy. They kept Victoria with them and the King asked her how she was enjoying this visit of her German cousins.

Victoria declared that she was enjoying it immensely. Her cousins were so amusing and so friendly; she was going to miss them sadly when they went home.

"You ought to come and see your Cousin George. He is very interesting and amiable too."

"I know; and I love to be with him. *And* with my cousin George Cumberland. I daresay he needs cheering up."

"I will arrange some parties for you," said Adelaide.

Victoria was longing to dance but it seemed she was expected to sit with the King and Queen and talk; and just as she believed she was going to dance, the Duchess of Kent swept up and told their Majesties that the Kensington party was about to leave.

"Oh, Mamma . . ." began Victoria, but a look from the Duchess silenced her.

The Queen was too bewildered to speak, because the ball,

which had been given in honour of the visitors, had scarcely begun.

"The Princes are so fatigued," said the Duchess. "They have been to a review in the park this afternoon."

"But they look . . ." began the Queen.

"Fatigued," said the Duchess promptly, and Victoria was startled that Mamma could so interrupt the Queen.

Fortunately the King, busy talking to one of his naval friends, had not heard this; and the Queen who hated any form of conflict was trying to hide how surprised she was. If the Duchess was going to make trouble, she wished to pass over it as quickly as possible. She could not allow the King to be upset on such an occasion. There was enough whispering about him as it was, and people had not yet forgotten that scene at the Royal Academy.

"So," said the Duchess firmly, "we must leave without delay."

"I should like the Princes to come and stay for a few days at Windsor," said the Queen. "You must make up a little party from Kensington."

"I'm afraid we cannot do that," said the Duchess. "They have engagements."

"But they are not going to leave us just yet?"

"They have engagements for the whole of their stay," said the Duchess almost rudely.

The Queen said nothing; and the Princes at the Duchess's request came up to say good-bye to the King and Queen before they left.

The King's looks were black as he remarked audibly he was always glad to see the back of that woman. Adelaide behaved as though it was perfectly normal for guests of honour to leave a ball almost as soon as it was started, and the Kensington party went to their carriages.

Victoria was silent as they drove along.

What a disappointment! She glanced at the Duchess who was seated in the carriage beside her, her hands clasped in her lap looking as though she was a General and had just won an important battle.

The Duchess laughed hilariously when she and Sir John were alone.

"That will show them how big a part I intend they shall play in our affairs."

"The Queen was docile, of course," mused Sir John. "But there is the King to consider."

"He's half mad. He'll be put away soon. He can't stay around much longer. And then . . ."

"Ah, and then . . ." said Sir John, smiling into her eyes.

"They will be asking us again before long, you see, and then . . ."

"And then we shall not be here."

"Oh?" Her eyes were alight with speculation.

"The Princes will want to see something of the country before they leave. What about a trip to the Isle of Wight? We could take the *Emerald* and have a very pleasant time."

"An excellent idea! And by the time their Majesties command us to come to St. James's, we shall not be at home."

"It is well that the Princes should realize Victoria's standing in the country. We'll have royal salutes fired on every possible occasion and we'll fly the Royal Standard over the *Emerald* to let all know that the future Queen is on board."

The Duchess was gleeful.

"We'll show their ridiculous Majesties what we think of them. How amusing . . . no matter how furious they become they can never shift Victoria from her position."

"As usual," said Sir John blandly, "you put your finger on the real issue. I often think how carefully we should have to tread if they had that power."

"But they have not. That is why we can do exactly as we want. And that, my dear Sir John, is what I intend to do."

What a gloriously exciting morning! Victoria had been up since just after five o'clock, for they were leaving Kensington Palace at seven. The Duchess and Sir John had made hasty plans which were to be kept secret because the Duchess wished it not to be known that they were going away until they had gone.

"How I shall love to be on the dear *Emerald*," said Victoria to Lehzen over breakfast. "I have been telling Alexander about it."

Alexander was the favourite, thought Lehzen; she must report this to the Duchess. Or should she? She had served the Duchess well but she did deplore her friendship with Sir John, and Sir John was no friend to Lehzen, any more than he had been to poor Späth. Späth was happy enough now with Feodora and her children, but she did feel the break with Vic-

toria sadly; and as for Lehzen, there was no one in the
world whom she could love as she loved Victoria and to
be separated from her . . . I would prefer death, thought
Lehzen dispassionately, for she was not given to dramatizing
situations and the fact was that she sincerely would. And
Sir John had tried to separate them.

What Lehzen wanted most of all was Victoria's happiness;
and if that was to be achieved her husband must be chosen
with the greatest care. Victoria was inclined to love any member of her family with enthusiasm, and she was particularly attracted by young men, and when those young men took such
pains to please her—for they were fully aware of what a
prize might come to one of them—she was in a state of
enchantment.

Victoria was affectionate by nature. She wanted to shower
love on all those around her. In the last year there had been
frequent visits to the opera and the ballet and the accounts
Victoria gave of these in her Journal were ecstatic—one
might say hyperbolic. She would describe in detail what the
dancers and singers wore; she would write of their beauty;
her delight in them was profound and she expressed it with
the utmost frankness.

Her greatly beloved child was so spontaneous, so delighted by the world around her, thought Lehzen, that she
was ready to fall in love with the first young man who was
presented to her. It must be the right one. George Cambridge was a delightful boy but Lehzen thought that being
brought up so near to Victoria had made her regard him
as a brother. Poor George Cumberland since his accident
had aroused her overwhelming pity and perhaps because of
this had become a little more popular than Cambridge. But
these glittering cousins with their precise German manners
and their overwhelming ability to please had been taken
right to her heart.

"God bless my dear child," prayed Lehzen nightly; and
now as she listened to Victoria's excited chatter at breakfast she thought: God give her happiness.

"I shall take them walking along by the sea. They tell me
they love the sea, although they did not greatly enjoy the
crossing. But this will be different, I tell them. Dear little
Dashy does not seem very well this morning, Lehzen. Oh
dear, I do hope he is going to be well enough to travel."

"He can go with the grooms," said Lehzen. "I daresay
he will soon be better."

"The sea air will be so good for him. Alexander loves Dashy. He did like him so much in his jacket and trousers, but I think they are too hot for this time of the year and they annoy him."

She is only a child yet, thought Lehzen. And this visit is just a preliminary one. There are the other cousins to be seen and she may like them better. At least there will be four of them and I expect she will be allowed to choose within the quartet.

It was time to leave. Sir John went into the first post-chaise and led the way, and Victoria followed in the next with the Duchess; after that came Lehzen's landau, with the cousins following in their carriage; and the rest of the party after them.

The sun was shining and the road was clear; and in an hour's time they were changing horses at Esher. As they drove the Duchess talked to Victoria about the manner in which she should conduct herself with her cousins, and Victoria listened somewhat listlessly, murmuring: "Yes, Mamma," now and then, as she revelled in the beauties of the countryside. She wished she could have ridden with the cousins, but she supposed that would not have been very proper.

What fun it was to be towed over to the *dear* Isle of Wight, and Admiral Sir Thomas Williams whose barge they were using accompanied them and stood with her and her cousins as they slowly left the mainland for the island.

"I shall always *love* the dear island after this," she said, and Alexander declared he would do the same.

"And so shall I," said Ernest, not to be outdone by his brother. And he added: "I hope I shall come here often."

Carriages were waiting to take them to Norris Castle in Cowes where they were to stay for a while. Victoria was secretly pleased that the Conroy family were not to stay at the Castle. Sir John had a house on the island, and he with Lady Conroy and the children were to stay there. It was called Osborne Lodge and when Victoria saw it she was delighted with it, and but for the fact that it was Sir John's and he was there, would have liked to stay in it herself.

What a glorious time they had! Everyone wanted to see Victoria and do honour to her. The people cheered her wherever she went; guns were constantly firing salutes; the Royal Standard flew from Norris Castle; and the Princes were very impressed with the importance of their young cousin.

Alexander was a little jealous of Ernest and Ernest of Alexander; but as they were so amiable, they did not allow their jealousy to spoil the happiness of the days only to enhance it.

I am growing up, thought Victoria; and one of the most pleasant things about growing up was the attention of young men. She tried to bestow favours equally on them because she liked them both; but if she were asked to choose which one she preferred, it would be dear Alexander.

And there was the beautiful *Emerald* which Victoria looked upon as her own ship, waiting for them. How she looked forward to entertaining the cousins on the ship. She was so beautiful with the Royal Standard flying bravely above her.

The Queen, reading the papers at breakfast, gave a little gasp of dismay.

"What's this?" asked the King.

For once Adelaide's equilibrium was disturbed and she was flushed with annoyance. It was a few days after the ball when the Duchess had discourteously left early.

"The Württemberg Princes spent the whole of yesterday at the Zoo," said Adelaide. "And I was told that they had so many engagements that our invitation to Windsor must be refused."

William laid down the paper he was reading and banged his fist on the table.

"That woman," he said, "is getting beyond endurance. You ask her to a ball which is to be given in honour of *her* relations and she comes here and behaves as though she is some sort of Empress and we are subjects whom she is honouring. I won't stand it, Adelaide. I tell you I won't." William had begun to declaim. "Who is the woman? Widow of some obscure German Prince before she married Edward; and when Edward died she behaved as though she were the head of the family. She has to be taught a lesson and I'm going to teach her a lesson."

Adelaide wished she had not spoken.

"The best thing is to ignore her," she began.

"Ignore her! When she goes about parading that girl as though she is already Queen and I don't exist. Oh no. I'll not ignore her. I'll humiliate her . . . publicly, that's what I'll do."

His face was growing scarlet.

He shouted for his secretary.

"William, what are you going to do?"

"I'm going to summon her to St. James's in such a way that she dare not refuse and then I am going to command her to bring those young men here. I'm going to tell her that they are guests in *my* Kingdom and if I wish to entertain them I will."

"William, don't you think . . ."

"I know what I think, my dear, and that is that this woman has gone too far."

His secretary arrived and he dictated a wordy command to the Duchess to come to St. James's without delay.

When the messenger had left William stalked up and down rehearsing what he would say to That Woman when she stood before him. Adelaide watched him fearfully. Words flowed from him a little incoherently. She was terrified; and then greatly relieved when the messenger returned to say that the Duchess and her guests had left Kensington the previous day and her servants were unsure of her destination.

William was not to be appeased. "Royal progress," he said. "Flaunting themselves all over the Kingdom. Staying in country houses! Whig houses most of 'em! That woman seems to believe that her daughter is the Queen and she is the Regent. For she is the one, you know. She is the ruler. The poor girl does what she's told. Royal Salutes popping all over the place. There's going to be an end to this popping."

"Perhaps," suggested Adelaide, "if they knew your wishes they would stop having these salutes fired."

"I shall command them to stop their poppings. Who ever heard of such arrogance? I'll send for Earl Grey and tell him."

"Yes," said Adelaide. "I think that would be an excellent idea."

When Earl Grey came he said that in view of the great popularity of the little Princess—and although he did not add the lack of popularity of the King although this was what he implied—he thought it might be a good idea to *ask* the Duchess first to stop having the salutes fired.

"Ask?" cried the King. "Why should I ask favours of that woman?"

"Just as a matter of form," suggested Earl Grey; and Adelaide was nodding.

The King hesitated. "Do it how you like," he said, "but the salutes are to be stopped."

Adelaide was relieved. She did hope the matter could be settled amicably.

"Do you think," said the Duchess to Sir John, "that too much adulation is going to Victoria's head?"

"There is certainly a change in her since the arrival of the Princes."

"She is too fond of admiration."

Sir John looked slyly at his Duchess. "It's a common enough failing."

"There is no room in the life of a Queen for common failings. She is becoming vain. I have caught her twice looking in the looking-glass; and worse than that, she seemed to have quite an idea of her own importance."

"Since she receives royal salutes wherever she goes and the people cheer her and make much of her, and she has two handsome young men both eager to be chosen as her husband—to say nothing of those paternal cousins whom the King and Queen would favour—I suppose a little vanity is understandable."

"She frowned when I criticized her. I do believe she thinks that she is of more consequence than *I* am."

"That may well be," said Sir John.

"She will have to be checked."

"Lehzen spoils her."

"In her own stern way perhaps."

"Nevertheless it is spoiling."

"My dear, she would make such trouble if I sent Lehzen away. She would appeal to William and Adelaide."

"You have snapped your fingers at *them* quite often."

"Yes, but we must remember that until William is acknowledged to be mad he is still the King and he could be difficult. Nevertheless I am determined not to allow Victoria to imagine she can command us all . . . yet."

A messenger had arrived with a letter for the Duchess. Sir John watched her while she opened it and read it.

When she had done so she threw it on the table with a

sarcastic laugh. Sir John picked it up and read it.

"They suggest that you stop the salutes."

"Impertinence," said the Duchess.

"Well, hardly that."

"I shall certainly not stop them. Victoria has every right to be saluted. She will be the Queen as soon as William is dead."

"My dear Duchess has overlooked one factor. William is not dead."

"I shall write back and tell them that I have no intention of depriving my daughter of her rights. As soon as this pier is opened I shall write to this . . . er . . . person and tell him so. Now I believe it is time we left."

Victoria was seated in the carriage with the Duchess, who was regarding her critically. The child was smiling at the people who were cheering her and looking decidedly complacent. Yes, that was the word. Indeed, she was getting out of hand and it would have to be stopped.

"Mamma, when I open the pier . . ."

"*We* are opening the pier."

"Oh," said Victoria, and stopped herself saying more. She had heard that the pier was to be opened by the Princess Victoria; there had been no mention of the Duchess of Kent.

"You must not imagine," went on the Duchess, "that the people are cheering *you*."

Victoria, who must have the truth at all costs, said: "But, Mamma, they call my name."

"It is the Crown they are saluting."

"But that is Uncle William's."

"You're in a most perverse mood, and I must warn you against arrogance."

"But I don't *feel* arrogant . . . only pleased that the people are so loyal and seem to like me."

"You think *that* because you are arrogant. You seem to forget that they are cheering me as well as you. And the Princes and . . . er . . . the rest of the party."

"But they say Victoria," said the Princess stubbornly.

"Really, you are becoming most difficult."

The carriage had stopped at the pier and the Mayor was waiting to greet them. The Duchess was helped from the carriage, followed by Victoria, and there was the Mayor seeming not to see the Duchess and going straight to Victoria all smiles, followed by the town Councillors.

"Long live the Princess!" called someone in the crowd. "Long live our little Princess Victoria."

The Duchess might have been one of the Princess's ladies-in-waiting for all the attention they paid to her. They hadn't a thought beyond Victoria. It was preposterous.

She waved an imperious hand at the Mayor.

"I have decided," she said, "that my daughter shall *not* open the pier. I will do it myself."

The Mayor and his astounded councillors stared at her, unable to hide their dismay. The Princess stood very still; her face had turned pale; there was glitter in her eyes, but she was determined that no one should know of the sudden fury which had seized her.

"Your Grace," stammered the Mayor, "the people are gathered to see the Princess perform this ceremony."

"Then they will see me perform it instead."

"But the people . . ."

"Come," said the Duchess, "let us proceed with the affair. Our time is limited, you know."

In silence the ceremony was performed. Victoria could not believe that Mamma would so humiliate her in public; but she knew that the Mayor and all those present were as angry with the Duchess as she was.

Sir John, watching, thought it a mistake; but he shrugged his shoulders; nothing could alter Victoria's accession and the more cowed she was the easier she would be to handle.

There was to be a luncheon to follow the ceremony and the Duchess coolly said that she would be unable to attend this. As the ceremony had taken place in Southampton and she was staying in the Isle of Wight it had been necessary to cross the water and that had not agreed with her. Therefore she did not feel she could take luncheon.

"Perhaps the Princess . . ." began the unfortunate Mayor.

"The Princess cannot attend ceremonies without her mother," said the Duchess coldly.

It was a disastrous occasion. It would be talked of, written of, and Victoria was heartily ashamed.

Mamma had spoilt this wonderful time they were having; as long as she lived she would remember the humiliation of being treated like a child in public.

A voice inside her said: "You hate Mamma. You know you do. Why not admit it?"

But she had sworn to be good and good people did not

hate their Mammas. At least they silenced little voices within them that insisted that they did.

The Duchess was in a bad temper which was not improved when they returned to Norris Castle and found a letter from Earl Grey. There was a new regulation regarding salutes to royal people. In future the Royal Standard must only be saluted when the King and Queen were in residence.

What a sad day, thought Victoria. Her cousins were leaving.

They were still in the Isle of Wight and she loved the place but it would not be the same without them. How I shall miss dear Ernest and even dearer Alexander! she sighed. How sad that they must go! But they had stayed for about a month and it had seemed like a week. Such fun they had had! She could not wait to write in her Journal:

> "They were so amiable and pleasant . . . they were always *satisfied, always good-humoured*. Alexander took such care of me getting in and out of the boat; so did Ernest. They talked about such *interesting* things . . . We shall miss them at breakfast, at luncheon, at dinner, riding, sailing, driving, walking, in fact everywhere."

But one must say good-bye quietly and whisper to dear Alexander—and Ernest—"Please come and see us again soon."

Alexander looked at her with longing in his eyes and said he would not be happy again until he did.

And so the visit of the Württemberg cousins came to an end and she missed them sadly.

But she seemed much older than she had before they arrived. That month had changed her. She wanted the society of amusing young people; and although she tried not to, sometimes she thought of Mamma in a manner which shocked her because she was sure it was not good to dislike one's own mother.

The Beautiful Blind Boy

❦ THE KING and Queen were at Kew and this was a very sad occasion—a farewell dinner to the Duke and Duchess of Cumberland and their son.

The King was subdued; he was a family man and all the resentment he had previously felt towards his brother Cumberland was now suppressed because of this terrible tragedy which had overcome him and his Duchess.

"Their only son," he said to Adelaide. "I feel for them."

"Oh, William," replied the tender-hearted Adelaide, "if only I could believe that this Baron Graefe could do something for the boy!"

"We can only hope he will. They say he's a clever fellow; and he didn't do badly with Ernest."

"But Ernest lost his eye. He couldn't save that."

"No. Well, we'll see. We've got to speed them on their way and hope, that's all, my dear."

"Poor Frederica. This has changed her."

"For the better," said William bluntly. "I always wondered whether she had a hand in murdering those husbands of hers."

"There are always rumours," said Adelaide sadly. "Few of us escape." She was thinking of Earl Howe, still attached to the Household but no longer in the position of Chamberlain.

"H'm," said the King. "And there have been some particular nasty ones surrounding my brother Cumberland and his wife."

"The whole world is sorry for him now," said Adelaide. "But we must go to greet our guests. I shall feel like weeping when I see dear George."

But she managed to smile when Frederica came towards her leading her poor blind son.

"My dear, dear George," said Adelaide, and kissed him tenderly.

"Why, Aunt Adelaide, it is good of you to ask us to say good-bye to you before we leave for Germany."

He was smiling. He had grown beautiful in his blindness; the gentleness had increased and his smile was very sweet. Adelaide had heard him referred to as the "Beautiful Blind Boy." Dear George, so young and yet to have acquired this special and so admirable quality which enabled him to bear his affliction more easily, it seemed, than those about him.

"Here is the King, dearest," said Frederica.

And George turned to William, who, the tears rising to his eyes and his face growing redder than usual, embraced him warmly.

"Dear nephew, this German fellow is good . . . the best in the world."

"So they tell me, Uncle William."

"You'll be back . . . right as rain."

Adelaide had taken his arm. "Come, dear George, we will go in to dinner."

It was an informal party as only a few close friends were fellow-guests and Adelaide and young George talked of the old days and visits to Bushy and Windsor when all the children had had such fun. The King and Cumberland talked politics together; and the Duchess of Cumberland's eyes scarcely left the face of her beautiful blind boy.

When the meal was over the King rose to his feet and drank the health of the Duke and Duchess of Cumberland.

"We all know for what purpose they are leaving us and our heartfelt prayers go with them. You will all pray, I know—as the Queen and I do—for the success of this mission. May our nephew return to us with his sight fully restored. I can say—and the Queen is with me in this—nothing would give us greater delight."

The Duchess of Cumberland was weeping quietly, and the Duke stood up and in a voice rent with emotion thanked the King for his goodness to him, his wife and his son. They would go on their journey with hope in their hearts and they would find comfort in remembering this evening.

All were deeply affected except young George, who sat smiling amid their tears—a look of happiness on his face. Adelaide wondered whether this was because he was certain of being cured, or whether it simply meant that the qualities which he had recently discovered in himself had brought him such consolation that he could be happy even in blindness.

How fortunate I am in my relations, thought Victoria. There were the dear Württemberg cousins, those other cousins she had not yet met from Saxe-Coburg but of whom she had heard much—they were already dear Ernest and Albert in her mind—and now there was dearest Feodora who was writing to say that her husband—another Ernest—was talking of a visit they might pay to England. Oh, what joy to see darling Feodora and the dear babies. They were increasing rapidly. Little Charles followed by Eliza, then Hermann and now another baby, Victor. Her brother Charles had upset everyone by marrying Marie Klebelsberg and they had a little son. Such fun it was to think up presents for the children. We are a great present-giving family, thought Victoria. Feodora's letters were a joy; they were full of the antics of the children who already loved their Tante Victoria. But dearest of all the relations was Uncle Leopold.

It was long since she had seen him but she remembered him as being the most handsome man in the world. He wrote to her regularly, stressing the fact that he wanted to help her, to guide her; she was his "dear soul" and he wanted her to turn to him for any advice she needed. She knew now that she would one day be a great Queen; she was very young, and it was likely that she would still be young when the Crown came to her; he wanted her to know that her Uncle Leopold, though he might be far away, was never far off in spirit. She could write her innermost thoughts to him. They were as one. He had believed that he would always be at her side, but fate had made him the King of the Belgians and that had meant that he could no longer live in England. Thank God, they could both wield a pen with some skill. Thus separation need not be an obstacle, although he would give a great deal to be with her, to embrace her once more. Did he remember how she used to sit on his knee and watch his lips as he talked as though she loved the very words which came forth? He was always at the disposal of his dearest Victoria.

"How fortunate I am to have such an uncle," said Victoria to Lehzen. "I believe him to be the most noble as well as the most handsome man in the world."

Lehzen was silent. There were facts about Leopold which

Victoria did not know. If he had been so devoted to his niece why had he not stayed with her? He should have said ambition rather than fate had made him the King of the Belgians. He had not behaved with what could be called nobility towards that poor girl Caroline Bauer. She must regret the day when she first saw Leopold, King of the Belgians, for as far as Lehzen could gather Fräulein Bauer had been a considerable actress on the German stage and fame and fortune were within her grasp. But Leopold had seen her; he spent many hours with her telling her of his sad life and how he had lost his wife so soon after their marriage and that the only woman whom he had ever known who reminded him of her and who could therefore take her place was Caroline Bauer. She was the niece of his friend and physician, Dr. Stockmar, and the fact that she had her mother with her seemed to give a respectability to the liaison. He had brought her to England, installed her in a little house and when he visited her would give her an account of his ailments and his sorrows; and then he would expect her to read to him for hours to save his eyes until the poor actress and her mother longed to escape the dreary life to which Leopold had condemned them; and when he decided to accept the Belgian crown they had with relief returned to Germany.

Of these matters Victoria knew nothing. Lehzen often wondered whether it was wise for the dear child to retain her fairy-tale view of life. Perhaps awakening would come fast enough; perhaps the Duchess herself was breaking it; for Lehzen was fully aware of the changing feelings of Victoria towards her mother.

Meanwhile one of the greatest pleasures in Victoria's life were the letters from dearest Uncle Leopold. She knew that dearest Aunt Louise was a *good* wife to him, and in this she rejoiced. It was her greatest hope that she would see them one day, and this, Leopold assured her, was a certainty.

Aunt Louise was going to have a child and how excited that made Victoria.

"You see, Lehzen, it will make up to him for Charlotte and her dear baby who never lived at all."

When Louise lost her baby Victoria wept bitterly for her.

"Dearest Uncle Leopold, how he must suffer! and I suffer with him."

Tears fell on to the watch cover she was embroidering for him. It was beautiful, with pansies in a lovely mauve shade.

"It must be done in time for his birthday," she told Lehzen. "He loves flowers."

"Pansies," said Lehzen. "They are sometimes called two-faces-under-a-hood."

"So they are, Lehzen. And that means a two-faced person, which in its turn could mean a deceitful one."

"A very appropriate gift for some statesmen," said Lehzen.

"But not for dear Uncle Leopold. I think I like the French names for them better. Pensées. Thoughts. He will know that I have chosen pansies for his watch cover because all the time I am working them I am thinking of him."

"And he will be right."

"Dear Uncle! I hope he is not too unhappy. Loving people makes one very sad sometimes because one not only has one's own troubles but theirs also."

Lehzen was suddenly emotional—which was rare with her.

"You are a dear good girl," she said.

"Oh, Lehzen, my dear, *dear* Lehzen, don't think I don't appreciate all you do for me."

Lehzen turned away. She did not want to show her tears. Her darling was growing up. Soon she would have no need of a governess. Victoria seemed to read her thoughts for she said: "Oh, Lehzen, you will always be my very dear friend."

And she was sad again, thinking of those days ahead when she would be grown up and no longer in need of Lehzen's services. Poor Lehzen!

It seemed that one could not love people without suffering with them. All the same one must be grateful for dear friends and relations.

"It will soon be Victoria's fifteenth birthday," said the Queen to the King. "Do you remember last year's ball? It was a great success. Victoria enjoyed it so much. I shall do the same this year."

"Excellent, excellent," said the King. "Like to see the children enjoy themselves. You remember the ball you gave for those Württemberg boys and how That Woman behaved."

"I shall never forget it," said Adelaide.

"Who but Madam Kent would have the effrontery . . ." began William, his face beginning to redden.

Adelaide said quickly: "It is Victoria of whom we must think. That child has a great capacity for enjoyment, and that is rather pleasant."

When the Duchess of Kent was told that the Queen was arranging a ball for Victoria's birthday, she told Sir John that although she had allowed Victoria to write a note of thanks to the Queen, she was determined that the Princess was not going to the ball.

"But what excuse can you make?"

"I shall find one. Leave it to me. You know what would happen at this ball . . . if she went. She would open the dancing with George Cambridge. Leopold has written to me that he feels a husband from our side of the family is essential. It is to be either Alexander or Ernest Württemberg or Ernest or Albert Saxe-Coburg. They are so much more suitable, Leopold says. And I agree with him."

Sir John agreed with the Duchess. Victoria must be kept in leading strings. She must make him her secretary when the time came, and the Duchess would be Regent if she were under age—if not her chief adviser; and if she had a husband who owed his success to the Princess's mother he would have to be grateful to her—and Sir John, the Duchess, with Leopold in the background, would continue to control the Princess . . . or Queen as she would then be.

The Duchess soon found her excuse.

"My poor brother has lost his child. We must go into mourning and that of course means no frivolities for a while."

She wrote to the Queen. The Princess Victoria was grateful to Her Majesty for offering her a birthday ball but in view of the fact that Kensington Palace was in mourning for the Princess's little cousin, she could not accept it.

When the King heard this he stormed; and Adelaide was terrified that he was going completely mad. Other people infuriated him temporarily but the exasperation and dislike with which he regarded the Duchess of Kent was perpetual.

"Let's forget it," said Adelaide. "After all, neither of us wants to entertain the Duchess. It was Victoria we were thinking of."

"One of these days," said the King, "I shall tell that woman exactly what I think of her. I'll banish her from England. Why should the King be constantly insulted by this . . . this . . . upstart of a Duchess?"

"She is the most difficult of women," sighed Adelaide, and began to talk about one of the grandchildren to turn his thoughts to a more pleasant subject. And as he was vitally interested in everything that concerned these young people she managed it successfully.

Poor Victoria, thought the Queen when she was alone. She was no doubt going to have a wretched birthday and all because of this stupid idea of mourning, which Adelaide knew full well had been thought up so that the invitation need not be accepted. If Victoria were not the heiress to the throne and it was their duty to bring her forward as much as possible, Adelaide would have washed her hands of Kensington Palace and its most troublesome inmate. But she often thought of that young girl who looked so wistful sometimes.

She wrote to the Duchess of Kent. Since there could be no ball for the Princess's birthday she would call at Kensington Palace on that day to give the good wishes of herself and the King to the Princess in person.

Who would believe anyone could be capable of such discourteous, ungrateful and arrogant behaviour? The Duchess of Kent apparently could; for she wrote back to the Queen. It was so kind of her to offer to call at Kensington Palace, but being in such deep mourning for her brother's child the Duchess was unable to receive anyone.

So there was no ball for the fifteenth birthday; but there was a letter which made Victoria very happy. It was from her sister Feodora, who wrote that she longed to be with her sister on this important day but the reunion would not be long delayed. A few days after Victoria's birthday, Feodora with her husband and two elder children would set out on the journey to England.

What joy, wrote Feodora, awaited her. Her little sister who had been but nine years old when she last saw her was now a young lady of fifteen. What changes there would be; and she had heard that Victoria had grown up very pretty. As for herself she had grown stouter and was really an old Mamma. She feared Victoria would get a great surprise when she saw her; but she would not wait for the day.

The great day turned out to be June 5th. Victoria was up early awaiting the arrival of her sister and her family long before they were due.

She chattered to Lehzen while her hair was being done. "Have I changed much, Lehzen? Do you really think I have grown prettier? Of course I am not very tall. But then nor is darling Feodora. Oh, I wonder if she has changed! And how

I long to see the dear, dear children."

Lehzen was moved too. She had been Feodora's governess before she was Victoria's, and she loved the elder sister only a little less than her present charge.

"You must curb your impatience," she said.

Victoria laughed and threw her arms about her governess. "And you, my dear Lehzen, are finding it very hard to curb yours."

At eleven o'clock the visitors arrived at Kensington Palace. The Duchess was there insisting on a little ceremony and that she be greeted first; but her maternal instincts were strong and she was delighted to see her elder daughter. Her love for Feodora being less calculated was more spontaneous and as she embraced her daughter and exclaimed with delight at the children she was genuinely moved.

Feodora's eyes were on Victoria. They flew at each other and hugged and kissed, tears in their eyes. Tears of happiness, said Victoria, for it was the most wonderful thing to see her darling sister again.

And the babies. They were enchanting. How tall little Charles was—and only four and a half! Who would believe it! He studied his Aunt Victoria very intently. "He has heard *so* much about you," Feodora explained.

"Oh, the darling."

"He remembers the whip you sent him. He talked about it for days before it arrived. Oh . . . but Eliza wants your attention. She does not intend to be left out."

Victoria had knelt down to embrace the little girl who was a year younger than Charles. Such a little beauty! Those enormous brown eyes, so big for her age and with such a merry, happy smile!

"What adorable children!" cried Victoria. "Oh, Feodora my dearest sister; how happy you must be."

"And never more so since I left Kensington than at this moment."

"You must see your rooms," said the Duchess, for once like any humble hostess. "Come, we will all go together." So the Duchess took young Charles by the hand, and Victoria held little Eliza's and with her arm linked in that of Feodora they went to the apartments which had been assigned for the family.

Feodora's husband, Ernest, Prince of Hohenlohe-Langenburg, looked quite old, Victoria thought, but he was kind to Feodora who loved him and he loved her and the children adored him, so Victoria was very ready to take him to her own affectionate heart.

The children were a source of amusement and delight; they were so well behaved and far from shy. They chattered away and were already very fond of their Aunt Victoria. They thanked her for all the presents she had sent them—no doubt primed to do this by Feodora and their nurses—but they did it so prettily that Victoria was very touched.

"I daresay," said the Duchess that afternoon, "that Lehzen would like to have her two girls to herself for a while. Victoria, you could take your sister for a drive and Lehzen could accompany you."

So off they went through the park with Lehzen sitting with them, laughing and recalling incidents from the past. "Do you remember?" they were constantly asking each other; and Lehzen sat there, her cheeks flushed, her lips quivering now and then with emotion and her eyes unnaturally bright as she listened to the light-hearted chatter of the two she loved so dearly.

Feodora was happy in her marriage. She saw that and was grateful. May Victoria find happiness as great, was her prayer.

Back at the Palace they dined and during dinner Charles and Eliza were brought in to say good night. How excited they were to be in England with the relations they had never before seen. How gay and happy they were! Eliza was much taken with her Grandmamma's appearance; she loved all the bows and ribbons and the jewels which adorned the Duchess's person. Victoria had rarely seen her mother so naturally happy as she was with these darling grandchildren.

How I wish it were always like this! she thought.

They had arranged to go to the Opera that evening, but Feodora said that she could not keep her eyes open.

"My love," said the Duchess tenderly, "it has been a very tiring day for you. You must go to bed early. The others can go to the Opera without you. As long as Victoria is present it will be all right."

Victoria was glad it had been decided for her because she loved the Opera—in fact Italian Opera gave her more pleasure than anything, even drawing and writing in her Journal —but at the same time she would have enjoyed staying behind to be with Feodora. But the Duchess said they had weeks ahead of them to chatter and Feodora was tired, so to the Opera went Victoria.

It was Rossini's *L'Assiedo di Corrinto* and Giuletta Grisi—

Victoria's very favourite artist—sang superbly. The Princess was entranced; and when Taglioni danced in *Les Sylphides* afterwards she felt that she had rarely enjoyed a day as she had enjoyed this one.

Moreover it was ten minutes to one when the party returned to Kensington Palace—a very late night to end a perfect day.

It was impossible for the Duchess to decline the Queen's invitation for her visitors to go to Windsor for the Ascot races. It would indeed have been a slight to her daughter and the Prince of Hohenlohe-Langenburg if they had not been received by the King and Queen.

The children did not go, but remained at Kensington Palace with their nurses. How sad! thought Victoria. Aunt Adelaide would have loved them.

Windsor, restored by George IV, was very grand; but Feodora was delighted to find the Queen as homely and kind as ever—although when she had left Adelaide had been merely Duchess of Clarence; and the King was kind too and delighted to see Feodora "with a nice little family, eh? Four of them. Good going. Like to see them. You should have brought them. Nothing like a family!" It was rather a tactless remark to make in the presence of the barren Queen but Adelaide was used to him by now.

It was going to be very amusing at Windsor, Victoria was sure, as long as Mamma did not offend the King or he her. She found herself becoming very uneasy when they were in the same company and watching them both, which did spoil the enjoyment a little. But the Duchess had changed with the coming of Feodora; she did love the granchildren so perhaps she was in a happier mood and not worrying all the time that it should be remembered she was the mother of the future Queen.

They went riding in the park together. How Victoria loved the park, and loved riding and dancing and everything that accompanied a visit to Windsor for the races. Victoria took her sister to see the recently erected statue of George III.

"There is a wonderful view from Snow Hill," she said, "and really poor Grandpapa does look very grand up there."

"Poor man!" said Feodora.

"It was all very sad," added Victoria. "They didn't tell me

for a long time. In fact I had to find out for myself. They are inclined to treat me as a child."

"*Poor* Victoria! I know what it can be like. Now that I have escaped from Kensington . . ."

"Escaped, Feodora? It sounds as though you think it like a prison."

"There were so many restrictions."

"There still are."

"And you, of course, are specially guarded. But, my dearest little sister, it will be different when you marry."

"Seeing you with dear Ernest makes me feel that there is a lot to be said for the married state."

"Our cousins came to see you a little while ago. Did you like them?"

"Oh . . . immensely."

"I think you might like the Coburg cousins even better."

"Do you, Feodora?"

"They are more . . . what shall I say . . . *manly*. Ernest is my favourite of the two."

"Do tell me why?"

"He is so honest and good-humoured."

"Oh, isn't Albert?"

"Oh yes. But he is more handsome and I think much more clever."

"I like handsome clever people."

"You will have a chance to see them soon, I daresay."

"I have not heard that they are coming."

"They will, Uncle Leopold is very anxious that they should."

"In that case I shall give them a special welcome."

"You see, my dear little sister, you are fifteen. It is quite old for a royal person."

"It certainly seems very old. In three years time I shall be of age. Think of that, Feodora. I shall no longer be . . ."

She did not finish the sentence. It seemed wrong to criticize Mamma even to Feodora.

"Sir John is always in such evidence," said Feodora.

"We cannot escape from that man."

"He seems to be a permanent inmate of the household."

"That is exactly what he is. And Lady Conroy too, although she is meek."

"She would have to be," put in Feodora.

"And Jane and Victoire are quite pleasant. But until a little while ago I saw very few young people besides them. The boys are sweet. I quite like them, but . . ."

Feodora sighed. "Never mind. Three years time and . . . then freedom."

Much as she would have enjoyed to carry on this conversation, Victoria felt that it was disloyal in some way, so she began to talk of Sir Richard Westmacott's bronze statue again and how fine it looked there in the Park, and how Uncle George had done so much for Windsor as well as Buckingham House which she believed was almost ready for occupation.

"Do you remember the time when we came to Windsor and he took me riding in his carriage? 'Pop her in,' he said when we met him in the Park, and Mamma was so frightened; but I loved riding so fast between him and Aunt Mary. I called him Uncle King and he was very kind; and he liked you, Feodora . . . he liked you particularly. I thought he wanted to marry you."

Feodora laughed. "Fancy if he had."

"You would have been the Queen of England."

"And that, my love, is a title reserved for you."

Now they had begun the fascinating game of "Do you Remember?" which lasted throughout the ride.

The company was assembled for dinner with one notable exception. The Duchess of Kent had not appeared. The Queen was waiting for her, because she did not feel that she could lead the guests into the dining-saloon without the Duchess, who was one of the most important guests.

Victoria was growing nervous. Why did Mamma not come? She knew the answer. The Duchess had been angry because not enough respect had been paid to her. Everywhere they went it was always the King, the Queen and Victoria. It was Victoria who sat between the King and the Queen, Victoria whom everyone watched and the Duchess did not like it. Victoria might be the future Queen but she was a child and while she remained a child the Duchess was a deputy for her. Nothing infuriated her more than to be treated as merely an honoured guest. She was *the* guest of honour—as representative of the heir to the throne. Next to the King and Queen should come the Duchess.

She believed the King deliberately slighted her and Victoria had heard her remark to Sir John that she had had enough.

Now she was keeping the house party waiting, to show that they could not go in to dine without her, and therefore must await her pleasure.

The Queen, who was anxious to avoid any trouble, had at first pretended not to notice her absence; but now of course she could not do so. Dinner could not be postponed for half an hour without there being a reason.

The King was getting testy. At any moment Adelaide knew he would command that they go in without the Duchess; and that would be an insult. "Half an hour late for dinner. Damned bad manners," growled the King.

He said in an audible voice to the Queen: "We're waiting for that woman, I suppose."

"I am sure she will be here very soon now," soothed Adelaide.

"If not we'll go in without her." The King's face had reddened. He shouted: "That woman is a nuisance!" Just as the Duchess, glittering and feathered, made her entrance.

Victoria held her breath with horror. What would happen now? The King was glaring at the Duchess who seemed blithely unaware of him and so sure of her right to keep the company waiting if she so wished to.

Dear kind Aunt Adelaide put an end to the scene in her usual gentle tactful way.

"Let us go in to dinner," she said, as though nothing upsetting had happened.

That was the only incident which spoiled the visit.

What fun to drive off to the races—herself sitting with Mamma and the King and Queen. Mamma was gracious on that day because she was in the first carriage; and although the King did not look at her, the Queen behaved as though nothing had happened and she and Victoria laughed and chatted together, which was comforting. Dear Feodora rode in the second carriage followed by the rest of the carriages—so many of them that Victoria did not know the number. There were people of all kinds on the race-course and the royal party aroused great attention as it went on its way to the King's stand.

How excited Victoria was by the races! She stood beside the King and clasped her hands and wanted to shout to the horses as so many people did.

Aunt Adelaide on the other side smiled at her and whispered that it was the greatest fun, and Victoria knew that it was her pleasure which delighted Aunt Adelaide as much as the races themselves.

What a happy day! Even riding back to Windsor with the carriage windows closed to keep out the rain which had come pelting down.

"How I love racing!" announced Victoria.

The Duchess remarked that she must not develop a taste for gambling.

But Victoria scarcely heard; it had been such a lovely day and she had quite forgotten that horrid scene before dinner on the previous night.

She wrote in her Journal. "I stayed up till a quarter past eleven. I was very much amused indeed at the races."

The days rushed by and the visit was over. How terribly sad to have to say good-bye to dear Feodora and the darling children.

"When shall I see you again, dearest sister?' asked Victoria, with tears in her eyes.

"There must not be a long parting," Feodora declared. "For I could not endure it. We are not so very far away."

"*You* must come again," Victoria insisted, for she knew that she who was not allowed to sleep alone or ever be alone would never be allowed to visit her sister.

"Remember . . . three more years and you will be of age," whispered Feodora. "You will make your own decisions."

Victoria understood. Feodora was comforting her. She knew the difficulties of life in a household governed by a domineering Duchess and she was telling Victoria that it would not be long.

They embraced for the last time and blinded by her tears Victoria watched the carriage drive away.

"How very sad I felt at breakfast," wrote Victoria in her Journal, "not to see the door open and *dear* Feodora come in smiling and leading her dear little girl; and not to get the accustomed kiss from her. At one we lunched. I missed dear Feodora here again terribly. I miss her so much today. At three we drove with Lehzen. How dull the drive appeared without dear Feodora! We dined at seven and after dinner

Aunt Sophia came. We passed a sad dull evening. I stayed up until a quarter to nine."

All she could do was look forward to Feodora's next visit and take small comfort in the fact that Feodora missed her as sadly as she did her dear sister.

It was wonderful to have such *dear* relations, she told Lehzen, but at the same time, so sad.

Owing to the dissension his Irish policy had caused his Cabinet, Earl Grey took the opportunity to resign his office and called on the King to tell him of his decision. Grey, whose family life was exceptionally happy and interesting— he had ten sons and five daughters and was on the best of terms with them all—had long desired to leave public life and retire to the country. This seemed the moment.

The King sent for Lord Melbourne and asked him to form a government.

William Lamb, Lord Melbourne, had not enjoyed the same domestic felicity which had been the lot of Earl Grey. In fact some years before, his wife, Lady Caroline, had behaved most scandalously and there had actually been a separation. Caroline Ponsonby, the only daughter of the Earl of Bessborough, had been one of the great beauties of the day but she had been so strange even in childhood that her grandmother, Lady Spencer, had consulted a doctor because she feared Caroline was unbalanced. She was right.

Melbourne's tragedy was that he married her; but no one could live in harmony with such a woman, not even the calm, intellectual Melbourne; and when Lady Caroline was involved in scandal with Lord Byron he could no longer live with her in any circumstances. They were separated; Caroline had died some six years before, and Melbourne, now a free man, devoted himself to art, literature and politics, and to his son, George Augustus, who was mentally defective.

Melbourne gave no indication that he had passed through such a tragedy. He was suave and handsome, and politically ambitious.

He accepted the King's challenge and set about forming a government.

There was no great excitement about Grey's departure. Melbourne was a good Whig and the Whigs had passed the Reform Bill. As long as Wellington—that arch enemy of Reform—was not brought back, the people were content.

Adelaide had a cough which persisted and William was worried about her.

She worked too hard, he said. That Reform business had upset her. She did not understand the English; she had believed that the country was on the edge of revolution and she was to be executed like poor Marie Antoinette.

She needs a holiday, said William to his daughter Lady Alice Kennedy, who had made Windsor Castle her home and brought her children there with her.

Lady Alice, who like all the FitzClarence family seemed to have grown very resentful of Adelaide since she had become Queen, said that a trip to her old home would be a good idea. There was that old mother of hers who could not live much longer; she was sure Adelaide would like to see her.

"I'll tell her she shall have a holiday," said William.

"Will you go with her?"

"A King has to govern his country, Alice. He can't go dancing all over the Continent."

"I thought so, but she'll protest and say she can't go without you. You should arrange the trip for her and then tell her what you have done. She'll be grateful to you for doing it that way and it will do her the good she needs."

"Capital idea," said William. "Leave this to me."

He sent for Earl Howe who was still a member of the Queen's household and, although at the time of the passing of the Reform Bill he had been forced to resign from the office of the Queen's Chamberlain, he continued to serve unofficially in that capacity.

"I want a trip arranged for the Queen," said William. "She's not well. She wants a holiday. She shall go to her old home and see her mother. It'll do her good."

"Has her Majesty agreed to this, Sir?" asked Earl Howe incredulously.

"No, no. It's a secret. I shall just present her with the finished plans."

Earl Howe was dubious as to the success of this, but he knew that the King was in too touchy a mood for him to suggest he might be wrong.

The King had been behaving even more oddly than usual lately and upsetting all sorts of people. Only the other day at a dinner where he insisted on making one of his interminable speeches he had talked of the changes in the Navy and how it was possible now to rise from the lowest rank to the highest. On his right, he pointed out, was a member of a family as old as his own, on his left, his good friend an Admiral who had risen from the dregs of society. The speech was received with astonishment and acute embarrassment by the Admiral on his left, but William was unaware of it. It seemed that there were times that if he could blunder he would do so. And he appeared to pass through periods when his mind was really unhinged.

No, decided Earl Howe, he dared not disagree with the King.

When Adelaide heard what plans had been made she was dismayed. As for the King his asthma had been worse than usual and he had felt most unwell. He hated the thought of losing her and would never have thought of a separation—however brief—if Alice had not persuaded him of the Queen's need for a holiday.

"I don't want to go," Adelaide told him, when he explained the plan to her.

"You must. You need a rest. That cough of yours . . . I don't like it."

"I feel I should be here with you."

"I'll miss you," said William. "I can't think how I'll get along without you. The Government . . . this fellow Melbourne . . . It's all very shaky. I shouldn't be at all surprised if the Government fell, and you know what, Adelaide, the people would blame you for it. They always blame you. They seem to have got it into their silly heads that I'm a dolt you lead by the nose."

"They're fond of you," Adelaide told him. "They want a scapegoat so they've chosen me as the French chose Marie Antoinette."

"It's not the same. You don't know the English. Still, I'd rather you were away. There are those fellows from Tolpuddle . . . or some such place . . . those six Dorsetshire labourers taking oaths about trade unions . . . They've been transported and the people are making something of it. It's nothing. Talk . . . just talk . . . All the same it upsets you, but I wouldn't want you to be here. You'd like to see your mother, wouldn't you? And your brother's coming over to travel with you. I've arranged for it all. There, you'll like to see your home."

"My home is England now," she said. "My pleasure is in looking after you."

He was deeply affected. "I don't know what I shall do without you. There are a hundred ways in which you are useful to me."

"Then I shall stay."

"No, no, I can't allow it. You must go. It'll do you good. Go . . . and come back soon."

So she left St. James's with her brother, the Duke of Saxe-Meiningen, and some members of the FitzClarence family; among the party was Earl Howe.

The Cumberlands had come home from Germany very sad because Baron Graefe had been unable to do anything for George.

Victoria wept when she heard the news.

"Poor, poor George Cumberland. I must ask Mamma if I may call on him. He will be in need of comfort."

The Duchess thought there could be no harm in Victoria's visiting her cousin. No one would expect her to marry a blind man, she said to Conroy.

So Victoria called on her cousin and found him not in the least depressed. He knew that he would never see again. Victoria tried to imagine it. Never see the flowers and trees, never to embroider, never to see Feodora and the dear children, Lehzen, Uncle Leopold's letters, the beautiful singer Grisi. How tragic. How very, very sad.

"Oh, Lehzen," she cried, when they were driving back to Kensington, "he looked so beautiful, so serene, it made me want to weep."

"The Queen Has Done It All"

WHEN Adelaide returned to England after her trip on the Continent it was to find the King ill and fretful. He was, however, delighted to see her, and when she arrived at St. James's Palace hurried out to welcome her and embrace her warmly.

"I'm glad to see you back," he cried. "It's not the same without you."

It was a wonderful welcome home.

Many ceremonies had been arranged for her and by the end of a week she was exhausted; so that when the day came for her to go to the City to receive a congratulatory address on her safe return she was unable to attend and the King went alone. Adelaide's detractors preferred to see this as an insult to the City although it passed off without much comment.

The FitzClarences had grown to dislike her actively, the main reason being that she had been so good to them, and their arrogant natures would not allow them to admit her generosity while they did not hesitate to accept it. Adelaide was the Queen; and they were the children of their father's mistress. This was a fact they could not forget. They hated her for being in the position which they reckoned should have belonged to their mother; and they were constantly reminding each other of what life would have been if their parents had been married. The fact that the King acknowledged them as his children, that they had titles and honours, did not satisfy them. They wanted more, and to appease their frustrated anger, like the people, they chose meek Adelaide as their scapegoat.

At one moment she was a fool with no intelligence; at another she was possessed of great cunning. She led the King and she was responsible for his opposition to the Reform Bill; she was an alien—a German, and there had been too many Germans in the royal family.

Those who had accompanied her to Saxe-Meniningen reported that the Castle of Altenstein where she had spent her childhood was certainly not worthy to be known as such. They had seen the room which Adelaide and her sister had shared —a little room without a carpet and containing two small beds with *calico* curtains. An English maid would complain at being given such a room. And this was the woman who sought to manage the affairs of England!

While aware of this hostility Adelaide pretended not to see it because she did not wish to upset William. He loved his wife; he loved his children; in the early days of his marriage the harmony which had existed between them—and which was of Adelaide's making—had delighted him; and his mind was not strong enough, Adelaide decided, for her to introduce new conflicts. She must forget the unkindness of William's children and delight with him in the adorable grandchildren who made no secret of their love for her.

Windsor Castle and St. James's were the homes of many of them; they ran about shrieking and playing their games, and no one restrained them, for the King and Queen enjoyed hearing their noisy play; and if there was silence began to fret that they might be ill.

Soon after her return London was shocked by the fire which destroyed the Houses of Parliament. The King grew overexcited and many people said it was an omen. The verdict was that had the fire been dealt with promptly the building might have been saved. But nothing had been done and a minor outbreak had resulted in a mighty conflagration.

There should be some means of preventing fires spreading, the Government decided; a kind of brigade which could go into action with the minimum of delay was needed.

William was excited and discussed it with Adelaide.

"They seem to think there should be some sort of Fire Brigade—men just waiting for a call with everything ready to deal with the flames before they've done too much damage."

Adelaide thought this was an excellent idea; and was very interested in the formation of the London Fire Brigade.

It was much more comforting to discuss the building up of such an organization than the depressing affairs of the Government.

"That fellow Melbourne has been to see me again," William told her. "He says he can't get the support he needs and that he thinks the Government will have to make concessions to these radical ideas if it's to stay in power."

"They cannot make concessions. It will be the Reform Bill all over again."

"That's what I tell him, but he stands firm. Melbourne will have to go."

"Will this bring Wellington back?" asked the Queen hopefully.

"We'll have to see."

Shortly after this the King dismissed the Melbourne Ministry, an action which was ill-timed, for he had played straight into the hands of the Queen's enemies.

It was well known that she had opposed the Reform Bill; she had no sooner returned from her trip abroad than Melbourne was dismissed. It was easy to see that the Queen wanted to bring back the Tories and that she was against reform.

The Times was the first with the news.

"The King has turned out the Ministry and there is every reason to believe that the Duke of Wellington has been sent for. The Queen has done it all."

It seemed that all London was against the Queen. The FitzClarences discussed her in their Clubs and the houses of their friends with venom. The dismissal of Melbourne was an attempt to obstruct a Government influenced by the people. And this had been brought about by an ugly woman with a German accent who had come from a "doghole" in Germany and had slept in a room which an English housemaid had scorned!

Adelaide was wretched. She almost wished that she had stayed abroad. William, oddly enough, was less excitable over major events than over small domestic difficulties.

"Stuff!" was his comment.

The people were parading the streets with banners on which were painted the words: "The Queen has done it all."

"You see," said Adelaide, "that is what happened in France. They chose the Queen because she was a foreigner to them, just as the people here have chosen me. I hope that I shall be as brave as Marie Antoinette when my time comes."

The King's "Stuff!" was some consolation. "We all get mud thrown at us now and then. My brother George was the most unpopular man in the country but he died in his bed. Stop fretting."

Wellington advised that the King should send for Sir Robert Peel and ask him to form a Government, and messengers were immediately sent to Rome where Peel was at that time. Meanwhile Wellington became First Lord of the Treasury and Home Secretary, and carried on the Ministry until Peel's return. Then Wellington took on the post of Foreign Secretary.

Such a hastily formed Government was an uneasy one, although it sufficed to carry the country through a rather ugly situation; it did last for four months, and the campaign against the Queen subsided.

The Times even went so far as to publish an apology to her, and the Queen was relegated to the position of a rather stupid woman, a nonentity who had failed to give the King the heirs to provide which he had married her, who was not even handsome enough to grace ceremonies; and therefore was to be regarded with contempt.

The FitzClarences added their criticism. She was a fool; she had an execrable German accent; she was no use nor ornament to the throne.

Adelaide, painfully aware of her unpopularity, grew thinner and her cough returned to trouble her.

Buckingham Palace had now been completed and even that was used as a condemnation against the Queen.

There had never been such a lack of taste displayed in any of the royal palaces. Did the people remember George IV? He might have been extravagant and a voluptuary controlled by women, but at least he had good taste. Think of Carlton House; think of what he had done to Windsor; think of the buildings round Regent's Park and Nash's Regent Street. And then think of Buckingham Palace!

"Every error of taste imaginable has been committed." The pillars—and there were many of them—were painted in a shade of raspberry. Thomas Creevy, the old gossip, had had a look over it and said those raspberry pillars made him feel sick and that instead of being called Buckingham Palace it should be called Brunswick Hotel.

The most vulgar thing of all was the wallpaper for the Queen's apartments which she had chosen herself.

And this was the palace on which a million pounds had been spent!

William himself did not like it when he went to look over it with Adelaide.

"I suppose we'll have to move in. They'll expect it of us . . . after all that money's been spent on it."

William was thinking of the FitzClarence grandchildren playing hide and seek behind the raspberry pillars. They would not like it he was sure. Not like Old St. James's for all its gloom, or Windsor for all its grandeur. And there was nothing like Bushy with its homeliness and memories of the old days with Dorothy when the children were all growing up and were much more respectful and affectionate towards the Duke of Clarence than they were to the King of England.

"Why not offer it to the country?" suggested Adelaide. "It could take the place of the Houses of Parliament."

"Capital!" cried the King. "That's what we'll do."

He was disappointed when the Government announced that it did not believe that Buckingham Palace would be suitable as the Houses of Parliament. Moreover, plans were hastily going ahead to rebuild them on that spot on the river where the old ones had stood.

How glad Adelaide was to go to Brighton for a respite! It was so pleasant not to have to worry every time she drove out that she would be confronted with one of those horrid placards about herself. The sea air was good too, even though it was autumn and the winds blowing in from the sea were bitterly cold.

One of her greatest comforts, apart from the grandchildren, was George Cambridge, who was growing into a very handsome boy, and was devoted to her. There was *one* who showed gratitude. But she had to face the fact that he was growing up and she supposed he would have to take up some training—military perhaps, which would entail his going away, probably to Germany where it seemed to be the custom to send royal Princes. But that was not yet and she would enjoy this period in Brighton.

The FitzClarences, however, would not allow her to be at peace, so they started a rumour that the Queen was pregnant.

When the Duchess of Kent heard this news she was wild with rage. She stormed up and down her drawing-room declaring that it was impossible. It could not be. That poor pale sick creature! How could it possibly come about? There was a mistake. Sir John must tell her it was a mistake.

Sir John did; but he shared her horror. If indeed it should be true, if Adelaide produced that child and it lived . . . then this would be the end of all their hopes.

Victoria said to Lehzen: "Do you think this story is true that the Queen is going to have a child?"

"It has been neither denied nor confirmed," said the judicious Lehzen.

"Lehzen, think what it will mean! I shall not be the Queen after all."

"My dear Princess, will that make you very unhappy?"

Victoria was thoughtful. "I think I shall be very disappointed. You see, everything that has happened has been leading up to that. But I can't help thinking of Aunt Adelaide. She is a sweet kind woman, you know, Lehzen, and I love her dearly. I know what she wants more than anything in the world is a baby of her own. Oh, she loves all the King's grandchildren—whom *I* am never allowed to see—and she loves the Georges and I believe she loves me too—when Mamma allows her to see me—but she does long for her own baby. So if I lost the throne and Aunt Adelaide gained a baby . . . Really, Lehzen, I can't *honestly* say, but I think I should feel happy for Aunt Adelaide."

Lehzen was moved to comment. "You have your storms and tantrums, but I think you have great honesty and that is a very fine characteristic to have."

Victoria smiled. "I can't help thinking too that George Cambridge has a much happier time than I do. He is not told he must not do this and that; he is allowed to be alone sometimes. So perhaps I feel too that there is a great deal to be said for not being the heir to the throne."

Lehzen said calmly: "I am glad you see it in this way, because if you should not be Queen you will still make a very happy life for yourself."

The Duchess was far less philosophical.

"This is monstrous!" she cried. "That old fool could not beget a child. And who is the man who is always beside the Queen, eh? Earl Howe. She is known to have a fancy for him. If the Queen is with child, then depend upon it, Earl Howe is the father."

The Duchess's suspicions were of course those of the Fitz-Clarences'.

"She is two or three months gone," said the Earl of Munster, that George FitzClarence whom Adelaide had nursed during her honeymoon when he had broken his leg. "There is going to be a big scandal over this."

It was whispered of in the streets. A fine thing. This German "frow" who had lived in a housemaid's bedroom before she came to the Court of England was about to give birth to a bastard and foist him on to the throne of England.

At length the rumours came to Adelaide's ears. How had they started? she wondered. Why did people make up these cruel stories about her? If it were possible for her to be pregnant, how happy she would be! But alas, it was not so. She would never be a mother now.

And how dared they say such cruel things about her relationship with Earl Howe? It was true theirs was a tender friendship; he treated her as though she was an attractive woman, something which for all his affection the King had never done. But the Earl was just a dear friend; she had been too rigorously brought up, she was too conscious of her duty for it to be otherwise.

There was nothing to do but show the King the newspapers which she knew his secretaries had been keeping from him.

He read them and threw them from him in contempt.

"Damned *stuff*," he said.

And when the scandal was proved to be groundless it was forgotten.

The Duchess of Kent regained her serenity. "How could we have thought that poor creature possibly could! No, it can never happen now. The throne is safe for Victoria."

The Duchess complained continually of her apartments in Kensington.

"Really," she said to Sir John, "it is a scandal. We are expected to live in these rooms which are scarcely better than servants' quarters."

This was far from true but Sir John never contradicted his Duchess unless it was absolutely necessary to his interests to do so and the Duchess's antagonism towards the King was never that.

"I think I have been patient too long. Good Heavens, doesn't that man realize that Victoria is the heiress to the throne?"

"It can scarcely be called my dear Duchess's fault if he does not," replied Sir John with one of his ironical smiles.

"I have long thought we should have a larger apartment. Why not? There are plenty of rooms available in the Palace. Why, therefore, should we be confined to these miserable few? I have decided to write to His Majesty and tell him that I require a larger apartment. There are seventeen rooms which I could take over and no one would be the worse for it. Then I might be able to provide apartments for my daughter comparable with her rank."

"Why not write to the King and ask his permission to take over the rooms you have chosen?"

"Oh, how infuriating. To have to ask the permission of that . . . of that . . ."

"Buffoon?" supplied Sir John; and they both laughed.

Dear Sir John! What a blessing that with all she had to put up with from her most tiresome brother-in-law, she had Sir John with whom to share a little jocularity.

"I shall write immediately," she said. "I see no reason to delay."

As Sir John did not either, she sat down and wrote her request to the King in her usual imperious manner.

When the letter was put before William, his eyes bulged with rage.

"So the apartments are not good enough for Madam Kent, eh? She would like more space. She will take over seventeen more rooms and she has already chosen them. By God, that woman will go too far one of these days. Write to her. Ask her when she proposes to take over St. James's and when she would like me to vacate Windsor so that she can move in. Or perhaps that's not grand enough for her. Seventeen rooms! No, I say. She will stay in her present apartments. And the answer to her request is No, No, No!"

When the Duchess received his reply she was so angry that she tore it up and flung it from her.

"Ill-mannered, uncouth, vulgar . . ." she stammered.

"Buffoon," supplied Sir John, smiling tenderly at her.

She laughed.

"But," she added, "I shall never allow the creature to get the better of *me*."

A Visit from Leopold

VICTORIA's sixteenth birthday would soon be with them.

"Dear me," said the Duchess, "how time is flying. Two more years and she will be of age!"

Sir John admitted this, with some gloom. "I hope that she will be . . . amenable."

"My dear Sir John, what *do* you mean? Of course she will do as she is told."

"There are the little tantrums. I fancy a certain resistance is growing in our Princess."

"It must be crushed," said the Duchess with the air of a general about to go into battle.

"She has spirit. If she fancies she is being . . . crushed she will refuse to be. I have seen that much in her eyes. Lehzen encourages her. It was a mistake not to get rid of her with Späth."

"My dear Sir John, I am sure that would have been disastrous. Victoria more or less threatened to go to the King."

"The King is an old fool."

"But a stubborn one and Adelaide is not such a fool as people believe her to be."

"You are right. But trust me in this, my dear Duchess, do not attempt to force the Princess. Coercion, persuasion . . . that is what we need. And when the day comes . . . and it must soon . . . we shall be there."

"The King must die before the next two years are up. How I wish she were a year or two younger."

"But she is not. So . . . let us try to please her. I believe she has a notion that we wish for power for ourselves. This is alienating her. It is her birthday. Think of something she really wants and give it to her. She likes music better than anything. Why not invite some of her favourite artistes to the Palace to give a concert for her. I am sure there is nothing she would like better. She grows lyrical about that Grisi woman; I am sure an invitation to give a concert here would send our Princess into rhapsodies of gratitude."

"It is an excellent idea," said the Duchess, "and shall be carried out."

It had been a wonderful concert, and it was the Duchess's birthday present to her. What a truly wonderful present. She could not have had anything to please her more.

"How very thoughtful of Mamma," she remarked to Lehzen.

She wrote of it in her Journal—how she had sat in the front row with the family, joined by poor Aunt Sophia and the Duchess of Cambridge—George's mother—who was now in England because George was going to be confirmed and later with George Cumberland to receive the Order of the Garter. The singing was heavenly; and what a joy to see Grisi off the stage—so tall and pale with such a lovely mild expression; her eyes were dark and beautiful and her eyelashes long. She had definitely not been disappointed in dear Grisi. Victoria was transported with delight when she sang *Tanti affetti* from *Donna del Lago*. There were other artistes, too, for Mamma had determined to bring in all her favourites. But there was none to compare with Grisi—dear, beautiful, talented Grisi!

She found it difficult to stop writing of the concert; she described it in detail reliving it as she did so.

"Now," she told Lehzen, "I only have to read this account of it and I shall hear it all again. Aunt Sophia loved it. Poor Aunt Sophia, she had never heard any of the singers before! But nobody was as enchanted as I was. I shall never forget it. What a wonderful, wonderful birthday present."

"A great success," said the Duchess when she read the Journal. But she was less pleased when she read the entry of a few days later.

"Sunday, 24th May. Today is my sixteenth birthday. How very old that sounds; but I feel that the two years to come till I attain my eighteenth are the most important of almost any."

Yes, those words were ominous. Victoria was thinking of that important eighteenth birthday when she could, should the King die, become the Queen, when she could, if she wished, demand that her mother cease to control her, when she could refuse to sleep in the same bedroom, and insist that she was alone when she wished to be.

"She is becoming too much aware of her position," said the Duchess. "We must be more watchful than ever."

There was the usual present-giving on the birthday and Victoria was awake soon after six with the delicious anticipation which birthdays always gave her. Mamma was ready with the presents.

"Oh, but, Mamma, you gave me the most wonderful of presents. That beautiful . . . beautiful concert."

The Duchess kissed her; she was always softened at present-giving time. She had had a brooch made containing a lock of her hair.

"I thought you would like it as it is *my* hair."

"Oh, Mamma, it is beautiful."

There were other gifts from the Duchess, of course, including a bracelet with a lock of her hair to match the brooch, a shawl and books; Lehzen's present was a lovely leather case containing little knives and pencils. The King sent a pair of sapphire and diamond ear-rings, and there was a Bible from a bookseller named Mr. Hatchard.

All day long the presents were arriving. She wondered where she would put them all, she confided to George Cambridge who sat beside her on a sofa—closely watched by Mamma—while they looked at the drawings in the album which was his birthday present to her.

She was very happy when she went to bed—and it was only half past nine so she wrote in her diary while it was all fresh and she had all the presents about her so that she would not forget one.

"My *dear* Mamma's great present was that delicious concert," she wrote, "which I shall never forget."

Yes, the concert was a great success. Victoria had written of her mother as *dear* Mamma; and that was something she rarely did.

"Today," thought Victoria when she awoke on that July morning a few weeks after her sixteenth birthday, "is one of the most important days in my life."

Lehzen and the Duchess had impressed upon her the importance of it. She was going to be confirmed. After today she must make a very special effort to be good; she must try to be a good daughter as well as a good Queen—when the time came. That would be necessary if she were to be a good Christian; she must comfort Mamma, and try to understand her.

She was full of good resolutions.

On the table near her bed she could see the books which Mamma had given her yesterday. *A Method of Preparation for Confirmation, An Address to the Candidates for Confirmation,* and *An Address to the Students of Eton College who are about to Present themselves for Confirmation in 1833.* She had not had time to read them yet but she would, and hereafter she would try to be a good Christian in every way.

She had done a rather good drawing yesterday and she was going to give it to Mamma with a very pretty pin in memory of this day; for Lehzen she had a ring. They were after all, the two who had prepared her for this and she must show her gratitude.

For an hour she lay thinking of this until Lehzen came in to say it was eight o'clock and to ask when she was going to get up.

"Oh, Lehzen, I have been thinking of the importance of today."

Lehzen agreed that it was very important and laid four prints on the bed; they were pictures of Saints and biblical subjects.

"They are very pretty, Lehzen, and so *suitable.*"

Lehzen said that she thought so.

After breakfast Victoria put on the white lace dress which had been specially made for the confirmation; and there was a white crêpe bonnet trimmed with white roses. Lehzen wept openly when she saw her, and Victoria threw her arms about her. "Dearest Lehzen, I am still the same. I shall not change. I shall still be your affectionate child even though I am a good Christian."

Which made Lehzen break down altogether.

The carriages arrived and Victoria and the Duchess took

their place in the first of them and drove off to St. James's.

In the King's closet the Queen embraced Victoria and whispered to her that she was not to be alarmed, because it was going to be a beautiful ceremony. The King kissed her too and said she looked pretty. How kind they both were! How she wished there was not always trouble between them and Mamma; and the older she grew the more she was inclined to blame Mamma for it—which was not a very *Christian* thing to do when she was so close to confirmation. I shall have to curb myself, she thought.

The family had assembled in some force for this very important occasion. The kind Duke of Cambridge with his pretty Duchess was there and she told Victoria that her son George was to be confirmed very shortly too. Both the Duke and Duchess of Cambridge were very anxious for her to like their son and she told them she did very much. The Duke of Cumberland, looking very sinister with his odd wicked face, watched her intently; she asked him about poor George and he told her that Victoria's visits to the beautiful blind boy were what he looked forward to more than anything. The Duke hoped she would spare the time to bring a little comfort into his son's life. And Victoria felt like weeping to think of being blind and unable to see the sun and the flowers—and even the Duke of Cumberland who was *not* a very charming sight.

The King had taken her hand and was leading her into the Chapel where she stood at the altar rail between him and her mother. She took off her bonnet and was bareheaded for the ceremony.

The Archbishop of Canterbury was very stern and after the ceremony he read aloud a warning to Victoria. Her life he said would be burdened by the most serious responsibilities. She must fulfil a destiny which would leave little time for pleasure.

He thundered on, warming to his subject; he was, thought Victoria, like a fearsome avenging angel. She was going to face great conflicts; her spiritual as well as her temporal life would be threatened. She would find her life no bed of roses . . . It sounded formidable, a future of misery.

She was trembling with horror at the prospect of it. Oh dear, she thought, if only Aunt Adelaide had had a child it would be different; I should have a pleasant happy confirmation, the sort that George Cambridge will doubtless have. As it was the future loomed before her, dark, gloomy, full of terrors. Her eyes had filled with tears and she had begun to weep.

Mamma at her side pressed her hand firmly, and she felt suddenly drawn to her and wanted to turn and fling her arms about that flamboyant figure and cry out: "Don't let me be Queen. Let them choose someone else."

Seeing the effect his address had had the Archbishop was satisfied and stopped as the King was looking impatient and was obviously about to tell him to bring his diatribe to an end.

"Well," William said, "that's done with." And he took Victoria into the closet with the Queen and the Duchess following.

He pressed her hand. "Priests!" he said. "Don't want to let them frighten you. Lot of *stuff*. You come and see what I've got for you. A nice present for a nice little girl."

"Oh, Uncle William," sobbed Victoria. "You *are* so kind."

That pleased him and in the closet he took up a set of jewellery; the emeralds glittered through her tears and she cried out that they were lovely.

"There, there, and you'll look very pretty in them. The Queen has something for you too."

The Queen's present was a tiara of matching emeralds.

"Dear kind Uncle William and Aunt Adelaide!"

Aunt Adelaide whispered that these ceremonies were very tiring and Victoria must not become too affected by them. If she was kind and good that was all she had to worry about, because everything would come right then; and she knew Victoria *was* kind and good, so it was not going to be so very difficult.

Victoria drove back to Kensington with the Duchess and wept a little on the latter's shoulder.

"You must learn to be a little more humble," said the Duchess. "You must listen and take advice, because now you are getting older you will most certainly have your duties. The Archbishop was trying to frighten you, but there is no need to be frightened because you have your mother beside you."

And for once there was some comfort in that.

Back at the Palace the Duchess had a present for her daughter. A bracelet containing a lock of her hair.

"Something very special to remind you of me," she said.

"I shall always remember this day, Mamma, when I look at this bracelet."

That was not the end of the excitement of that day. During the afternoon a messenger arrived from Langenberg.

The Duchess seized on the letter avidly and calling to Victoria cried: "Feodora has a little daughter. They are both well."

"Oh, what a happy day after all!" cried Victoria.

She was enchanted at the thought of having another niece; and the baby was to have her name too—Adelaide, Victoria, Mary, Louisa, Constance.

She could not be called Victoria, of course. That would be a little confusing. She would be known as Adelaide—a rather pleasant compliment to the Queen.

Victoria was wildly excited. It was the happiest of days because she had heard that Uncle Leopold was to pay a visit to England with his wife Aunt Louise, of whom Victoria had heard much and never seen.

Uncle Leopold could scarcely wait to clasp his darling Victoria in his arms and Victoria could scarcely wait to be clasped. For so many years they had been in touch only through letters, but their affection, they were often declaring to each other, had never waned. Leopold's letters had been full of advice for the future Queen of England, and again and again he expressed the hope that she would never cease to consult him. Hers had been full of gratitude and professions of her enduring love.

"And now the prospect of *seeing* him, Lehzen, makes me so happy that I can scarcely *bear* it."

"You must not get too excited," warned Lehzen. "We have to make the journey to Ramsgate, don't forget, and you wouldn't want to be upset and not ready to greet them,"

"What a terrible terible tragedy, dear Lehzen. But I will try not to get over-excited and think about the happiness which will be mine when I see my dearest Uncle."

A few days later the Duchess's party left Kensington for the leisurely journey to Ramsgate. Victoria was delighted to be in *dear* Tunbridge Wells which she had always enjoyed, but of course all the time she was eager to get on to Ramsgate for the arrival of Leopold and his wife.

They had taken a house overlooking the sea. It was small and unpretentious and the Duchess was angry because the King would not allow her to fly the Royal Standard. Victoria tried to soothe her mother.

"The King is right, I think, Mamma, because after all I am not the Queen."

The Duchess was so startled that Victoria should disagree with her that she had no words ready to reply and Victoria went on: "He hates what he calls my Royal Progresses and I do understand, because it makes it seem as though he is dead already and the last thing I want is Uncle William to die. He is always kind and it would upset dear Aunt Adelaide so."

"You talk like a child," said the Duchess angrily.

"Well, Mamma, you often tell me that I am one. But I do not think Uncle William was pleased with our last trip to the North."

"He is jealous . . . jealous of your youth and your popularity with the people. You must not allow yourself to be influenced by jealousy. You heard what the Archbishop said. You have a very difficult road ahead and if you are going to allow yourself to behave without dignity because of the jealousy of some people I can see you are soon going to be in trouble. You must be ambitious . . . in the most honourable way of course. And you must not give way."

But for all the Duchess's talk she dared not flout the King's authority and the Royal Standard was not flown over the house.

Such petty troubles, however, were forgotten with the arrival of Uncle Leopold and his wife. The streets of Ramsgate were decorated to greet him and Victoria received the usual acclaim in the streets.

"What an enchanting sight!" cried Victoria to Lehzen. "All the flowers and the flags . . . and to know that they are for dear Uncle Leopold, and the people are so glad to see him. And the sea looks so beautifully blue. I have always loved Ramsgate but I shall love it doubly now."

The Duchess said that they would see the arrival of the steamer better from the Albion Hotel than from the house and as it was so close she had not ordered the carriages; they would walk.

So accompanied by the Duchess, Lehzen, Lady Conroy and Lady Flora Hastings, Victoria set out for the hotel; and as they reached it she could see the steamer in the distance. Victoria found it difficult to control her impatience.

What excitement to sit at the window and wait for the steamer to arrive. Victoria saw it clearly, with the Belgian flag flying from its mast.

"You must control your excitement, Victoria," said the

Duchess sternly; but she was not really displeased; she liked Victoria to show appreciation of her Coburg relations of whom Uncle Leopold was the most important.

"I am trying, Mamma," replied Victoria."But it is so long since I have seen him."

"Four years," said the Duchess.

"Four years and two months," Victoria corrected her; and on that occasion the Duchess merely smiled to be corrected.

How the people were cheering! How pleasant it was to know that they appreciated Uncle Leopold! And so they should, for he had lived for a very long time in England and when he had married Princess Charlotte he had been very popular.

Then she remembered that he had a wife. She only hoped the new Aunt Louise was worthy of him. Perhaps that was expecting the impossible, but she did believe that Aunt Louise was a very good wife and that Uncle Leopold could not have done better.

The steamer had now entered the harbour and the cheers were deafening. Soon now she would be face to face with him.

"I cannot *bear* it if he has changed," she whispered to Lehzen.

There followed a quarter of an hour of acute suspense and one of the waiters came in and bowing to the Duchess said: "Your Grace, their Majesties are almost here."

They rose hastily to be at the door to greet them; and at last there was Uncle Leopold arm in arm with a very lovely lady whom Victoria knew at once was her Aunt Louise.

His eyes were searching for someone among the party. She knew who that was.

"Uncle Leopold!"

"My dearest love!"

They embraced; they looked at each other. "Oh," cried Victoria, "you have not changed at all except to become more handsome."

That pleased Leopold. He brought his Queen forward.

"You two must love each other."

"We do already," cried Victoria impulsively. "Oh, Uncle Leopold, dearest of all uncles, how happy I am to see you again."

The Duchess would not allow Victoria to monopolize the scene. *She* must be the centre and for a while she was; but Victoria found Uncle Leopold's eyes coming back to her;

she told Lehzen afterwards that she read *volumes* of love there which made her very *very* happy; and the years of separation were forgotten in this wonderful reunion.

Later there was time to make the acquaintance of Aunt Louise who was determined to charm Victoria since she was so important to Leopold.

Victoria was thinking of what pleasure she would have describing this scene in her Journal.

Aunt Louise had a slim and pretty figure and lovely fair hair; her nose was a little aquiline and her eyes a beautiful shade of blue. She wore a light-brown silk dress with a sky-blue bonnet and possessed that simple elegance which was to be expected of a Frenchwoman and the daughter of Louis Philippe. She was very pretty and what was even more important far from formidable. She seemed young and Victoria felt that she had lots of high spirits which were longing to bubble over, and if they could meet at a less ceremonious time they might do so for Victoria.

What an exciting meeting! On the way back to the house she chattered all the time to Lehzen about the charms of Uncle Leopold and his wife.

Uncle Leopold's visit was, alas, of short duration; but he was frequently in Victoria's company and contrived that they, should be alone.

What joy to go hand in hand along by the sea with Uncle Leopold; there they could not be interrupted so easily as when they were in the house.

"My love," he said to her when they were alone, on one of these occasions, "when I left, you were but a little girl. Now you are grown up. In two years you will be of age."

"Yes, Uncle, it sobers me to think of it."

"It is right that it should, for great responsibilities rest on the shoulders of Sovereigns."

"You must tell me how I can be a good Queen."

"I shall. I have made a study of royalty. Your cousin Ferdinand is betrothed to the Queen of Portugal and I have given him plenty of advice. You will meet him and his brother Augustus shortly, I hope. I want you to know your cousins."

"I *loved* Ernest and Alexander Württemberg."

"Very good boys. I shall be interested to hear what you feel about Ferdinand and his brother Augustus. But I particularly want you to like your cousins Ernest and Albert."

"What lots of boy cousins I have. There are the Georges on Papa's side too."

"Ah yes, but you will find your German cousins much more mature. My darling, *I* wish you to like them better than you do Cambridge and Cumberland."

"Then I am sure I shall . . . if only to please you."

"No, no, it must be to please yourself."

"Then I know I shall. You were going to tell me how to be a good Queen."

"Take advice from those whom you trust and are in a position to advise you."

"There is you, Uncle Leopold."

"Always," he said fervently.

"Apart from you there is no one." She hesitated; she realized that to go on would somehow be disloyal to Mamma.

But Uncle Leopold was insistent. "You must hold nothing back from me, my love."

"I do not wish to, Uncle, but . . ."

"Oh come, my darling. I want you to tell me everything . . . to be absolutely frank. You were going to say that there was no one whom you could trust but me. Was that so?"

"Yes. I was going to say that. There is Lehzen, of course, who is my dear *dear* friend, and I know that all her loyalty is for me. I was not thinking of Lehzen, for she would not advise me in the way you mean."

"Then you were thinking of your mother."

Victoria coloured hotly. "I love Mamma. I know she thinks constantly of my good."

"But?" insisted Leopold.

Victoria hesitated; then she blurted out: "But I think she listens too much to Sir John Conroy."

"Ah," said Uncle Leopold with a long-drawn-out sigh.

"I daresay I am wrong," began Victoria.

"I daresay you are right," said Leopold. "You may be absolutely frank with me, my darling. *I* understand. I know what is going on. You have to act with caution and discretion. Your position is an irksome one. I know it well. Try to accept it. It will not be for long. In two years' time, my child, you will be of age. Always remember that. Be prudent. You know that I am watching over you. Never be afraid to confide *all* in me. Be patient, my dearest love, and all will be well, you will see."

"Oh, Uncle, what comfort you bring me! When I think

it is only two more years I should be a little frightened if I did not know that you were there."

He pressed her hand, and told her that he had been looking forward so much to seeing her and he had not been disappointed. She was still his darling child. He now knew that she had lost none of her affection for him and that made him the happiest man in the world.

She was enchanted with Aunt Louise who was, after all, Leopold's wife. Leopold loved her; and Victoria must love all those whom Leopold wished her to. She must love her maternal cousins better than her paternal ones. But of course she would since they were closely related to Leopold. She had loved the Württemberg cousins very much; and she was prepared to love Ferdinand and Augustus—but best of all she must love Ernest and Albert because Uncle Leopold loved them and wanted her to do so, too.

Aunt Louise's English was fluent and her French accent pretty. She had such lovely clothes and Victoria was fascinated by them.

One day Aunt Louise took her up to her room and they tried on all her clothes which were very elegant having been made in Paris. Aunt Louise showed her how to wear them and they were large on Victoria—but not so very large, for Louise was slight and shorter than the Duchess.

"How pretty you will look in some lovely clothes!" cried Aunt Louise.

"I am always dressed like a little girl."

"That will not always be so. I will send you some clothes from France."

"Oh, Aunt Louise, how lovely. I wonder if Mamma will let me wear them! But of course she will, because Uncle Leopold will approve. I should so love to look like you, Aunt Louise. But I never shall because I am not so pretty."

"Nonsense, nonsense," said Louise. "We are as sisters . . . Ah, that is pleasant. We shall be sisters. Could you think of me as such?"

"Oh, Aunt Louise, I could, I could."

She was sober suddenly.

"What is wrong?" asked Louise.

"I was just thinking how sad and dull everything is going to be when you and Uncle Leopold have gone."

And the end of their visit was coming near, Victoria tried not to think of it, but it was impossible not to.

"I almost wish," she told Lehzen, "that it had not all been so perfect, then I should not be so sad."

"Come, come," said Lehzen. "You will see them again. They will visit you."

"They did not for more than four years."

"But your Uncle writes you lovely letters and your Aunt will now that you have met."

"I feel so sad," sighed Victoria. "I could weep."

"You must be gay for their last days."

But Victoria found this difficult. She had a headache and she felt sick.

She braced herself to be gay for the next few days; and when Leopold and Louise took their leave and she, with her party, saw the steamer with the Belgian flag sailing away, she could make no more attempts, and Lehzen taking her hand cried out in horror.

"How hot you are! I think you are letting this departure upset you too much."

"They have gone," sobbed Victoria. "It is all so *dull* without them."

"I should go to your room and lie down," said Lehzen. "I will sit with you."

Victoria felt too listless to disagree. She allowed Lehzen to lead her to bed and when she was there she sank into a sleep immediately.

In the morning she felt faint and sick and in great consternation the Duchess called in her doctor.

Within the next few days it was known that the Princess had an attack of typhoid fever.

An Intruder in the Bedroom

LEHZEN was in constant attention, snatching only a few hours sleep each night. The Duchess was unsparing of herself; Victoria was ill; all her hopes rested on this girl; Victoria must get well. She could not be submitted to ordinary nursing; Lehzen alone was to be trusted with the precious creature and between them the Duchess and the Baroness nursed Victoria.

All through those dark October days in Ramsgate Victoria lay in her bed—not aware of where she was or what was happening to her. Lehzen cut off her hair and wept to see the thin little face—so unlike her blooming charge's. The flushed face, over-bright eyes and incoherent babbling terrified her.

The climax of the illness came at length and with great relief the Duchess knew that it was only a matter of building up her daughter's strength and convalescence.

"She is scarcely recognizable," said the Duchess to Sir John. "This has been a sad fright for me."

"She'll recover. Our Princess has a very firm grip on life."

"Indeed she has. Poor Lehzen! She has not slept for nights but she's almost gay—if you could ever imagine Lehzen gay —now that she knows the worst is over. She hardly likes *me* to be in the sickroom. As if *I* would disturb her darling. I suppose I should be furious with the creature but I know it is only out of her devotion to Victoria that she behaves like a tigress with her cub."

"And whose cub is she?" asked Sir John with a smile. "Lehzen has too high a conceit of herself. I've always thought we could do without her."

The Duchess sighed. It was one matter over which she had had to stand out against Sir John. It was an indication too that Victoria already had some power; because both the Duchess and Sir John knew that to attempt to remove Lehzen would set Victoria completely against them; and there was no doubt that she would enlist the help of the King and Queen which would be readily given. In fact the King would like to take Victoria from Kensington and have her brought up in his household. A fine prospect, to have her running wild with the "bastidry" and indulged and pampered by the foolish Adelaide.

"Well," went on Sir John, "she is on the way to recovery now. And when I think that in less than two years she will be of age I am very apprehensive."

"Perhaps we concern ourselves too much."

"Most young people turn against those who have directed them in their youth—once they have escaped from that vigilance which has maintained them. I feel sure the Princess will be no exception."

"I shall see that she is!"

"She will be surrounded by those who seek places. I do think we should make sure that we are at hand to guide her. You as her mother will certainly be, but I think I should have some post which will ensure that I am at her side."

"What post do you want?"

"I think if I were her private secretary I could look after her, and you, my dearest Duchess, could be sure of seeing all important documents that came into our hands."

"Then you must be her private secretary."

"She of course will be the one to decide on whom to bestow the post."

"Then I say she *shall* bestow it on you."

"She will know that it is in her power to refuse; and she may go to the King."

The Duchess looked angry. "Disobedience . . ."

"Remember, my dear Grace, that she will be of age and the Queen. She will no longer be your dependent little girl. We have to go carefully."

"I do hope she is not going to prove *ungrateful*."

"I will speak to her, while she is feeble, and try to persuade her. There is a change in her. She will be less arrogant, more amenable on her sickbed."

The Duchess nodded.

"So I have your Grace's consent to make this request to her?"

"But of course. And it is, like all your plans an excellent one."

There were long shadows in the room. She was supposed to be sleeping. Beside her bed Lehzen sat dozing. Poor Lehzen who refused to go to bed and must be on call day and night for her Princess. Victoria had seen her often sitting by the bed when her eyes refused to stay open; and Victoria smiled when she actually slept.

She thought: This is the nearest I have ever been to being alone.

She watched poor Lehzen now—the piece of needlework fallen from her hands, her head lolling forward. Dear Lehzen, let her rest.

I have been very ill, thought Victoria. Indeed, she felt very weak and quite hazy. Only this morning when she had awakened she had not been sure where she was. How glad she would be to be back in Kensington. It seemed years ago that Uncle Leopold and Aunt Louise were here. When she had looked at herself in the mirror which she had insisted on Lehzen's bringing to her, she scarcely recognized herself—she was so pale and her eyes looked so big and protuberant; and her hair . . . which used to be so thick was now thin and lifeless.

Lehzen had assured her that it would soon grow thick again.

She felt so tired—too tired to think of how old she was getting and that she would soon meet some more cousins from Germany whom Uncle Leopold was so anxious for her to like.

She half dozed and then awoke with a start, for the door of the room had quietly opened and someone was standing there.

She wanted to scream for in her weakened state it seemed to her that evil had entered the room. He stood smiling at her—bold and wicked, for she was sure he was wicked—with that half-sneering smile on his face. Sir John Conroy, the man whom she had hated, had come into her bedroom and she was unprotected, for Lehzen, worn out with exhaustion, was fast asleep in her chair and she herself, weakened by her serious illness, was unable to do anything but stare at him in fascinated horror.

He put his fingers to his lips and, glancing at the sleeping

Lehzen in a way which angered Victoria, he came closer to the bed and sat down on it on the opposite side from that at which Lehzen sat.

"What . . . do you want?" stammered Victoria.

"To speak to you," he whispered.

"Not here . . . in my bedroom."

He laughed softly—that beastly laugh which she hated.

"It's as good a place as any and you happen to be here."

"I am not strong enough to receive visitors. Lehzen will tell you . . ."

He laughed again in contempt of Lehzen. "I'm not an ordinary visitor, am I?"

That was true. He was certainly not like the Queen or the Duchess of Cambridge or poor old Aunts Sophia, Augusta or Mary. She did not feel well enough to see them, but at least they would come with the kind purpose of cheering her up. This man was sinister.

"I am tired," said Victoria.

He laid a hand on hers which made her shiver.

"Then we will settle our little business quickly."

"Yes, please," she said pointedly.

"My dear Princess, I want you to make me a solemn promise."

"I should want to know first what you are asking me to promise."

"You are going to need a great deal of help in a few years time. You will need someone you can trust to be at hand. A position which will be of the greatest importance will be that of your private secretary. I want you to give me your solemn promise now that when you are Queen that post shall be mine."

"I can give no promises," said Victoria.

"My dearest Princess, you are very weak at the moment . . ."

"And in no condition to be approached about such matters."

"There is a certain urgency."

"I see no urgency."

"You have to prepare yourself for something which could happen at any moment."

"I shall be prepared."

"You do not understand these things. You are a young and charming girl whose thoughts are taken up with pretty clothes from Paris."

"I can give my attention to other matters when it is necessary."

"It is necessary now. Just say the word. That is all I ask. Your solemn promise. And I will draw up a paper to which you can put your signature . . . It will all be so easy."

"No," she said firmly. And then: "Lehzen. Wake up, Lehzen."

Lehzen opened her eyes and stared at Sir John who continued to perch jauntily on the Princess's bed.

"What are you doing here?" demanded Lehzen.

"Madam?" replied Sir John with the utmost haughtiness as though to ask how a mere governess could dare to speak to him—the Duchess's adviser and friend—in such a manner.

"I feel so tired," said Victoria.

"The Princess is not well enough to receive visitors," declared Lehzen, getting up and dropping her sewing on to the floor.

"Except members of the household, of course," said Sir John, "and I am in that category."

"I think you should leave now."

"I intend to have a word or two with the Princess first."

"The Princess will see you when she is well."

"This is important business, Madam. The Duchess and I have decided it cannot wait."

"I cannot have the Princess disturbed."

"The Duchess's orders are that she is to receive me."

Victoria sat forward; her head was swimming but her eyes were brilliant with defiance. "I shall myself decide," she said, "whether or not I shall receive visitors. The Baroness has asked you to leave."

"Oh come," said Sir John, "all this excitement about such a little matter. We don't want a storm over a friendly visit."

"I have told you that I do not wish to receive," said Victoria. "And no matter how much you talk I shall not appoint *you* as my private secretary."

"So that is what it means," said Lehzen.

"Yes, Lehzen," replied Victoria, "and I wish to rest. Goodbye, Sir John."

Sir John's eyes were angry, his mouth tight. He looked as though he would like to murder Lehzen; but she stood still glaring at him while Victoria pretended to shut her eyes but they were only half closed; she wanted to see Sir John go.

He saw that there was nothing more that he could do then, so he bowed abruptly and went out.

When he had gone Victoria cried: "Oh, Lehzen, I *hate* that man."

"Thé craftiness!" said Lehzen. "And I was asleep."

"You are worn out with nursing me, dear Lehzen. And I only had to call you. I am so glad I was *strong*. At one moment I felt I would say anything to get rid of him."

"So he was trying to make you promise to have him beside you when you are Queen?"

"That was it, Lehzen. I never would. Once I am able to make my decisions my first will be to get rid of that man. Sit down, Lehzen. Take up your sewing. He has gone now. Let us be cosy again. But the thought of him lingers, doesn't it?"

She put out a hand and Lehzen took it.

"Dear, dear Lehzen, who takes such good care of me. Oh, how I hate him! There is something evil about him."

She could not forget him; she would wake in the night because she had dreamed that he had come into the room.

As she grew stronger the dreams were less frequent. Lehzen said that if she took the nourishing food she prepared and rested and allowed Lehzen to take very good care of her she would soon be well.

It was not until January that they returned to Kensington Palace. It had been a bitterly cold journey, and after spending a night at Sittingbourne they arrived at Kensington in the early afternoon.

The Duchess took Victoria's hand and with Lehzen hovering showed her the new apartments which would now be hers.

"The others," said the Duchess, "were far too small. Most unbecoming. Now that you are convalescent you need more airy rooms."

"But it is quite magnificent, Mamma."

The Duchess snorted. "I think sometimes that old buffoon at the Brunswick Hotel forgets that you are a Queen."

"But I am not, and if I were it would mean that he were dead. Poor Uncle William. I hope he will live for many years."

The Duchess grunted. She was a little unsure of her daughter since Sir John had reported on that rather alarming scene in the bedroom. They had to remember that she was growing up. She would be seventeen this year and she was well aware of her importance. It would not be possible to command her now—only to arouse her sense of loyalty and persuade her what she must do out of gratitude in the future for those who in the past had done so much for her.

"It is very kind of His Majesty to give us these lovely rooms," went on Victoria, at which the Duchess laughed.

Victoria went into the bedroom (which she was to share with the Duchess) and admired its lofty ceiling, its spaciousness and the pleasant furniture. It was a great improvement on the old room.

"Seventeen rooms!" she cried. "Why, Mamma, what a lot of space we shall have."

"There is a sitting-room for you and a study. Lehzen can have our old bedroom."

"She will like that," said Victoria, flushing with pleasure in anticipation of Lehzen's.

"I venture to think," said the Duchess, "that these apartments are a little more worthy of the future Queen."

Victoria could not wait to hear what Lehzen thought of the changes; but Lehzen was clearly more interested in getting Victoria strong.

"You'll have to get back your appetite. Dr. Clark said you must eat more bread and butter and I shall myself cook you some nice boiled mutton and make some orange jelly."

"Oh, Lehzen, you have this pleasant bedroom and you talk of boiled mutton and orange jelly."

"You're a little wraith and nothing more," scolded Lehzen.

"I used to be rather plump, didn't I? And look at my hair. There's scarcely any of it. You remember how thick it used to be."

"It'll be thick again and you'll soon be plump. You just trust Lehzen."

And Victoria threw herself into Lehzen's arms. "I do," she said. "I do trust you . . . more than anyone in this Palace I trust you."

Then she felt guilty of disloyalty to the Duchess and so did Lehzen for listening. But they hugged each other and understood; for it was true.

The Cumberland Plot

✦ THE DUCHESS of Cumberland, considerably softened since the blindness of her son, was worried. She knew what was going on in her husband's restless mind. He was not the man to see his plans frustrated and meekly accept that; and she knew that until Victoria was firmly on the throne he would be considering means of preventing her reaching it.

He still confided in her although he was fully aware of her resignation. She had said that if only George's sight could be restored to him she would ask nothing else of life. Her mother-love had subdued her ambition and he was not sure whether or not he admired her for this. He missed the scheming woman he had married; but he was glad to find the devoted mother. He too cared only for the two of them—wild Frederica whose past had been as devious as his own, and young George whom blindness seemed to be turning into a saint.

But he was not going to give up his ambitions.

"Ernest," said the Duchess to him one January morning when Victoria was still by the sea recovering from her attack of typhoid fever, "why don't you accept what life has given you? You will find the kingdom of Hanover very much to your taste."

"My taste is for a larger kingdom."

"I know, but a small one is better than none."

"Do you think I should stand aside and let that woman govern England, for that is what she will do if Victoria is Queen."

"How can you do anything else but stand aside?"

"I am not without influence."

"Are you thinking of the Orange Lodges?"

"Of course I am thinking of the Orange Lodges. My hopes

lie with them. There are 145,000 men in England who would be ready to spring to arms to defend the Protestant cause."

"But the King is not a Catholic."

"He is very friendly with Mrs. Fitzherbert."

The Duchess laughed. "Oh come, Ernest, you can scarcely expect me to be taken in by such talk. You know there is no danger of England's becoming Catholic and your Orangemen need not leap to her defence. Why not admit the truth . . . that you are ready to fight to wrest the throne from William . . . or at least to take over on his death?"

"You know what this means. Victoria is too young to rule; that mother of hers—that nuisance of a Duchess—would be virtually ruler of England. The country would rise up and call blessed one who averts such a calamity. Victoria . . . a minor. That woman Regent."

"William is not dead yet."

"No, but he's half way to madness they say. He'll have to be put away sooner or later like his father."

"Ernest, you must be careful. You have suffered a certain amount of notoriety. The country would not welcome civil war."

"When the people saw that it put a real King on the throne they would think it worth while."

"How much better if William appointed you his heir."

"How can he? That girl comes next. We ought to have the Salic law in this country. Women should be excluded from the throne."

"At least, she won't have Hanover."

"Hanover. Who would not barter Hanover for England?"

"But you cannot have England while Victoria lives."

The Duke narrowed his eyes. Is it true, wondered the Duchess, that if he had an opportunity he would murder Victoria? A fearful thought but the girl meant nothing to him but an impediment that barred his way to ambition. The Duchess shivered. Ernest would go too far if he attempted to remove Victoria, who was already winning popularity. If she suddenly died of some mysterious illness Ernest would be suspected. Oh, why had her darling boy had to have this terrible accident! If he had not been stricken with blindness and had married Victoria Ernest might have been satisfied.

But now he was extremely dissatisfied and she was afraid of what he would do. He had these men ready to follow him. Besides the English there were 125,000 men in Ireland.

It was to have such an army at his command that he had joined the Lodge and become its Grand Master. There was no end to his ambition.

"This country needs a strong man," he said. "Any means to bring him to the throne should be employed."

"Any means, Ernest?"

"Any means," he repeated firmly.

"She is quite a pleasant creature—Victoria."

"She is a child, governed by that impossible nuisance of a woman. Anything is permissible which would prevent Madam Kent having a hand in government."

The Duchess said: "Remember . . ."

And he knew what she meant. Some years ago he had had a plan to get rid of Victoria; he had wanted her at Windsor where he was living at that time in the household of George IV; and he had set rumours in motion that the child was a weakling, not expected to live. But her mother had foiled that by parading the child in the park—"plump as a partridge," as it had been said, glowing with health. His schemes had reacted on himself and sinister rumours had again surrounded him.

It would be unpleasant if the rumours that he was planning to murder Victoria were started up again.

He avoided his Duchess's eye. He said: "I am commanded to dine with the King at Windsor. He is not well." He laughed rather unpleasantly. "Every time I see William I wonder how much longer he can live . . ."

"Out of a strait-jacket?"

"I was thinking of the grave."

"Poor William. I'd rather the grave than the strait-jacket."

"I think that was what our father always thought—but he had both. And if William doesn't die soon it'll be the same for him. He would have been put away by now but for Adelaide."

"I don't think we consider Adelaide enough. She's much less insignificant than is generally believed."

"It's true, but once William has gone she will have no significance whatsoever. I don't concern myself with Adelaide. It's Victoria I have to think about. That chit should be set aside. A girl . . . what good is a girl to a country that needs a strong man?"

"People might recall Queens Elizabeth and Anne."

"Bah!" said the Duke. "They weren't brought up by the Duchess of Kent."

"It is time you left for Windsor," said the Duchess. "And, Ernest . . . have a care."

The old fellow was certainly looking ill, thought Cumberland. And the Queen was a poor thing, too.

"She works too hard," said the King. "And her cough's troublesome."

"She must take greater care of herself," replied Cumberland.

Adelaide wanted to know how young George was.

"He is unchanged," said his father; and the Queen's eyes filled with tears.

"Is there nothing that can be done?"

"If Graefe can do nothing, nobody can."

"Poor, poor George! I know how the Duchess suffers."

Cumberland thought: This is not like a royal court. William has no idea of kingliness and Adelaide is too domesticated. She means well but what a travesty of royalty.

He began to think of how different it would be when he was King. It was so easy to enrage people. They hated Adelaide already. If he could make them believe that there was a danger of that poor old dotard William's turning Catholic, his coup would succeed in a few days—weeks at the most. As for Victoria . . . she might be agreeable to stand aside. What did a chit of a girl want with a throne?

The King said it was time to go in to dinner and in his usual informal way he went among his guests exchanging greetings with them as though he were some country squire rather than the Sovereign of a great country.

Surely, thought Cumberland, these people must be laughing at him behind his back. Surely they would be pleased to see a real monarch on the throne.

After the meal, Ernest as the King's brother proposed the royal toast. He noticed that those assembled drank it without a great deal of enthusiasm. This made Ernest daring. He would make an experiment; he would see what the reaction would be.

He rose and raising his glass cried in a loud voice: "The King's heir, God bless him."

William stared at him, his face growing red with sudden anger. He had heard the rumours; he knew what an ambitious man his brother Cumberland was. Did he think he was going to do away with tradition? Did he think that he was going to sweep away the true heir to the throne? William could not abide the Duchess of Kent; in fact he hated the woman more than he hated anyone; but that did not mean that her daughter was not the rightful heir.

He stood up and lifting his glass and glaring at his brother he cried: "The King's heir, God bless *her*."

For a few dramatic seconds the two brothers stared at each other. Cumberland was very well aware that the company was with the King, and that he had committed a major error in betraying his ambitions so blatantly.

This affair of Cumberland's toast was widely discussed in political and Court circles.

The Duchess realized that her husband had once more through his impetuous conduct spoiled his own game. So it had been when he had set rumours in motion about Victoria's health. It had been so easy to refute these by parading the child. If he had wished to woo the public he should not have accumulated such a fearful reputation, so that the world was ready to believe the worst of him.

What did Cumberland mean by such a toast? The King's heir, God bless *him*. It could only mean one thing—that he believed that the Princess Victoria was either going to die or be deposed. This was a man who had been suspected of murder. What did it mean?

A certain Joseph Hume, a careful Scotsman who had risen from somewhat humble origins—his mother had kept a crockery stall in Montrose—and who was a man of great energy and determination, decided that this was a good opportunity to attack the Orange Society. Hume, whose mother's hard work had enabled him to become a surgeon, had later gone into Parliament and had called attention to himself by exposing abuses.

He had long been aware that the Orange Lodges were a menace, and considering the association of the Duke of Cumberland with them he believed that they were to be used in an endeavour to change the succession. He decided to raise a question in the House of Commons regarding the purpose of the Orange Lodges and the Duke of Cumberland's connection with them.

So once again the Duke's hasty action had foiled his own plans.

He immediately capitulated. He declared that the rumours

concerning him and his motives were entirely false. He had never thought of changing the succession. Such a thing, he declared, was impossible. He could not understand how such rumours had started.

Shoulders were shrugged. They knew their Duke. Was he not the Grand Master of the Orange Lodges?

"No longer," he declared, "for I have resigned that post."

The Government decided that as a safety measure the Orange Lodges should be disbanded; and to show his innocence no one was more indefatigable in bringing about their dissolution than His Grace of Cumberland.

Frederica sighed. How much wiser, she thought, to resign oneself. He would in due course be King of Hanover. She would be rather pleased to go back to Germany; and their dear blind boy would follow his father on that throne. Life would be more peaceful; Ernest would enjoy it more when he had ceased to scheme for something which could not be his.

Some Coburg Cousins

HOW pleasant it was to be back in Kensington and well enough to return to the well-tried routine.

"I so missed the times when my hair was being done and we did our reading," said Victoria. "Oh dear, what a lot of time I have wasted."

"You can soon catch up on your reading," soothed Lehzen, "and if you do all Dr. Clark and I tell you you will soon be strong again."

"And my hair will grow thick and my cheeks pink again," said Victoria with a smile. "And it will be wonderful to go to the opera again and perhaps see a play. I am longing to go back to my own singing lessons."

"You know the doctor said you were not to strain yourself."

"I know, but I believe that pleasure is good for the health and singing gives me pleasure."

Lehzen smiled and Victoria picked up the Irish history from which she was reading aloud.

Later that day the Duchess sent for her; she was in a very good mood, Victoria noticed.

"I have here a letter from your Uncle Leopold."

Victoria's eyes shone at the mention of that beloved name.

"We're to have visitors. Your Uncle Ferdinand is coming to stay with us and he is bringing his two sons with him. Your cousin Ferdinand is on his way to Lisbon."

"I know that he is betrothed to the Queen of Portugal. How strange, Mamma. She is about my age and she is already a widow."

"You would not surely wish to be the same."

Victoria laughed at the idea, and then she was serious. "Oh no, but I suppose I might think that I may soon be a wife."

"It is something you will be made aware of when the time comes." Victoria looked a little sullen and the Duchess went on: "I am sure your Uncle Leopold would say the same."

At the mention of his name the sullen look passed as the Duchess knew it would. It was a little exasperating that after all she had done she must come after Leopold. Of course she trusted Leopold to look after the family affairs—but this adoration for him was a little childish. Sir John had said that Victoria was apt to be a little too whole-hearted in her devotion to some and her dislike of others. It must be watched.

"We shall entertain my brother Ferdinand and his two sons. I am sure you will like Ferdinand and Augustus and be a good hostess to them."

"Oh yes, Mamma, I shall do my best; and I know I shall love them as I did my Württemberg cousins."

"There is a letter for you from your uncle."

"Oh, thank you, Mamma."

"Are you not going to open it?"

"I think I will read it in my sitting-room."

The Duchess frowned but said nothing and Victoria went out clutching the letter to where Lehzen was waiting to conduct her to her sitting-room.

She opened the letter with that slight tremor of the hands which the dear handwriting always aroused in her. As usual Uncle Leopold assured her of his undying devotion to his "dear soul." He wanted her to like her cousins who would be shortly paying her a visit. They were charming young men;

she would find them both good-looking and clever. They were a little "new in the world." New in the world! what a *wonderful* expression and how apt and how like Uncle Leopold to explain so *exactly* that she understood immediately. They were not worldly young men; she was glad of that; she would like them the better for it.

Uncle Leopold went on to say that he hoped she would have a visit from two more cousins very shortly. These she would admire even more. He was sure of it because he knew his dear little soul. He wanted her to like these two Coburg cousins even better than Ferdinand and Augustus whom of course she would like very much. Ernest and Albert would be coming later in the year. Uncle Leopold was very fond of them and he naturally wanted her to be the same. He hoped she would like Albert particularly.

Of course she would. She was determined to like whomsoever Uncle Leopold wished her to.

The Saxe-Coburg cousins, Ferdinand and Augustus, arrived with their father Ferdinand, and how charming they were and how exciting it was to have such guests! There was so much to show them, so much to talk about and how attentive they were to their young cousin!

Victoria loved her Uncle Ferdinand; with her father's relatives there always seemed to be some conflict, but this was not so with the Duchess's family. All was harmony and the Duchess herself softened considerably in their company. They were so proud of her because of the grand marriage she had made and the Duchess was pleased with herself too while she seemed to dislike or despise almost every member of the family into which she had married.

But Victoria was delighted with her German relations. How amusing the young men were with their German accents and their habit of shaking hands every time one met. They thought her clever and pretty and charming, so how could she help loving them?

Besides, they so admired Uncle Leopold and they saw a great deal of him and Aunt Louise. Ferdinand admitted that he loved Aunt Louise very much and that Uncle Leopold had been so wonderful to him teaching him how to be a good King when he reached Portugal and even laying down a set of rules for him.

"Uncle Leopold," cried Victoria, glowing with pride and

happiness, "is the wisest and most noble of Kings. Belgium was a poor little country when he took it over. Now it is of great consequence. He is an example to all. Oh, how lucky we are to have him."

Augustus said that when he next saw Uncle Leopold he would tell him what Victoria had said.

"My great regret," she went on, "is that I cannot be often in his company. His recent visit was so very short that the pain of losing him almost equalled the pleasure in seeing him —not quite, that is, for it was wonderful to see his dear face again."

They were such happy days; everyone was gay and seemed to love each other, and Victoria, whose young heart was so eager to love all her dear relations, to help the poor, to be kind and good was happier than she had been for a long time.

There came an invitation for the Duchess to bring their relations to Windsor.

Oh dear, thought Victoria, I do hope everything is going to be all right. Aunt Adelaide is so kind and so is the King; and yet the thought of a visit to the royal household filled her with apprehension.

Adelaide was worried about the King. He was very breathless and seemed to be suffering from more than his usual asthma. What worried her most, of course, was his peculiar behaviour. She was always terrified that he was going to say something outrageous to some important person and that it would be reported and get into the papers. He never seemed to think before he spoke; he often rambled on, and he would not give up the distressing habit of making long speeches. The disrespectful press delighted in caricaturing him—always with the same-shaped head which had been likened to a pineapple. "What could one expect from a man with a head like a pineapple," commented one anonymous writer. Although others compared the head with an egg—an addled one at that.

There were the dear grandchildren to comfort him. Thank God for them! thought Adelaide. He would listen to their childish troubles as though they were important matters of state and they did much for him. When they lived simply, shut away from affairs, William was like a normal grandfather —getting on in years, it was true, a little feeble, a little inclined to sudden outbursts of anger, but on the whole an ordinary man.

On one occasion he said: "Adelaide, how I wish we could get away somewhere in the country . . . you . . . myself . . . and the babies!"

Adelaide wished it too.

If only his children would be kinder to him! Who would have believed that Dorothy Jordan's sons could be so cruel and so acquisitive. It was not as though William had ever attempted to disown them; he had given them honours, but the more they had the more they seemed to want. Unnatural children indeed. George FitzClarence, the Earl of Munster, would not come to see his father because he considered he had been badly treated. Monster would be a better name than Munster, someone had said, and Adelaide was inclined to think there was something in this.

The King was very sad because he loved George dearly; he was constantly telling Adelaide how proud he and Dorothy had been of their eldest son. "What a little rascal, eh?" cried William. "I taught him how to use his fists when he was two. Dorothy doted on him. He was a good boy to her, too. It's since I've been King that everything has gone wrong."

Adelaide did her best to soothe him.

Lord Frederick FitzClarence was another son who had actually written abusively to his father in such terms, the King's secretary confided to the Queen, that he had decided against showing the letter to His Majesty and had answered it himself, for he feared that it could serve no useful purpose and would only upset the King when he was in one of his less healthful phases.

There were complaints also from Lord Augustus FitzClarence, who declared that the King did more for others than for his own sons.

The daughters were kinder, particularly Sophia, who had become Lady de l'Isle and Dudley. She with her family was constantly in the King's company and gave a great deal of comfort to him. She was one of the few FitzClarences who were kind to Adelaide, and the King was very fond of her. She had come to Windsor when Adelaide had left for the Continental trip and William declared he did not know what he would have done without her. But he mourned for the unkindness of his sons.

The Queen said to him, "Ferdinand has his two sons at Kensington."

"I know. That young boy's going to marry Maria de Gloria and be the King of Portugal. Leopold's spreading his relations all over Europe."

"I think Leopold is a very shrewd politician."

"A cunning fellow. Can't stand him. He never takes wine. Drinks water. I don't want people drinking water at my table."

"No, but he does seem to have plans for the Saxe-Coburg family."

"H'm. And bringing these young nephews over now. You know what he's after, don't you? He wants Victoria to marry one of her German cousins. Well, she is not going to. She's going to have George."

"I hope she will. George is such a darling."

"And all the time that woman does what she can to prevent their meeting."

"Well, Ferdinand is clearly not intended for her. I don't know about Augustus; but I think it's the other cousins Leopold has his eye on—Ernest and Albert."

"If he tries to bring those fellows over here I shall forbid them to enter the country."

"Oh, William, can you do that?"

The King's eyes bulged. "I'm the King."

It was better not to pursue that. "I suppose," said Adelaide, "that we must ask Ferdinand and his sons to Windsor."

"I don't want them here."

"I know, William, but I believe it is expected of us. You forget sometimes how important your invitations are."

"You're right, my dear. You always are. Let's have them, but if that woman starts her capers in my Castle . . ."

"We will try to make it an enjoyable visit."

The King nodded dismally. "A pity we can't ask Victoria without her mother and that man . . . I won't have him in the Castle, Adelaide. She can entertain her lover elsewhere."

"We are not sure that Conroy is her lover."

"N . . . no," agreed the King. "She's a cold-hearted vixen."

"Well, I shall see that the invitations are sent out. It will be a very short visit."

The King nodded and went off to finish his letter to George FitzClarence which he hoped would help close the rift between them.

"My affection for yourself and all your brothers and sisters is, and ever will be, unaltered; and the only difference which has risen between you and me has been that you have not considered that I have a double duty to perform as King and father. Whenever you feel inclined to return to my roof, the Castle at Windsor, the Pavilion at Brighton and the Palace at St. James's will be opened to you and yours with perfect satisfaction on my part. God bless you, and I ever remain, dearest George.

Your most truly affectionate father,

William R."

Adelaide was determined that the visit should not be marred by discord between the King and the Duchess. Ferdinand and Augustus were two charming young men and there was no difficulty about entertaining them. William received them kindly; and there was no doubt that he was delighted with Victoria. There was something so fresh about her, so affectionate that it was impossible not to be fond of her. The King wanted to make it very clear that his quarrel with Kensington did not extend to his young niece.

He took her hand and led her into dinner; the Duchess of Kent walked on the other side of him but he did not look at her. It was arranged that Victoria should sit between William and George Cambridge—which, Adelaide had said, will give the young people a chance to talk together and discover how very charming they are. It was also significant of the royal wishes.

Victoria liked George Cambridge, but she had known him for a long time and he was not as new and fascinating as her German cousins.

"Are you looking forward to the ball, eh, my dear?" asked the King.

"Oh yes, Uncle William," cried Victoria. "I love to dance."

"So you should. You should dance more. The Queen's always saying to me: 'We'll give a ball for Victoria.'"

"I *love* the Queen's balls, Uncle. Aunt Adelaide always gives the best parties."

"She knows what young people like." His eyes were filled with tears and so were Victoria's for she knew that he was thinking how sad Aunt Adelaide was because she had no children.

After dinner Victoria danced three quadrilles—the first with Ferdinand as he was the guest; and then with George

Cambridge and after that with Augustus.

She wrote in her Journal: "I stayed up until one. I was much amused and pleased."

The visit was a brief one. Young Ferdinand must go to Portugal to celebrate his marriage to the little widowed Queen, and Victoria must say good-bye to them.

"How very sad," said Victoria, while her hair was being done and the book from which she was reading lay unopened before her.

Lehzen said that there would be other visits.

"I look forward to them. I am very fortunate to have such *good* cousins. The more I know Ferdinand the more I like him. He is so sensible, so natural and unaffected, so unsophisticated and so truly *good*."

"And Augustus?"

"I love him too. He is so distinguished-looking and unaffected. He is so amiable and quiet and gentle."

"They have certainly made an excellent impression," replied Lehzen.

"How I wish they were not going so soon! You know, Lehzen, I think Ferdinand more handsome than Augustus. There is something quite beautiful in his expression. I think he is superior to Augustus and more advanced for his age."

If, thought Lehzen, he were not going to marry the Queen of Portugal and they had wished him to be Victoria's husband, they would have had little difficulty in persuading her to take him. She was so ready to love and be loved.

"Let us get on with the book or we shall miss our reading," said Lehzen.

Dear Albert

✿ THE cousins had left. How she missed them! There was no one to dance with.

"You must never dance with anyone who is not royal," said the Duchess, which meant a dearth of partners. But with her cousins Victoria could dance round the schoolroom at any moment of the day when she was free. She could ride and walk with her cousins; she could show them her drawings; they could help her seal letters, which they did, and it seemed a great joke when Augustus burned a letter during the process. Everything seemed gay and amusing when shared with them.

And when they had gone she felt that she had stepped back into captivity. It was the old routine, never to be left alone, always supervised.

She was now openly showing her hostility to Sir John who was growing very uneasy and seeking to placate her; she believed she disliked his oily hypocrisy more than the sneers of the past.

She would never forget that moment when he had come to stand by her bedside and almost forced her to do what he wanted. She had written and told Uncle Leopold who was most shocked and did not feel so kindly as he had once towards Sir John. With the support of Uncle Leopold she felt bolder. A certain coolness had crept into her attitude towards her mother. After all, she was growing up. She was just over a year from independence, and the Duchess and Sir John knew that if they did not get the Regency set up and Victoria in leading strings before her eighteenth birthday they never would.

The Duchess sent for her daughter. She still sent for her but whenever she received a summons Victoria thought: "It will not be for long. Very soon *I* shall be sending for people."

"My dear child," said the Duchess, who called Victoria "child" frequently in the hope that by so doing she could ignore that fast-approaching eighteenth birthday, "you miss your cousins sadly, I know."

"Yes, Mamma, I do."

"Well, here is a letter from your Uncle Leopold. He suggests that I invite our brother Ernest's sons to Kensington."

"Ernest and Albert?" asked Victoria. "Uncle Leopold has already mentioned them."

The Duchess inclined her head. "I have already sent an invitation." Her smile was a little coy and Victoria guessed what this meant. After all, Uncle Leopold had hinted at it.

The visit of these two cousins was more important than any other because one of these boys could be her future husband.

"You will greatly enjoy their visit," said the Duchess as though this was an order; and Victoria was too excited to feel resentful.

"I'm sure I shall, Mamma," she said; and a pleasant little refrain started up in her head and would not be dismissed. "Albert or Ernest—Ernest or Albert."

Feodora, happy in her Langenburg Castle, wrote loving letters to Victoria which bubbled over with cosy domesticity. Marriage was clearly a desirable state, thought Victoria— happy marriage that was. There was Feodora with her drawing and painting, her reading, her devoted husband and her growing family whose little ways were so lovable and diverting.

Her life was dull, she wrote, compared with that of Victoria, but she was very happy. The two eldest children had just paid their first visit to the theatre. They had been so excited that they had laughed merrily all the time and the audience had been more diverted by them than what was happening on the stage. The babies were well and merry and content and they talked often of their Aunt Victoria. Of course Feodora discussed this aunt constantly and the children felt that they knew her. They were very interested in all she used to do and quite consoled that sometimes she was just a little naughty. In fact they liked the stories of Victoria's bad behaviour better than her good. Perhaps because those stories were so rare.

And now she had the news that their two Coburg cousins were coming to Kensington. Victoria would like them, she was sure, even more than Ferdinand and Augustus. They were more *manly* in Feodora's opinion; she was very fond of them both.

"Ernest is my favourite, although Albert is much more handsome and cleverer too, but Ernest is honest and good natured. I shall be very curious to hear your opinion of them."

Victoria read and re-read the letter.

So Feodora preferred Ernest. But she loved them both.

"I shall use my own judgment," she told herself resolutely; but in her heart she knew Albert would be favourite with her because that was what Uncle Leopold wished.

"So," cried the King in fury, "she's bringing these Coburgs over. That water-drinking fellow has arranged this! They know I want her for George Cambridge so they bring over these Coburgs."

"Do sit down, Papa," said Sophia. "You are getting far too upset."

"Upset. That woman is enough to upset anybody. I'll send her back where she belongs. She can leave Victoria to Adelaide. Adelaide will look after her better than that feathered vixen."

"She is her mother, dear," said Adelaide gently.

"More's the pity. I won't have those young fellows here. They seem to forget I'm the King. Why should I have these foreigners in my kingdom when I have no wish to? They're not going to be asked to Windsor. They're not even coming to England."

Lady de l'Isle and Dudley exchanged glances with the Queen. When he was in this mood it was better to let him work out his fury rather than frustrate him. Later, between them, they would persuade him that it would be a major affront to a foreign power to refuse the Princes of Saxe-Coburg admittance to England.

In his heart he knew it; but he was disappointed. He liked young people. He had no heir of his own body; he would have enjoyed fathering Victoria. He liked the girl. He wanted to have her here in his household like his daughter. That would have been pleasant. They could have been seen more together. The King and the heiress to the throne! It was what the people wanted; it was good for the Monarchy. But that woman at Kensington had spoilt everything.

He went on at length about his intended refusal to permit the landing in England of the Saxe-Coburg Princes. Victoria was going to have George Cambridge. A nicer boy there could not be. He would rather see her married to blind George Cumberland—a charming fellow if ever there was one and a boy who had overcome his handicap. Why shouldn't he be the Queen's consort? "No reason," said the King. "No reason at all."

Then he laughed. "I've only got to live a little longer, Adelaide, and that child will be eighteen. Once she is, that mother of hers will have no power over her whatsoever. It's clear what I've got to do. I've got to live till after Victoria's eighteenth birthday."

"It's only next year, William, and you've got years ahead of you."

"I'm a sick old man, Adelaide. But I am going to do everything in my power to foil that woman. She is never going to be Regent of this country. I am going to see Victoria Queen . . . then I'll die. Not before."

At length Adelaide succeeded in persuading him that he could not forbid the Saxe-Coburgs to come to England. He then devised another plan.

It made him laugh so much he almost choked.

"I'll tell you what I'll do, Adelaide . . . and I've done it. I didn't want you persuading me. You're too good a woman, Adelaide. That Kent woman is a she-wolf and you're too good to know it. Time and time again you've smoothed things over for her. I know. You've shielded her. You've kept me from knowing. That's what you've done. Well, now I'll tell you what *I've* done. I've invited the Prince of Orange and his son over. They'll be here the same time as those Coburgs. That will put their German noses out of joint."

"But you don't like the Oranges overmuch."

"But the Water Drinker will *think* I do. He'll be in a panic. He'll think young Orange has been brought over for Victoria."

"But it's our George . . . George Cambridge who is to have Victoria."

"Of course it is. But let Leopold think it's going to be young Orange. That'll shake him. That'll make him see that I won't have him interfering in my Kingdom."

So there was nothing the Queen could do. At least she

had averted a major quarrel with the Saxe-Coburgs; and now
she would do her best to entertain the Oranges without
alienating the Saxe-Coburgs and the Duchess of Kent.

When Leopold heard that the Prince of Orange and his
son had been invited to England he was furious. This was a
double insult. There had always been an uneasy relationship
between himself and the Prince of Orange, for Orange had
been one of the Princess Charlotte's suitors. She had rather
brusquely jilted him and when Leopold arrived had fallen
passionately in love with him. It was something which made
Orange regard the King of the Belgians with a certain pique.

And to invite him at the same time as Leopold's protégés
were in England was, Leopold considered, an insult to himself.

Leopold had long decided that the husband for Victoria
was Albert of Saxe-Coburg-Gotha. Albert was his protégé as
Victoria was. Leopold's great hobby was the guiding and
directing of his young relations. He was not only a King but a
maker of Kings and Queens. He had written a treatise on how
to govern for young Ferdinand; he had tutored Victoria since
she was a child; and he had been equally watchful of Albert.

Albert was three months younger than Victoria—a baga-
telle, said Leopold. They were of an age.

Albert had taken to Leopold when he was a little fellow
just over a year old. His enormous blue eyes had regarded his
uncle with adoration; he had shown his pleasure to be near
him and had constantly put his arms about his uncle's neck
and kissed him. This was gratifying to Leopold who greatly
desired the adoration of the young members of his family.

After the divorce between Albert's parents, Leopold had
felt himself to be even more the boys' guardian and had kept
in constant touch with him as he had with Victoria. He was
determined on a marriage between his nephew and niece;
everything told him that they were ideally suited; moreover,
they both turned to him naturally and that would mean that
when Victoria was Queen and Albert her consort there
would be no diversity of opinion between them, for they had
both been brought up to trust and adore Uncle Leopold.

Some time before he arranged for the cousins to meet,
Leopold had sent his friend and physician, Baron Christian
Friedrich von Stockmar, to Albert. Leopold trusted Stockmar
more than any man he knew; and he wanted his opinion of

Albert and for him to be with Albert to advise him in the difficult role which Leopold had chosen for him.

The Baron at this time was some fifty years old; he was a native of Coburg, and had been in Leopold's service even before his marriage to the Princess Charlotte. Stockmar was no respecter of persons, no seeker after favours. He was just the man on whom Leopold could rely in the delicate task of bringing these two young people together.

His report on Albert was encouraging:

> "He is a fine young fellow," he wrote to Leopold, "well grown for his age and with agreeable and valuable qualities; and who, if things go well, may in a few years turn out a strong handsome man of a kindly, simple yet dignified demeanour. Externally, therefore, he possesses all that pleases the sex, and at all times and in all countries must please. It may prove too a lucky circumstance, that even now he has something of an English look."

Very encouraging, thought Leopold.

Stockmar, who was of course well aware of his master's intentions, wrote later:

> "But it must be made *sine qua non* that the object of the visit must be kept strictly secret from the Princess as well as from the Prince, so as to leave them completely at their ease."

But of course Stockmar did not know Victoria. The very fact that she knew Leopold had chosen Albert for her would predispose her in his favour; as for Albert, his grandmothers had talked so often of the possibilities of a match with England that he could not think of the Princess Victoria in any connection than as that of a possible wife.

These two young people were Leopold's creatures and they had been so accustomed to regarding him as a superior being that they would continue to do so.

And just as he was about to set his plans in motion that old fool of a King had decided to frustrate him. Victoria's uncles had seemed a poor lot to Leopold. His own father-in-law, George IV, had disliked him from the start and had done all he could to frustrate his match with his daughter, but at least he had been a man of taste and culture. William was a coarse sailor and a fool at that. And if he were not careful the plan he had had brewing for years could be frustrated.

Orange! No, it was too much to be borne. He did not fear Cambridge half as much; and Cumberland, being blind, was out of the running. The Duchess had made sure that Victoria did not see much of her cousins on her father's side; naturally she was all for a husband from her own side of the family. And he could trust his sister. But if the King brought Orange in, who knew what could happen? What sort of a man was the Young Prince of Orange? Victoria was so impressionable, her mother said. So she was; the dear child was brimming over with affection. But no, he, Leopold, had made it clear that he wanted her to choose Albert. He could trust Victoria.

He took up his pen and wrote to her:

"I am really astonished at the conduct of your old uncle the King. This invitation to the Prince of Orange is very extraordinary . . ."

His anger was so great that the pen was shaking in his hands. The Duchess had told him that Victoria was inclined to be very fond of her Aunt Adelaide and that she had an affection for the King too. They were on the spot. They might have some influence. Leopold was well aware that Victoria was leaning farther and farther from her mother, and that her dislike of Sir John Conroy was growing into hatred.

"I had a communication hinting that it would be highly desirable that the visit of *your* relatives should not take place this year . . . I have never heard of anything like it and I hope it will arouse your spirit. Slavery has recently been abolished in the British colonies. I do not understand why you should be kept as a little white slave in England for the pleasure of the Court. I am not aware of the King's having spent a sixpence on you; and I have no doubt that in his passion for the Oranges, the King will be excessively rude to your relations. This will not signify much. They will be *your* guests not his."

Angrily he sealed the letter and sent it off at once. Then he felt better. Once Victoria knew what his wishes were she would act accordingly.

Victoria and the Duchess stood in the hall waiting to greet their guests.

Victoria's heart was beating wildly beneath her rather prim white dress. "Albert and Ernest" it seemed to be saying. "Ernest and Albert"—the cousins whom dearest Uncle Leopold so fervently wanted her to love.

And here they were—Uncle Ernest a few paces ahead of them, embracing Mamma, and Mamma looked younger, tender and very, very happy. Now it was her turn.

Uncle Ernest held her tightly against him. It was too emotional a moment for ceremony.

"And your cousins are longing to kiss your hand."

Ernest first because he was the eldest—tall, dark-haired and very, very handsome. "Dear cousin Ernest, what a joy for us to meet at last!"

And Albert. As tall as Ernest she noticed, but not so dark —more my colour with big blue eyes—such beautiful eyes— a little stouter than Ernest who was just a little too thin—and a handsome nose and mouth and such white teeth.

They were charming and so clever and intelligent—both of them.

Her hand was held and kissed and the large blue eyes of Victoria met those of Albert and she wondered a little apprehensively if he thought she was as handsome as she found him.

"Let us go upstairs," said Mamma.

She led the way with her brother and Victoria fell into step between the two cousins. They smiled at each other and the cousins talked to her in English which they spoke well and she thought how poised they were, what men of the world, far more sophisticated than Ferdinand and Augustus. Oh yes, Ferdinand and Augustus were "new in the world"— not so dear Ernest and dear Albert.

Upstairs in the drawing-room Ernest was telling his cousin Victoria that he would be eighteen in a month.

"My seventeenth birthday is only a few days away," Victoria replied.

"Then Albert is the youngest for he will not be seventeen until August."

Victoria smiled at Albert. She rather enjoyed the idea of being a little older than he was.

Uncle Ernest said he had a present for Victoria and the Duchess ordered that it be brought into the drawing-room. It turned out to be a lory which was so tame that she was able to hold it in her hand.

"You may put your finger in its mouth and it will not bite you," Albert told her.

She promptly did so, laughing with delight.

"Such glorious colours," she cried. "Purple and brown, red, blue and yellow. I shall sketch and paint him afterwards. Oh, I love him already. He is bigger than your grey parrot, Mamma."

The Duchess agreed that he was, and they all went to see the grey parrot and Victoria told the cousins how Mamma had bought him from a man on the roadside when they were taking one of their walks.

"You must not forget," said the Duchess to Victoria, "that you are dining with the Archbishop of York."

Victoria looked so downhearted that everyone laughed.

"It appears to me," said the Duchess in a pleased voice, "that you would prefer the company of your uncle and cousins."

"It's true," admitted Victoria.

"So soon?" asked Albert who, she noticed, was never at a loss.

"Yes, so soon," she replied.

The Duchess thought: A good beginning. Leopold will be pleased.

What a happy visit! What a pleasure to wake up every morning and think: My cousins are here. What shall we do today? I can go riding with them. I can sketch with them. They could both draw well—particularly Albert. They loved music and could play the piano. This they did charmingly. Particularly Albert.

How they laughed together! They were so easily amused and yet they could be so grown up.

They were the most fascinating cousins anyone could have.

Her seventeenth birthday came. But there was little time for writing in the Journal now. She did record it though.

"I awoke at seven. Today I completed my seventeenth year; a very old person I am indeed."

A very old person! One more year and she would be
quite grown up. She was really looking forward to that very
much.

Then she began to wonder what life would be like when
the cousins had gone. How desolate! Not to walk with dear
Albert . . . and Ernest; not to listen to their merry jokes
and marvel at the way they suddenly became very solemn
and grown up and talked about serious matters!

I shall be far more sad than when Ferdinand and Augustus
went, she thought.

"I'll not have those damned Coburgs at Windsor," said the
King.

"Perhaps a brief visit," suggested Adelaide.

"Just a brief one," Lady de l'Isle backed her up.

The King growled and supposed he'd have to receive
them. He had to entertain the Oranges in any case.

"But they'll not get a ball," he insisted.

Never mind. He received them and there was no friction
during their brief stay at Court.

They and Victoria were glad to be back in Kensington
where the Duchess gave a ball for them and Victoria had
the pleasure of dancing with her cousins.

Albert secretly found it all rather tiring. He was not fond
of the social life and he thought the rooms overheated. He
would have liked to be in his room reading—perhaps to
Victoria—but not dancing which he found rather fatiguing.

He tried not to give any indication of this; he was aware
that Uncle Leopold—that oracle of wisdom—wished him
to like Victoria and her to like him, and he was determined
to do his duty. Apart from the physical exertion required
this was no hardship, for Victoria was an enchanting girl;
she was so eager to please. He liked the times better when
they talked or played the piano or sang and sketched together. The manner in which he was expected to stand at
levees tired him considerably. He did not like the late hours
which so delighted Victoria; he longed for his bed. Stockmar
had said he was growing too fast and that was why he was
so drowsy early in the evenings. Once he grew so pale and
looked ready to faint that Victoria noticed. She was all

concern and there was that sweet anxious voice beside him. "Dear Albert, are you sure you feel quite well?"

He assured her that he did and that it was merely the heat of the rooms which had overwhelmed him. He did not tell her that he was fighting off the desire to go to sleep all the time.

After that he saw his cousin regarding him anxiously. But he could always make her laugh with his quick wit, and even the way he played with Dash amused her. He wished that she did not enjoy dancing so obviously. What a pleasant companion she could have been if she only cared for the less demanding pleasures of life. But she was charming and he could not help being eager to please her.

At last the day came for the departure. When the last farewells had been said Victoria wept bitterly. Her only comfort was her Journal.

"At nine we all breakfasted for the last time together. It was our last happy, happy breakfast with this dear uncle and those dearest cousins whom I do love so very very dearly; much more dearly than any other cousins in the world. Dearly as I loved Ferdinand and also good Augustus, I love Ernest and Albert more than them. Oh yes, much more. Augustus was like a good affectionate child, quite unacquainted with the world, phlegmatic, and talking very little; but dearest Ernest and dearest Albert are so grown-up in their manners, so gentle, so kind, so amiable, so agreeable, so very sensible and reasonable and so really and truly good and kind-hearted . . . Albert is the more reflecting of the two. They like talking about serious and instructive things . . .

"At eleven dear Uncle and my *dearest beloved* cousins left us . . . I embraced both my dearest cousins most warmly, also my dear Uncle. I cried bitterly."

She had written to dear Uncle Leopold. She knew that he would be eagerly waiting for her verdict on the cousins and particularly on Albert; and that very soon he would be seeing her uncle and cousins and asking them their opinion of England and her.

So before they left she had given Uncle Ernest the letter and asked him to hand it to Uncle Leopold when they met.

"I must thank you, my beloved Uncle," she wrote, "for the prospect of great happiness you have contributed to give me in the person of dear Albert . . .

"He possesses every quality that could be desired to make me perfectly happy. He is so sensible, so kind, so good and so amiable too. He has, besides, the most pleasing exterior and appearance you can possibly see. I have only now to beg you, dearest uncle, to take care of the health of one so dear to me and to take him under your special protection . . ."

When he received her letter Leopold smiled complacently. He had known he could rely on Victoria.

The King's Discovery

❀ WHEN the cousins had left the Duchess decided that they would go and stay for a while at Claremont. Victoria was delighted. She loved Claremont—the home of dear Uncle Leopold where he had once been so happy with Princess Charlotte; and she could enjoy it even better now because Uncle Leopold was happily married to Aunt Louise —and even Charlotte, Victoria decided, could not have been more charming. So now there need be no sad thoughts at Claremont.

She had tried to adjust herself to the daily routine after the departure of the cousins and found herself talking of them constantly to Lehzen, of how Albert had done this and that and how very sensible he was.

"Darling Dashy misses him. Oh, Lehzen, wasn't he funny when he played with Dash?"

Lehzen thought: She has too much affection. She is ready to believe the best of everyone and love them. She is inclined to think that all people are as honest as she is, as kind and eager to be good.

What a credit the Princess was to her, for Lehzen believed in her heart that the Princess's excellent qualities were the result of her upbringing rather than the Duchess's. Charming, young, with a defined sense of duty—what a Queen she would make!

The Princess's face was flushed with pleasure now because a singing lesson was due. She wished, she had said, that she had singing lessons every day. She admired her singing master with all the fervour of her nature. He was the great operatic singer Luigi Lablache and when he sang Victoria laughed and wept with delight.

She would talk of him endlessly if Lehzen permitted it.

"He is such a patient master, Lehzen. So good-humoured, pleasing and I'm sure he's so honest. It is such a pleasure to hear his fine voice and to sing with him is a privilege. Throughout my life I shall remember my lessons with him. How the time flies when we are together. How active he is for his size. I feel so very small beside him, I love the way he comes in and gives that wonderful dignified bow."

"You are too ready to admire people," chided Lehzen.

"Oh, Lehzen," cried Victoria mischievously, "is that why I admire you?"

Victoria was laughing as she went off for her session with *dear* Lablache.

And now to Claremont where *dear* Louisa Lewis would be so excited because she was coming. She could curtsy in that slow dignified way which was different from the way other people curtsied; and then when Victoria had made her quite sure that she was still the same girl who had sat and watched her eat her breakfast in her own room at Claremont, the barriers would be broken down and Louisa in her white morning dress looking so neat and clean would tell stories of Charlotte as she always did; and she would somehow imply that Victoria now had the place in her heart which had once belonged to Charlotte.

Dear Claremont!

The King's health had deteriorated in the last months and Adelaide was constantly urging him to rest.

"A fine one to talk," he said indulgently. "That cough of yours doesn't get any better. I'm a good few years older than you and I have a right to be ill at my time of life."

"I only want you to take care."

"I know. I know. You've been a good wife to me, Adelaide. In the beginning I didn't want you . . . I didn't want you at all. But then I grew to love you."

Tears filled his eyes and she smiled at him.

"We have done well together, William."

"And we'll go on, eh? I'm not finished yet. Don't you think it. I've got to live till Victoria's of age. I'll refuse to go until that woman hasn't a chance of the Regency."

"That'll be next year. You must go on long after that."

Sometimes he wondered, but he mustn't worry Adelaide.

"I will, you see," he assured. He added to change the disagreeable subject: "It'll be your birthday on the thirteenth. We'll celebrate it with a ball and we'll let the celebrations go on until mine, as the twenty-first is so close."

"We should ask Victoria."

"Oh dear, that means that woman."

"I can't see how she could possibly be left out."

"For two pins I would leave her out."

"It would be impossible. We must ask her; and I hope that she will behave well."

"That's where you're asking the impossible, my dear."

Adelaide sighed.

"The Coburg visit went off all right."

"And don't think I don't know how hard you worked to make that happen. You're too good, Adelaide. I've told you so before."

"It's just that I hate quarrels and I think they do the family harm."

"The greatest harm the family ever did to itself was to bring that woman into it. The pity is that she is the mother of Victoria."

"Perhaps she would have been more bearable if she had not been. In any case I will write to her and invite her to the Castle and pray that during her stay all goes well."

When the Duchess received Adelaide's invitation she laughed.

"So," she said to Conroy. "I am graciously asked to go to Windsor to celebrate Adelaide's birthday. She forgets mine is on the seventeenth. Mine is, I suppose, of no importance. I shall go, of course, to the King's because that is an occasion at which the heiress to the throne should be present."

"You will refuse an invitation from the Queen?"

"My dear Sir John, do you doubt it?"

"Of course I don't."

"You will see."

She sat down at her desk and wrote to the Queen.

She could not come to Windsor at the date the Queen suggested because she wished to celebrate her birthday at Claremont. She would, however, come on the twentieth, which date would not conflict with any of her arrangements.

When she had written it she showed it to Sir John.

"Well?"

"It might be the Sovereign writing to one of her subjects."

"I shall soon be the mother of the young Sovereign."

"And Adelaide is, of course, only the wife of the old one."

They laughed together; it was so gratifying to know that however rudely she behaved William and Adelaide could do nothing to oust her from her position.

The King was in a bad temper. He had come up from Windsor to prorogue Parliament. He was finding breathing difficult and was feeling irascible as he always was when he was not well.

That Woman again, he thought.

Adelaide would have kept the letter from him if she could have done so; she always wanted to save him irritation. But of course he had to know that she had declined the invitation to celebrate Adelaide's birthday. It wasn't that they couldn't do without her. They could—most happily. It was the effrontery, the impertinence. He had demanded to see the letter and when he had read it his face had grown scarlet; the veins in his temples had stood out, and he had almost choked with rage.

She wanted to celebrate *her* birthday. No mention of Adelaide's! That was what maddened him. It was an insult to Adelaide. When he came to think of it that was why she angered him so. It was because she was continually insulting

Adelaide. He wouldn't have Adelaide insulted. She was a good woman, the best wife in the world, and people must pay proper respect to her or answer to him.

The ceremony was boring and tiring. He complained of everything to Lord Melbourne. He was scathing in his comments on this fellow and that minister. Melbourne wondered what had happened to him.

William was glad when the ceremony was over and he was on his way back to Windsor. Passing Kensington Palace he remembered the Duchess and his anger returned. She was staying at Claremont now from where she would deign to come over to Windsor. He ordered the coachman to stop. He would call at Kensington Palace; he would inspect the Duchess's apartments. She would not be there, but she would hear of his visit and it would let her know that the apartments she used belonged to him, and that if he had much more impertinence from her he would turn her out.

That woman needs a good lesson, he thought.

There was consternation among the servants. A royal visit. And they had had no notice of it.

He was amused to see their dismay.

"I've come to see the apartments I allow the Duchess of Kent to use," he said in his free and easy way. "No, no need to take me—I know the way." He went to see those which he had allotted to her.

To his amazement they were empty. He called: "Here. Come here. You, fellow. Where are the apartments of the Duchess and the Princess Victoria?"

"If Your Majesty will come this way . . ."

If he would go that way! He would! And as he went he knew what had happened.

These were the rooms she had asked for and he had denied her. She had made alterations in *his* Palace. How many rooms had she taken? He was going to count for himself. Seventeen. The number for which she had asked; and she had turned the gallery into three rooms—without consulting him, going against his orders.

How dared she!

He went through the entire set of apartments . . . the bedrooms, the sitting-rooms, the dressing-rooms and the receiving-rooms. Trust her to make the place fit for a Queen.

He could not speak; he thought his anger would choke him.

He got into his carriage and growled the order: "To Windsor."

The journey to Windsor seemed longer than usual. It was nearly ten o'clock when he arrived. The house party was assembled in one of the drawing-rooms and he went straight to it.

When Adelaide saw him she knew something terrible had happened. He greeted her and his eyes went round the room until they rested on the Duchess of Kent who was standing with her daughter waiting to be greeted *first* because of her rank.

The King ignored her and held out his hand to Victoria.

"My dear child," he said, "I am very glad to see you here. I am sorry I do not see you more often."

Victoria was smiling her open affectionate smile and returning her uncle's kiss warmly; she had not noticed that he was seething with rage.

He turned to the Duchess and bowed coldly.

Then he said in a voice which every person in the drawing-room could hear: "A great liberty has been taken with one of my palaces. I have just been to Kensington Palace where apartments have been taken against my express commands. I do not understand such conduct." He glared into the Duchess's flushed face. "Nor will I endure it, for it is quite disrespectful to me."

He then turned to Victoria, who was trembling. So they had no right to those beautiful rooms! She had thought that her mother had asked for them and that the King had granted her request. How dreadful to think that Mamma had taken them against the King's wishes. It was like stealing.

She would never enjoy them again.

The King was smiling at her. He wanted her to know that he did not include her in his disapproval.

"So you're at Claremont, eh. A lovely place. Always liked it. Reminds me of Bushy. Ah, I spent many happy years at Bushy."

But there were tears in Victoria's eyes and while she answered the King she thought: "Oh, Mamma, how dared you. All this trouble is your fault. Yours and that man's . . . who persuaded you to it."

The evening was brought to a hasty close. The King was tired and he was not fond of late nights in any case. Abruptly, he turned to Adelaide and said they would go to bed.

When he had gone, the Duchess led Victoria away; and Victoria knew that as soon as they had gone there would be an excited buzz of conversation as to what steps the King would take to punish the Duchess of Kent.

Adelaide was alarmed. The King's anger had not been soothed by that outbreak in the drawing-room. In their bedroom he raved against the Duchess. He detested her, he said. If they had been living a couple of hundred of years ago he would have sent her to the block. "No power nowadays," he mourned. "Kings . . . they're controlled by Parliaments. But, by God, I won't have that woman controlling me."

Adelaide said: "In less than a year Victoria will be of age. Then everything will be different."

"Yes, by God, and I'll see it is. But don't let her think that in the meantime she can rule us."

"I am sure you made her feel very uncomfortable tonight."

"Good! Good! And I'll make her a damned sight more uncomfortable before I've finished with her."

"William . . ."

"Don't you worry, Adelaide. Leave this to me. A King must have some say in how things should be done."

"It's your birthday tomorrow. You should be at peace with the world."

"Nothing's going to make me at peace with that woman."

The next morning his anger had not abated.

Lady de l'Isle who was pregnant tried to soothe him. William was particularly tender to his eldest daughter because of her condition but he would not swerve from his resentment.

When Lord Adolphus FitzClarence called to wish his father a happy birthday William embraced him warmly, always delighted to have the family call of their own accord, always ready to forgive their slights and insults of the past, but he went on grumbling about that outrageous creature who was actually here in the Castle at this moment.

All through that day his anger smouldered but when it was time to go in to dinner he seemed much calmer. There were a hundred guests all come to celebrate his birthday and as it was to some extent a ceremonial occasion everyone must be seated with some concessions to precedence. It was very unfortunate that the Duchess of Kent must be placed next to him.

Adelaide watched the King with apprehension; he was smiling and talking to Victoria, but she could see that the Princess was uneasy, no doubt remembering the King's remarks of the previous evening.

All went well through the dinner except that the King did not address a word to the Duchess of Kent, and then Adelaide expressed the desire that the King's health should be drunk. This was done and the King rose to thank his guests. They believed that there was to be one of his long rambling speeches and were unprepared for what happened.

He began to shout and to the consternation of everyone he began his attack on the Duchess of Kent.

"I trust in God that my life may be spared for nine months longer, after which period, in the event of my death, no Regency would take place." He paused and pointed at Victoria who sat as though petrified, unable to take her eyes from his purple face. "I should then," he went on, "have the satisfaction of leaving the royal authority to the personal exercise of that young lady, the heiress presumptive of the Crown, and not in the hands of a *person* now near me, who is surrounded by evil advisers and is herself incompetent to act with propriety in the station in which she would be placed. I have no hesitation in saying that I have been insulted—grossly and continually—by that *person*, but I am determined to endure no longer a course of behavior so disrespectful to me. Among many other things I have particularly to complain of the manner in which that young lady has been kept away from my Court; she has been repeatedly kept from my Drawing-Rooms, at which she ought always to be present, but I am fully resolved that this shall not happen again. I would have her know that I am King, and I am determined to make my authority respected and for the future I shall insist and command that the Princess do upon all occasions appear at my Court, as it is her duty to do."

His eyes were on Victoria and suddenly his anger passed from him and they were glazed with tears for Victoria was openly weeping; and the Duchess sat very pale and silent, which was very unusual for her.

Adelaide, looking horrified and uncertain, rose and led the ladies from the room.

As soon as they had left the men the Duchess turned to the Queen and cried out that she had been publicly insulted. Never had she been so treated in her life. She would not endure another moment under this roof. Her carriages must be ordered without delay.

Victoria, in tears, was trying to plead with her mother not to be so rash. The King's displeasure had already been aroused; they must now act with decorum.

"Oh, how right!" cried Adelaide. "You cannot leave to-night. Please, try to calm yourself. I am sure the King will repent having reprimanded you so publicly, but you must not go tonight."

The Duchess did not relish a night drive to Claremont so she allowed Adelaide to persuade her not to leave immediately but to wait and see what the morning brought forth.

They retired to their rooms, Victoria in a state of extreme nervousness. She could not understand how her mother could have taken the rooms when the King had forbidden her to do so. It was wrong of her. No subject should ever so flout the Sovereign's authority.

That night Victoria had moved even farther from her mother; and she was glad on the ride back to Claremont the next day that the Duchess behaved as though nothing unusual had happened, although her lips tightened from time to time so that Victoria knew that she was then remembering the King's outburst.

"That damned woman's gone," said the King, "and by God, that's something to be thankful for. The brazen creature. I couldn't believe it, Adelaide, when I saw those rooms . . ."

"Don't think about it," soothed Adelaide. "It's done now. You've made your protest and she will think twice before she defies you again."

"Not that woman. By God, I could have thrown my glass of wine into her insolent face."

Adelaide could at least be thankful that he had not done that.

"She'll go back to Kensington and think up some way to plague me."

"She's at Claremont now."

"Yes, but she'll be back at Kensington in due course."

His daughter Sophia came in and Adelaide was glad, for his mood immediately softened.

"How is my Sophia today?" he asked anxiously.

"Very well, dear Papa."

"You must take care," He was always a little worried when any of his daughters were pregnant. He thought of the difficult times Adelaide had had.

"I'll be all right, Papa."

"Of course you will. You're like your mother. She'd be on the stage a few days before the babies were born."

Adelaide had long since become accustomed to hearing of the perfections of Dorothy Jordan, the mother of his adored children, whom he had deserted a few years before her death. She believed he had forgotten that desertion now; she hoped he had because she knew at one time his conscience had plagued him about it.

"You'd better stay at Windsor, Sophia, though I'd like you to be near us when we go to St. James's." His eyes narrowed. "What's the name of that housekeeper woman at Kensington Palace?"

"You mean Mrs. Strode?" asked the Queen.

"Mrs. Strode, is it? H'm. She's getting old."

"Poor creature," said the Queen. "I don't think she's long for this world."

"The housekeeper at Kensington Palace . . . it's a very comfortable post."

"She's really the custodian," said Adelaide. "Housekeeper sounds as though she is in a menial position. The truth is far from that."

"I'm a plain-speaking man, my dear. Custodian, then. It would suit Sophie. Good apartments, good air. I always like the air of Kensington myself."

"But do you mean Sophia should take over from Mrs. Strode?"

"In due course perhaps," said the King. "You'd like that, Sophie."

Like most of the FitzClarence family Sophia had her mischievous side. She knew what the King was implying.

She might go to Kensington and spy on the Duchess. It appealed to her.

"I should indeed, Papa."

"But you could not of course turn Mrs. Strode out," said Adelaide quickly. "It would be too unkind, particularly as she is so old and ill."

"But if she should die," said William, "and if it should be necessary to find a new *custodian* at Kensington . . ."

Sophia laughed; and William laughed with her. Adelaide sighed faintly. It was amazing how his children could put William into a good humour.

At *dear* Claremont Victoria could forget that horrible incident at Windsor for something wonderful had happened. Uncle Leopold had come for a short visit.

He wanted to talk in person with his "dear little soul," he said. Letters were all very well, but how much greater understanding could be reached in conversation.

He wanted her opinion of Albert; what exactly had she thought?

It was all true, she told him, what she had written to him. She loved Albert; she loved all her cousins but there was something *special* about Albert.

He had seemed a little delicate, Uncle Leopold feared, but there was nothing really delicate about him. He had merely grown too fast. He had an alert and wonderful brain. Did she not think so?

She thought Albert the cleverest young man she had ever met.

Uncle Leopold was satisfied.

Oh yes, in her Uncle's company she could easily forget unpleasantness. He was like her second father, she thought. No, her only father for he was indeed her real father because she had none other.

How grateful she would always be to Uncle Leopold.

Uncle Leopold must go back to his own country and they must go back to Kensington, although they returned to Claremont for Christmas. Since *His Majesty,* said the Duchess, speaking with exaggeration to indicate contempt, thought that the heiress of the throne occupied too *much* of Kensington Palace, they should show that they had another home and that Claremont—the house which belonged to the Duchess's brother Leopold—was always at their disposal.

The news came that Mrs. Strode had died and that the King had appointed Lady l'Isle and Dudley as the custodian of Kensington Palace.

The Duchess was furious.

"That woman! At Kensington Palace! And in such a post! How characteristic of That Man. He has no sense of royalty."

"Mamma," pleaded Victoria, "it is the King's command and there is nothing we can do about it."

The Duchess studied her daughter quizzically. The child was beginning to criticize her own mother. Could it be that she was taking sides with the King against her!

"So," she said coldly, "you have no objection to sharing a roof with . . . with the bastidry!"

Victoria said, with that newly acquired dignity which was giving her mother and Conroy such uneasy qualms, "I think, Mamma, that we must accept the King's commands."

Incident in the King's Drawing-Room

WILLIAM sat at his desk, the letter in his hand, his eyes glazed with memories.

Maria Fitzherbert was dead. Another link with the past had snapped. He felt he was a very old man and there was little time left to him.

Adelaide came in and found him and understanding the cause of his grief mourned with him.

"She was the only woman George ever loved," declared William. "What a sad thing that they parted. How foolish George was . . . not to appreciate the love of a good woman. I thank God, Adelaide, that I have more perception in that respect. I don't know what I should do without you. I've had the love of two good women in my life and that's a good share, you know."

"She was old, William. It had to come."

"Oh yes, she was older than George. She must be over

eighty. Poor Maria Fitzherbert. She was magnificent, Adelaide, magnificent."

"And she was good," added Adelaide.

"A good handsome woman—a rare thing, Adelaide, a rare thing."

Adelaide winced. She knew she was plain; the press were continually calling attention to her lack of physical charms; but she was foolish. She was getting old and she should be accustomed to William's tactlessness by now.

"Death!" said William. "It's claiming so many of the people who were young with me. My turn can't be far off."

"Don't talk of it," she said quickly.

"All right, all right. I've got to live for a long time. I've got to live until Victoria is of an age to stand on her own, for, by God, I'll not have that Duchess as Regent."

"Yes, you must live, William. You are needed not only by your country but by me."

William felt suddenly happy. He had a good wife and he loved her; and he was fortunate, for how many men were so blessed in that respect? Two good women had loved him —his incomparable Dorothy who had given him his dear children and Adelaide who could give him none but instead gave him a devotion which even Dorothy had been unable to give. He had always believed that with Dorothy the children came first.

A lucky man, he thought. Two good women and ten children—and if at times they were cruel to him, they had given him the darling grandchildren. Yes, a lucky man.

Death was in the air. News came from Saxe-Meiningen that Adelaide's mother was very ill and not expected to live. She was asking for Adelaide.

"You must go, my dear," said the King. "You'll not have any peace if you don't. But don't forget the King is missing you, so come back to him as soon as you can."

"I don't think you're well enough to be left."

"I'm all right. The girls will come and stay with me."

"Sophia's at Kensington."

The King grinned. "And I hear Madam Kent is not very pleased about that. Not Sophia, no! In any case she's expecting the child in April. She'll stay at Kensington. But Mary could come, and I daresay my sister Augusta will be here too. I'll be in good hands. Now you go and see your mother and come back to me soon."

Adelaide was more aware than most that the strange moods of the King had intensified, which they did at certain periods, and at such times she appeared to be the only one who could comfort him.

So with misgivings she left England.

Lady de l'Isle had been finding the last weeks before her child was due rather trying. She was very much aware of the Duchess of Kent in her grand apartments, which the King had not taken from her, and although normally she would have been able to deal with her, she felt too ill and listless to do so.

The Duchess, whenever possible, humiliated her; she made constant references to the fact that although Sophia was the King's daughter she was illegitimate.

"Good gracious," cried the Duchess, "if all the Kings' bastards through the ages were lodged in royal palaces we should have to start building rapidly to accommodate them."

Victoria's eighteenth birthday was only a month or so away, and she was uneasy. How would Victoria behave when she was her own mistress?

"Eighteen," she cried indignantly to Sir John, "is far too young for a girl to manage her own affairs. Victoria should ask the King to let a Regency continue for a while after she comes to the throne, for I am sure she will be far too young."

"It's a difficult letter to write," Sir John warned her, "because the assumption must be that the King is dead before she comes to the throne."

"The old fool must know that he can't last much longer. *I* have no compunction in reminding him of that."

"I know, but *he* might object."

"Ridiculous old fool," snapped the Duchess. "But draft a letter to Melbourne and tell him that Victoria wishes me to continue as Regent for a while after she comes to the throne."

"Shall you consult Victoria on this point?"

"Good gracious me, no! In her present mood she might refuse."

There was no harm in drafting the letter, Sir John supposed. His position in any case was even more desperate than that of the Duchess, so they might try everything however wild and devious. Victoria showed quite clearly that she disliked him and never would take him into her service, but the Duchess as her mother could not be so easily disposed of, however much Victoria might long for the disposal.

Yes, thought Sir John, they must try everything.

Really, thought the Duchess, such a bother! And all because a *bastard* was about to give birth to a child. Carriages arriving at the Palace; the King's own physician calling; the King himself. It was most absurd. People would think that *she* was ill or perhaps Victoria. Such a fuss was made they would believe it must be someone who was *important*.

She was having a dinner party that night and she did not like all this activity in the Palace, even though it was not in her own apartments.

Victoria had said: "Mamma, don't you think that in view of Lady de l'Isle's condition you should postpone your dinner party?"

"Postpone my dinner party! Sometimes I wonder at you. What has the confinement of this . . . this . . . woman got to do with *my* dinner party, pray?"

"It is just that at such a time perhaps we should be quiet. I have heard that all is not going quite as it should."

"That rumour is put about merely to call attention to her. She is like her mother . . . that common actress. They're like gypsies. They could have babies by the roadside."

"Gypsies deserve as much consideration as anyone else, Mamma."

"What, Victoria?"

"I believe that the King's physicians are rather anxious about Lady de l'Isle. Oh, I do hope all goes well. Uncle William will be so distressed; and think of her little children."

"You say the oddest things," said the Duchess coldly. "You should thank God that I am constantly at your elbow to remind you of what is expected of a Queen."

I am not that yet, thought Victoria, and perhaps when I am you will not be at my elbow.

But she said nothing.

Later that day Lady de l'Isle died.

"Certainly," said the Duchess, "I shall *not* cancel my dinner party. What have this woman's affairs to do with me?"

Victoria took her usual refuge in tears. She had had Lady

de l'Isle's children in her rooms and tried to amuse them with her sketches to take their minds off what was happening.

Oh dear, she thought, Mamma *cannot* give a dinner party while the King's daughter lies dead in the Palace. But apparently she could.

The King was demented.

"My little Sophie! But what were those doctors doing? She was well enough during her pregnancy. My Sophie! Why her mother had ten children and there was never any trouble."

He wept and there was no comforting him. He told everyone how Sophie had been born and how he had loved her. She was his eldest daughter and had been the most enchanting of little girls. He and Dorothy had been so proud of her. No, this was too cruel. He couldn't bear it.

Melbourne thought he was going mad and wondered how he was going to control a young Queen who was not yet of age. But she would be in a few weeks' time. He had received a letter from her mother in which she stated that Victoria wished for an extended Regency. He could scarcely approach the King on this matter yet. So the Princess felt herself inadequate to rule without her mother!

"God help us!" groaned Melbourne. "How shall we work with the Duchess of Kent!" A young girl would be easier to advise and control and from what he had seen of Victoria he believed her to be intelligent, by which he meant that she would be wise enough to realize her lack of experience and listen to her Prime Minister. But the mother!

He would shelve the letter for a while, at least until the Queen came home. What ill luck that she should be abroad at this time when the King needed her. If she did not come home soon his sanity would desert him. Only those who lived close to William knew how much he depended on Adelaide.

He sent a despatch to the Queen urging her to return to England.

Adelaide's mother had meanwhile died and she came home with all speed.

"Oh, Adelaide, how glad I am! How I missed you! And this terrible terrible news about Sophie. Who would have thought it possible?"

"Dear William, it is heart-breaking. And the children?"

"They are still at Kensington. Young Victoria is being very good to them and they seem to be fond of her. They say they are happier with her than they would be anywhere else."

"Dear Victoria. She is so good. And it's true. She will be gay with them and gaiety is what they want, poor mites."

The King nodded. "My little Sophie, Adelaide . . . my eldest . . . I'll never forget the day she was born."

Adelaide soothed and comforted and the King's health recovered a little. His ministers noticed and were relieved.

Adelaide, however, was really ill. Her cough had become much worse and the journey to Saxe-Meiningen on such a dismal mission had sapped her strength.

She must rest, the doctors told her. She must take great care of her health and remember how important she was to the King.

The Princess Augusta was at Windsor and she assured Adelaide that she could take over many of her duties. Adelaide's chief one at the moment, as the doctors had told her, was to get well.

"You see what happens to William when you're not there, Adelaide," Augusta reminded her. "For Heaven's sake, guard your health. William needs you."

"There is the Drawing-Room . . ."

"But think what effect Drawing-Rooms have on you. I know you have to bandage your knees to help with the swelling."

"Oh, Augusta, I feel so foolishly weak and ineffectual."

"You are certainly not ineffectual. And if you could know what William is like when you're away you'd be fully aware of how important you are. No, I will take your place at the Drawing-Room and you will rest."

Sir John had persuaded the Duchess that she must attend the King's Drawing-Room. He had expressly said that Victoria must appear at Court and that he was going to insist on her doing so. Therefore to ignore this invitation would infuriate him, and, moreover, they must remember that he was the King and had certain powers.

The Duchess was not averse. She would show them that she cared nothing for the King, that she was fully aware that very soon he would have departed this world and her daughter would be the Queen and herself Regent.

She was taking Sir John with her to let everyone see that

she would have whom she chose about her. She was well aware of the King's dislike of Sir John—he had referred more than once to her evil advisers—but that was of no importance. If she wished Sir John to accompany her he should do so.

Victoria, sitting beside her mother in the carriage which was taking them to St. James's for the Drawing-Room, was conscious of her mother's truculent mood.

In a few weeks' time I shall be eighteen, she kept telling herself. Everything will be different then.

In the Drawing-Room the Princess Augusta, deputy for the Queen, received them; and then the King came in.

The Duchess chuckled inwardly. He looked ill and was quite tottery; it was a long time since she had seen him looking so *old*.

He was having a word or two with a guest here and there and when he came to the Duchess he looked through her as though she did not exist. It was a deliberate insult and everyone was aware of it.

Old fool, thought the Duchess. Much good that will do him. Victoria will soon be Queen and he can't alter that. The sooner he is in his grave the better for everyone. He looks as if another step or two will take him there.

The King had seen Sir John Conroy. That fellow . . . among his guests! He had no invitation to appear at his Court. If that woman thought he was going to receive her paramour in his Drawing-Room she was mistaken.

He called: "Conyngham! Conyngham!"

The Lord Chamberlain hurried to his side.

The King's face had grown very red and there was a deep silence throughout the room as William pointed to Sir John Conroy.

"Turn that fellow out!" he said. "I'll not have him here."

There was a gasp of amazement. Everyone was wondering what the King would do next as Sir John Conroy with a shrug of his shoulders and a sneer on his lips was escorted out of the King's Drawing-Room.

William was telling Adelaide all about the incident in the Drawing-Room. Adelaide, her head aching, her cough worrying her, listened and was relieved at least that she had not been present.

"These terrible quarrels between you and the Duchess are

doing you no good, William," she said.

"You aren't suggesting I should let her have her own way."

"No, but perhaps it would be better to ignore her."

"Adelaide, that woman is a fiend. What that child of hers has suffered, I can't imagine."

"Poor Victoria! I don't think she had much fun as a child."

"I'm sure she didn't. But she'll be of age next month."

"She must have a very special celebration."

"The child is very musical. I've heard that she likes singing and playing the piano better than anything else. I shall give her a grand piano for her birthday."

"Oh, William, that's a lovely idea."

"I knew you'd think so. And there'll be other things, too. I've only got to live a few more weeks, Adelaide, and I'll have had my wish. One thing I was determined not to do was to die and let that woman have the Regency."

"You're going on living for a long time yet."

"Yes, yes," said William soothed, but he was not so sure in his heart.

He went on to talk to Adelaide about the Drawing-Room. He believed his feud with That Woman gave him a zest for living.

He had thought of something else. "Now that my darling Sophia is dead my daughter Mary shall go to Kensington. She'll keep an eye on Madam Kent. By God, she'll be appropriating the entire Palace if we don't look out. I wonder when she'll want to move into St. James's and Windsor?"

He was growing excited again and Adelaide talked of the grandchildren to soothe him.

An Important Wednesday
in May

✼ AT the beginning of May the King's health deteriorated rapidly. At a public luncheon he was seen to be very ill and looked as though he were about to faint. The Queen was at hand and managed to guide him through the meal, and afterwards he did actually faint.

"You must rest from all functions for a few days," she told him; and he was feeling so ill that he allowed himself to be persuaded.

The Duchess was delighted when she heard the news. "Not long now," she told Sir John, but Sir John, still smarting from that public rebuff, was inclined to be morbid. What Victoria would be like when she reached her majority he was not at all sure. There had been so many signs of rebellion lately. They had kept her almost a prisoner for eighteen years but in doing so they had failed to win her confidence. They should have dismissed that doting Lehzen with her stern ideas of duty and her caraway seeds. Victoria clearly regarded her as the one person in the Palace whom she could trust.

Leopold was keeping her in leading strings but they had to stretch too far across the Channel to be as effective as they might have been. Leopold was the first to realize this and as the great moment was coming nearer and nearer he decided to send Baron Stockmar to England to report on the situation there and guide Victoria.

Stockmar arrived at Kensington Palace to be warmly welcomed by Victoria because he brought letters and messages from Uncle Leopold and in these letters she read that she must love and trust Stockmar for Leopold's sake.

This she was very ready to do. She had a new idol; she listened to everything he said; she was certain of his wisdom.

If he was not Uncle Leopold he was the next best thing.

"Baron Stockmar," she wrote in her Journal, "is one of the few people who tell plain, honest truth, don't flatter and give wholesome and necessary advice, and strive to do good and smooth all dissensions. He is Uncle Leopold's greatest and most confidential attaché and disinterested friend, and I hope he is the same to me, at least I feel so towards him."

When she had written that she thought of Lehzen who would read her Journal and think of all the years that they had been together. She wanted Lehzen to know that there would never be another friend for her like her dear Baroness so she added: "Lehzen being of course the *greatest* friend I have."

Stockmar was delighted with his pupil. Her frank acceptance of him, her innocent belief in him because Uncle Leopold had sent him, and afterwards because she sensed his great qualities, pleased him.

He wrote back to Leopold of his enthusiasm for her. She was bright and intelligent. She was above all aware of her inexperience and eager to learn.

"England will grow great and famous under her rule," prophesied Stockmar.

So during those weeks which she felt to be so momentous Victoria was relieved to have Baron Stockmar close at hand.

At last came that Wednesday in May of the year 1837 which was Victoria's eighteenth birthday.

"How old!" she wrote in her Journal. "And yet I am far from being what I should be. I shall from this day take the firm resolution to study with renewed assiduity to keep my attention always fixed on whatever I am about and to strive to become every day less trifling and more fit for what, if Heaven wills, I'm some day to be."

It was a solemn time, waking in the familiar bedroom and thinking: I am now of age. I am no longer a child. Everything will be different from now on.

But first there was a birthday—the most important of them all—to be celebrated. To her delight she suddenly heard the sound of singing beneath her window; and she recognized the voice of George Rodwell, the Musical director of Covent Garden, who had composed a special piece of music for her birthday. She leaned out of the window and clapped her applause.

Lehzen said it was a very pleasant compliment and it was time she dressed.

The presents were laid out on her table and she eagerly examined them and thanked everyone; and the gift which delighted her most perhaps, because it showed that however angry the King might be with her mother he had an affection for her, was the beautiful grand piano which was delivered with His Majesty's affection and best wishes.

"Oh, it is beautiful . . . beautiful!" she cried; while the Duchess looked at the piano as though it were some loathsome monster.

But Victoria thought: She cannot forbid me to accept it or to play it. She cannot forbid me to do *anything* now!

It was an intoxicating thought. Freedom! There was no gift as desirable as that.

She was realizing how important she was. The heiress to the throne and of age!

During the morning the City of London sent a deputation to congratulate the Princess on coming of age. Victoria received it with her mother standing by her side and when she was about to thank them, the Duchess laid a restraining hand on her arm and herself addressed them.

She told them that she, a woman without a husband, had brought up her daughter single-handed and she had never once swerved from her duty nor forgotten the great destiny which awaited the Princess. When her husband had died she had been left alone, not speaking the language, almost penniless with such a great task ahead of her. This she had not shirked . . .

Oh, Mamma, Victoria wanted to scream. Be silent.

In the afternoon Victoria and the Duchess, with Lehzen, drove through the streets and everywhere the flags were flying in her honour. The day had been declared a public holiday and people thronged the streets, and when her carriage passed a great cheer went up.

And later she went to St. James's for the state ball. She was terrified of how the King would behave towards her mother and she towards him; but in her heart she believed that now that she was of age everything was going to be different.

She was very sorry to learn that the King was unable to attend because he was so ill; and that the Queen was not well enough to come either. Her aunt, the Princess Augusta, received them and she consoled herself that at least there would be no unpleasantness.

She could give herself up to the pleasures of the ball. How delightful to dance to heavenly music. The first dance was with the Duke of Norfolk's grandson and he danced with great skill and told her she looked beautiful.

There were many other dances and it was a wonderful ball; and when she entered her carriage to return to Kensington the people had come into the courtyard to cheer her.

A wonderful birthday, an *amusing* ball, but she knew it was more than that. It was the beginning of a new life.

Her Majesty

LORD Conyngham, the Lord Chamberlain, called at Kensington Palace to be received by Sir John Conroy.

"I have," said Lord Conyngham, "a letter here from His Majesty to the Princess Victoria."

Sir John held out his hand for it. There had been no reply from the letter the Duchess had sent to Lord Melbourne and he believed that it had come to the Prime Minister's ears that the Duchess had not spoken to Victoria about an extended Regency, in which case the Prime Minister would tactfully pretend that he never received such a letter.

But a message from the King to the Princess must of course be seen first by Sir John and the Duchess.

Lord Conyngham, however, did not pass over the letter. Instead he said: "I have His Majesty's instructions to put this letter into no hands but those of the Princess Victoria."

Sir John sent one of the pages to tell the Duchess that the King's Chamberlain was at the Palace with a message from the King.

The Duchess swept in, greeted Conyngham haughtily and held out her hand for the letter.

"I am sorry, Your Grace, but the King's instructions are that his letter is to be given to none but the Princess."

The Duchess flushed angrily but could do nothing but send a message to Lehzen to bring the Princess Victoria to her drawing-room without delay.

When Victoria arrived Lord Conyngham bowed and handed her the letter.

"It is from His Majesty, Your Highness."

Victoria took it.

"Are you not going to open it?" asked the Duchess, coming to stand beside her and obviously using great restraint in not snatching the letter from her daughter.

"I think," said Victoria, "that I would prefer to read it in my own sitting-room . . . by myself."

The Duchess was affronted. The Princess Victoria had never been allowed to be alone even and now she was proposing to read an important letter without sharing it with her mother.

There was a new dignity about the Princess, an assurance; she had crossed the bridge between restraint and freedom and she was safely on the other side.

She took the letter, she read it. The King wrote affectionately that now she was of age she might wish to have a separate establishment from her mother's and he was prepared to allow her ten thousand a year of her own.

Gleefully Victoria accepted.

Life was changing rapidly. She was becoming independent. Not that her mother would allow that without a fight; and the King was growing so ill that nothing was done immediately about her separate establishment. The Duchess wrote to the Prime Minister to the effect that ten thousand a year was too much for Victoria and she thought she should have a share of it.

But everything else was set temporarily aside because the King's condition was so rapidly deteriorating. It was clear that he could not live long; he had lost the use of his legs and had to be wheeled wherever he went. The FitzClarence children were at Windsor, all rancour forgotten. George, Earl of Munster, had given up quarrelling with his father; his daughter Mary was constantly with him; and Augustus read the prayers every morning; but it was Adelaide who was constantly at his side and if she were not in the room he became uneasy.

He knew he was dying. It was as though he had made up his mind that he would live until Victoria was of age. Now that day had come; he had had his revenge on the Duchess and would depart in peace.

"Any day now, it will be the end," said the courtiers, the ministers and the people in the streets.

But the King lingered on.

The Duke of Cumberland could not give up hope. He was excited. Surely his moment had come. The King was dying and the heiress to the throne was a girl of eighteen. Something must be done.

Surely the people would rather have a strong man at the head of affairs.

Frederica, grown philosophical, said: "You're crazy, Ernest. The people want Victoria. A young girl like that . . . providing she's got the ministers behind her, can bring back respect to the Monarchy. I hear William said that sailors and soldiers will enjoy having a girl-Queen to fight for. It's true, Ernest. Why can't you be content? The day William dies you'll be the King of Hanover."

"I want to be the King of England. I want England for George."

"Our beautiful blind boy will be content with Hanover," said Frederica.

But the Duke would not believe this. He had grandiose plans. The Orange Lodges had been disbanded but he would not give up.

He went to see the Duke of Wellington.

"It's wrong," he told him. "Why should the Salic law apply in Hanover and not in England?"

"Because it's not an English law," said Wellington. "You should be careful. The people are in no mood to support those who stand against Victoria."

"This girl . . . this child . . ."

"The true and only heiress to the Crown," said the Duke. And added: "God bless her."

"If I raised an army I'd have plenty to follow me."

"They would follow you," said Wellington ironically, "to the Tower of London."

Ernest gnashed his teeth. All his plans had gone wrong.

He had been foiled by a simple girl who somehow had the country behind her. These people wanted a girl-Queen; they were ready to shout for Victoria and call traitor any of those who opposed her.

He went back to Frederica who smiled at him rather cynically.

"You should have taken my advice and been content all these years. Never mind, Ernest, in a short time now people will be calling you 'Your Majesty . . . Your Majesty of Hanover.' The second prize but very acceptable for all that."

The King awoke one Sunday morning and said to Adelaide: "This is the eighteenth of June. I should like to see the sun of Waterloo set."

"You will, dear William," whispered Adelaide.

"A great victory," added William. "Yes, I should like to live through Waterloo Day."

His family came; he recognized them and was happy to see them. He talked a little incoherently of their childhood and Dorothy and the days at Bushy and when George arrived he wept openly, for George had brought the flag which Wellington always sent to William on Waterloo day.

William took the flag and kissed it.

"A great and glorious day for England," he said.

His children did not leave him; they sat around his bed; but Adelaide must be there; he was not happy unless his hand was in hers.

When she asked if there was anything he needed, he shook his head. "Only to have you . . . and the children near me, my dear."

And because he knew she was weeping he pretended to feel better.

The next day in fact he did revive a little. The Dukes of Cumberland and Sussex came to see him; but he was unable to talk to them.

When they left he said good-bye to his children and all the time he would not release Adelaide's hand.

"Don't cry, Adelaide," he whispered. "Nothing to cry for. We were happy. Didn't want it . . . but it was right . . . it was good . . . my dear, dear Queen. Bear up, my dear. Bear up."

It seemed right that the Princess Victoria should be sent for but Adelaide would not allow this for she knew that the

Duchess would not permit the Princess to come alone and her presence would greatly upset the King.

So she sat beside him as for the last week she had been sitting day and night and her only consolation was the knowledge that her presence there comforted him.

All the time he was concerned for her, anxious that she should not grieve, trying to pretend that he was going to get better . . . for her sake.

It was past two in the morning of the twentieth that he called her name.

She who was at his side bent over him. She put her arms about him and leaning against her he smiled.

And she knew soon afterwards that he was dead.

It was six o'clock.

"Victoria," said the Duchess of Kent. "Wake up."

She started up in bed. She knew of course. Some instinct told her, but then for some days now she had been expecting it.

"The Archbishop of Canterbury and Lord Conyngham are at the Palace. They have come to see you."

"To see me . . ."

"You had better get up. They are in your sitting-room. We will go to them at once."

She put on her dressing-gown and she said firmly: "I will go . . . alone, Mamma."

The Duchess was about to reply but she did not. There was something in Victoria's manner that forbade it.

And with her hair hanging about her shoulders, her dressing-gown buttoned about her little figure, her feet thrust into slippers, she went into the sitting-room.

At the sight of her, they knelt.

"Your Majesty," they said.

And so she knew that she was no longer the Princess Victoria but Queen of England.

Bibliography

Queen Victoria's Sister: Life and Letters of Princess Feodora	Harold A. Albert
V.R.I., Queen Victoria, her Life and Empire	The Duke of Argyll
National and Domestic History of England	William Hickman Smith Aubrey
Queen Victoria	E. F. Benson
Letters of Queen Victoria	Edited by A. C. Benson and Viscount Esher
The Youthful Queen Victoria	Dormer Creston
Victoria (Queen and Empress)	Richard Davey
Memoir of Queen Adelaide	Dr. Doran
The Girlhood of Queen Victoria (A Selection of Her Majesty's Diaries between the years 1832 and 1840)	Viscount Esher
The Greville Memoirs	Edited by Roger Fulford
Hanoverian Queens of England	A. D. Greenwood
Unsuccessful Ladies (An Intimate Account of the Aunts of the Late Queen Victoria)	Jane-Eliza Hasted
Queen Adelaide	Mary Hopkirk
Life and Reign of William IV	Robert Huish
Early Court of Queen Victoria	Claire Jerrold
Victoria R.I.	Elizabeth Longford
History of the Four Georges and William IV	Sir Justin McCarthy
The Sailor King, William IV, His Court and Subjects	Fitzgerald Malloy
Queen Victoria as I Knew Her	Sir Theodore Martin

The House of Hanover	Alvin Redman
The Life and Times of Queen Adelaide	Mary F. Sandars
Victoria of England	Edith Sitwell
Life of Queen Victoria	G. Barnett Smith
Dictionary of National Biography	Edited by Sir Leslie Stephen and Sir Sydney Lee
The Mother of Victoria	Dorothy Margaret Stuart
The Patriot King (Life of William IV)	Grace E. Thompson
British History	John Wade

Jean Plaidy

"Miss Plaidy is also, of course, Victoria Holt." —PUBLISHERS WEEKLY

☐ BEYOND THE BLUE MOUNTAINS	22773-1	1.95
☐ CAPTIVE QUEEN OF SCOTS	23287-5	1.75
☐ THE CAPTIVE OF KENSINGTON PALACE	23413-4	1.75
☐ THE GOLDSMITH'S WIFE	22891-6	1.75
☐ HERE LIES OUR SOVEREIGN LORD	23256-5	1.75
☐ LIGHT ON LUCREZIA	23108-9	1.75
☐ MADONNA OF THE SEVEN HILLS	23026-0	1.75

Buy them at your local bookstores or use this handy coupon for ordering:

FAWCETT PUBLICATIONS, P.O. Box 1014, Greenwich Conn. 06830

Please send me the books I have checked above. Orders for less than 5 books must include 60c for the first book and 25c for each additional book to cover mailing and handling. Orders of 5 or more books postage is Free. I enclose $_____ in check or money order.

Name_____

Address_____

City_____ State/Zip_____

Please allow 4 to 5 weeks for delivery. This offer expires 6/78.　　A-33

Victoria Holt

Over 20,000,000 copies of Victoria Holt's novels are in print. If you have missed any of her spellbinding bestsellers, here is an opportunity to order any or all direct by mail.

☐	BRIDE OF PENDORRIC	22870-3	1.75
☐	THE CURSE OF THE KINGS	Q2215	1.50
☐	THE HOUSE OF A THOUSAND LANTERNS	X2472	1.75
☐	THE KING OF THE CASTLE	X2823	1.75
☐	KIRKLAND REVELS	X2917	1.75
☐	LEGEND OF THE SEVEN VIRGIN	X2833	1.75
☐	LORD OF THE FAR ISLAND	22874-6	1.95
☐	MENFREYA IN THE MORNING	23076-7	1.75
☐	MISTRESS OF MELLYN	23124-0	1.75
☐	ON THE NIGHT OF THE SEVENTH MOON	X2613	1.75
☐	THE QUEEN'S CONFESSION	X2700	1.75
☐	THE SECRET WOMAN	X2665	1.75
☐	SHADOW OF THE LYNX	X2727	1.75
☐	THE SHIVERING SANDS	22970-X	1.75

Buy them at your local bookstores or use this handy coupon for ordering:

FAWCETT PUBLICATIONS, P.O. Box 1014, Greenwich Conn. 06830

Please send me the books I have checked above. Orders for less than 5 books must include 60c for the first book and 25c for each additional book to cover mailing and handling. Orders of 5 or more books postage is Free. I enclose $_____ in check or money order.

Mr/Mrs/Miss_____

Address_____

City_____ State/Zip_____

Please allow 4 to 5 weeks for delivery. This offer expires 6/78.   A-3